L.H. BOLTSON

The Modified Ones.

First published by L.H. Boltson 2025

Second edition

ISBN: 979-8-218-72871-7

This book was professionally typeset on Reedsy.
Find out more at reedsy.com

Contents

Prologue v
Chapter 1 1
Chapter 2 7
Chapter 3 16
Chapter 4 19
Chapter 5 33
Chapter 6 38
Chapter 7 44
Chapter 8 52
Chapter 9 55
Chapter 10 68
Chapter 11 82
Chapter 12 87
Chapter 13 96
Chapter 14 101
Chapter 15 105
Chapter 16 114
Chapter 17 117
Chapter 18 123
Chapter 19 128
Chapter 20 133
Chapter 21 142
Chapter 22 158
Chapter 23 161
Chapter 24 164
Chapter 25 166

Chapter 26 169
Chapter 27 172
Chapter 28 181
Chapter 29 193
Chapter 30 197
Chapter 31 207
Chapter 32 211
Chapter 33 215
Chapter 34 219
Chapter 35 222
Chapter 36 224
Chapter 37 231
Chapter 38 238
Chapter 39 245
Chapter 40 247
Chapter 41 252
Chapter 42 256
Chapter 43 257
Chapter 44 258
Chapter 45 265
Chapter 46 268
Chapter 47 270
Chapter 48 272
Chapter 49 274

Prologue

June 27th, 2079 - SANTOS

Red and blue lights appear in the distance along with the shriek of sirens. The sun is setting, making a perfect summer backdrop in the beautiful coastal city of Beaufort, South Carolina. Despite their quick movements, the additional emergency service vehicles won't come in time. Lieutenant Santos quickly clears out the small coffee shop of the few that remain inside, but not before taking their names and telling them to head to the police station. The teenage employees are required to head to the break room and wait patiently for him. He'll deal with them in the aftermath, hoping for more answers. Even with the vision of the scene now burned into his brain, he remembers to confiscate their cell phones and asks them not to talk about the incident until he is able to speak with them later. His mind is moving a million miles a second to try and remedy the situation. He quickly starts to survey the scene one final time before making the call.

A young, dark-haired mother is curled up in the corner of the bitter smelling shop with her baby wrapped tightly in her arms. Tears stream down her mocha-colored skin and onto the top of the baby's peach-fuzz head. When he first arrived at the scene, Santos thought this was just another racial incident—something rather common in the south despite the country claiming to be fighting against inequality for the last few hundred years. 'History repeats itself until a revolution occurs', his abuelita would always tell him in his younger years. He thought about her words a lot throughout his career, mostly every time he saw something that could haunt his dreams at night. Unfortunately, he is positive that this will be one of those times that replays as a nightmare.

He turns his gaze away from the mother and toward the two men sprawled out on the ground. Both of the men are surely dead by now, he silently confirms to himself. The first man, an average height, thick, pale white man with a deep stab wound directly in the stomach—knife still protruding from his body cavity. The other, a dark-skinned man with gunshot wounds. One bullet in the shoulder and the other right between the eyes. Even though Lieutenant Santos wasn't there when the fight broke out, he can replay the scene in his mind based on his crime scene knowledge and the few blurts he heard from the coffee house staff when he arrived.

The men got into a verbal argument causing most to naturally clear out of the coffee shop in fear that the tension between the two would escalate to an eruption. Santos silently thanks those who left early to make his job of cleaning up this mess easier. He gathered that the verbal argument became a pushing match according to the pimply, varsity blues looking teenager behind the cash register upon arrival. The stab wound must have come first followed by the shot to the shoulder and then the head shot. It is the only way the scene makes any sense. The scene itself is always the easy part to understand in situations like this. Why these situations escalate is always the harder part to comprehend.

Lieutenant Santos has observed countless violent acts without any real cause since he started in the police force. He tries to not give too much weight as to the 'why' at this time, knowing he likely will never find out the true cause. He begins to finish eyeballing the situation and realizes that this is going to be a costly mess for the coffee shop. The chairs thrown around the small storefront had broken the glass pastry windows, dented and scuffed the walls, and even cracked the large street view window. Not to even mention the deep red colored puddles of blood seeping into the worn wood flooring as he stands witness.

With the sounds of the ambulance sirens now closer, he moves himself to the distraught mother in the corner who is shielding her baby. At first this attempt is to console her, but as he approaches, he's caught off guard by the look of the child. He's heard rumors of such a child being born, but he's never laid his eyes on one. Deep down he thought that the rumors were all a hoax to stir up more turmoil between the northern and southern states.

Up until this moment he would have bet his life against it being true.

His gaze moves up until he is making eye contact with the devastated woman, but this time he doesn't just see sadness. He sees a new level of fear in her dark eyes. He can tell that the terror in her stare is not because of what happened to her husband but is directed towards what could be coming next. The lieutenant slowly retreats from the mother and stands up as the EMTs enter the shop. The police sent to work the crime scene enter immediately following them. He directs the medical professionals to check the men to ensure they have departed. Once confirmed the police officers begin their crime scene routine and everything gets roped off before pictures are snapped and samples get taken. While everyone is busy with their role, Santos directs the woman to the bathroom in the back of the building and asks her to wait in there until he comes to get her. He slowly picks up a nearby fallen chair and sets it inside the bathroom for her to rest on. She nods at his request without making further eye contact. He is thankful that she does so. He doesn't know if he could handle looking at her or that baby for one more second.

It feels like forever to Santos before the bodies are taken out in body bags on the stretchers and the runts of the police department's crime unit begin to clean up the destruction left behind by the altercation. Finally, everyone assisting in the investigation has been ushered out of the building and Santos locks the entrance and pulls the shade down on the large entry window. He takes a deep, much needed breath before he walks back to the bathroom and releases the woman and the now sleeping baby. As she leaves the hallway and makes her way into the open space that she was previously in, her eyes scrunch up and the lieutenant can tell that the smell of the bleach and other cleaning products have reached her. He pulls out a chair at one of the tables and motions for her to sit. He turns away from her when he remembers the staff is still in the break room. He rushes toward the break room and tells the three employees that they need to make their way to the police station and to wait there for him with an added gentle reminder to not discuss the events that happened here today. He apologizes for the delay, as it was originally his intention to talk to them here and promises that he will have food waiting for them at the station.

He picks up his cell phone and calls the station. A deputy picks up and he relays the necessary information regarding the employees that are heading his way. He kindly asks the man on the other end of the phone line to order some pizzas to the station for the teens. As the word 'pizza' leaves his mouth he wonders if it can really be even called pizza anymore. Fresh ingredients are so limited now along the coast that even pizza places began purchasing ingredients from factories and everything pretty much tastes like plastic with seasoning on it. At least pizza still resembles the round shape and texture that it used to, unlike most of the foods now, he reminds himself. He shakes the thought of food from his mind easily when he remembers why he is here. He picks up the phone to make just one more call. This is the moment he has been dreading.

June 27th, 2079 - FRANK

No one ever told Frank Roy that being mayor would be easy. In fact, many people in his life tried to push him towards other career paths, his mother and wife included. This is partly why he resented them both when they told him how proud they were of him at the after party for his election three years ago. If you would have asked Frank in his election year if he could ever understand their concern he would have brushed off the question with a cocky smirk, but two minutes ago when he ended his phone conversation he came to the realization that he finally understands the concern that his wife and mother had for him all along. This job will change who he is.

Frank redirects his attention to the task at hand. He slips on his navy suit jacket and slides his phone into the pocket. Slowly rising from his chair, he can feel his weight shifting and putting pressure on his knees. As the pain throbs in his left leg, he takes a mental note of how old he feels and that he should finally go for the physical he'd been meaning to get. As he walks through his office doors he nods at his secretary, June, and lets her know that he will be heading home for the evening and to please cancel his morning meetings. She barely lifts her gaze off of her calendar, but shouts that she will take care of it in an irritated voice. He knows that he has relied a lot on her lately and promises himself that he will find a way to show her his appreciation soon—surely another lie to help him sleep at night.

When Frank gets in his car, instead of setting the auto-drive feature to his home, he sets it to the coffee shop, True Beans, in the center of town. He loves True Beans coffee and has June pick it up for him almost every morning. It is one of the few places that hasn't changed over the years in Beaufort. The shop owners figured out two or so decades ago how to transplant coffee bean plants that they bought from overseas and have been growing them in the small greenhouse behind the building ever since. This was really lucky since shortly after that most of the imports from other countries were cut off or slowed. They don't have a huge supply of coffee beans, but it has always seemed like enough for the little city of Beaufort.

The car pulls up and parks itself right outside of the shop. Frank does not get out immediately. He pauses to think about what should come next. Having one of *those* kinds of people in his city is bad for business, but it is even worse if word gets around that it caused a double murder. He has to cover this up...at least the murder part, in order to keep local tempers at bay. Luckily, Frank has his loyal soldier Santos to count on for this, but this would be a big ask even from Santos. He's done several 'shady' jobs for him in the past to help him to get where he is today, but this favor will be different. It will take Santos crossing several lines to make this go away. Frank will have to reward him handsomely for this one.

After several minutes of contemplation, Mayor Roy makes his way to the coffee shop and finds the door is locked. He gently knocks on the glass pane. Before he is even done with his second knock, he hears the lock unlatching. He enters the room to find a young woman sitting at a table facing away from him. He looks up at Santos, his lackey who slowly turned into his friend, who shakes his head in a disapproving way. The two men join the young woman at the table. They wait several seconds for her to acknowledge their arrival at the table, but she refuses to look up at them.

Mayor Roy breaks the silence, "We know this must be really hard for you given what you've just experienced, but we have to talk about the next steps. It is important for the three of us to be on the same page to ensure the safety of the town, yourself and," he pauses, "…your child".

After several minutes of conversation, the mayor makes it clear to the woman that if she agrees to never speak of this incident again, he will provide funds and transportation for her to move with the child to another city of her choosing. Roy looks over at Santos and he can see that he is shaken but is trying to stay strong since he is the intimidation piece of this puzzle right now. The young woman, after some time, agrees that putting all of this in the rearview mirror and never looking back is what is best for her now.

By now it is dark and Santos very discreetly puts the woman and child into the back of his cruiser. Roy stops him outside of his car and whispers to him, "Once this cover up is done, we are in this now as a team, forever. There can be no turning back. This is bigger than just us, and we have to protect what we are building. It was our only real choice, so I don't want you to go on stewing about this. I do, however, worry that this is only the beginning. More and more of them are going to keep popping up and we are going to have to make sure that doesn't become a problem."

As Frank Roy inches closer to Santos, he can see him conceding with his eyes.

Mayor Roy continues to speak with newfound authority in his voice, "As a reward for your continued loyalty and friendship, you'll become the next sheriff when Samuels retires in August."

April 2nd, 2082 - AVA

The bedroom door slowly creaked open and the loving mother of two peeks in. She sees the light from the moon enter the room and drape across her oldest son's face. His bright blonde hair is illuminated in the beam from the bright beacon in the sky. The view from the window is breathtaking. She lingers a little longer trying to take in the majestic way the moon reflects on the water of their beachfront property.

From across the room something catches her eye and panic consumes her. She does a double take, trying to squint in order to see across the room. She freezes and tries to convince herself that what she just saw is impossible. She takes a deep breath and quietly pushes the door open a little wider so she can squeeze through without making much noise. The petite woman creeps towards her son's bed and bends over to get a closer look. Time seems to pause while she considers everything that she knows about the world.

The world has gone through a lot of changes in the past few decades. The effects of global warming are still getting worse, and society is now burdened with the lack of consistent attempts to slow the process. Many of the world's scientists have worked hard to come up with ways to slow or reverse the demise of the Earth's biosphere, but due to the largest companies working actively against them in order to maintain control over the economy, they have been unsuccessful.

Pollution has tripled in the United States, primarily in the southern, factory-ridden half over the last thirty years and it isn't turning around anytime soon. Over the past quarter century or so it started to become very apparent that capitalist America has a tight hold on the government officials and legislation. Everything began to come from factories, including most food. Most farms have been shut down due to changing weather patterns and market vendors outsourcing to larger corporations. It is rare to find fresh food now unless you are near a coastal area that still uses primitive methods to catch seafood. Without a lot of positive changes being implemented by the world's top scientists and activists, humans have had to adapt in other ways in order to survive.

Several children in the United States were born over the last couple of years with adaptations that can only be described as some sort of evolutionary reaction to the environment. Scientists speculate this is because of the rising sea levels along the coasts and the extreme changes in temperatures. Once the news of the evolution of these humans made it to national television there were outcries from the north, who, at that time, had no *Modified* births. Fear, intrigue, disgust, excitement and pretty much every other emotion under the sun was, and still is, being provoked by the media.

Parents of children born with these *'modifications'* who are now being called MODs, a term developed by the younger generation to refer to the *'modification'* or evolution of the human body for survival, are now terrified of what may happen to their children. People from the north are becoming more intolerant of those who are *Modified* and some protests and riots filled with violence have been sparked. The lack of government action compromises the integrity of society and that is now being felt in all areas of the United States.

Ava's thoughts travel even deeper into her childhood memories of her mother sharing her recollection of the 2020 riots and protests that she had experienced as a young person due to political, social and ethical strain on society. The mental retelling of her mother's childhood lore has her wondering if the United States can make it through another rough patch in its history with the north becoming increasingly volatile towards the southerners and their media faked acceptance of the MODs. Surely, she decides, that the United States can once again overcome such things and stay united even though everything feels like it is falling apart around them.

Upon hearing the news of *Modification* the rest of the world immediately closed entry to travelers from the United States. The media spewed that other countries are concerned about the state of politics, health, and wellness of the American people. People naturally are scared of the unknown and treat it like a contagious disease. Another similarity to the saga her mother told her about.

Social media sources and news outlets were taken over by the government making it so all users can only interact with those inside of America in hopes to keep the hysteria under control. No average citizen in the United States has been able to hear news from overseas for the last several years now.

The thoughts drift out of her head as she stands in disbelief of what is before her eyes. It is impossible, she thinks, for a child of eight years old to become M*odified*. All of the children in the news have been born with their *modifications*.

MODs began making headlines back when the first baby to be born with adaptations made headlines in 2079. Frog Baby is what the headlines began calling the child, she recalls, remembering how cruel of a nickname she thought it to be. The government and scientists all noted that it was an evolutionary change that was coming with the new generation of babies. Since the northern people had no reported MOD children at the time, it was thought that the warmer weather, reliance on seafood, and new profound pollution in the south has triggered a DNA mutation to occur during gestation as a way to better handle what Earth is becoming. If all of these things are true, then how could it be that she is standing here in front of her primary school aged child witnessing what looks like the beginning of the modification process.

She moves in even closer to the platinum blonde boy's soundly sleeping body and brushes his hair away from his forehead in a gentle swift motion as she has done countless times throughout his life. She takes her soft fingers and gently presses them to the boy's neck. A small amount of air escapes through her fingers with each breath that he takes. A quiet whistling noise moves through the limited space between her pointer and index finger barely making it to her ears. She rubs her index finger over tiny holes forming on each side of his neck to feel the rough texture. This is how it begins...with the gills.

Chapter 1

April 25th, 2082 - KATIE

Katie Kleug, Junior Administrator for the HBRF (Human Biology Research Foundation), a branch of the United States government's Scientific Research Department, wakes up to her phone ringing at 5:46 a.m. on Saturday, April 25th, 2082. She is startled by the loud, insistent vibration on her nightstand table. Katie opens one of her eyes to look at the lock screen. She pauses and lets the call go to voicemail. The screen displays that she has missed three other calls this morning. It was her boss, David Bruner, calling—all of the times. Her mind begins wheeling about what could be going on. She is exhausted, but knows she has to call him back within the next ten minutes or he will just call again or even worse, come to her house. Her head is now filled with mixed emotions, could he want her back again or is something happening at work?

Thinking back, Katie knew it was a bad idea to get involved with her boss, but he was magnetic when he talked and she fell for his charm every time. His persistence with her was, of course, appealing. But it was really how ambitious and career driven he was that really got her going. A career like his is something she always desired for herself. She looked up to him in so many ways. He was at the height of his career and his confidence was proof of that. Part of her didn't know if she cared more about him as a person or the insight he could offer her to help her bring her own career to the next level. Maybe it was a little of both.

She uses her fingers to wipe away the morning from her eyes. She decides to check the forecast before calling him back. The soft tip of her index finger taps the weather app on her cell phone. Another cloudy day ahead. She rolls her eyes, annoyed that spring can't ever just let the sun shine over Washington D.C. She pauses for a minute to think about why she moved to such a drab place anyways. Katie immediately shakes off her annoyance and reassures herself it was the right choice for her career path and quickly grabs the remote off of the nightstand and turns on the news.

Within seconds anxiety consumes her body. She's heard the rumors swirling around her for several days now about a young boy who has evolved, but she was hoping that it was just another hoax that the conspiracy theorists were spitting at the gullible people of the world to sell more merchandise and products. A child born without the *modification* and then developing it has been unheard of until now. This type of development has the potential to drive fear into an already collapsing society, showing that no one is safe now.

The news station shows a scientist confirming it is possible for someone to develop the *modification* without being born with it. The reporter is stretching what the scientist said in his interview, blowing the lid right off of the fear that had been slightly contained before when the word 'rumor' was associated with it. Reporters always do things like that; try to twist the words of others for views. Unfortunately for the scientific community the twist of words will work, and fear will fill the hearts of millions of viewers.

Katie decides that the media wants to test the bounds of loyalty and patriotism in the United States to see if it can withstand anything. Not that it matters much now since United States citizens are barred from all travel outside of the country. People can't leave even if they want to.

Katie knows now why David was calling her and her stomach sinks. She feels as though she swallowed a rock, and it is just sitting in her abdomen. She gets up from her bed quickly and instantly becomes dizzy. Barely able to stand, Katie plops herself back on her bed and closes her eyes for a second. She convinces herself that everything will be fine and picks up the phone to return David's call. Katie instantly notices the change in David's tone on the phone. Normally he is always so smooth and collected when he talks, but this time his voice is shaky, and she can tell he is shook. He tells her that they can't talk over the phone, and they need to meet at the office in twenty minutes. She reluctantly agrees and rushes out the door.

Katie arrives at the office looking slightly disheveled. Her ash blonde hair is thrown up in a quick bun at the top of her head. Little tousled strands that she missed when styling her hair found a home against her delicate neck. She didn't have time to put on any makeup or even wash her face. Even so, her creamy, white skin remains blemishless. Being in such a rush, she barely bothered to get dressed. She threw on a clean pair of yoga pants that were lying on a chair in her room and grabbed a sweatshirt to put over her less than flattering pajama top.

Her feet feel heavy as she drags them into each step on the way into the office building. Her stomach is in knots, but she can't decide why. She knows what is coming next isn't going to be easy, and isn't going to be good news, but deep down she knows her hesitation could be because she hasn't seen David in months.

She's been avoiding him since he broke it off with her for the third time. Luckily for Katie it was easy for her to evade the sight of David since his office is on the seventh floor and hers is on the second. He rarely needs to contact her in person and can just email her when things come up. Katie has been happy with this method of communication so far. It means she can ignore her feelings for a little longer.

Katie pops into the elevator in the lobby and clicks the button for floor seven. She tries to think about the last time she pressed that button, but nothing comes to mind. Her stomach twists and turns like she is on a rollercoaster as the screen in the elevator counts up and pauses at the illuminated seven on the tiny screen.

Katie thinks back to her choices of past boyfriends as the elevator halts. She has always made terrible decisions when it comes to men. She doesn't really know why. Her father is a wonderful man who has provided her with nothing but love and affection since the day she was born. He isn't a perfect husband to her mother, but she has always been able to tell that they love one another, and he is a good role model. Since she was a little girl, she has aspired to find someone like him one day to share her life with.

When she met David, she thought maybe she had finally found someone to settle down with. Someone to really love her for her. Each and every time they called it quits, she couldn't figure out why they could never make it work between them and blamed herself for not having what it took to make him happy.

As she steps out of the elevator, she catches a glimpse of the back of David's dishwater blondish-brown hair across the room. She immediately feels torn inside. The rock in her stomach seems to dissipate and left in replacement is an ache of longing for him to hold her. She shakes off the uncomfortable feeling and begins to approach him, hoping she can act natural and mature. With every step she takes she can feel his presence coming closer. The tiny hairs on the back of her neck begin to stand up as a chill runs down her back. The sweet smell of his aftershave and particular deodorant fills her nose and brings back the memories of the mornings they would lay in bed talking about their hopes and dreams and the world around them.

Katie recalls David rolling over in the bed that they shared and brushing the hair from her face so he could kiss her good morning. David had asked her where she wanted to be in ten years, and she couldn't think of any place other than in his job. She envied how easy it was for him to take on such a demanding position. He never brought any work home and he never complained, not even once, about anything work related. It was like he took this position and turned it into whatever he wanted it to be without any real effort.

No matter how many nights they spent together, Katie couldn't tell him that she hoped to be as successful as he was in ten years. She also couldn't tell him that she thought she could be better at his job than he was. He took his job seriously, but never really tried to make any substantial difference in the world with the power he has. David wasn't the kind of man who wanted a woman who was equally as successful as he was. Instead, she told him that she wanted to be married with kids and own a comfortable house that she could make into a home. It wasn't a lie. She did want those things. She had wished that these things would come sooner than ten years and she hoped David would be the one to give them to her.

CHAPTER 1

Thinking about her past causes her eyes to well up and she tries to pinch her nose to snap herself out of this emotional coma she feels herself slipping into. It is over between them, and she needs to accept it. They are toxic together and she needs to move on, but each time he calls her she seems to fall in love all over again. His voice pulls her in and she forgets all of the disagreements and pain she felt when she found out that he didn't want the same things as her.

Her heart broke the day he told her that he had met someone else and was leaving her. They had broken up before—several times, but the reasons never involved another woman. Their arguments always stemmed around how David didn't respect the amount of time Katie spent on her work. He needed her attention, but her work always preoccupied her and came first. Katie knew that she was a workaholic and driven to move up the ranks, but she couldn't see why David wouldn't be happy for her if he really cared about her and wanted to be her partner. She hoped that this time would be like all the others, and he would be back to her in a matter of weeks, making up in her apartment late at night like they always had.

This current breakup, however, feels more final. She made a point to unfriend and unfollow him on every social media app she could so she wouldn't be inundated with pictures of him and his new girlfriend. She never liked social media much anyways. It is impossible to tell what is real and what is an illusion. Still, she hopes that the girl in the pictures is more fake than real.

With each step towards David, Katie tells herself to shake it off and focus on why she is here. Her job needs to take precedence, like it always has. As she gets closer, she notices she can hear David talking to someone. Immediately she regrets not taking the time to put on something more flattering and professional. She quietly curses herself for being so careless about her looks.

As she rounds the corner of the cubicle outside of David's office, she sees he is standing near someone, a man with shaggy, dark, brown hair, rounded glasses, and a little face stubble. Although he isn't what she would normally consider her type, something about the way he looks rumpled is slightly attractive and intriguing to her. The man immediately stands up and sticks his hand out to greet her. She studies him for a second longer. He looks so familiar. She has seen him before but can't quite put her finger on where.

Katie hesitantly shakes the man's hand as David begins to introduce them. Before David can finish his sentence, she remembers where she's seen the man before. His image was on the news this morning when she turned the TV on.

"Pleasure to meet you Ms. Kleug, I'm Dr. Nicholas Cyrus, but please just call me Nick," he says.

Chapter 2

April 24th, 2082 - NICK

Nick Cyrus wakes up on Friday, April 24th, 2082, to an influx of emails that he has yet to read. His field of study is more talked about now with the information flying around all media platforms about the people that they call *'The Modified'*, but he had no idea if the rumors were true about the newest developments. His inbox tells him all he needs to know. The boy who evolved well into childhood must be real and he now has a big job to do. Even though big companies are trying to poach Nick with giant salaries and signing bonuses to head up their research departments, he wants to work with one of the government's departments in order to help keep order and provide accurate information to the public. Salary doesn't matter. This could finally be the big break in his career that he has been hoping for. The grants provided for research are what will make the biggest difference in terms of the trajectory of his future. He could finally do something *serious* with his degree. Something life changing.

Nick has always been a do-gooder. Even from the time he was in elementary school he was always the rule follower who took very little risk. He grew up with a single mother, who he adored. She worked late most nights, often leaving Nick home alone. Without having much company around the house, Nick began researching things that interested him. The evolution of animals is what intrigued him the most. There were even times when his mother would come home late into the night, and she would find him asleep in bed with his digital book projection still on his ceiling or with his personal room bot playing sound clips of old lectures from the

EDUvision app. His mother could never get upset with him for staying up late because his dedication to learning everything about evolution and biology was monumental and she knew he would use his knowledge for greatness one day.

By high school, Nick was in all of the honors classes and on track to go to a good college to double major in Biology and Biochemistry. He continued to work hard and ended up going to Northwestern in Chicago. When he was a junior wildcat, his mother called him and told him she was diagnosed with skin cancer. She requested that he not worry too much because it wasn't that serious. He believed her and stayed at school, working harder than ever.

When Nick returned home for the summer before his senior year, he found that his mother wasn't all that honest about how serious her diagnosis was and how her treatment was going. Within a few weeks she severely declined, and she was gone before the summer ended. His heart had broken into a thousand pieces that summer break. Not only did he lose the most important person in his life, but he felt that scientific advancements within medicine had betrayed him by not being able to save her. He decided that it was more important than ever to find a path in the sciences so that he could really help people.

He returned to school that fall more invigorated than ever to work hard and after graduation he felt his education was not completed. He decided to go forward and pursue his doctorate degree. Completing his educational goals came easy to him and before he knew it, he was Dr. Cyrus. Great networking happened throughout the program and Nick was able to land an internship as a biochemist at a cosmetics company that was trying to solve the aging crisis for upper class women.

Working as a biologist for MoonCycle, the leading cosmetics company in the United States, wasn't a dream come true for Nick, but it was really hard for biologists to get a job right out of college, and he felt lucky to be asked to stay after his two-year internship. He also hoped that if he was able to move up in the ranks, he would eventually be able to create a product that really helped people—people like his mom, rather than just those who wanted to look and feel better about themselves. Biologists didn't have the best reputation in society when he graduated or even a few years later when he completed his internship. A lot of people turned away from their faith in the sciences due to political division and the spread of false information by media sources. A miracle product would have to hit the market in order to bridge the gap between those who valued the sciences and those who did not.

The biggest divide was and still is linked to those who believe climate change is real and those who think it is brewed up as a ruse to control and disjoin society. This is a tale as old as time. Climate change becoming a problem was predicted in the year 1896 but really began gaining some traction through discussion in the late 1980's and never really died down after that. Almost two hundred years later, it is still at the forefront of most discussions and news stories.

From the moment his mother died, Nick believed that somehow the inaction on climate change, his love of biology, and the lack of medical advancements of the time period were linked. He just didn't know exactly how it all fit within his life. He did know one thing though. He knew that he didn't want to work in the cosmetics lab forever. He hoped that he could one day make bigger scientific strides to save people and cure some of the disease that riddled the world. He dreamed that he could become the one to cure types of cancer, like his mother suffered, or other terminal illnesses through his passion and bring back society to the belief that science and education are important. A cosmetics company was helping people in a way, Nick justified, when he began to get some serious credit for his work. He was the lead scientist on the groundbreaking product that was released in 2080, Half Moon. Most scientists only dream of receiving world recognition for their contributions, but Nick became one of the few who get a chance to feel appreciated.

Half Moon is a product unlike any other ever released by a cosmetics company or really any company for that matter. It works to slow visible aging. Other companies have claimed their lotions and creams can get rid of wrinkles or crow's feet. Some of those creams even work a little bit, but Half

Moon is something different. Half Moon is a liquid that is taken by mouth using a syringe each week. It is absorbed into cells and actually slows the aging of the cells, and even modifies their DNA, and in turn slows the aging of the people who are taking Half Moon. It is truly a medical breakthrough.

While academics and job success were always something that came easily to Nick, social interactions are not and have never been his strong suit. He has been so busy focusing on growing his career that he missed out on developing relationships with peers along the way. This is likely why he hasn't really had any friends except a few close colleagues. He hasn't even had a girlfriend since he graduated high school. Not all of his social ineptitude can be linked to his strong work ethic. Some of it has a lot to do with the times, as the older generations say, "people don't interact the way they used to anymore".

Nick's high school, college and graduate level courses met in person, but not in the way they had with earlier generations. Students would show up to their assigned classroom but bring themselves into their soundproof computer pod to listen to the lecture and complete their coursework and discussions. A professor would be available for conferencing, but that was the only verbal back and forth found in the classroom. This distraction free tech pod helped most students to be more focused on their coursework, but didn't offer any help when it came to getting to know one another. Most interactions between students happened on the weekend at parties, but Nick isn't the kind to partake in such events.

Nick's mother had always taught him to work hard, but she also desired for him to start a family and find someone to share his life with. Nick didn't understand this want that his mother had for him. She always seemed so content not to be attached to anyone other than him. When he was younger, he even resented a little bit that she didn't want to find someone to be a father figure to him. His resentment disappeared when he got older and found his success came much easier without having to worry about others. Now with his recent fame in the scientific community, he knows he can become even more successful without being distracted by silly things like relationships.

Nick opens the mail app on his phone and scrolls through the inbox. He sees an email from the Human Biology Research Department. An overwhelming feeling of mixed emotions comes over him. The Human Biology Research Department of the United States government is the best research facility in the world. Having David Bruner, who oversees all scientific research for the government, reach out to him personally is very flattering. He quickly scans the email:

Dr. Cyrus,

Please call me immediately regarding a position the government is requesting that you fill. The Human Biology Research Department is moving quickly to get started on research and will need your response before the end of the day. For security reasons we will need to meet in person to discuss the opportunity. I can be reached via phone today to confirm your travel and hotel accommodations if you are interested in hearing about the position.

Thank you for your consideration,

David Bruner
President of Operations
The Human Biology Research Department
555-887-9852 extension 2008

Even though the email is cryptic, Nick knows it's about *'The Modified'*. No one seems to be able to talk about anything else once again.

A few years ago, when the first MOD children were born, the news didn't seem to report about anything else. The engrossment with the MODs eventually died down and it became more accepted, at least in a few southern cities, as time went on. Now that there is word of a child evolving in later childhood, Nick is mentally preparing to hear about this for the next several months…if not years.

He begins to get nervous about the prospect of being a part of something so large and encompassing, but this is something he's been waiting for his entire life. He is happy to finally be free of his position at MoonCycle. After waiting for his contract to expire with them for so long he finally has the chance to do something he feels passionate about.

He wipes his clammy hands on his boxer shorts and gets out of bed. He rummages through his bedding to find his phone and walks over to his desk to get comfortable. Somehow he is able to find a piece of paper and pencil on his cluttered desk to take down the contact information from the email Bruner had left him. He dials the number, and David Bruner picks up on the first ring—which startles Nick a little as he thought he'd have another few seconds to prepare.

"Bruner's phone!" David spat into the phone. Nick is immediately thrown off by the daft way Bruner answered the phone.

"Uh, hello there Mr. Bruner, this is Dr. Nicholas Cyrus. I received your email this morning." Nick says, beyond flustered.

"Ah yes, of course Dr. Cyrus, thank you for getting back to me so promptly. As you have gathered from my email this is a classified conversation, and I will not be able to discuss anything with you over the phone. However, I am able to tell you this is about the evolutionary changes that I'm sure you have been hearing about." David calmly states.

"Yes, I assumed as much. I am interested in hearing more about the government's take on things," Nick, now finally calm, declares.

"Wonderful, I am looking forward to meeting you. I have arranged for your flight out of Chicago this evening to Washington D.C. It is my understanding that you have a phone call with NBC news this evening. I have made sure that you will be able to make it to your flight after that. I will have someone pick you up at DCA and bring you to your hotel accommodations at Hotel Washington. Unfortunately, since we are on a very tight time crunch, I will need you to get settled quickly and meet me early tomorrow morning so we can get started. I will have my assistant forward you all the necessary travel documents."

"Thank you, Mr. Bruner, I will see you tomorrow morning."

Both parties hang up the phone. A wave of anxiety falls over Nick. He has to begin packing now in order to leave tonight and still be able to fit the call with NBC Chicago in.

Nick throws some clothes in a bag. He never really cared much for packing. He always saw people travel to the airport with three or four suitcases full of items for their trip, but he could never understand how someone could need that much stuff. He decides that as long as he has a couple pairs of shorts, a few t-shirts and at least one semi-dressy outfit that it would be sufficient. He can always buy something if he needs it, he decides.

Nick phones into the NBC line at 5 p.m. sharp. The role that NBC pitched him was to come on as one of the lead scientists to talk about his success at MoonCycle and what he thought would come next now that he had left the company. He tried his best to prepare for questions he thought he would be asked, but he could never be really sure about the route that the journalist would take. He decided to also be prepared for any questions about MODs that may come up given the current news climate.

He sits on hold for several minutes before NBCs top journalist, Lila Whitt, picks up saying, "We now have Dr. Nicholas Cyrus with us. Can you hear us Dr. Cyrus?"

He confirms, "Yes, I can hear you quite well. Hello, Lila and hello Chicago."

Lila doesn't waste any time with small talk and jumps right into her interview with the doctor.

"Dr. Cyrus, you've had quite the last two years. You were on top of the world with HalfMoon when it was released. I have even heard that you were listed as one of America's top scientists to watch for this decade. How do you feel about being free to pursue other interests and opportunities now?"

Nick was obviously expecting this question and had come up with a nice generic response with hopes she wouldn't be able to ask any follow-up questions about it.

"I've been waiting a while to be able to pursue some new opportunities and I'm hopeful that I will be able to find something soon that appeals to my specialties. As of right now I'm really just weighing all my options, and I can't really give you more than that at this point."

Lila tries to pry a bit more to see if she can get Nick to give information on any of the offers that he's received, but he doesn't budge. She finally moves on after what feels like forever to Nick.

She then tries to dig a little into Dr. Cyrus's personal life, but he isn't having any of that either and shuts her down quickly. After finding no real information out from the interview she decides to drop a real bomb of a question on him.

"Dr. Cyrus, there have been some rumors swirling around in some of the southern states about people becoming *Modified,* or as most of us know them as MODs, without being born with the traits. Have you heard this to be true?"

Nick is really thrown off by this question and doesn't know how to respond. He thought that he would be asked about how the children could develop in the womb with these traits without their parents having them because even as the years passed most civilians still didn't understand the process, but he is not prepared to talk about rumors that he doesn't know to be true. He can't believe that the producer would let the anchor put him in this position on national television.

"I don't really know much about the rumor that you are presenting to me, but I suppose it is possible. We haven't seen anything like this yet, but I also haven't done extensive research on the topic of *Modification* as I have been working for a cosmetics company for several years now."

Lila decides to take his words out of context and run with it. She thanks him for his time and says that he was very helpful in confirming that there is a very good possibility that the rumors of a child becoming a MOD are true. He is disconnected from the call feeling like he probably made a huge mistake by even agreeing to do this interview. He decides that this is the last time he is going to talk to the media, watch the news, or even check social media.

Waking up Saturday morning, Nick surprisingly feels refreshed and enthusiastic about the prospect of new research that he may be able to start soon. He is meeting Bruner at 5 a.m. this morning so he has to rush. After a brisk shower he hurries to brush his teeth and throws on some khaki shorts and a button up blue madras shirt. Once in the lobby, he is lucky to find that even though it is so early, there's a coffee station ready to go. He pours himself a hot, plain black coffee and heads out front.

Chapter 3

April 25th, 2082 - DAVID

David notices Katie taking a long look at Nick as he introduces them. He feels jealousy burning in his throat. He ended things with Katie because he wasn't ready to get serious with her and she wanted to settle down, but he isn't ready for her to look at someone the way she is looking at Dr. Cyrus right now.

David begins to tell Katie that she will be working closely with Dr. Cyrus on the research project as his point person. She is to provide him with anything that he needs throughout his research and to keep in contact with David on all developments.

Katie lifts her gaze off of Dr. Cyrus and turns back to David. Her face is expressionless. David can tell she is uncomfortable around him, but that doesn't matter now. At least he hopes it doesn't. The job that they need to complete is a big one. If they can't get this job done it could mean the end of all of their careers and that is honestly not even close to the worst thing that could happen.

David sends Nick along with his assistant, Kenny, to get situated in the lab. He requests that Katie stay back for a moment so they can clear up some of the arrangements for the work assignment. In reality, he just wants her to stay a bit longer so he can try to patch things up with her enough so she will trust him again. When he called things off with her, he didn't anticipate needing to keep her so close just for work purposes. Of course he still has feelings for Katie, but the feelings won't ever really transpire into anything serious. He has a new girlfriend now—a super-hot girlfriend, as all his friends keep assuring him. Katie will always be too 'girl-next-door' for him. He needs adventure and thrill and that just isn't Katie.

It isn't that Katie isn't attractive. That isn't it at all. She is one of the most beautiful people David has ever seen, but she's too simple. She doesn't want anything from him; she doesn't stroke his ego the way he needs her to. He wants a woman he can take care of. Someone that needs him and will treat him as such. Katie will never be that for him. Maybe that's why it stung so much when he saw Katie looking at Dr. Nicholas Cyrus. He thought for a second he saw in her eyes that she could maybe one day need him in a way she never needed David.

David always tries to play everything off so cool. This scenario will be no different. Of course he can't let Katie see he is bothered at all, but at the same time he needs to keep her close. Even if there is not a chance that they will ever be getting back together he needs to make her think there is so that she will confide in him during the next steps of the assignment.

"How have you been Kitty-Kate?"

Kitty-Kate. His pet name for her since their first rendezvous. She smirks. His heart melts a little. David tries to stay focused. He knows he can't get hooked on her again. They are really over this time so he has to make it into a game.

"I've been good, David. How have you been?" She responds promptly and without enthusiasm.

"I've been fine. Thank you for asking. I just wanted to tell you that I don't want things to be awkward between us. I will always have feelings for you. I want us to remain the best of friends. We used to be so close, and you've been slipping away," he says with intentional sadness in his voice.

Katie feels the heat on her cheeks. She doesn't know why, but David is always a soft spot for her. She wants to be free of him for good this time and she feels like this time is different, but that doesn't mean he still doesn't have a bit of a spell over her.

"I'm sure we can still be friends still, David. I would like nothing more," Katie says, acting unaffected by him.

He is going to have to try a bit harder to keep Katie close. He leans into her giving her a tight, lingering hug. Her head impulsively rests on his shoulder. A few seconds pass by before she even realizes what is happening and pulls away from David.

Chapter 4

April 25th, 2082 - NICK

Nick is on his way to the lab to get everything situated. He was told by Bruner that he needed to be set up by the afternoon because there would be a delivery for him of more materials and even some samples he could use for his research. It is his job to find out why and how evolution is occurring in the southern and southeast regions. It isn't explicitly asked of him, but he knows that if he can figure this out, he will also be able to find out why it isn't happening at the same level in the north and why the modifications in the regions vary so much.

The north doesn't have as many factories as the south has. This has been true since the second industrial boom in the early 2050s, but the north still has its fair share of pollution as well as weird weather patterns caused by climate change. If Nick is able to pinpoint the direct correlation of the increased evolution to the southern region, the news may be able to finally give people answers and smooth over the northern and southern conflict. This discovery could maybe even help the United States get back on good terms with the rest of the world. Much of the media is strictly controlled by the government so Nick isn't sure that MODs exist overseas, but if they do it comes to his mind that maybe he can help them too.

By late afternoon Nick feels like the lab is organized to his liking enough to get started. It's lucky that he works so quickly because David Bruner walks into the lab to offer him even more to work with. He tells Nick to get into his hazmat suit so he can show him the sample brought in for him to analyze. Nick isn't worried about catching the "*modification*". He knows that isn't how evolution works, but etiquette calls for him to follow Bruner's lead. He zips himself inside of the hazmat suit and follows his boss out of the lab.

As Nick follows David through a long dimly lit hallway he begins to get a sense of discomfort for the situation, but he can't quite put his finger on why he is feeling this way. He has always felt comfortable in research buildings and scientific situations, but something about this interaction is making him feel a way he hasn't felt before. As soon as they reach the end of the hallway Nick spots the word "quarantine" on the door they are about to enter. He now knows why he is feeling so uncomfortable. It becomes clear at this point that the sample Bruner brought in isn't just a sample, but rather a person.

They enter the quarantine room with their hazmat gear on to find a small blonde-haired, blue-eyed boy sitting on an examination table. Nick eyes the boy up and down and determines that he can't be more than seven or eight years old. A few things cross Nick's mind at this point. He realizes that he is very irritated that Bruner didn't tell him he would be working with actual MODs, but at the same time he is also mesmerized with the boy on the table. He had only ever heard of children who were recently born of having the "*modification*", but this boy isn't even close to being an infant. Nick knows now that the rumors are true, and he is looking the rumor right in the face now.

David meets Nick's eyes and notices that he is perplexed by the situation. He whispers into Nick's ear that he needs to go check in with other units of his department and that he will return. He then exits the room taking all of the air in it with him.

"Hello there, I am Dr. Nick Cyrus. What is your name?" Nick gently asks the young boy.

Without making any eye contact and keeping his eyes to the floor, the boy whispers, "I am Adam."

"Adam, what is your last name?"

Adam lifts his head and meets Dr. Cyrus's gaze and responds, "Ardi".

"Thanks for meeting with me, Adam Ardi. Are you feeling a bit nervous about being here?"

"Yes, I want to see my mom. Do you know where my mom is? The man that was here before said I could see my mom soon, but it has been a really long time," Adam says frantically.

"I promise that I will figure out where your mom is after we talk and I evaluate you for a few more minutes, is that alright with you, Adam?" Dr. Cyrus asks with gentle eyes.

Adam agrees and Dr. Cyrus begins to examine him.

On Adam's neck there are small slits forming. With each breath that Adam takes in, Nick notices that there is a little air escaping through the slit that bulges and opens slightly. He asks Adam where he is from, but he doesn't need to. He knows that he is from the southeast. Likely one of the Carolinas or what's left of Florida given the type of *modification*. That is where most of the MOD births have been occurring and it is obvious, too, that he isn't from the north. The northern people facing evolutionary changes look different from what the southern MODs have been experiencing. The northern MODs are being born with thick, rough looking skin to withstand the extreme cold temperatures that now come in six month waves.

Nick recalls the first time he first laid eyes on a northern MOD. He remembers that he was on one of the moving sidewalks that he traveled from work to his home each day on the busy Chicago streets. The end of the sidewalk was backed up with people and a crowd started forming. The sidewalk that continuously runs made a sharp buzzing noise and came to an immediate halt. He tried to move around the crowd, but police officers pushed in front of him to try to break up the crowd. That's when he saw the young girl. She couldn't have been more than 6 months old. Her mother had lifted her up from the expensive all-seasons hover pram and placed her tightly into her arms. She became fiercely protective as the crowd moved in closer to her. Some of the bystanders began shouting names at the mother and child, calling the baby an abomination, a sin, and deformed among other nasty comments. While Nick was shocked to see the child with the pale blue, rough and even slightly jagged skin, he could never imagine calling a child the things he heard that day. He eventually made it through the crowd and onto another moving sidewalk to complete his journey home, but regretted later that he didn't stay longer to ensure that the mother and child found safety away from the forming mob. That memory stuck with him day in and day out whenever he traveled that sidewalk home.

Nick pulls himself away from his regretful memory and focuses on the young MOD before his eyes. Adam explains to him that he is from South Carolina and that he lives in a house on the beach with his mother, father and little brother.

"Adam, were you born with these slits on your neck?"

"No, they showed up a few weeks ago."

"What do you mean they showed up?"

"Well, one day I woke up and my neck felt sore, like a sore throat, but it was on the outside. I told my mom about it and she took me right to the doctor. It was kind of weird though. She didn't seem to want to take me like she did when I was sick other times. On the way to the doctor I looked in the mirror in the car and I saw these two wide dots on each side of my neck, kind of like little holes," explains Adam, with his breathing slowing now.

"So the slits on your neck were smaller than this at some point?"

"Yes, sir. They were a lot smaller. When we got to the doctor he looked at me and took my temperature and all those things doctors do and then he took my mom outside to talk to him. I don't know much of what happened after that. The only thing I know is that my mom kept getting phone calls over and over and she would not answer them. The phone just kept ringing and ringing. She even changed her phone number. I wasn't allowed outside anymore. She wouldn't even let me go to school anymore. She said she needed me to stay home to keep me safe ….I don't really understand why she said that since I didn't feel sick at all anymore," Adam explained matter of factly.

"Then what happened?" asks Dr. Nicholas Cyrus, truly interested in what the boy has to say.

"After a long while a man came to my house and told us that mom and I have to come with them. They said if we didn't then the police would make us come. My mom said no for a minute and then she said yes. I don't think she wanted to though. She told me the whole time in the car over and over that everything would be alright and she wouldn't let anything bad happen to me. I didn't want to tell her, but that made me even more scared.…I was so scared I didn't even tell her about this…"

Adam stops talking and lifts up his shirt to show his ribs. Along each side of his rib cage are little slits forming. They look smaller like what he had explained happened to his neck when it first formed.

Dr. Cyrus adjusts himself trying not to show his discomfort.

"Adam, I am going to do everything I can to help make you feel less scared, but I am going to have to look at these spots on your body a little more later. We have to do a bit of research as to why and how these things are happening to your body."

"OK, but can I please see my mom now? It's been a really long time." Adam pleads.

"Let me see what I can do, stay here and I will be right back."

Dr. Cyrus walks out of the quarantine room and back down the hallway until he reaches a door with a window that says 'waiting room'. He doesn't even realize that he has been holding his breath until he reaches the door. He lets out a deep breath that sounds more like a sigh.

As Dr. Cyrus opens the door to the waiting room, a short, tan woman turns around and he can instantly tell she is Adam's mother. She has the same bright blonde hair and deep blue eyes as Adam. Nick walks over to greet her and explain who he is. Her aura screams 'overwhelmed'. Despite the defeat and exhaustion in her eyes he can tell she is strong and determined by the toughness in her voice. The woman introduces herself as Ava Ardi. She expresses to Dr. Cyrus that she was forced to come here by the Department of Defense and that they told her they would take Adam away from her if she wasn't more willing to participate.

Nick thinks it is best to get an adult perspective on what happened to Adam, but as Ava starts speaking, he realizes no one really, not even his mother, knows what happened to Adam other than he just started developing gills one day. Ava's best guess is that he was evolving because they lived in South Carolina, so close to the beach. She wonders if she let him spend too much time in the sun and sand. She explains that Adam spent every waking moment that she would let him on the beach and in the ocean. Even on the cooler days when he couldn't get in the water he would just sit and play in the sand for hours. There are times she said he would eat breakfast and beg to go straight to the beach and then they wouldn't even head inside sometimes until supper time. She said sometimes he wouldn't even want to come back for supper despite eating only a few bites before running out the door that morning.

As Ava describes her son playing on the beach, Nick thinks back to his own childhood. The joy in Ava's voice as she talks about Adam reminds Nick of his own mother when she was still alive. He thinks about how his mother would boast about him and his accomplishments over the phone to her friends and distant relatives even before he did anything noteworthy. She was always so proud of him for working hard and of the person he had become. She was the reason he worked so hard to become the best he could in his field. She was also the reason that the money didn't really matter to him now and it never really would. It wasn't about the money; he wanted to make her proud even if she wasn't around to see his accomplishments anymore. Nick can tell that Ava will be the same role model and inspiration for Adam as he grows into manhood.

Dr. Cyrus tries to keep positive thoughts about what is going to happen over the course of the next few weeks, maybe even months, but seeing Ava Ardi in that room pacing and waiting to see her young son makes him feel like there is more to the situation than he was told by Bruner. He starts to feel his morning coffee rising back up in his throat as he excuses himself from Ava. It crosses his mind that he hasn't eaten much since he got the call from Bruner. He can't tell if the nausea is being caused by an empty stomach or the uneasiness he feels about the moments to come. He tells Ava that he will check back in with her very soon and that Adam is doing alright as he heads through the waiting room door.

The walk back to the quarantine room is interrupted by Bruner's assistant, a young man in his early 20's that goes by the nickname Kenny even though his company name tag says Kendrick. Kenny Nash is someone that Nick feels like he can relate to. He can tell Kenny is smart by the way he speaks, and he can also see that he lacks confidence similarly to Nick himself. His voice is calm, and he seems almost as if he is too shy to even make eye contact with the doctor.

Kenny tells him that Bruner wants him to head over to his office and fill him in on his take on the sample that was received today. That word. Sample. It makes Nick's blood boil. He knows that Kenny is just repeating his boss's words, but it stings just the same. He isn't a sample. He is a little boy and he should be treated and talked about as such. He shrugs off Kenny and walks past him to re-enter the quarantine room.

Adam is still sitting there on the cool, metal table, but now he is shivering. Cyrus can't tell if it is because he is cold or because the room speaks to you in an empty way that can strike fear into the manliest of men. The room is just as dim as the hallway that had led him here. The artificial light hanging above Adam doesn't help to make the room feel more comfortable. Instead, it makes it seem like a setting straight out of a 2040's horror film. Looking over at Adam sends an icy-cold sharpness up his legs causing him to want more than anything to help the boy and his mother to feel warm and safe again.

Dr. Cyrus wants to spend another few minutes with Adam before he goes to Bruner. There is no need to assess him anymore, but he wants to tell him that he saw his mother and that she is doing well. Most importantly he wants to tell him that everything will turn out alright.

From the smile on Adam's face you can tell he appreciates that his mother is still nearby. Cyrus promises Adam he will be able to see her soon and that he will do whatever he can to reunite them.

Directly after he leaves Adam, Cyrus begins to make his way to Bruner's office, as suggested by his insistent assistant. Outside of the office he is once again greeted by young Mr. Nash. Nick begins to think that Kenny is spying on him since he has been seen hovering around quite a bit this morning. Cyrus decides to dig a little into the situation, hoping he can get some insight into the workings of the department. He thinks Kenny should be an easy target given his awkward state when it comes to conversations.

"Ken, how long have you been working for Mr. Bruner?"

"The name is Kenny. Please do not call me Ken. That is my father's name, and I assure you, I am not my father. I have worked for Mr. Bruner for going on three years now. Please head into Mr. Bruner's office now. There's no time to waste and I don't have time for a chat right now."

Kenny's shortness is quite a surprise to Nick. He can tell that his first judgment about Kenny was wrong. Kenny isn't shy at all. He's just hardheaded and knows what he wants. He begins to wonder what else he could be wrong about. He assumed Kenny lacked confidence because of his small stature and the way he seemed to hang his head when he walked, but it hadn't occurred to him that Kenny being a young, intelligent, black man who moved up quickly in ranks probably has quite a bit of confidence in what he brings to the table.

Nick decidedly shuffles past Kenny and promptly makes his way into Bruner's office. To his surprise it isn't just David in the office, but Katie Kleug too. Katie greets Nick again with a soft smile. He instantly decides that he likes Katie. She seems confident, but humble. She reminds him of his mother in all the best ways. His mother had always been bright but never acted as though she were smarter or better than anyone else. She always made everyone around her feel comfortable and welcome. That is the same vibe he gets from Katie. She is a simple, pure beauty. He can feel the calmness and kindness radiating off of her.

Bruner begins the conversation without any small talk or how do you do's, "Well Cyrus, what do you think of the sample?"

Nick's eyes squint a bit and his jaw slightly clenches when he hears the word 'sample' again. He can tell Katie picked up on his discomfort because of the way her eyes immediately dart away from him to the carpet.

"He's not a sample. He's a young boy and he's very scared. I did have a chance to assess him a bit and I would appreciate it if you would let him see his mother now. Please keep them close—they shouldn't be separated right now. He's not contagious. You can't catch what he has," Nick declares with sharpness in his voice, still angry at the inhumane treatment of the young boy.

Bruner's face turns a slight twinge of pink, almost as if he is both angry and embarrassed.

"How is it that you are sure he is not contagious? We haven't seen any children become *Modified*, not unless they were born that way. He's the oldest child we've seen evolve," Bruner notes with a hint of arrogance in his voice.

The words hit Nick like an empty cloud. Of course, Nick knows that about Adam. He has been paying attention to all research and work on MODs since the whole thing started 4 years ago and not one child over the age of 2 weeks has ever *Modified*.

"I can assure you that he is not contagious, I don't have time to explain the logistics behind how evolutionary changes take place right now, but his mother has been with him everyday and she would have contracted it anyways if he was contagious so just let them be together," Nick spits out exasperatedly.

Bruner reluctantly agrees and picks up his phone, presses a button and speaks concisely to someone on the other line explaining that Mrs. Ardi could join her son, but she has to wear a hazmat suit until further notice. Nick rolls his eyes as the words exit Bruner's mouth, and he can tell Katie picked up on that too. A witty little smile pops up on her face but disappears quickly as Bruner hangs the phone up.

Nick can't tell if David understands how his actions look. His decisions make no sense. If David really thinks Adam is contagious there is no way he would have allowed his mother to be separated from him in the beginning because it would have been possible that she could be contagious too after spending so much time with her son. David, of all people should know how contagions spread given he runs a biology department for the government.

As soon as the phone hits the hook, Bruner's voice begins again, "We have to move quickly on this. I've gotten word that there is going to be a press conference soon by the Mayor of Beaufort, the town Ava and Adam are from. I guess the word has gotten out about Adam. Some of the people in the town have seen Adam and heard things coming from the rumor mill and it has gotten a lot more suspicious now that the entire Ardi family has gone missing from the town. Of course they're not actually missing, but we can't tell them that. The husband and other child are held up in a secure location and we have security watching over them so we will have no further leaks to the media."

Katie's eyes widen as David Bruner is speaking. This is obviously the first she's heard of this as well. She must be in the dark on a lot of what is going on around here too, he thinks. He finds it interesting that Bruner isn't keeping her in the loop since he handpicked her for this assignment. He can also sense some tension in the room between Katie and David. The way they won't exactly let their eyes meet make it seem like the history between them isn't exactly all sunshine and rainbows.

Katie wonders aloud, "What exactly do you need us to do?"

With uncertainty on his face, Bruner quietly marches over and pushes the door shut the last centimeter until he hears the click of the door perfectly fitting into the jam.

"I need you both to work together to try to figure out what is causing this. I know I didn't make the assignment entirely clear when we spoke last, but I've now been instructed to put all force behind this. We have to stop people from *modifying* or at least figure out why it is occurring now. Tension is growing in all of the northern states. This is a top-level clearance. As of right now the two of you are to keep all information you obtain classified, top secret and you'll report only directly to myself or my assistant, Kenny," Bruner proclaims with confidence, even though his face is now white as a sheet.

Nick finally speaks up, "Are you worried about a civil war breaking out? I've been following the news, and it seems like people in the north have been growing intolerant of the south, not attempting to slow the rate of MODs coming from this region and not trying to figure out why it's happening. It also appears that people in the south have grown just as tired of the north, not even attempting to slow climate change, but rather blame it entirely on those in the south despite being equally responsible. I've even heard of hate groups outside of Chicago—in Illinois and Indiana. The groups are fighting for segregation again! Can you believe it? Segregation! They're acting like we are living in the 1800's. They want all of the *Modified* people to not even be able to interact with the *Unmodified*. It's just a rumor, but I heard someone even mentioned a petition to the Supreme Court to make it illegal for *Unmodified* and *Modified* to marry in the future. They're children! How can people be so obtuse?"

Judging by Katie's expression she isn't all that surprised by what Nick has just said. Her lips remain pursed, and her eyebrows furrowed. She must have been hearing similar things through news outlets and personal connections to make her so immune to his outrage.

David pauses for a long while. He doesn't seem surprised by Nick's inquiry, but rather somewhat unsure of how best to proceed. To Nick, it seems most like he is pondering whether or not to answer the question at hand: Should they be worried about a Civil War?

David takes a deep breath, it seems like he is going to divulge some big secret, but instead he just notes, "There are a lot of crucial concerns we need to consider right now. The most important thing I need you to worry about is figuring out why this is happening and how we can stop it. The latter being the more important part. I will take care of the rest. You will be working together. Ms. Kleug is going to be able to help facilitate anything you need and gain you access to a lot of our facilities. I'll need a follow up from you, Ms. Kleug, at a minimum of every 48 hours."

Katie nods her head and begins rummaging through her bag looking for a pen and pad to begin taking notes. Her thin, delicate fingers fumble around for a few moments before she finds what she was looking for. Both men watch closely at every move she makes, almost in awe of her ability to get directly down to business.

Nick likes that Katie is old school enough to use a pen and paper, but he won't come out and tell her that in fear that he would make a fool out of himself. Most businesspeople from the northern region now-a-days file their thoughts, to-do lists, and any miscellaneous notes on their virtual assistant. Nick refuses to use one. He thinks it's bad enough that everyone spends most of their time on electronics as it is, he doesn't want anything attached to his body. He hates that the artificial intelligence on the device is aware of his mood and needs. He thinks it would feel like someone is reading your mind. The lack of privacy is terrifying to him.

The fact that the virtual assistant gets implanted into your neck behind your ear seems a little too close for comfort to him. They don't even do the procedure in a medical setting. It is installed now at the device store when you purchase it. They have people who are "trained" on the implantation process. He understands how the technology works, of course, but he feels it's just a little too personal and doesn't want anyone, even if it's a computer, to have that much information on him. He considered using it at one point, but only if he could remove it each time without having it implanted. It turns out the only way it works is if it is implanted so that the technology can help manage your life for you by doing things like seeing if you're in distress to call emergency services or reminding you of things without others hearing. One conscience is enough for Nick.

Three years ago, when this technology came out he figured it was like any new technology that would eventually be obsolete as soon as people were once again reminded that their phones, watches, computers, and numerous other devices could do the exact same thing for less cost. Instead, the virtual assistant became a status symbol.

When Dr. Cyrus first met David Bruner; he could immediately tell that Bruner was wearing a virtual assistant device. He talked to himself, pressing the button behind his ear, leaving notes about practically nothing in front of Nick just to seem important. This flex wasn't lost on Nick, but it didn't bother him because he had met many men like this during his time working at MoonCycle. Everything about MoonCycle is a status symbol down to the very products that are sold in stores.

Katie Kleug could easily afford a virtual assistant device based on her status at the company, so it was a breath of fresh air to see that she didn't have one. This small piece of information about her makes Nick feel like the two of them are on the same level.

Cyrus takes a step back from his thoughts and focuses on what Bruner had just said. He nods in agreement to Bruner's directions for them to get started and the pair exit Bruner's office together. Katie is next to him with her paper pad in hand. She brushes up against him as they are walking. As their arms touch Nick feels a shock. He takes mental note of the spark between them but pretends not to notice.

As they walk down the corridor to the elevator to head back to the lab, Katie says something that surprises Nick, "I'm really worried about this assignment. A lot seems to be riding on this, much more than I had initially been led to believe. I have a feeling that this thing is coming from much higher up than David Bruner. In all the time that I have known David, he has never seemed insecure."

Nick has never worked in a lab where everyone seems to be acting in secret before. He initially thought it was because it is a government lab and they have protocols, but it seems to be much more than that. It appears to be that the government is acting in its own interest, but he can't quite explain why he feels that way yet. He doesn't want to alarm Katie, so he keeps his thoughts to himself. He is surprised that she expressed how worried she is even though she seemed so collected in the office. Besides, he doesn't really know her that well yet. He did however, take a mental note when she said, 'In all the time I've known David'. He decides he will read more into that mental note later when he has more time.

"I agree, we need to work quickly in order to get everything sorted out not only for the boy, but for society as a whole," Nick admits, feeling a little less alone knowing he has Katie to help him.

Katie jots something down on her notepad and then glances up at Nick. Her mood immediately changes.

"Alright Mr. Scientist, what is our first step?" She excitedly blurts.

He smiles at her. She definitely knows how to shift the energy in a room. Any apprehensions about Katie's previous dealings with David and any anxiety about what is to come next is put on the backburner. Nick takes a second to think about what he had learned about Adam. It appears that the only thing that links Adam to being *Modified* is that he lived near the beach and the coastal cities have seen the highest numbers of MODs. Maybe we start there then, he thinks. Nick begins to explain what he had learned about Adam to Katie and asks her to arrange for them to travel to Beaufort,

South Carolina so they can do a little more digging.

Chapter 5

April 26th, 2082 - FRANK

Mayor Frank Roy of Beaufort, South Carolina decides it is time to take action. It has been endless days of continuous phone calls and interviews at City Hall. People want to know if being *Modified* has somehow become a transmittable disease. Mayor Roy doubts it, but the last 72 hours have worn him down and he doesn't know what to believe anymore. Now with Sheriff Santos standing next to him getting ready for this press conference he feels a sense of fear knowing this is going to be a new stage of something he wishes he was never a part of.

Rodrigo "Rio" Santos leans over and whispers into the mayor's ear, "Are you alright? You're sweatin' bullets and lookin' pretty clammy too".

Frank takes out his pocket square and dabs his forehead. "I can't take this heat," he mumbles.

"Frank, are you sure you're alright? It's actually pretty cool out today for it being late April. Weather only calls for a high of 72 today," Sheriff Santos recalls.

"Not that heat, Rio. I can't take all these government officials swarming around. Everywhere I turn I feel like I'm being watched. Likely because I am! If it ain't one of you-know-who's men then it's a constituent coming to complain. This press conference is not a good idea. I think it's going to do the opposite of what they want it to do. I think it's going to rile people up even more," Mayor Roy says matter of factly.

"Frank, listen, I know this isn't the right call and it definitely isn't the most comfortable of situations, but we just have to play ball for a little longer.

The people of Beaufort need to know we are here to protect them and give them a piece of mind that we are doing everything we can to find the Ardi family," Santos notes with a sting in his voice.

"I hear what you're saying Rio, but I'm lying to everyone around me. I can't sleep; I barely can eat. My wife thinks I'm having an affair because I've been acting so unusual. These people elected me. They count on me. Everything I am doing is a disservice to them," Mayor Roy's tone drops.

"We are a small town and if you don't want any of the bigger fish coming to visit and making a stink around here then I think we better just get on with it," Rio huffs.

Frank Roy knows Santos is right. He better get on with the press conference so the people can find some solace. Some of the bigger fish Rio mentioned had already made their debut in Beaufort a few years back when this all started, but they might come back if he doesn't get things under control. They warned him that he couldn't let things get out of control while they were working on a solution and so far he has been doing a good job as mayor keeping order in the small city.

The microphone squeals and crackles as he begins to speak. "For those of you who tuned in and came out to hear me speak, I appreciate it. As you know, being a mayor is not always easy. Sometimes I have to deliver news when there is no news to deliver. As of late we have had many people come out to the police station and to city hall to share their concerns about things they believe are going on in Beaufort. As an elected official I love having people take part in their community and expressing their concerns. It's what makes us one of the best towns in America in my biased opinion. That being said, Sheriff Santos and I have spent a lot of time looking into the concerns that have been presented to us. We have analyzed all aspects, and the police have been diligent in their field work regarding the topic of the Ardi family. It is unfortunate for me to have to stand up here and let you know that as of right now we do not know where the Ardi family is and we are still conducting the search with all of our manpower behind it. At this point in time we do not believe there has been any foul play, and we do not believe the community to be at risk. In addition to our search for the Ardi family we have been hearing a lot of concern about one of the Ardi children, Adam. A rumor has spread throughout the community that Adam Ardi has become a *Modified* without being born with his adaptations. We currently believe this is all a hoax. There has been no proof to show that Adam Ardi is or ever has been a *Modified* or holds any characteristics of a *Modified*. We do take all of your concerns very seriously and will not close the case on this, but we want you as the community to know there is no risk to your safety at this time. I am going to step away now and let Sheriff Santos answer any questions you may have."

Mayor Roy steps away from the podium and a wave of relief comes over him. For the first time in days he can breathe again. Real deep breaths instead of his worried shallow ones. He heads back into City Hall hoping to make it to his office uninterrupted to find some silence and get his head straight, but instead when he enters he sees his secretary, June, pacing in front of her desk.

June spots Frank coming in through the door and quickly shuffles her way over, her feet barely lifting off the carpet with each tiny step. Her forehead appears wrinkled in fear and her hands are shaking, ever so slightly. Frank becomes immediately concerned. June isn't someone to be shaken up easily.

In the lowest possible tone her voice can carry, she says, "You have a visitor in your office. It's one of the men from before. The younger one. I told him you were busy and all—giving the press conference, but he wouldn't take no for an answer. He just waved me off and told me he will wait until you return. He walked right into your office and sat down. I couldn't do a thing to stop him!"

June's head scans the room quickly as if to check if she is being watched. Frank Roy nods and takes a large gulp as he walks through the entrance to the office. He can feel June's eyes following him with concern until he closes the door shut tightly.

"Good afternoon again Mr. Nash! Nice of you to come visit again. What may I ask is the reason for this impromptu visit?" Mayor Roy questions. He has to politic extra hard to make the words seem sincerely welcoming coming out of his mouth.

"Ahhh, please call me Kenny, Frank. I've never been much for formal introductions when it comes to myself. I've been instructed by Mr. Bruner and some of our other acquaintances to just oversee that the press conference went well. You had a wonderful turn out," Kenny notes.

"Yes well, I've been very lucky that most of my constituents are very loyal and trusting," Roy says with disdain in his voice.

There is a long, uncomfortable pause before Kenny speaks again, "Listen Frank, there's been some developments. We have now employed that scientist we were talking to you about, Dr. Cyrus. He's going to do some digging around here. I want you to watch over him and make sure he doesn't go rogue. He can be our key to completing our objectives if we can get him on our side. Do you understand where I'm going with this? Make sure you take care of this, Frank."

Frank closes his eyes for a moment and takes a deep breath. He is too far in now and has no choice but to cooperate, if not for him, for his family. He doesn't want his grandchildren to see what kind of man he's actually become; the kind of man who takes bribes and lies to everyone around him.

Frank gives a forced smile and nods in agreement. Before Kenny leaves he hands him a folder with everything he may need in it. Once Kenny Nash is out of the room, Frank pours himself a glass of whiskey from a bottle he keeps in his bottom desk drawer, to take the edge off. He sits back and opens the navy folder. He takes note that even the folder that was chosen for this seems formal. Couldn't they have just chosen a normal, plain folder, he thinks with irritation growing inside of him. Somehow this fact makes everything seem worse to Frank. It is a reminder that he stepped away from his average, happy, small-town life into something bigger. Something he didn't really want at all.

As he sips his whiskey he thinks about the day he was approached by David Bruner. It was right before the incident at the coffee shop back in 2079. MODs were rumored to be popping up along the eastern coast at this time. Within a few months social media outlets started speculating that there were close to thirty babies born as MODs in the southeast region right below Beaufort alone. This was all, of course, speculation. In fact, the baby in the coffee shop was the first MOD that Frank ever laid his eyes on. David showed up in his office just six days before the murders in True Beans took place. At that time David told Frank that it was reported that at least one MOD was born in Beaufort and that because of this, it was important he work extra hard to keep emotions in check. David briefly glossed over why he was involved in this project. He didn't need to go into detail because once he told him where the orders came from, Frank knew he didn't have any option other than to play ball.

He finishes downing his smooth whiskey and finally looks inside of the folder. He finds many documents. Documents that describe everything one needs to know about Dr. Cyrus. It explains where he lives, where he went to school, his work history, lists of distant relatives, so much information that he is surprised it doesn't tell him the last time Dr. Cyrus took a piss. As he flips through the documents, he finds the documents are not just about Dr. Cyrus, but also about a woman, Kathryn Kleug. There is just as much information on Ms. Kleug as there is on Dr. Nicholas Cyrus. Great! More people I have to include in my circle, he thinks. After he reaches the end of the documents of information regarding Cyrus and Kleug, he finds a post-it note from Bruner.

In the very limited interaction that Mayor Roy had with David Bruner, it always seemed that David conducted his business very formally. He either always sent Kenny Nash to speak in person so no paper trail would be left or if he was speaking on the phone, he was very cryptic as if not to give out unnecessary information. For those reasons the post-it note struck a chord with Frank. He picks up the crinkled, yellow post-it note to examine it a little closer.

"Don't let anything slip past you. Your fate rests on your actions." - Bruner"

Chapter 6

April 26th, 2082 - NICK & KATIE

Before today, Nick never had the opportunity to fly private before. It is a really odd experience for him. Part of him is kind of enjoying having someone wait on him. The stewardess is constantly seeing if he needs another drink, a snack or pillow and blanket. The other part of him just wants to be left alone in silence so he can think about his next move. He wants to be able to come back to D.C. with new information so that he can help Adam and Ava.

He glances over at Katie and tries to get a read on what she is thinking. She looks so calm and innocent sitting there reading and then re-reading her notes. Her blonde hair is smashed up into a messy bun at the top of her head exposing her soft, milky looking neck. This must be her signature hair style, he determines. Nick is trying not to stare at her in fear that she will notice, but somehow, he just can't look away. The way she chews on the end of her pen while she is thinking is so attractive to him. He finds her focus on her work to be impressive, and he admires how important doing her job well means to her. He abruptly decides that if he looks at her any longer there is no way she won't notice, so he decides he better make conversation to ease the tension growing inside of him.

"Are we all set for when we get to Beaufort?" He blurts a little louder than he expected.

Katie jumps a little in her seat.

"Ohhhh for Pete's sake! You scared me! I was so focused that I didn't see you were trying to get my attention," she laughs a little as she tries to collect herself after being petrified.

"Yes! We are all set to go. We are scheduled to meet the town's sheriff and mayor at 3 p.m. so they can brief us on everything that's been going on over the last few days. Unfortunately, while we have been up in the air, I guess there was a press conference and Q&A going on in Beaufort and we will have just missed it."

Nick can tell that Katie is more anxious about it than she is letting on. He can hear her overcompensating with her sweet voice. He tries to comfort her with his eyes. Katie notices this and melts a little bit inside. She doesn't want to get too close to him. The last time she felt a strong connection with someone was with David and that didn't end well at all.

She hates that she still has to sporadically see and talk to David because her job requires her to. The worst part is that the people she normally interacts with on a daily basis still spend time with David at events, so she ends up hearing about him often, despite trying to stay away. She thinks about quitting at times, but she loves her job. Katie worked hard to get where she is today. She started off as a project manager for a small tech company outside of Pittsburgh and eventually networked enough to get hired on by the Human Biology Research Foundation when they sold them some of their computer software. She's been climbing the ladder at the foundation ever since. She's finally in a strong position in her career and she doesn't want to let David or any man take that away from her.

Something feels different in the way that Nick looks at her, though, unlike any other man. It isn't just a lust for her, as it had been when David looked at her. There is a softness in his eyes and voice when he speaks to her. Even though she barely knows him it makes her feel safe. Despite feeling this connection with the stranger she's been assigned to spend all this time with, she doesn't want to get involved. She needs to stay focused. This could be the biggest task she'd ever take on in her career and she can't let a man ruin it, no matter how desirable he looks sitting across from her.

The wheels hit the ground in Beaufort and Katie is already hard at work. She is organizing hotel accommodations and making sure they have access to a local governmental facility that they can use as a pop-up lab. She works quickly and diligently. Nick is beginning to feel useless. Up until this point all he's really done is watch Katie work. He doesn't even know what he could do to seem useful at this moment. He was never good at planning and with his job he didn't really need to be. The systems put in place at labs are pretty straight forward and organize themselves. For this, he is thankful. He still wants to feel more useful and asks Katie if there is anything he can do to help. Luckily, she finds something for him to do while she stays in the SUV and makes all the other arrangements. She delegates to him the task of checking out the Ardi's house and the surrounding area to see if there was anything worth noting that can be helpful to their research.

Once the car pulls up at Ardi's residence, the side door swings up and Nick hops out of the black, fully loaded SUV and takes in his surroundings. It is a beautiful sight. He has been along the coast before, but he forgot how truly breathtaking the views could be. The sun shining down on the sand makes it appear almost as though a field of glitter is touching the ocean.

He walks along the path that leads to the house and looks around. It appears as if life is frozen in time in the yard. Water guns laying in the grass. Beach towels hanging out to dry on the porch railings. Toys sprawled all over the place as if the children just called it quits only for a moment to take a snack break, intending to return.

Once Nick reaches the house he tries to peek through the windows on the door, but the frosted glass makes it impossible. He makes his way around the porch to the ocean side of the house and peers through the large wall of windows. Everything inside looks the same as it did on the outside–abandoned. The counter still has juice boxes with tiny straws sticking out and half eaten sandwiches on it. The Ardi's were obviously not expecting their unannounced guests to whirl them away in an instant. This makes him wonder where the rest of the Ardi family is being held. He assumes that since Adam and Ava were taken in to be held at the lab that her husband and other child were taken in and put in some containment area as well, but he didn't see them anywhere near the lab before he left for Beaufort.

Standing on the porch looking out at the beach, Nick feels a wave of uneasiness wash over him. The type of feeling where you don't feel alone even though no one is in sight. He scans the horizon and the areas to the north and south of him, but nothing catches his eye. He takes a moment to take a few deep breaths to calm himself down. Maybe he is just being paranoid. The conversation that Bruner had with him put even more pressure on him to get to the bottom of things and put a stop to the changes before the tension in the world hits a tipping point. The pressure, he decides, is what is making him feel crazy.

The truth is that Nick doesn't really see anything wrong with people becoming *Modified.* He actually thinks it is a positive thing from a scientific standpoint, but he can never let anyone know that he feels that way with how controversial things have become in the media and even among friends and families. Nick decides it is time for him to shake off all of the reservations he is having and to get down to business, but even as he tries to set his mind to it, he still has an overwhelming feeling he is being watched.

Just as he begins to head down to the beach to look around a bit more, he sees something move out of the corner of his eye. Nick stops, trying not to act spooked so he can figure out what caused the movement without scaring whatever it is back into hiding. He heads down the stairs to the sandy beach that lay in front of the picturesque beach cottage and peers out of the corner of his eye to the north of him to see a large man standing in between two large bushes where the shade gathers. The man's eyes and most of his face is shaded by the hat that he is wearing, but Nick can tell he is looking directly at him. The thought crosses his mind that maybe he is just being paranoid. It can very well be a neighbor looking out onto the beach to take in the scenery. That thought, though, is quickly destroyed when the man moves from that set of bushes into another set closer to the water as Nick moves across the beach. He is now positive that he is being followed, but why, he wonders. He has been sent here by the people he figured would be the ones doing the spying, so why would they enlist him for this project if they don't trust him? Nick resets his thoughts and realizes that he, too, in a way, is the one doing the spying and acting suspiciously on someone else's property.

Nick doesn't want to be found out by the man who is peeping on him through the bushes, so he tries to act as casual as possible. He bends down and evaluates the sand and takes a quick sample. Then he slowly makes his way closer to the water where the wet sand tends to stick between your toes. There he pauses to look at the remains of crabs that have washed up on the shore. He kneels down to take some of the small crab pincers left behind by the deceased crabs as samples as well. He is hoping to find some turtle eggs on the beach, but it isn't quite their nesting season yet.

He decides he needs to get several water samples as well. He takes a sample of the shallow water right along the beach then he kicks off his socks and shoes and treads in the water a few feet where he takes a couple samples as well. Luckily, he was smart enough to have taken his phone and wallet out and put them in his shoes on the beach because now his shorts are soaked up past his pockets. The waves aren't particularly large, but they keep crashing into him saturating more and more of his clothing.

After he gathers the samples, he makes his way back to where he left his shoes. The wind blowing along the coast causes the wet hair on his legs to dry quickly. He peers up again to the north to see if the man is still watching him from the bushes, but he doesn't see anything or anyone now. A little relief washes over him, but not knowing where the man was doesn't offer him much comfort.

Nick gathers his materials and makes his way back to the high-end SUV to find Katie ending a phone call with from what he can tell, the mayor or someone in his office. He slides into the seat next to Katie. Her nose crinkles up and a cringed look appears on her face.

"Why are you all wet?" She inquires.

She slides a few inches away from Nick so as to not get any of the wetness on her own clothing.

"We need to meet with the mayor and the town's sheriff in thirty minutes, and you can't really go like that, can you?"

Nick makes an 'I don't know' gesture with his hands. Katie laughs out loud at how he doesn't even think about what being wet could mean for their schedule today and how silly he looked when she questioned him about it. He explains that he had to gather some samples and it only made sense to get some in the water not directly along the shore for the sake of accuracy. She nods, but Nick can see a little annoyance still on her face. She had asked him to do this task, but then didn't like the way he had done it. Then she smiles and laughs at him when he can tell she's actually annoyed. He definitely doesn't understand women, he decides.

This in part is why in the past Nick never had relationships that he could follow through with. One minute he would feel like he has a connection with a woman and the next he would feel the connection run cold. He wasn't sure if this was what all relationships were like or not, but he never stayed around to find out. It was always easier to be on his own, do things his own way and never answer to anyone else.

This assignment will cause him to view his interactions with women differently. His job now requires him to work closely with a woman who isn't exactly considered his boss, but for all business purposes she will take the lead on this work assignment. He decides that to make things run smoothly he will try to be more considerate of her in the future and be clear about what he's going to be doing.

Nick sits silently in the car for several minutes trying to figure out how to explain what he experienced at the beach.

Pulling the conversational band-aid off he whispers to Katie, "I think someone was watching me while I was out there. I saw a man in the bushes. It wasn't a neighbor or anything like that. I could tell that he didn't want me to see him. Do you think I'm just being paranoid?"

A confounded expression stays on Katie's face for some time. Nick can almost hear the thoughts spinning in her head.

Chapter 7

April 26th, 2082 - KATIE and NICK

Katie asks their assigned driver, Mr. Preston, to make a quick stop at the hotel that she arranged so Nick can change his shorts. Nick appreciates that Katie is willing to accommodate him. He decides that he probably should have thought about informing Katie that he was going to take samples in the water before he had done it. He changes quickly into some khakis and decides to top it off with a clean polo even though the t-shirt he was wearing came out of the ocean unscathed. He figures he might as well make an effort since he is meeting with the town's mayor after all. Once changed he moves as quickly as he can through the hotel with the awareness that he is likely putting stress on Katie by almost making them late to their appointment.

In front of the hotel, Nick spots the SUV and promptly climbs in. On the way to city hall Nick and Katie decide to come up with a game plan for their meeting. Katie suggests that she take the lead on everything. Nick is happy to let this happen as he already feels awkward and they haven't even arrived yet. He doesn't want his social anxiety to get the best of him and make him look like a fool in front of Beaufort's mayor and sheriff.

Katie determines that their goal should be to see where the police investigation is at currently, but to not give too much information to the sheriff about what they are doing in Beaufort. She doesn't quite trust anyone with the sensitive information they gathered from David, and she doesn't quite know what the mayor's role is in the project yet.

Normally, Nick would have said that Katie is being overly cautious or even crazy, but his tune changed the moment he saw the man watching him from the bushes. Nick realizes he never did see where the man went and that thought puts his stomach into knots. He decides from then on that he is going to keep his eyes peeled and his suspicion high in case the man following him shows up again.

Nick exits the car first and offers his hand to Katie to help her out of the vehicle. She smiles at him with the most beautiful, genuine smile he has ever seen. As she grabs his hand, he feels the tension between them rising. He doesn't know exactly how to deal with the feelings he keeps catching anytime he is in the presence of Katie. He has never felt so close to someone so quickly before. Once she is safely on the ground, she holds his hand a little longer than necessary and he senses she may be feeling something also.

Inside the historical building Katie and Nick sit patiently in the waiting area of Mayor Roy's office. Roy's secretary, June, tries to make the wait more bearable by offering Nick and Katie some sweet tea. It is the sweetest beverage Nick has ever tasted. He has, of course, had sweet tea before, but it was not nearly as sweet as what he is drinking right now. It is almost as sweet as a cola. The first sip brings him back to the last cola he had drank back when he started going to grad school. It has been close to a decade since he last had a cola because artificial sweeteners were outlawed in 2073 due to medical research proving severe health risks associated with the consumption of them. Now with the FDA approved recipe using real cane sugar again, which is not easily grown in the United States, the price increase makes it hard to justify as a purchase. Despite so much time passing, Nick remembers the sweetness of cola as if it were just yesterday and this tea feels pretty close to it. The deliciousness filling every taste bud and awakening them one by one.

He can tell instantly that Katie isn't from the south either as her eyes grow and her lips pucker at the first taste of the tea. He likes the way her lips look all puckered up. He can't turn his eyes away as she licks the sugary drink from her lips.

As he watches her drink, a small piece of her hair falls in front of her eyes. Instinctively, he reaches over and brushes it out of her face. He shocks himself a bit by this action. Katie is a little surprised as well, but she doesn't want him to think she didn't like it so she plays it off cool. She reaches over and touches the hand that is resting on her face, and their gaze holds for a second before the door to the office opens and interrupts the moment.

Katie pulls away and sits up straight. Nick freezes for a second, processing what just occurred. He can still feel the sensation on his hand from when she gently embraced it. He looks down at his hand hoping the feeling of her soft skin on his would stay a little longer.

Mayor Roy enters the room with his voice booming a generic greeting. To Nick, he resembles a cartoon character. Exactly the type of man you would expect to be a mayor of a small town. Mayor Roy is an older, rather tall, pale man, maybe in his mid-50s, with graying hair and a small grandpa belly to match. He kind of reminds Nick of Santa Claus, if Santa Claus shaved his beard for the summer and gained a southern accent.

The high-spirited mayor ushers Nick and Katie into his office. June scurries behind asking if anyone needs anything else. Mayor Roy waves her off as he introduces them to Sheriff Santos who was already inside of the office.

Sheriff Santos is an intimidating looking man. His slicked back dark hair shines in the light from the window. Nick decides that he can't be too much younger than the mayor, but his leanness makes it hard to put them in the same generation. He looks very clean cut aside from the very little stubble on his cheeks leading to his thick mustache. He isn't taller than Mayor Roy, but his presence somehow seems larger. Santos stands and shakes hands with Nick and Katie, then everyone finds a seat to begin their conversation.

Mayor Roy starts off the conversation like any good host would. He asks how the flight was and if they feel their accommodations in his quaint little town are to their liking. All of this is, of course, just for show. No one in the room actually cares to discuss these things but, unlike the north, it is how things work in the south. There has to be small talk before the real business can be discussed.

After a few minutes of bland ice-breaking conversation, Katie finally pipes in, "Mayor Roy and Mr. Santos, I hear that you held a press conference this morning. How did that go? We've heard there are some growing concerns about the rising tension in South Carolina when it comes to the *Modified*. I'm sure that the Ardis going missing has not helped the situation."

Mayor Roy clears his throat, but before he could begin to speak Sheriff Santos chimes in, "The press conference seemed to go well. Most of the people just want to know they are safe. We can offer them that much. As for the concerns over the *Modified*, I'm sure you've seen on the news that things have been becoming physical. There have been a few rallies, protests and sit-ins to express concern over MODs playing a bigger role in society. Violence has even struck some of the towns in the form of riots. Luckily, we here in lovely Beaufort haven't had that happen to us. We are concerned, but we think it is in check. Our top priority right now is to keep the fact that the Ardi's are missing under control. If the rumors continue to spread about the Ardi boy becoming a MOD, I don't know that we can keep the people of Beaufort or the surrounding areas from starting some of their own protests as well. Things down here are very conservative. People don't like change, and they certainly don't like to feel threatened in any way."

Mayor Frank Roy adds his two cents, "Mr. Santos is correct in saying that things are under control, but as far as I know the reason the two of you are here is because your boss believes you can figure out what happened to the Ardi boy and stop all of this before it becomes something we all need to worry about."

Nick watches Katie the entire time that both Sheriff Santos and Mayor Roy speak. He is trying to get a read on whether or not she trusts them. It seems as though she does by the way she intently keeps eye contact and makes appropriate facial expressions to match theirs. Nick hasn't said a word since introductions, and he doesn't plan to. Katie has it under control and she knows much more about the relationship that David may have with Mayor Roy than he does. Besides, she is much better at social interaction.

Katie responds to both Mr. Santos and Mr. Roy in one breath, "Thank you for filling us in. David briefed me a little before we left D.C. We are definitely here to help, but first we need to know where the investigation by the police department has landed."

Santos adjusts his body in his chair as if to show his discomfort. As he speaks it becomes clear that he was expecting this question. He starts up in an almost robotic response, "the investigation is ongoing, but I'm sure you know that already. We do not know where the Ardi family is, but we do know that it has something to do with the boy, Adam, becoming *Modified.* I'm sure you all already have this information since you're here now. I'm sorry the police department doesn't have any updates for you."

Katie winces. She can tell Santos is holding back something. He is not making eye contact with anyone other than Mayor Roy and sweat beads are forming on his forehead. It is the first time since the conversation started that Nick can tell she isn't pleased.

Sheriff Santos must have picked up on Katie's facial expression because he forces his eyes to meet hers and follows with, "Mrs. Kleug and Dr. Cyrus, the Beaufort Police Department is at your service, and we are hoping to help you in your research in any way while you are here. We would like to think of us all as one big team. We help you and you help us. After all, we all have the same goal in mind—to keep the peace in the south and find a way out of this mess."

Katie and Nick nod in agreement. Neither of them can tell whether the other actually bought what was said but they know as much that social conventions mean that a nod will end the conversation sooner than later.

After a quick exchange of direct line numbers Nick and Katie head out of the office and back to the SUV waiting for them in front of city hall. Once they enter the car, for the first time since meeting one another, there isn't any awkward silence. Katie begins talking right away. She tells Nick that she is glad to have the opportunity to work with him. He agrees and it feels nice to have someone he can talk to and trust as a partner. He wants to address the moment that they had earlier in the waiting room, but he feels it is better just to move on.

Katie points out that it seems rather odd that the police department doesn't seem that concerned about clearing up what is happening with the Ardi family to the public. She isn't even sure why the mayor and sheriff wanted to meet after the press conference since there is no new information to share. She speculates that Mayor Roy and Sheriff Santos know exactly where the

Ardis are and how they got there.

Nick does find it a little odd how willing Sheriff Santos said the police department is to become partners in the research with them. In his experience police are never really open to being helpful without direct orders from the top of the totem pole. Plus, Sheriff Santos gives him an eerie feeling. However, regardless of how they feel at this time, Katie and Nick have no proof of anything, so they have to tread lightly, ensuring that they keep every connection in the town intact in case they need it for later.

Nick suggests to Katie that it is time to bring some real evidence into the equation, and they head to the pop-up lab that they have secured to run these samples. Before they know it, they arrive in front of the local governmental medical lab, likely the only one in the small town of Beaufort. Nick hops out of the car quickly, antsy to get started. He opens the trunk and carefully checks his samples in the bag to make sure they traveled well in the bumpy ride. Despite it being a small town with a small population, the city of Beaufort has quite a bit of potholes that made the ride less than what he would consider smooth. Just from observing the town and the people in it for a few minutes, Nick is surprised that the residents of Beaufort allow the road quality to be so poor.

When he opens the bag, he is shocked to see that there are only seven samples. He distinctly remembers taking nine. He counts in his head again. One in the dry sand. Two in the wet sand. Three crab pincers. One in the water on the shore. Two in the 'deep', the less shallow part of the ocean. That's nine, he confirms. He looks closer at the labels on the test tubes. The two samples that are missing are from the 'deep'.

Nick closes the case to the samples and scans the area around him suspiciously. It doesn't seem as though anyone but himself, Katie, and the driver are around, but he can't be sure. He was followed earlier, afterall.

Nick shouts up to the driver, "Mr. Preston did you happen to see anyone near the vehicle while we were in city hall?"

Mr. Preston exits the vehicle and walks around to the back of the car. The driver straightens his chauffeur hat and thin, oddly short, navy tie and responds, "No, Dr. Cyrus, I didn't see anyone at all. However, I did take a quick trip to grab a cup of coffee while you were in the meeting and the car was unattended during that time. I couldn't have been gone for more than five minutes though, is something missing, sir?"

Mr. Preston looks as white as a sheet at the notion something could be missing under his watch.

Nick can see sweat forming on his forehead and down his thick neck. Upon taking another look, Nick notices that Preston has a virtual assistant device behind his ear. It is the first one he's seen since he arrived in the small town of Beaufort. Nick is a little surprised to see that Preston has a virtual assistant because he doesn't quite seem like the big city, fast-paced, generally wealthy type, like most virtual assistant owners. The device is a big purchase for a man who works for a driving service.

The driver's body tenses up before Nick, waiting for his response. Nick takes in the magnitude of the man. Mr. Preston is one of the largest men Nick has ever seen. He looks like he could have been a professional wrestler in another life. Even with his size, Nick finds him to be one of the kindest, most polite, helpful, easy-going people he has ever met, even in the brief time since they were introduced. He doesn't want to make him feel guilty for taking a coffee break, no matter how suspicious the situation feels after his encounter with the man between the bushes earlier.

Nick shrugs it off and says, "Oh no worries, Mr. Preston, I must have miscounted the number of samples I took. These should do just fine for now and if I need more I can go back." Mr. Preston pats the sweat on his neck and forehead with a detailed handkerchief he pulls from his pocket and smiles.

On the way into the lab Nick glances at Katie, who missed the whole ordeal because she was on the phone updating Kenny on the meeting they just had with the mayor and sheriff. He stands near the door and waits patiently until she ends her call. After several minutes the call finally ends, and she puts her paper and pen into her bag and makes her way to the door that Nick is waiting outside of. They make eye contact as she comes close and he informs her that they need to go somewhere to talk in private. Katie nods skeptically as she holds the door for Nick who was carrying the case of samples in. Once they get into the building instead of heading directly into the lab, they find an empty conference room on the main floor and decide to occupy it for the time being.

"Nick, did something happen?"

The question is rhetorical. Katie knows something happened. She is just looking for confirmation. Nick begins to open the case.

"I took nine samples from the Ardi's beach property. There are only seven here. The driver, Mr. Preston, said he didn't see anyone near the car while we were away, but he also said he stepped away for a few minutes to grab a coffee." Nick sputters out exasperatedly. As the words exit his mouth he realizes Mr. Preston's alibi sounds even more simple and rehearsed than he initially thought, making it all the more suspicious.

Katie mulls over what Nick said for a moment. "Are you positive you took nine? It could be a simple mistake that anyone could make. Maybe you just miscounted," she asks, not even really believing it is a possibility.

"Katie, I'm absolutely positive. Something is not right here. I know I took nine." Nick explains to her the order in which I took the samples. He tells her that the samples from the 'deep' were likely the most important ones and he would not have forgotten to take a sample in the water since that was the entire point of him collecting them in the first place.

She agrees that something doesn't seem right. She remembers his shorts were wet when they left the Ardi's beach cottage, so it makes sense that he didn't forget to take samples in the 'deep' of the ocean. The more she thinks about it the more she believes someone broke into the car and stole the samples, but she can't justify why someone would want to do that.

"We need to go take more samples of the water to replace the ones that are missing. There's obviously a reason someone doesn't want you to see what is in the 'deep'," she says.

Nick agrees. Someone is trying to keep whatever was in the water from them and he wants to know why.

Chapter 8

April 26th, 2082 – FRANK and RIO

Frank Roy sits down and releases the tension in his shoulders once Dr. Cyrus and Katie Kleug leave his office. Sheriff Santos, too, seems to relax a bit.

"What happens if they find out about the water, Roy?" Santos asks, already knowing the answer.

Roy throws his hands up in an exasperated attempt to say, 'we are screwed'.

"They're going to find out, Rio. Cyrus isn't an idiot. Bruner sent them here to find out what is going on and the water is the obvious first place to check. It's our job just to stall it a bit. Bruner wants them to find out everything, but he needs them on our side first so Cyrus will participate in the next steps. David said he would step in if it became necessary. I guess he has his hooks in the girl. Bruner said that Dr. Cyrus is a do-gooder. He's a smart man, but he's not quite smart enough to help himself out if it means others have to suffer. He may have to use his play on the girl if all else fails," Roy explains.

He continues growing more and more out of breath with each sentence, "we have to show them that we are cooperating, but we have to set boundaries. Once he finds out about the water we are going to have to make it clear what the best option is moving forward. With or without pressure—if you know what I mean."

Rio nods, annoyed with the words coming out of Frank's mouth and at the penetrating sound of his voice. Of course he knows what he means. Doesn't mean he has to like it.

CHAPTER 8

Since the *Modified* began making more headlines in the south his job has gone to shit. Being an officer, upholding the law used to be something he was proud of. Even though he sacrificed his marriage to all the late nights at work he knew his son was still proud of him and the work he was doing. From the time his son, Javi, was in elementary school he always told his dad that he wanted to grow up to be a police officer just like him. Nothing made Rio happier than hearing that. Up until the last few years that dream was not just of Javi's, but Rio's as well. Rio wouldn't wish this job on his worst enemy now.

As he looks over at Frank Roy, someone he used to consider a close friend, he feels resentment building up inside of him. Rio had always trusted Frank. They've known each other since primary school, but their true alliance began in high school on the football field. Frank has really let himself go since then, but Rio still sometimes can see glimpses of the man his dear friend used to be. The old mayor's passion sometimes still shows up when he talks about the town he's lived in and loved his whole life.

Rio Santos helped out with Frank's campaign when he ran for mayor. He went around town telling everyone that they wouldn't be able to find a more trust-worthy, honest man than Frank Roy. At that time, he really meant what he was preaching to all of his neighbors and community members. He didn't know at the time that he would regret those words.

It doesn't really matter to Rio that their friendship is now unrepairable. That isn't really the issue that causes soreness in his heart. He has lost friends before and survived. Hell, he's even lost his wife and survived. The real issue is that he can't trust himself now. He likes to blame all of his problems on Frank, but the truth is he liked the perks he got from aligning with the mayor even if it meant doing things he didn't believe in. He has to make things right even if it isn't for himself and only for his son, Javi. He doesn't want Javi to learn about the kind of man he has become. His reputation is all he has now.

Rio looks at Frank's exhausted face. He realizes he would turn on him in a second if it meant he would be absolved of all the wrong doing. If all the lies would go away he would gladly say goodbye to his old friend. What kind of person does that make me? He wonders. It's not like it matters; it doesn't seem to be in the cards anyways.

Partners until the end, he thinks, the resentment building inside of him. He knows that the other set of partners they need to enlist won't come to their side as easily as Frank thinks they will. He stops and questions himself for a moment. If everything boiled down to violence in the next few days, could he do what needed to be done? Even Rio, himself, is scared to find out the answer to that question.

Chapter 9

April 27th, 2082 - NICK AND KATIE

Starting with a fresh day ahead of them, Nick and Katie decide it is best to take the samples again together. They see safety in numbers. It also is clear to both of them that they can't quite trust anyone else yet. Mr. Preston, their driver, drops them once again in the driveway of the Ardi's beach cottage.

Nick arrives a bit more prepared this time with wading boots. He doesn't want to lose another pair of shorts to this endeavor. He slips the waders all the way up to his waist and heads into the 'deep' of the ocean. The tide is coming in a bit now that the hours have passed so he doesn't need to go out as far as before to feel the water approaching his waist. He takes three samples this time in different sections of the deep before he heads back to the dry, sandy area of the beach. The entire time Nick is in the water Katie stands in the center of the beach front property just scanning her surroundings. Her head turns from left to right and back again. She decides she doesn't care if it looks suspicious that she is looking all around her. It is her job to ensure the project goes as planned. Plus, she is tired of this guessing game they are playing already and wants to get back to the lab to figure out what is going on.

Instead of putting the samples into the trunk this time, Nick decides to hold the case on his lap throughout the drive back to the lab. He doubts that whoever took the samples the first time would be stupid enough to do it again but holding them close still makes him feel more comfortable. His knuckles turn bright white as he wraps his hands tightly around the case. He feels a bit of relief for the first time since he spoke to Bruner. He knows that this water will tell him something. He doesn't know if it will be good news or bad news, but he knows it will be news, nonetheless. Any information at this point can help him to determine how to move forward in helping Adam.

The thoughts in his head are broken up by Katie's voice, "How are you feeling, Nick? I know this entire thing seems like a hot mess and I don't think either of us are used to feeling like this."

She's so considerate, he silently thinks. He can't remember the last time someone asked him how he was doing and sounded like they truly wanted a real answer.

"I'm doing the best that I can to keep cool. I'm sure it doesn't seem cool at all though, does it? Me running around in those waders and you acting all suspicious the whole time. We're quite the pair, aren't we?" Nick says with a little laugh at the end. He hopes the laugh hides how nervous he is to talk to her.

Katie smiles a big, toothy smile. This is the Nick she has been feeling a connection with. She likes that he can make light of something even in the worst of times when uncertainty rules their thoughts. She wants to say more, but nothing comes to her. Instead, she just giggles and gives him a little, playful slap on the chest. When she sees him smile back at her she feels the butterflies in her stomach rise and move around a bit reminding her of his hand on her cheek back in Mayor Roy's waiting room. The thought of his skin touching hers causes her mouth to dry out and her heart to beat faster. Before either of them have the chance to speak again they pull up in front of the lab.

Mr. Preston jumps out of the car so quickly it seems as if the car hasn't even come to a complete stop before he exited it. He rushes around and opens the door for Ms. Kleug. She scoots out of the seat followed by Dr. Cyrus in the same fashion. Preston tips his hat at them as they pass by him. For a moment, Katie feels a rush of uneasiness when Preston looks at her. She, too, notices that he has a virtual assistant. She hasn't seen anyone in Beaufort aside from him with one. She has no reason other than his ownership of expensive technology to second guess him as a person. He has always been kind, but something in her mind screams there is something off about him.

The pair make their way to the lab. Although Katie doesn't really need to be in the lab, they decide that sticking together and following through with the project as a team is the best option. Even though she works for the Human Biology Research Foundation, she doesn't really know much about science. She, of course, knows the basics and had taken courses in it in college, but she is more on the business end of things now, when it comes to her position. As a junior administrator her job really is to oversee any projects that David sends her way. In general, she doesn't spend a lot of time in labs and is seen more as a point person for things the scientists and project leaders need. Nonetheless, she offers help in any way that Nick will have her.

He carefully analyzes each sample he has collected. Katie is in awe of how focused he has become. It is as if there is no one or nothing in the world that can get in between him and what he is doing. She admires his dedication. She has never met anyone who cares about their job as much as she does and it is refreshing to see the passion in his eyes. He handles each sample with such care that it makes her feel like maybe he could care for a person in that same way given the right circumstances. She wonders if maybe she could be that person and these could be the circumstances.

Nick's expression doesn't really change much throughout the process. He remains focused until he gets to one of the 'deep' water samples. Katie notices his brow as it furrows followed by his eyes opening to their fullest extent. Katie knows better than to break his train of thought by speaking. She watches him fumble with the other samples and run through each one of them one more time. Each time he looks at one his eyes somehow open wider.

"There's something in this water, Katie! Let me show you. Please hand me that filtered water sample that's right there on the table so we can compare them."

Katie hands him the water sample and peeks inside of the microscope. She looks at the tap water sample but doesn't really know what she is looking at.

Then he shows her the water in the 'deep'. She looks into the lens, focusing as hard as she can. While she still has no idea what she is looking at, it is clear the samples are very different. Katie looks up at Dr. Nicholas Cyrus trying to explain with her eyes that she has no idea what she was looking at or why it is important.

Nick clearly understands her cryptic message and begins to explain, "I'm sure you don't look at samples often Katie, but I can tell you saw the difference. To be honest, I do not know exactly what is in this water yet, but there's definitely traces of something in it and I think it may be the key to what is happening with the Ardis. I'm going to run some more tests to figure out what it is. At first glance, my guess is some sort of chemical compound."

Nick pauses for a second, realizing that Katie still doesn't understand what he is talking about. Even so, it is nice to have someone listen when he talks.

"Do you want to grab us some lunch while I keep working? I'm starving!" He begs.

Katie nods in agreement. Her stomach feels as though it has started eating itself. She hasn't even noticed that since they've been in Beaufort they've had nothing but a few snacks to eat. Katie isn't feeling like much help in the lab anyways so she figures this could be her contribution to the team. She remembers she saw a row of shops down the street and decides to walk over there to grab a couple of sandwiches, hoping to make it quick.

In the small town of Beaufort there are not a lot of options for a quick meal so when she sees the little cafe with only a few cars parked outside of it, it is a no brainer. They don't have these small-type cafes in the big cities in the north anymore. In fact, most of the things she notices now can't be found in the northern regions.

She walks up the narrow street taking in everything around her. It all reminds her of an old timey TV show or an antique painting you'd see in a museum. Everything seems so surreal. She realizes that this might be because she is from Pittsburgh, a considerable sized city, but walking down the street seeing kids playing at the park without an adult in sight and old men having coffee on park benches seems very dystopian to her. She sees people stop when they pass one another just to catch up and it feels like every single person in this town knows one another on a personal level.

This isn't how things are where she is from. People go outside of course, but it is really just to get from place to place and maybe for occasional exercise or for holiday parades. The latter being the only time you really see crowds of people anymore as if it is a tradition kept only to remind people of better times. Kids rarely come outside for activities anymore. They can communicate through their computerized watches and gaming devices. School in person has become optional and a lot of students choose remote, online learning as their method of education. Those who choose to attend in person still mostly complete all of their work online and have their own individual workspace pods, similar to colleges except she's heard that high school students call their pods 'cribs' now. She thought that was an odd name when she first heard it, but the more that she sees the world change she realizes it is just another form of prison to keep people in and separated from one another. Other students who don't feel strongly one way or another about their learning flip back and forth between remote learning and in-person learning based on societal and environmental issues in their areas.

Most kids in the north have even given up organized outdoor sports to play in online tournaments. She doesn't understand the want to play online rather than in person, but that is how the latest generation communicates. She chalks a lot of the generational changes up to how erratic the weather has become and how unpredictable storms are in the northern regions.

Torrential rainfall has frequented the northeast over the last several years and lasts for days in the late summer and fall months, causing people to lock down in their homes for safety. The news reports that the Midwest has been plagued with terrible blizzards in the winter months over the last five years. The temperature drops so low during these "frozen storms" that people can't leave their homes for days for fear of freezing to death. If that isn't bad enough, the summers in these areas can get so incredibly hot or sometimes be so unnotably mild, but a lot of times meteorologists are unable to predict the temperatures of the season ahead of time so planning for things is nearly impossible. Katie isn't too sure about how the south has been affected by climate changes over the past several years, but she knows one thing, the south can get very hot in the months of June through October. She's heard that the temperatures can sometimes reach one hundred and thirty degrees Fahrenheit, which is still much hotter than what the north would consider "incredibly hot".

Just from the short time Katie has been in South Carolina, she can tell that outdoor recreation is one of the major differences between the north and the south. Southern people still take their football games very seriously. From what she has gathered the southern states have had to shift the football season to be played in cooler months due to the climate change, but they refuse to let the game go as a whole. For over a century and a half, football has driven society in the south and there isn't a chance the southerners will let the declining environment take that from them without a fight.

As she approaches Cafe a la Beaufort she peers into the window. She is taken aback when she sees Mr. Preston, her driver, sitting at a table with Sheriff Santos. It appears to be a very serious conversation. Sheriff Santos looks irritated and is using hand gestures that make her feel as though he is yelling at Mr. Preston or at the very least giving him a good talking to. She can't tell for sure from far away, but Mr. Preston looks upset. His head is hanging down and his shoulders are slumped forward. It looks like all confidence is drained from his body. She remembers back to when Nick told her that the samples were missing and the driver confirmed that he left the car unattended for a second. She decides to enter the cafe as quietly and unseen as possible to try to hear some of their conversation.

Katie opens the cafe door and to her dismay, the bell at the top of the door signals her arrival. She rolls her eyes at the sound of the bell. Places in Pittsburgh are too crowded to have bells ring each time people come in or go out, even with most people having their food delivered to their homes. The continuous sound would drive people crazy, like it was doing to her right now. How perfectly 'small town' of this cafe, she thinks with judgment filling her head.

Before she can even make it over to the counter, Mr. Preston and Mr.

Santos look up and conclude their conversation. Mr. Preston bounces up from his seat and hurries over to see if Katie needs anything.

"Ms. Kleug, I'm so sorry! I should have offered you and Dr. Cyrus some lunch, even at this late hour. I just got so hungry from sitting in that car that I decided to pop over to the cafe," he says practically panting.

Katie gives him a sweet smile even though she is feeling more suspicious than sweet. "Not a problem at all, Mr. Preston. Nick and I had realized we hadn't eaten a real meal since we arrived. This cafe was the closest thing to the lab that looked appealing. I saw you sitting with Sheriff Santos, are you old friends?" She pries.

Mr. Preston now looks uncomfortable but tries to mask his discomfort with a nervous smile. "Oh no ma'am, I mean I do know who Sheriff Santos is… as more of an acquaintance, but I wouldn't categorize us as friends. I just happened to see him come in for a sweet tea whilst I was sitting there alone and asked him how his press conference went. I didn't have a chance to watch it on the television," the nervous driver states very matter of factly.

Katie gives a forced smile hoping to show Mr. Preston that she is harmless. "Mr. Preston, would you mind me asking you something?"

The large man nods while giving a little chuckle, "Of course, ma'am. Happy to give you a little insight into my world."

"Do you know why Dr. Cyrus and I are in Beaufort?" Katie asks directly.

"No ma'am. It is not my job to know things. I just make sure people get to and from where they're supposed to go," the driver says plainly.

Katie tries to look deeply into Prestons eyes when he is speaking to get a read on him, but he looks to the left to break their eye contact. He turns away quickly and sits down.

Nothing in Mr. Preston's explanation seems out of the realm of possibilities, but Katie now has the inkling that she needs to dig a little more into the man who is driving them around and listening to their conversations in the car. He has been watching their every move and likely will continue to do so until they leave Beaufort. She orders her sandwiches to go and says a quick goodbye to Mr. Preston who is now at the counter eating a lobster roll, obviously avoiding Sheriff Santos.

Rodrigo Santos offers her a quick head nod on her way out and she returns the gesture. The bell rings once more as Katie exits the cafe. The 'small town' sound of it makes her cringe.

Katie power walks her way back to the lab. She is a bit out of breath when she arrives in front of the governmental building. The whole time she is walking, she's running a series of questions through her head. Her main question, the one she kept coming back to is: who is Mr. Preston?

She hasn't really received any information on Mr. Preston, other than he is the person that Kenny Nash, Bruner's assistant, set up to pick them up from the airport and chauffeur them around for the duration of their travels in Beaufort. She had always assumed that he's a hired driver from a car service. Every work trip she has taken prior to this one always had a driver like Mr. Preston assigned to her and they were always from an outsourced car service. Does she even know his first name, she wonders, searching the depths of her memory. She can't recall ever being told his first name, but there has to be a record of it somewhere in her files.

Outside of the lab building she finds a bench and decides she needs more information, and she needs it now. She pulls up her emails to see if any correspondence with Kenny can offer her any insight into the life of Mr. Preston.

After scrolling for some time, she comes across an email that notes Mr. Preston will be the one picking them up from the airport. Kenny explained in the email that Silas Preston is the name of the man that they could expect to take care of them for the duration of their trip. She is concerned that she let this detail slip. She wonders if her newfound interest in Dr. Cyrus is starting to cloud her brain. Before even reading the rest of the email she closes her email app and opens up her web browser to conduct a search on Silas Preston. Several hits come up with both the names Silas and Preston separately highlighted, but nothing about Silas Preston, well at least this not this particular Silas Preston, and nothing related to South Carolina. Katie tries to tell herself that this could all be a coincidence and that she is being paranoid. There's no proof of any wrongdoing. In fact, there is no proof of anything at all.

When she arrives back inside of the lab Nick is writing something down in a folder. She heads over to him to offer a sandwich, but she also wants to pick his brain about Silas Preston. Before she can get a word out, he sees her and immediately starts on his findings.

"Katie, you're never going to believe what I found out about the water we collected. In the samples of the water, sand, and even the crab pincers, I found something called Dibutyl and Diethylhexyl Phthalates. Finding small traces of it isn't unheard of, but the deeper the water the samples were collected from the more there was. I would imagine that has something to do with how the water current has been moving, but I'll have to research a little more into that aspect. This isn't a small amount. This is a serious amount. I'm surprised dead fish aren't winding up on the shore with six heads," he says, his voice filled with enthusiasm.

Katie's thoughts change quickly from Preston to the missing water samples. "I bet whoever stole those water samples didn't want you to find this." She blurts excitedly, realizes how loudly she is talking and continues with an inside voice, "what exactly can this cause? Could this be related to the *Modifying*?" She wonders aloud.

She can feel anxiety and thrill filling her up as she awaits his response. Nick enjoys seeing her get excited about his findings. This is the first time he really has someone to share his career successes with and it feels really good.

Nick tries his best to explain in layman's terms what he's found, "So basically Dibutyl and Diethylhexyl Phthalates can cause reproductive and hormone changes, which in turn can cause immune responses in certain circumstances. It's actually been banned for several decades in most of Europe because of this. Well...at least I think it is still banned. In the United States it isn't banned from products, but it's supposed to be monitored very closely. The amount I found in this water definitely exceeds anything that would be allowed in production and distribution to the public. This absolutely could have to do with the *Modification* occurring in Adam. I'm almost positive this triggered some sort of response in the human cells causing them to adapt to survive."

Katie's expression goes through a series of phases from surprised, to intrigued, to pure terror. She doesn't know what to say or what to ask.

Nick continues on, "my biggest concern right now is finding out where the phthalates are coming from. We shouldn't work on stopping it until we know what is causing it. If it's something we can control it would be helpful to know that. We need to keep a lid on this until we figure it out. We may need some assistance from higher ups to get access to records from the town. Do you think we can trust the mayor or the sheriff to take them up on their offer to help?"

Katie sighs. She explains to Nick what she just saw at the cafe and how uneasy it made her feel. Katie explains that she has worked with Bruner for a really long time and feels like she can trust him enough to reach out and ask for his input on how to go about things.

Nick agrees with her proposal, but he doesn't really trust Bruner. He knows he is technically his boss, but he could feel the tension between Katie and David when they all met in his office on his first day and he didn't like the way it made him feel. He can't decide if he didn't like it because he felt lingering feelings between the two or because David is a snake who is only worried about his own skin. A vibe he's got from many people working in high ranked positions throughout his career. He ends the debate in his head with the conclusion that both reasons are likely true.

Katie explains she will fly to D.C. very quickly to talk to David in person since he is easier to get a read on one-on-one rather than through the phone. Nick decides he will stay back to continue digging a little bit on his own while she is gone.

The two sit close to one another while they eat their BLT sandwiches that Katie was kind enough to grab for them. If you can even call them a BLT. With farms having struggled for so long, bacon has pretty much become obsolete. Most pig farmers have sold their land to corporations in order to survive during the long, unpredictable seasons. What people call bacon today is basically processed mystery meat that no one can be sure comes from a pig.

Nick picks at his sandwich, inspecting parts of it before pushing the rest aside. So much has happened since they had first met in Bruner's office that they haven't had much of a chance to get to know each other. Katie wants to know more about why Nick has agreed to work for the Human Biology Research Department when he could have chosen anywhere to work in the world with his experience. She prompts him slowly by asking how he knows Bruner.

He replies, "I actually don't know him personally. He sought me out and I wanted to help. I guess I should have seen being chosen by the government as a red flag given the strain on society right now, but at the time I found it more flattering."

Katie can understand being flattered by the job. She, too, desires more than anything to be sought after in her field.

"I can understand how that would be appealing to you. I would find it flattering too if people just started head hunting me for jobs because I was known to be the best. It is my dream to be the President of Operations one day. Once I do that, I can easily transition into working closely with the cabinet positions of the government. That's where people can really make a difference," she explains.

Nick is excited to hear about her goals. When he did interact with people, women specifically, around the labs they never talked about their goals. Part of that is probably because he never cared enough to ask, but in passing they always talked about where they were going out with their friends that night or what vacation they were planning to take. It is nice to hear from someone who has big goals and cares about making a difference.

"What kind of changes would you like to see if you could get into that type of role?" the doctor inquires, anxiously awaiting her response.

Katie thinks for a moment. She really hasn't had anyone care enough about or show interest in her personal goals or philosophies of life before. David stopped asking her about what she wanted out of life a long time ago and even when he had asked, he didn't seem interested in her responses.

"As long as I can remember there was always this political divide that science was in the middle of. There never was any reason as far as I could tell other than news outlets, media and politicians were giving mixed information just to get people on their side or gain followers. I've always found it to be a power play. I even remember when I was younger in primary school when we learned about history the teacher talked about how in the past people trusted science and there weren't really 'sides' to it because it was considered factual. I would like to try to bring that back. I know it was over a hundred years ago, but it seemed like a nice time to live in—the 1950's that is. Bruner has a lot of power and control, but he doesn't use it for anything worthwhile," Katie explains with passion and excitement in her voice.

Nick isn't surprised to hear that Katie's intentions are so pure and honest. He is delighted to find that he has met someone who wants to make the world a better, more informed place just like he does. He's also really impressed that her goals are so focused. Many people just want to move up in companies to make a lot of money, but Katie knows exactly where she wants to be and why.

"I'm really glad to hear you talk like that Katie. A lot of people don't use their opportunities for societal good. A lot of people don't realize it, but I was so happy once my contract with MoonCycle ended."

Katie leans in waiting to hear more. She isn't surprised at Nick's want for change, but it is hard for her to comprehend having so much success and wanting to leave it behind.

He finishes his thought, "I worked my whole life to make my mom proud. She did everything for me and never asked for anything in return. When she died I promised myself that I would do something worthwhile, not for the money, but to make a real positive change in the world. I thought it was a compliment to be considered by David Bruner for this position. I had worked so hard at MoonCycle to create something important while I was there and I did it, but it isn't going to cure sickness or make regular people's lives better. I thought I was finally going to get the chance to do that here. That is, before I saw Adam and found out this whole thing isn't what I thought it was."

Katie doesn't know what to say to make things better at this moment, but she knows she has to try.

"I'm really sorry to hear about your mom. I'm sure that's really hard for you. My parents moved to Arizona to be near my brother when he was in college, and they decided to stay long term. I feel so alone without them. I can't imagine how you feel," she stops speaking for a moment and puts her hand on his shoulder.

"I'm glad that we were put together on this assignment, even if I am not really sure why. David really could have chosen any of the junior administrators or project leaders from the department, but I'm glad he chose me. I think we make a great team. If we stick together, we will be able to figure this all out and come out ahead," she concludes with determination. She hadn't even realized how lonely she really was until now, sitting and talking with a man she can now call her partner and friend.

He is glad to hear her talking like this. Her compassion makes him feel whole again. This is the best work lunch he has ever had, and he is upset that it has to end, but they have a job to do and they have very limited time to do it.

Nick doesn't like the fact that Katie is leaving him alone in Beaufort. Not only does he not know anyone else here, but he will also miss getting to know more about Katie too. He has grown to enjoy being around her even in some of their awkward silences. As the moments pass, he feels more of a bond growing between them and selfishly he doesn't want to lose that. He doesn't know how he can be thinking of something like this at a time when he's supposed to be working on his biggest career assignment of all time with many repercussions if he messes it up, but here he is sitting across from her, just thinking about how beautiful she is when small wispy pieces of her hair fall across her soft, pink cheek.

Chapter 10

April 28th, 2082 - KATIE & DAVID

On her flight Katie puts some research into both Silas Preston and Rodrigo Santos. She begins to look into Mayor Roy too but knows she won't find anything on him because he would have cleaned it up before his campaign so as to not ruin his chances of getting elected. His name came up a lot through the search engine, but as she predicted, clean as a whistle.

Katie is having no luck with any of her site searches, so she decides to reach out to one of her old college friends, Patrick Janes—PJ to his friends, who now works as a police officer. She and PJ have kept in touch throughout the years and she knows he's trustworthy. She asks him to look into Silas Preston. She knows better than to ask him to look into Rodrigo Santos. It has always been her understanding that the police have a way of taking care of one another. She doesn't want to put Patrick in an uncomfortable situation with his colleagues. Patrick, of course, agrees to help and tells her he will get back to her as soon as he can. Now all she has to do is wait and try to enjoy the rest of the plane ride.

Relaxing on the plane ride is definitely easier said than done for Katie, an overthinker. Her mind keeps bringing her back to Dr. Nicholas Cyrus. She doesn't like to admit it, but she hasn't felt anything for anyone in years, other than David. There is something about Dr. Cyrus that keeps drawing her in deeper with each interaction. It is like he is magnetic, but in the most unintentional way.

Katie knows she has always been attracted to smart men who also happen to be sophisticated, but something is different about her attraction to

Dr. Cyrus. Nick definitely falls into the intelligent category, but he most definitely is not sophisticated. To her surprise, his lack of sophistication is what she thinks is most attractive about him. He doesn't really seem to give thought to what anyone else thinks of him. He is very down to earth and easy to talk to when she is able to actually get him talking, which isn't very often. He seems to like living mostly inside of his own head. He doesn't feel the need to make small talk without reason, unless he knows a specific situation really dictates that he makes an effort. He doesn't particularly dress nicely either. The man decided to wear khaki shorts and a polo to meet the mayor for God sakes! His clothing is much more dressed down than what she is accustomed to seeing from successful men. Everything about her attraction to him doesn't line up with her previous relationships and romantic interests.

Even so, she continues to think about him and how focused he was at the lab when she had last seen him. She desires to watch him work again. To see the passion and drive in his eyes when he puts his mind to something. She decides that even though it wouldn't be a good idea to get involved with Dr. Cyrus, given their working relationship, she wants to see if things can progress naturally when she gets back to Beaufort. She owes herself that much, she convinces herself.

As the plane is landing, she sends Nick a quick text, "About to land in D.C. I will let you know right after I leave Bruner's office so we can figure out our next steps together. Keep in touch if you find anything else out. See you soon." She even adds a smiley face emoji at the end of the text, hoping that he will get the clue that she is interested in him.

As soon as she is able to deboard the plane she heads directly to the office. It crosses her mind that she should have stopped back at her apartment to grab a few things, but she is too anxious to talk to David. She promises herself over and over on the flight that she won't let him suck her into his vortex again. Once he grasps her and gets his hands on her it feels like his nails are digging into her and she will never be able to escape his allure. Katie is hoping that since she now feels a connection brewing with Nick that she will be able to hold strong when the time comes to be face to face with David.

When Katie arrives at David Bruner's office and checks in with Kenny, she finds that David is not in the office. Kenny tries to pry out of Katie the real reason for her visit, but Katie won't budge. She has never really liked Kenny. Kenny always acts too much like a know-it-all. He always seems to be around lurking, ready to pounce on any opportunity that might move him up the professional ladder. The thought of him trying to capitalize off of her visit with David makes her sick.

Katie messaged David on her way to the airport just to let him know she will be arriving in person so they can discuss the next steps in the assignment, so she assumed he would be expecting her. Kenny explains that he was able to get ahold of Bruner and that he will be in within the half hour. Katie decides to stay and wait in the waiting room until he arrives. She sits patiently and watches Kenny from across the waiting room as he whispers something to his virtual assistant. 'That snake' she thinks and glares at him from across the room for no real reason other than she just doesn't like the way he is.

Whilst waiting, her text message notification goes off. Oh, how she hopes it is Nick! Luckily, it is him so she can finally stop wondering why he hasn't responded yet. Her heart flutters as his name pops up on the screen. She opens the message, "Glad your flight went well. Looking forward to talking to you. I found out something new. It's big. It has to do with a cosmetic company. You're never going to believe it. Talk soon." He ends the message with a saucy little wink emoji. Katie's heart warms at the sight of the emoticon. She hopes it means that he misses her. She can't believe how "middle-school" she is acting about a crush, but she has to admit it is exciting.

After the warm sensation begins to leave her body she starts to wonder about the cosmetic company that he mentioned. It makes sense that a cosmetics company would use chemicals like the ones they found in the water. Everyone knows that all these beauty companies use so many chemicals in their products even though they claim to be good for your health and good for the environment. She is eager to hear more about what

Nick found over the phone.

Within fifteen minutes of Katie waiting, David Bruner storms into the office like a hurricane. He seems so flustered from rushing. He whirls past Kenny who must have known he was approaching because he stood in the center of the room awaiting his arrival. Even Kenny, the snake, seems to be surprised at David's state of mind when he enters the room. He doesn't bother to look in Katie's direction as he shuffles his way through the waiting room and into his office, the door slamming behind him. Kenny shutters as the door slams and then grabs his tablet and enters the room only seconds after David.

Katie can't hear anything coming from the office. If they are talking in there, it has to be in a whisper. Merely thirty seconds later the door abruptly swings open and Kenny exits. David then approaches the door looking more put together and greets Katie asking her to join him in his office. On her way into the office she passes by Kenny's desk and he gives her the most sly smirk. Her gut immediately feels heavy, as if a rock replaced her stomach.

Katie enters the office and David is acting as smooth as ever. Katie doesn't know how he managed to come in a hot mess and come out looking like a million dollars within seconds. He leads Katie to a chair in front of his desk and asks her if she wants anything to drink. She can't even answer before he is on his intercom shouting for Kenny to bring her a Perrier. Katie looks at him in dismay. He doesn't even remember that she dislikes carbonated beverages. She begins to wonder what she saw in him in the first place.

He sits down in his chair and leans back with his fingers intertwined across his abdomen. "So, Kitty-Kate, you've got some news for me?" his voice purrs at her.

Instead of swooning over him the way she normally would, she sits straight up in her chair, full of confidence and responds as matter of factly as she can, "Well, Dr. Cyrus and I have done some research, and we have found that things in Beaufort aren't exactly what they seem. You see, since we've arrived things have felt 'off', almost suspicious. It's hard to explain why exactly. For starters some of Dr. Cyrus's samples went missing."

David doesn't budge. His expression doesn't change, not even a little. He remains diligently listening as Katie proceeds.

"Dr. Cyrus took some new samples and when he analyzed them he found a chemical presence in them. Something that shouldn't be in water and could cause damage. He thinks maybe this is what is causing the *modifying* to occur," she explains keeping eye contact.

Now David looks interested. David appears as though he is about to speak when a knock at the door interrupts him.

Kenny's head pops in, "Sir, I need to speak with you very quickly. It's rather urgent if you don't mind."

David rolls his eyes as the word 'urgent' comes out of Kenny's mouth. Katie can tell that even David doesn't particularly like Kenny, but he must keep him around because he is really good at his job or at least good at pretending he is. Kenny shuffles in quickly and sets a bottle of Perrier on the desk with a glass. Katie, frustrated at the sight of both the water and Kenny, finds herself frowning. Bruner stands up and leaves the room following Kenny, closing the door tightly behind him.

Katie looks at her phone while she is waiting alone in David's office. She notices she has a new email notification. It is Patrick getting back to her about her inquiry of Silas Preston. She opens the new email and begins to scan it.

"Katie,

So nice to hear from you! We will have to catch up the next time you're in Pittsburgh again. I did some quick digging and nothing too crazy came up on Silas Preston.

He has a record that was expunged, but it was nothing super serious. A misdemeanor charge when he was 23 years old in South Carolina. Looks like he got into a fight and was charged with aggravated battery, but the charges were dropped. A common occurrence among the young men in the south. The only other thing I found was his employer. He has worked for MoonCycle for the last four years. I'm not sure how you know him, but I don't see any red flags with him. If you need anything else, don't hesitate to contact me. I'd be happy to help.

- PJ"

Katie is trying to process what she read. Why would the driver that she is assigned by Kenny work for MoonCycle? All of a sudden it is as if a lightbulb appears above her head and illuminates itself.

MoonCycle is one of the leading cosmetics companies in the world. She begins to connect the dots. Things are falling into place like little puzzle pieces in her head. Nick had just texted her about a cosmetics company only a few minutes ago. Nick worked for MoonCycle prior to this new job. It can't be a coincidence. They must be connected. Kenny organizing Silas Preston as her driver can only mean one thing—MoonCycle and the Human Biology Research Department are working together or at the very least Bruner is working with the cosmetics company in some capacity.

Katie is trying not to panic knowing that Bruner could be coming back into the room at any second. She knows she needs to get out of the office without Bruner finding out what she knows so that she can sort through it with Nick and come up with a strategy on how to move forward since what she knows is all circumstantial. The connection she has with David could be a problem for her trying to leave without raising flags that she knows something.

David could always read her. It is as if he is inside of her head. When they were together there were times when she didn't even have to speak, and he immediately knew how to respond to her and her mood. She has to put on her best poker face before he comes back into the office. Katie knows now that David has set her up for this assignment because he wants someone on the inside, someone that he can control. It stings a little bit inside of her knowing he chose her because he thinks she is weak.

Katie sits still, trying to control her breathing. She replays the last two days in her head, hoping to make sense of why David would lie to her and put her in this position. Nothing she comes up with serves as a reasonable cause. What could David possibly be getting out of this arrangement to be taking such a risk with the research department, she wonders.

David has only been out of the room for five, maybe six minutes, but to

Katie it feels like an eternity. Her mind is wheeling. She has felt so many exciting emotions with Nick over the short time they've spent together that she begins to wonder if she has been too naive. Nick worked for MoonCycle in the past. Could he be hiding something from her as well? She fears. She quickly scans her memory of their interactions and decides that their connection feels too honest for him to be trying to deceive her. She opens her phone and decides to text the only person who she hopes she can still trust, "Nick, something is wrong. I haven't talked to David yet, but Mr. Preston works for MoonCycle. I'm guessing that's the company you're talking about. I feel like I've walked into a trap by coming to David's office."

She waits to see if the 'read' checkmark darkens near the text message. After a few seconds the checkmark fills in showing her proof that Nick is with her, and he is reading her words. Three dots appear showing that he is typing. They remain on the screen. She hears a noise and it begins to grow closer to the door. She turns her phone to silent as quickly as possible and slides it into her bag. The door handle turns slowly and David re-enters the room. He gently closes the door and locks it behind him this time.

David isn't looking as calm and collected as he had the few minutes she was with him before their conversation was interrupted by Kenny. She can't put her finger on what his emotion is with the way he is carrying himself now. He seems upset, angry, and irritated all in one. His cheeks turn a soft pink, and his eyes have a sting in them.

"Oh Kitty-Kate. You've been digging in places you shouldn't have, haven't you?" he sneers.

Katie's mouth opens, just slightly, in surprise. How could he know that? Like clockwork the gears in her head begin turning and now she understands.

"You've been looking through my phone?" she asks, now beginning to get choked up. The fear begins to burn her eyes and they start to water.

"Katie, it is a company phone and company email. We have access to everything. No need to get upset. We are all on the same side, Kitty-Kate. Let's chat about where to go from here. It's actually wonderful you dropped by, now I don't have to come to you," Bruner responds smugly.

Katie swallows, but it doesn't alleviate the lump in her throat. She has to be smart about how to proceed next in order to keep herself and Nick safe. She just doesn't know what being smart looks like in this situation. Katie leans back and situates herself into her seat, trying to make herself appear comfortable to David.

When they had first begun dating, David took Katie out to a restaurant in the city. It was one of the nicest restaurants Katie had ever been to, if not the nicest. It was the kind of restaurant where you walk in and the maître d' makes you feel like you're a movie star.

During that dinner one of the servers tried to seat David and Katie at a table along one of the walls close to the kitchen when David had specifically requested a window table. Katie didn't think it was a big deal at all. Honestly, she was just happy to be there with all of the "fancy people". The server explained that all of the window tables were already reserved and there was nothing that he could do.

David wouldn't let it go. He went and spoke privately to the maître d' and within seconds the maître d' himself came over and moved them to a window table and even sent a bottle of Le' Lux, the most expensive champagne in the world, over to the table to apologize for the mix up. When Katie questioned David about how he was able to get the table moved he only said, "You always play to your strengths, Kitty-Kate. That's how I've gotten to be so successful. My strength happens to be never accepting 'no' as an answer." Katie still doesn't know how David got their seats moved to this day, but she knows that David is smarter than most people think and he has a lot of tricks up his sleeve when it comes to getting people to do what they want.

Thinking back to that moment makes Katie realize she knows her play. Her best chance to get out of this situation is to play to their history and make him think they are partners as they always have been, that could be her strength. It isn't guaranteed to work because he knows her so well, but she has to give it a try.

"You know, David, I've really missed seeing you. Our friendship was always so solid. I hope after this assignment that you've sent me on wraps up we can grab dinner like old times. We can even go to that one restaurant you like so much, what's it called…Très Beau?" Katie says in the same raspy tone she would use with him when they would talk on the phone late at night.

David's eyebrows raise just slightly, almost as if he is intrigued by the thought of them spending time together. His sly smirk turns into a grimace. This catches Katie off guard. She has never seen him like this before. In all of the years she's known him he never once seemed sinister. Sure, he seems arrogant at times, sexy at times, even a little irritating, but never evil like this. This is a new look for him and she realizes she may not know him as well as she thinks she does.

"Katie, as I mentioned before, this is a company phone. We've seen the message you just sent to Dr. Cyrus, the emails you've sent, and the searches you've made on the device. It appears that neither of us have been truly honest about where we stand in this situation. I'm honestly disappointed in you, Katie," David says with an unwavering, strong tone before pausing and standing above her to show his dominance.

"This can go one of two ways, Kitty-Kate. Option one: you stay here and we monitor your communication with Dr. Cyrus. We need him on our side. This thing is bigger than you understand. It would do you good to partner up with us. We can protect you. Things are about to get bad in the United States. We've gotten word that there are various opportunist groups that are planning on taking to violence in order to cause disorder in this confusing time for everyone. Society is about as divided as it has been since the pandemic of 2019, maybe even as divided as the Civil War. Various groups want to come out on top of this thing to not only make money, but to gain power in the shift that is going to happen among the world's top players. You want to be on the right side of this thing Katie, trust me."

Katie listens intently, weighing all of her options now that she has been cornered. David knows that she doesn't trust him. Her plan has gone out the window. Now she needs to make another decision in order to save her skin.

"And option 2?" she inquires.

"Well, let's just say that option two is less desirable for all parties involved,"

David declares.

Katie knows things are getting bad in the big cities. She has heard of some violence occurring and about how divided people have become, but she didn't think they were on the brink of a 'species war', for lack of a better term.

On the news some people with *Modified* infants have reported being chastised in public. She recalls watching a news story about a woman from Houston, Texas. The woman couldn't have been more than 25 years old. She took her baby to the store with her just for a quick grocery run. The baby was born *Modified,* little gills showing on his neck. It was reported that when she was in the store people were giving her dirty looks and even trying to spit on her as she walked down the aisles. That wasn't even the worst part of the story. On her way to her car with her groceries she was egged by a group of men in the parking lot. She tried her best to cover the baby in the cart so he wouldn't be harmed. The men ran off before the authorities got there and because she was the only witness, the men got away with it. The grocery store manager even refused to give up the security camera footage from the parking lot. He said that the company wasn't legally obligated to help with the investigation. Katie remembers the young woman's face on the screen and how terrified and shook up she was that people in her community would treat her and her baby that way.

Despite thinking back to the frightening news story, she feels that David might be exaggerating how bad things actually are just to get her to join forces with him.

"What would you need me to do? Why do you need Dr. Cyrus on your side? It seems backwards that you purposely sent us to South Carolina just so we could find evidence that you obviously wanted us to find. Why didn't you just speak to Dr. Cyrus and tell him what was going on? I don't understand the need for these theatrics," Katie rattles off, finally finding her strength.

David looks surprised to hear Katie speak in such a strong tone.

"We needed Dr. Cyrus to be the one to figure it out. He worked for MoonCycle and knows how their cosmetics lab runs. He has what I believe would be considered an…." David pauses trying to think of the correct word to explain his take on the situation, "…allegiance, yes let's say allegiance, to MoonCycle since they are the reason he has become such a well-renowned scientist."

Katie wants to stop him right there. She doesn't like the way David is portraying Nick as some pawn in his game. She doesn't know everything about Nick, in fact, she only knows a handful of things about him, but one thing she feels sure about is that he has integrity and would never be a part of this if he knew people were being harmed or going to be harmed in the process.

David continues, "He is the only one that we think can quickly find a way to combat the chemicals that were dumped causing the *modifications* to grow at an alarming rate. We need to be able to end this if we need to. He's also the only one that makes sense to take the fall if things go south. He had to be seen in Beaufort or at least connected to Ardi's disappearance in some way, just as a contingency plan."

'And there it is', Katie thinks. The real reason that David enlisted Dr. Nicholas Cyrus on this project. It isn't because he believes in him, it is because he needs someone to take responsibility for what is happening and Nick would be the perfect person to do it. If someone comes out of the woodwork and explains to the public that they're responsible the heat will fall on one person and only one person, that person being Dr. Cyrus, a scientist seen lurking around Beaufort trying to cover his tracks for a mistake he made when he worked for MoonCycle. The bloodshed could then be spared and the tension between the north and south could all come down on one person instead of fueling an already divided nation. MoonCycle and the Human Biology Research Department would come out looking like heroes who saved the day.

"What if I can't get him to agree to everything you're saying?" Katie probes.

David knows Katie isn't stupid. She already knows at this point that either both of them cooperate or things go south quickly for everyone. David, however, underestimates how strong and determined Katie has become since she has met someone who inspires her.

David has an inkling that Katie already knows the answer to this question, so he ignores it and begins explaining more about the importance of Dr. Cyrus agreeing to work with MoonCycle again.

"If Dr. Cyrus decides to play ball and cooperates with us as he had agreed to do in this office with you standing here a few days ago then everything will work out. He may even win a few awards for his excellence in scientific research. It needs to look like MoonCycle and the Human Biology Research Department are working together on this, in sync. However, if he doesn't agree to cooperate, I'm not the person he needs to worry about. MoonCycle has some very rich and powerful investors who are not willing to take a loss on this one."

Katie pretends to mull over all the options presented to her. In her silence, Kenny opens the office door and rushes over and hands David a piece of paper folded in half. After delivering the piece of paper to his boss's hands he spins around and walks right out without saying a word. The stuck-up assistant doesn't even bother to look at Katie on his way out. David unfolds the paper and looks at it briefly before re-folding it and putting it inside of the pocket on the inside of his jacket.

Katie decides that she has heard enough. Neither option is a good option, but she knows she has to do whatever her conscience will be able to live with even if it isn't the safest option. Katie tells David she would like to choose a third option. She wants to excuse herself from this entire thing. She even agrees to sign a nondisclosure agreement if she needs to. She just doesn't feel like she can be a part of something where people are inevitably going to be hurt, one way or another. She hopes that David will agree and let her leave so she can somehow get in touch with Nick to warn him. She will have to be slick about it because if David lets her leave he will definitely have people watching her.

Katie recognizes that David wants her to take option one, but she doesn't really believe that was ever a real option. David knew her so well at one point that he could basically read her mind, so there was no way that he doesn't see that Katie wants to protect Dr. Cyrus at all costs and will warn him immediately.

David wants to agree with her proposal of a third option. He doesn't really want to hurt her. She is one of the best people he has ever met. Even in the midst of their breakup when he broke her heart he could tell she was still worried about him more than herself. He still can't let her leave as much as it pains him. His weak attempt at using whatever little control he has left over her did not work and he only has one option left.

"Katie, I can't let you leave here. You know that already, though, don't you? I knew you wouldn't agree to cooperate. I don't really even know why I offered you any options. You're just too selfless. It really is a flaw," he says very calmly.

"I'm going to need to confiscate your phone and any personal belongings you brought in here. Kenny is going to set you up in a room where you can rest until things calm down. You're not going to be able to have any contact with anyone outside of myself and Kenny for a while. I don't want to do this to you Katie, but this is the only way I can protect you and myself at the same time. I really hoped you would have just followed our original plan. Things would have gone smoother if you would have stayed in South Carolina to do your job and let me handle Cyrus in my own way, but this is the course we are taking now."

David clicks his intercom and begins speaking into it, telling Kenny it is time to get moving. Within seconds Kenny comes into the room and takes Katie's bag and ushers her out of the office. David sits down in his chair defeated. He slowly reaches back into his pocket to retrieve the note that Kenny had brought him just minutes earlier. He unfolds the creased paper and prepares himself to re-read it. The note is in Kenny's neat handwriting. David silently admires the way the letters are perfectly spaced. He momentarily finds himself mourning handwritten expression now that everything is so high tech now.

Mr. Bruner,

NP says he wants to accelerate things. He wants you to call him as soon as he can so he can catch you up on what is to come next.

- Kenny

Kenny must have notified him of the developments with Katie and Dr. Cyrus. Smart, he thinks. That is something that he would have done years ago when he was trying to show his importance to his boss. Kenny is definitely showing David that he is playing the long game. The note brings David back to when he was first given orders almost five years ago by the Department of Defense to begin research on the *Modifieds*. At first this was an exciting notion for David because he knew that if he were successful this could mean a lot for his career. He didn't at that time know that it would mean he would lose almost all autonomy in the position he worked so hard to get. He was so naive when he was first starting out, but that now has been corrected.

He stays sitting silently thinking about his future, hopeful to please NP, as he mourns the loss of his friendship with Katie. Although he never plans to get back together with her, part of him always thought they'd stay connected in some way or another. David hangs his head and covers his eyes with his hands trying to hide from everything, including himself.

Chapter 11

April 28th - 29th, 2082 - NICK

Nick is starting to get worried now. He can't figure out why Katie hasn't responded to his text message yet. He can tell that she read it. The little darkened checkmarks are proof of it. It has been several hours now and he needs to get some sleep, to get a fresh perspective on things. He dozes off with his phone resting on his chest just in case she messages him back.

A few hours later he wakes up in a sweat. He picks up his phone to check the time: 3:24 a.m. He checks his messaging app just to see if he missed a notification. Nothing. He still hasn't heard from Katie and it has almost been over twelve hours now since she messaged him with her concerns about Bruner and MoonCycle. He has since responded back to her saying, "Call me once you get out of the meeting and come back to D.C. so we can figure this whole thing out together. I knew something was suspicious about Preston. Be careful." He checks the message conversation again, hoping to see something different this time.

As he stares at the conversation on the screen, he decides he can't wait any longer. He knows it is late, but he tries to call her anyway. The phone rings four times before going to voicemail. He doesn't want to sound too needy when he leaves a message, so he keeps it short, "Hey, uhh, Katie, it's Nick. Haven't heard from you for a bit. I'm getting a little concerned. Please call me back as soon as you can."

He is way more than the "little concerned" he noted in the message. Over the last twelve hours or so of silence on Katie's end, it comes to his attention that he longs to talk to her. When he found out about MoonCycle, she was the first one, the only one, he wanted to share it with and it wasn't because they were working together. He genuinely likes the way she talks to him and the way she always gives her full attention when he is talking, like whatever is being said is the most important thing she's ever heard, even if it isn't.

He tries not to panic once he ends his voicemail, but he can't control himself and starts to text her hoping to see the 'read' check marks fill in, "Katie, I'm really starting to get concerned. Please message me back. I need to talk to you… I miss you".

He doesn't mean to add that last part, but the adrenaline caused by the fear of the situation isn't allowing him to make any well thought out decisions. He stares at the sent message for a few minutes hoping to get a response. The 'read' checkmark darkens on his screen. His heart beats faster as he sees the three little dots indicating that she is typing.

The message comes through abruptly. "Hi, I'm sorry I didn't respond back to you. I've decided I need to step away from the project for personal reasons. Please don't contact me any longer. You can reach out to David Bruner or Kenny Nash directly if you need anything for the assignment." He can't believe it, she just up and quit. He reads the message over and over trying to make sense of it.

After what seems like the thousandth time reading the message he closes the app. It doesn't make any sense. He doesn't think Katie would do something like this. Everything he has learned about her up until this point in time is the opposite of what he just read. She really cares about her job and he thought she cared about him too. Could he have been wrong about the vibe he has been feeling between them? He doesn't want to believe this to be true, but there it is in black, block text across his screen that she has given up and walked away. He wonders if his connection to MoonCycle has Katie thinking that he is part of whatever is going on. He hopes that he has left a good enough impression on her for her to see that isn't true. He lays back down trying to convince himself that a few more hours of sleep could do him some good. Things will look brighter in the morning, he thinks.

Nick is awakened by a pinging sound on his phone. It isn't a text message, but rather a voicemail notification. He doesn't know how he slept through the phone ringing. He must have been so emotionally drained that he slept deeply for the last few hours. His eyes feel heavy and his mouth is dry. He sits up and situates himself in the bed.

He checks the time: 6:56 a.m. At least he was able to get a few hours of sleep despite feeling so terrible, he reasons. He looks at his call log and it is a number he doesn't know. He sighs deeply. He had hoped that it would be Katie's number displayed on his screen. As he is connecting to his voicemail, he is hopeful that it won't just be another spam caller trying to sell a warranty for the latest technologies.

The voicemail message begins and it is Katie's voice coming through the speaker, "Nick, I don't have a lot of time. David is holding me here against my will. It was a mistake coming here. I told him I wouldn't help him get to you. He wants you to take the fall for MoonCycle if you are unable to find a cure for what is happening. They handpicked you for this all along. He alluded to the fact that there are bigger players in their game than we understand," she pauses. "Nick, they took my phone. I'm locked in a room in the Human Biology Research Department building. Don't worry about me, please just get yourself safe. They're going to try to get to you now and get you on their side. I've got to go now. I think someone might be coming. Oh and Nick, I really hope I see you soon and that you can figure a way out of this." The voicemail ends.

A small sense of relief washes over Nick. That text message wasn't from Katie after all. It must have been from David or Kenny. His heart skips a beat knowing that he is the one she called with her only opportunity. He needs to figure out how to reunite with her and fast. Nick knows he has to get back to Washington D.C., but he has to be smart about how he does it. If he has to help MoonCycle and team up with Bruner to save her then that's what he will have to do.

Nick hops out of bed and rushes to the shower. He turns the water cold in hopes to awaken him and provide him with clear thoughts. It doesn't help one bit. He can't stop thinking about Katie's voice and how he longs to save her.

Once he is out of the shower he packs up all of his samples and decides to travel on foot, hoping he won't be seen by anyone. Unfortunately, in a small town like Beaufort, it turns out you can't really go anywhere without being seen or word getting out about your whereabouts. Nick makes it only three blocks from the hotel before Silas's freshly washed SUV pulls up next to him.

"Going somewhere, Dr. Cyrus?" Preston shouts out the passenger window. Nick decides to play it cool. After all, it could be possible that Preston doesn't know Katie sent him a message about the truth of his employment. Unlikely, but still possible.

"Oh, just heading for a stroll, I figured I would check out different parts of the town to see if I should take any other samples that make sense to my research." Nick lies.

Silas Preston's thick cheeks grow plump as a smile forms on his face.

"Oh, Dr. Cyrus, that won't be necessary. You have a meeting with someone in a few minutes. Please get in the car and I'll drive you," Silas says with a determined tone.

The car comes to a halt. Nick knows that if he wants to save Katie then he needs to cooperate. He shrugs and opens the car door, entering the backseat. To his surprise, he isn't alone when he slides into the back of the SUV.

"Good morning, Dr. Cyrus. I hope you were able to get a good night's sleep in our peaceful little town," says the unwanted guest, Sheriff Rodrigo 'Rio' Santos.

Nick looks over and a chill runs down his back. A vision flashes into his memory. The man who had been standing on the beach between the bushes watching him, is now sitting next to him...Sheriff Santos. He didn't notice it was him when they had met in the mayor's office that day, but now with him sitting next to him and his hat on his head with a shadow draped across his face, he is positive it was him. During their meeting that day in the mayor's office, Nick didn't really feel like he could trust either of them, but he never could have imagined that the Sheriff would be working with MoonCycle too. Is everyone in this town corrupt?

Nick returns the meaningless greeting and tries his best to act unbothered by the Sheriff's presence. Sheriff Santos can tell Nick is uncomfortable despite his efforts to appear collected.

"Don't worry Dr. Cyrus, we are just heading to a quick meeting with a few common acquaintances," Santos says, trying to seem unaffected as well.

Nick is sure that Santos is talking about Bruner. Who else could he be talking about? Everything points back to Bruner playing a game that Nick doesn't quite understand yet.

The car comes to a slow halt at their destination and Nick is not at all surprised to see they are at a MoonCycle factory along the coast, just a few miles north of the Ardi's house. Mr. Preston gets out of the car and opens the sheriff's door behind him first and then walks around the back of the car and opens Nick's door. Nick carries his samples with him, just as a comfort item at this point.

They enter through a side door of the factory where they are greeted by a woman, a secretary, Nick guesses. She ushers them up the stairs to an office that overlooks the factory floor. The metal stairs clang with each step Nick takes. He thinks to himself that he should be more nervous than he is because he doesn't really feel anything at all now.

Sheriff Santos leads the group into the office, with Nick entering second and Silas Preston coming through last and softly closing the door behind him. Upon entering the office Nick scans the faces of the men who were waiting patiently for their arrival. David Bruner is not there. He thought he would feel relief knowing that he won't have to face David today, but the occupants of the room tell him otherwise.

Mayor Frank Roy is sitting in the corner and stands up to shake everyone's hand immediately upon their arrival, in true politician form. While Nick is slightly thrown off by the mayor's attendance in this meeting, it kind of makes sense with Sheriff Santos being involved and all. The two seemed thick as thieves the last time Nick saw them. The other guest is a little less surprising than it should be to Nick, given all that he's found out. At the desk in the center of the room is the one and only, Nathan Pierce, the CEO of MoonCycle.

Chapter 12

April 28-29th, 2082 - KATIE

Katie can't believe what just happened in David's office. He has lost his mind, she decides. The David that she just experienced a few minutes ago is not the David that she's known these past few years. She tries to replay in her mind what happened in the office while she follows Kenny into an elevator. The elevator doors close and Kenny stands facing them just grinning. She hates Kenny now more than she ever has. The moments in the elevator with this self-satisfied, coattail rider can't possibly pass any slower. Katie looks up at the number displayed above the doors and it counts down slowly…7…6 ….5 ….4 ….3. The number freezes at 3 and the doors creep open.

Kenny guides Katie out of the elevator first, ensuring that she won't try to make an escape. As she exits the elevator she notices a man, he is wearing a black suit. Katie begins to worry that this man is going to harm her in some way. From afar he looks intimidating and professional. His appearance reminds her of an old action movie she watched as a kid about a CIA agent. She has never seen anyone in the building that looks like him before even though she has worked here for years, so she is pretty positive that he isn't employed by the Human Biology Research Department. He must be a MoonCycle employee just like Silas Preston. Kenny escorts Katie slowly down the hall towards the man.

The closer they get to the man the less nervous Katie is about her future. The man looks smaller than he had at first glance and he definitely doesn't look professional or intimidating. Katie can tell that the man's suit is not the correct size. It is very obviously off the rack and not tailored. His coat sleeves are too long and hang past his wrists. The trousers the man is wearing have the crease in the wrong spot and look rather wrinkled. As she walks right up to him she can even see that the white of the man's collar has started to yellow with age of the shirt.

Katie Kleug has learned a lot of things from being associated with David for some time. She can now tell if a man is sophisticated and wealthy by how they dress and carry themselves. She learns from looking at the man a few feet from her that she is pretty good at telling the opposite of those characteristics as well. She shakes the judgment from her head. She doesn't know why she is worried about what the man is wearing. Before dating David she would have never judged someone based on their appearance or how much money they have. She hopes this is a one off and that she didn't pick up any other terrible habits from David. It would be horrible to be as shallow as he is. She decides that she may need to reboot herself to her pre-David version.

The power-hungry assistant doesn't think it is important to introduce Katie to the man, but rather he ushers her into the conference room nearby. Kenny explains to Katie that she will be staying in this room for a while and that he will have some things brought here for her to keep her comfortable for the time being. Katie scoffs at him and shoots him an evil look.

Kenny closes and locks the wooden door once Katie is inside. He hands the key to the man. Katie scopes out the room. There is a titanium, oval shaped table that takes up most of the room surrounded by black egg-shaped chairs. There isn't much else in the room. A huge touch screen hangs on a wall parallel to the table. She looks around to see if there is a phone in the room somewhere but then realizes there probably isn't a phone in this office and hasn't been one for at least a decade or two given how updated the screen and room look.

Even when Katie was little, seeing a landline phone was a foreign concept that pretty much only existed in old films. She remembered seeing one at her grandparents' house one time. They didn't ever use it, but she recalled seeing it in their attic when she helped her grandmother spring clean years back. Her grandmother showed her how it worked, and Katie was mesmerized by the fact that there had to be a cord that plugged into the wall. Grandmother called it a rotary phone, as she recalls. It was an antique even to her grandmother. Even as she got older and saw telephones in old films, she always found it an odd concept that one had to stay in the same spot to have an entire conversation.

She looks around a little more to see if there is anything in the room she can use for communication or even for entertainment. She doesn't have any luck so she plops herself down in one of the cushy, egg chairs. Katie hopes that whatever Kenny is going to have brought in for her will arrive soon. She isn't good at being alone with her own thoughts, especially in a room where there is literally nothing to distract her. Whoever had been in here before disconnected the touch screen from its power source and the power source is missing. She likely wouldn't have been able to watch or do anything on the techy screen anyways since it needs to be hooked up to a device to work. At this moment, Katie really wishes she would have agreed to the virtual assistant that David offered to buy for her back when they were together. She could have had a chance to be close enough to connect to her phone, wherever they took it, if she had the device. She decides that being stubborn and ungrateful when it comes to technology is, for the time being, her worst character trait.

The junior administrator spins around in the chair for several minutes before she can't take the silence anymore. She knocks on the door hoping someone will answer from the outside. She considers screaming for help but realizes that isn't going to help Nick or herself stay safe.

She knocks a second time, much harder than the first. She assumes the man in the suit is nearby, but she can't be sure. Someone on the outside returns the knock. Katie gets excited at the prospect of at least having someone she can talk to.

"Hello, I'm Katie. Are you the man who was out there when that little troll brought me in here?"

The sound of an animated laugh travels through the wooden door. The man responds, "Yes, I'm the same man you saw as you were coming. My job is to just wait here and make sure that you receive what the so called "little troll" considers necessities for you to survive for the time being."

The man has a lightness in his voice. He reminds Katie of Mr. Preston when she first met him—before she found out he wasn't really a driver by profession. She is filled with hope that she can befriend him and then he may be inclined to help her.

Over the next few hours she speaks to the man on the other side of the door, just trying to make friendly conversation. While her hope is that he will somehow aid her in her escape, she also just wants some company. The room is terribly drab and the silence makes her feel a level of despair she hasn't ever felt before. Somehow talking to the cheeky man in the wrinkly suit makes it more tolerable.

They chat about her job and how she ended up as a prisoner. She figures telling him everything can't hurt. He is already working for the enemy. She tells the man about how betrayed she feels by David and divulges a little of their past to him. He agrees that he'd feel a deep betrayal too after she tells him how the last few days transpired.

The man seems genuinely interested in what she is telling him, but she can't be sure because he is likely as bored standing on the outside of the door as she is sitting on the inside of it. Throughout the conversation Katie asks the man about himself, but he won't give her any information. She understands that he is just being cautious, after all he probably needs this job and he doesn't want to jeopardize himself or possibly his family. He won't even tell her his name. After a while she decides she will just call him "Panda Man" because the only thing she knows about him is the color of his suit. He finds it amusing when she refers to him in that way. He always gives a little chuckle when he hears the term slip through her lips.

Katie continues going on about the last few days, appreciative that Panda Man is even bothering to listen. She begins to tell him about the man she is lusting over, Dr. Nick Cyrus. Despite the only person listening being a man who is helping keep her captive, she is still glad to have another person's perspective on whether or not Nick might be interested in her the way she is in him. She tells Panda Man about all of the interactions that she felt the closest to him, trying to gauge if it might all be in her mind. She tells him about the text message and the emojis he ended it with, the long-held eye contact, and the touch of hands in uncertain times.

Panda Man says he can't be sure, but it sounds a lot to him like Dr. Cyrus is definitely interested in her. Hearing that she isn't just imagining their connection helps her to feel a tiny bit better about her current situation. Instead of focusing on being trapped in a conference room, she can't stop thinking of Nick and how he is doing. She envisions herself seeing him again and allowing their connection to flourish.

Katie looks up at the clock in the conference room and it has now been several hours since Kenny locked her in the room. At this point she doubts he is even going to send items up to keep her busy and comfortable. She hasn't heard anyone in the hallway outside of the door aside from Panda Man for hours. Her stomach is starting to growl and a wave of sleepiness is coming over her.

She decides to pause her conversation with her new wrinkly suited friend and try to get some sleep, hoping to pass some time. She requests a quick bathroom break before she calls it a night. He obliges and she is happy to see Panda Man's face again. This time when she sees him he seems different to her—more like someone she has known for a long time and can trust, more than just a stranger in a suit.

She is awakened early in the morning by voices coming from outside of the conference room door. She rubs her eyes, trying to focus them on the clock that hangs above. It reads 6:45 a.m. Katie is surprised to find she has slept through the night. She reasons that it must just have been because she was so emotionally drained that rest found her easily. She can't quite hear what is being said on the other side of the door. It is muffled and a little further away than Panda Man had been when they were talking last night.

The door begins to jiggle a little as someone on the other side is attempting to unlock the door. It creaks open and Panda Man enters carrying a black duffle bag, a few paper grocery sacks and a plastic bag of take out. As she stands up to greet him, she realizes she hasn't gone to the bathroom in almost eight hours, the last time being when Panda Man had accompanied her to the women's restroom right before she had called it a night. The urge to urinate fills her immediately. She requests to use the bathroom and Panda Man calls out into the hallway, "Bathroom Break". A man in a similar dark suit, but with a much less sunny disposition, appears in the doorway. He must be the man that delivered all of these items, she decides. Panda Man tells the other suited man to take Katie to the bathroom and then bring her right back afterwards. He explains he will be unpacking everything and getting her set up while they are gone.

Katie thinks about making a run for it on her way down the hall to the bathroom, but she realizes she wouldn't have anywhere to go nearby that David wouldn't know about. She also doesn't have any money. If she did escape and was able to get a hold of Nick then what would she do? Where would she go? Nick is still in Beaufort and even if he could get here within a few hours or even a day—David would surely be able to find her by then. She stops tormenting herself with 'what ifs' and makes her way to the bathroom to relieve herself. The man waits outside of the door and escorts her back down the hall to the conference room.

When she returns to what is becoming her makeshift apartment, she notices that Panda Man emptied quite a few things onto the conference table for her. There are snacks, a couple containers of food from a local Chinese takeout spot, some toiletries, and clothing. She is glad to see that there is some food because she has grown famished over the last several hours.

Panda Man tells her that he will be back in a few hours to bring her more food and let her use the restroom now that she has some personal items to keep her busy for the time being. He moves through the doorway and locks the door. She isn't sure if the other man who had taken her to the bathroom is gone or not, but she doesn't hear any noise outside the door so she guesses she is now on her own. With her stomach growling at regular intervals now she decides that she would start with the Chinese food since it smells somewhat appetizing and she can tell it was still warm because of the little streams of steam coming through the cracks of the containers.

Chinese food isn't Katie's favorite. In fact, she doesn't really like it at all, but she can tolerate it. The cuisine has gotten less appetizing over the years since the embargo on pretty much everything coming and going from the United States. Most business owners have done what they could with what they have available to them and the cuisine seems less authentic now. Katie looks back at the clock. Someone must have gotten this Chinese food last night and heated it up this morning. There is no way the Chinese spot down the street is open this early. Beggars can't be choosers, she determines, happy just to have something to eat now.

The takeout bag looks very familiar to her. It brings her back to when she was with David. He often ordered from Sichuan Pavilion—the place where this food before her came from. He never really even asked Katie if that was what she wanted or if she liked it. Now that she thought about it, he never really asked her much about any of her preferences. Each time over the last few days when she looks back on their relationship she notices there were a lot of red flags that she missed while under his spell.

She grabs the plastic bag holding the containers of what she guesses is orange 'chicken'—or at least something passed off as chicken—and spring rolls, the scent already making its way to her nose, and begins to adjust one of the rolling chairs so she can sit down. She looks back down at the table where the bag sat only a few seconds ago and notices a cell phone on the table. She immediately sets the Chinese food back down so she can focus. It looks worn in and she realizes it has to be Panda Man's phone. He is the only one that ever entered the room. She wonders for a second if he left it on purpose for her because they bonded through the door or if it is a complete accident. Katie decides the reason doesn't really matter and that she has to act fast because he will likely be coming back for it either way.

She picks up the phone, ready to call Nick. She presses down quickly on the phone app. She can't believe she can remember his cell phone number after only knowing him for a few days. She has only seen his number a handful of times in her notepad and files when she was preparing their accommodations for Beaufort, but when she was younger her mother drilled her cell phone number into her head before the first day of kindergarten—just in case of an emergency. Since then, she always found that remembering numbers came easily to her. She would see commercials, billboards, and park benches and be able to recite the numbers on them to the jingle or company it corresponded with easily. She punches the number quickly into the floating keypad that popped up above the screen. She realizes now that her mother's neuroticism and her own atypical compulsory behavior may play a role in saving Nick and maybe even herself now.

The phone rings on for close to 40 seconds before the voicemail clicks on. Disappointment hangs in the air. All she can do now is leave a voicemail, hoping he will check it soon. Katie knows that Panda Man won't leave the phone here long—even if he did leave it here on purpose he will have to return for it—claiming that he left it behind as a mistake. She talks quickly, worrying that her time is running out. She warns Nick of what she heard in David's office the day prior. She wishes him luck and tells him that she hopes he can figure a way out of this. She wants to tell him how she feels about him and she considers it for a moment since she doesn't know when she will see him again, but then she hears footsteps approaching the door and the handle moving ever so slightly as someone begins to unlock it. She ends her call and quickly goes back into the call log and deletes all traces of the last few minutes. She promptly places the phone back on the table slightly under the bag of Chinese takeout.

She grabs a container out of the bag and sits down hastily as the door creaks open. Panda Man stands in the doorframe taking in the scene. He announces that he must have dropped something when he was unpacking and that he has come to retrieve it. He makes the announcement so loudly that it seems like he is doing it for an audience that may be lurking by rather than for Katie's benefit. She leans back to peer outside but can't see anyone.

Panda Man leans over the table and begins searching for the cell phone. When his hand finds the phone he intentionally makes eye contact with Katie. Nothing is said, but Katie now knows for sure that he left the phone for her on purpose. The gleam in his eyes and the smirk on his face tells her everything. She found a friend in him somehow through their conversation and while he can't rescue her, he can give her the opportunity to rescue herself.

He retreats from his hunched stance and begins announcing his next move again loudly, "I'm going to head out now, but as I said before I'll be back to let you go to the bathroom and bring you some food in a couple of hours."

He backs himself through the door, opposite of how he had entered and relocks it. The sound of his heavy steps disappear second by second.

Katie opens the container that is in her hand and begins picking at the food with her fork. She's right, it is orange 'chicken'. She decides at that moment that she will enjoy this meal in honor of her new friend, the Panda Man. As she chews on the moist, citrusy chicken she feels a sense of accomplishment. Her voicemail may reach Nick and now everything is in his hands.

Chapter 13

April 29th, 2082 - NICK

Nick isn't entirely sure why he is shocked by Nathan Pierce being here, it is one of his factories afterall. Everything he's found out has led straight to MoonCycle so why wouldn't it make sense for the face of MoonCycle to be involved, he concludes. Nathan doesn't even bother to introduce himself. Why would he? Everyone in the room knows him, in fact, most people in the United States are familiar with him. Nick hasn't seen him in some time, not since he was recognized for being one of the top scientists in the Half Moon product development at a banquet dinner two years ago.

Nathan Pierce begins the conversation, speaking only to Nick, "It's good to see you Dr. Cyrus. Long time no see. It has come to my attention that you have figured out the little problem we are having with the water along the coast here in beautiful South Carolina. I'm so glad you have agreed to come back to assist your MoonCycle family in coming out on top of this terrible incident."

Nick forces a half-smile.

"I'm happy to be of service. Can you tell me if the spill from the plant has been contained? There are extremely high traces of chemicals in the water."

His stomach churns at the thought of the CEO's impending response.

Pierce quickly responds, "It wasn't a spill, the factory had been running the output into the water for some time. This, of course, was not something I was aware of. As of three days ago the output has been redirected and is no longer an issue."

Nick nods to show his understanding, but he doubts it is true. Pierce doesn't seem like a man who would ever allow himself to be surprised by something happening in his company. He is always involved in every aspect of everything. Nick had even seen him in the lab several times when he was working on Half Moon, just popping in to check on how things were going. Most CEOs would call in virtually or have an assistant check on things, but Pierce is completely hands-on in his companies. Whether or not the runoff is stopped would somehow be a calculated move by Pierce.

Nick's understanding of the situation doesn't really mean much. It is a terrible situation from every angle. The water in the area will eventually be washed out into the greater ocean and the chemicals will become diluted, but that won't help with the fact that many people have already come in contact with the water and they can't be sure of what the outcomes of that will be. That is, of course, if it's true that the runoff has been redirected and isn't still filling the nearby waters. It is also unlikely that in the event that it was redirected that the new location of the runoff is safe and not affecting any of the population. Every scenario that runs through Nick's mind ends with some sort of devastation.

"What I'm thinking here, Dr. Cyrus, is that this is the perfect opportunity for you to come up with a new serum. Half Moon was, and still is, so successful and we'd like the new serum to live up to the same hype. Now, I can guarantee you that our chemical additives in the water didn't start this whole *'Modified'* or 'MODs', as the young people call it, mess, but it definitely accelerated it and forced some sort of super immune response in people, like you've seen with your new friend Adam Ardi. What we'd like to do is create something to actually stop the process or dormant it entirely," Nathan Pierce says in a proud voice.

Nick looks at him and scowls. He is almost more smug than David Bruner when he speaks…if that's even possible. Did he just admit to me that he purposely forced immune responses in people using chemicals just so he could sell more products? Nick questions himself and runs back the conversation in his head to see if he is just imagining things. He really hopes that isn't the truth, but Katie says in her message that there are bigger players involved in this and she isn't wrong about that. People like Nathan

Pierce are so powerful and worried about losing that power that they will do almost anything to keep it. Pierce doesn't only own MoonCycle, it is just one of his many ventures. He owns several big companies that span across the entire market economy. There's unlikely a single person in all of America who doesn't own one of Nathan Pierce's products.

Dr. Cyrus thinks for a moment before responding, "Wouldn't it be dangerous to release a serum that could stop the *Modification* process? I don't mean dangerous in a physical sense, I already know that answer. What I'm asking is, wouldn't it be detrimental to society to do so since we are already struggling with what is thought to be a possible civil war brewing?"

Nathan Pierce is already shaking his head in disagreement before Nick finishes his question.

"Absolutely not, we are, of course, trying to take the path of least resistance. This could help the different parts of the country to move past their differences by providing a path that could offer not only a peace of mind for people, but an obvious health choice that can unite people like they were before all this MOD nonsense began. We know you're capable of developing something that modifies DNA, you've done it before," Pierce utters.

Nathan Pierce is right, Nick has done it before and he probably can do it again. His lack of confidence isn't really the issue here. The problem is that he doesn't know if he agrees that this is the best path to take. Nick takes a second to run through the scenarios in his head.

If he helps them create a serum and if that serum is distributed, but the public doesn't like the option, then MoonCycle will turn on him in a second and put him in front of the public as the evil genius who tries to fuel the fire that is the brewing civil war. Additionally, he can't guarantee that whatever serum he comes up with will have no side effects. There might be effects on the body that cause more changes than *Modifying* would.

On the other hand, if he doesn't help them, he could still be thrown to the wolves to take the heat for the chemical spillage in the water since it was only a matter of time journalists came digging in the small town of Beaufort. Somehow they would figure out a way to link all of this back to his Half Moon creation whether it was true or not. Plus, the entire community of

Beaufort had just seen Dr. Cyrus running around town and I'm sure they would corroborate whatever Sheriff Santos asked them to. Neither option is great for Nick, but he feels that if he goes with option one at least he has some control over the situation.

"I see what you're saying, Mr. Pierce. I appreciate you having so much confidence in me and my abilities. I would be happy to help work on a new serum, but I do have one condition," Nick says with a more genuine smile than before.

"Name it, my boy," Pierce replies.

"Well, I would like to be able to work at the Human Biology Research Department lab in D.C. That facility has a state-of-the-art lab and I've grown to really enjoy the area," Nick says plainly.

Mayor Roy breaks his silence, "I don't think that is such a great idea, Nathan. We won't have anyone in D.C. to keep an eye on things. As the Mayor, I have to stay here and keep tabs on what is developing in the town and extinguish some of these rumors before they grow into something much larger."

Pierce turns his head to the side a little to show that he is listening, taking in, and seriously considering what is being said.

Sheriff Santos agrees with Mayor Roy, "Nate, I'm going to have to agree with Frank. It seems a bit too risky—all just because the boy likes the scenery of D.C. No one actually likes the scenery of D.C. it is an absolute shit hole."

Nick doesn't like the way he is being talked about—as if he isn't in the room. He also isn't too keen on them calling him 'boy'. He is a grown man. Sure, all of the other people in the room are older than him, but that doesn't mean he isn't a grown man. Instead of wasting his time being offended at the chosen term, he decides to chalk it up to a 'southern thing' that he just doesn't understand, nor does he want to.

Pierce breathes deeply and replies in one long breath, "I hear your concerns, fellas. I do, but I'm going to go with the good doctor on this one. He made a small request and I think we can honor it. Besides, Silas will go with Dr. Cyrus to keep an eye on things, won't you Silas?"

Mr. Preston straightens his posture at the mention of his name as if he wasn't paying attention to anything happening in the room up until that moment. He shakes his head in agreement without speaking. Nick can tell Silas fears every person in the room except him. Seeing Silas as the odd man out of the group makes him more relatable and makes Nick like him a little more.

Pierce continues, "It's settled then, isn't it? Plus, Bruner will be there as well and that little pain in the ass assistant of his too—whatever his name is."

Both Mayor Roy and Sheriff Santos agree and laugh at the way Pierce referred to Kenny Nash.

Nick acknowledges that Kenny is, in fact, a 'pain in the ass', but it isn't really all that funny. Nick can tell immediately who the brain behind this operation is. It clearly isn't the two 'geniuses' running the charming little town of Beaufort. They are straight scared of Nathan Pierce. Nick understands their fear though, Nathan Pierce has a lot of clout, a lot of money, a lot of power and a lot of friends...important friends.

Chapter 14

April 29th, 2082 - NICK

The only reason Nick really wants to move to the lab in D.C. is to be able to get close to Katie. The lab isn't really that great. He has worked in much better labs throughout his career, but no one needs to know that.

It has now been nearly two days since he spoke to Katie, not counting the message she left him in the middle of the night a day ago. He needs to know that she is safe and this seems like the only way to do it. He doesn't want anyone in the meeting to know that this is his true intention for requesting the lab several states away and because no one called him out for it, he has a suspicion that David Bruner isn't exactly telling his 'friends' every detail of what has been developing.

Instead of heading directly to the airport from the factory, Nick requests of Silas—his now personal assistant, driver, and babysitter—that he be able to stop and gather many more samples along the beach so that he can use them in his development of the new serum. Nick has zero intention of using said samples or even cooperating with Pierce, but he decides that if he is going to play the part then he has to do it well otherwise he may compromise himself and even worse, Katie.

The car pulls up by the Ardi's beach as their first stop on the three stop request for samples. Nick gets out of the car and gathers samples the exact same way he did the first time. Another nine samples. Silas watches Nick's every move while he is on the beach. Nick feels like he is a reality television star and Silas is one of his fans.

When they make their way back to the car, Nick decides to ask Silas a question that has been burning a hole in his skull for days now. Nick is pretty sure he knows the answer, but he still feels the need for confirmation, "Mr. Preston, were you the one who took my samples the other day, the missing ones?"

Silas Preston's face develops a spirited little smile.

"Oh of course not, and please from now on, call me Silas. I think our friendship has moved past you referring to me by my last name."

Nick knows Silas is lying, but it doesn't matter because his smile tells the truth for him. Nick is hoping to find some sort of redeeming quality in Silas, but that doesn't seem possible now. He will be stuck with him for the foreseeable future and will have to figure out a way to make it work.

The next two stops to gather water samples are really just for show. Even if Nick were to use samples to create a serum he would never need this many. Silas doesn't know that though. He just needs Silas to report back to the big, bad bosses to let them know that Nick is doing exactly what he is supposed to be doing.

The second stop is along a port to the south. After gathering samples there, they head back to the hotel where Nick and Katie are staying to grab the rest of Nick's items and check out. Silas requests that they stop for lunch back at Cafe a la Beaufort before heading to their third stop. Nick can't really deny Silas this pleasure because he is also starving. He hasn't eaten anything since a few things that he grabbed out of the vending machine in the hotel last night. It was not even enough sustenance to be considered a meal, let alone dinner.

The two park the car and head into the cafe—and wouldn't you know it, there is Sheriff Santos, sitting right at the counter. He gives a hearty, "Hello Gentlemen" when he notices their arrival, which is signaled by the bell above the door. Nick can't imagine why anyone in the whole world would want everyone looking at them when entering a room, but apparently people around here like being noticed.

Silas greets Sheriff Santos and grabs the seat to the left of him. Nick decides there is no way in hell he will be sitting next to Sheriff Santos and grabs the open stool on the other side of Silas. The better of two evils, he thinks, trying to justify his choice.

Nick orders the cafe's fried 'chicken' with a side of fries—which their sign says they are famous for, and he is hungry enough to eat every last bite. He doesn't know if his body is capable of finishing so much food—the people down south must have bottomless pits for stomachs, but it is definitely hitting the spot.

Luckily, Sheriff Santos makes very little conversation with Nick while they are sitting there. Nick desires some peace and quiet, but he can handle listening to the little college football talk that Preston and Santos drum up to keep up appearances. Nick isn't much of a football fan himself, but he knows enough about college football and enough about the south to know how important it still is to the southern people. It is one of the only outdoor sports that is still around.

All the sports talk brings Nick back to his childhood. He was a huge baseball fan when he was younger. Baseball used to be America's favorite pastime, but all the outdoor stadiums had to install roofs to combat the changing weather patterns. The league still plays, but something about it isn't as magical as it had been years back and many fans stopped paying attention. Sitting inside watching a game just isn't the same as having a hot dog and cold drink in the sun while seeing an out-of-the-park home run.

Silas keeps going on about Clemson and how they are bound to have the best season yet despite some setbacks last year. Nick tries hard not to choke on the last few bites of his food when he hears Santos say he is a Gamecocks fan. Of course you are, thinks Nick. He can not eye roll hard enough when the words come out of the sheriff's mouth. Even Nick, a Chicagoan, knows that team is terrible, but somehow they still have a traditionally large fan base. Silas wraps up eating the burger he ordered and then pays the check for the both of them. Nick doesn't offer Santos as much as a goodbye on his way out.

The third stop on their tour of sample gathering is a little north of the Ardi's property. Nick creeps up along the beach and grabs a handful of samples before their quick drive to the airport. This time when they arrive at the airport there isn't a private government plane awaiting their arrival, instead it is a huge private plane that sports the MoonCycle logo along its body. Nick grabs his bag and the case full of samples and boards the plane thinking that it will be a truly tragic death if he dies in a plane with that logo on the side of it.

The flight itself is very pleasant. Nick is finally able to get some space from Silas, probably because Silas knows there is literally nowhere for him to go now that they are up in the air. Nick sits in the back row alone with his thoughts.

First, his thoughts go to Katie and how he really doesn't know what happened to her. She told him that she was in a room in the Human Biology Research Department building, but that was over a day ago now. Could she still be there? He imagines her leaving the voicemail for him. Her face disappointed that he didn't answer, but still as beautiful as ever with her hair in her signature messy bun and biting her lip like she does when she is thinking.

His mind shifts to Adam sitting in the quarantine room and his mother, Ava, worrying herself sick. He wants to help Katie more than anything, but Adam is in the back of his mind weighing on him. He can't stop thinking about how scared Adam probably is about what is happening to him. Whatever his next steps are, he needs to find a way to help the *Modified* children. They aren't choosing this life, they are being born into it.

He tries to wash his thoughts of her and Adam away in order to make a decision on how to proceed before the flight ends. He doesn't intend to actually help MoonCycle create a serum that would basically fuel a war that could very well destroy human existence in America, but he has to figure out another option while making them believe that is exactly what he is going to do. He spends the last forty-five minutes of the hour and half flight concocting his plan. He constructs something that will be risky but could force MoonCycle to take responsibility for their actions. All he needs now is to go get Katie before the plan can go into effect.

Chapter 15

April 29-30th 2082 - NICK

The flight ends and Nick is ushered off by Silas to the lab. Nick doesn't mind that Silas is in a hurry. He spent long enough on the plane stewing around in his own thoughts that now it is time for some action. Nick asks Silas if he can speak with Mr. Bruner before he gets started in the lab. Silas speaks quietly into his virtual assistant. Within seconds he shakes his head no.

From the first day Nick met Silas, he learned that he was a man of few words, but he is still kind of hoping for a little explanation as to why his request was denied. Nick decides not to pursue the request any further for fear that Kenny, the slimeball, will be the one that he has to deal with. Nick doesn't really dislike Kenny all that much, but he remembers Katie saying that she can't stand Kenny and because of that Kenny gained another enemy.

Nick enters the lab and gets to work immediately. He knows it is possible to take his Half Moon serum and develop it into another serum that is used to block the modification of DNA that is being caused by more than just environmental factors and also block the super immune response to the chemical waste that had been dumped into the water, but he isn't planning on doing it. Instead, he decides to begin creating something he likes to call 'an insurance policy'.

He found something else out about how he could use the water back in Beaufort that he didn't tell anyone, not even Katie. He has to keep this part to himself, just in case things go south. He convinces himself that it isn't lying because it could protect others. He feels terrible about withholding information, it makes him feel slimy, just like Bruner and Pierce, but he knows it could be used later if he really needed it.

While he is working in the lab, Nick becomes very aware of Silas' every move. He wants him to step away from the door he is guarding so that Nick could slip through to look for Katie for a little while, but Silas barely moves at all. If he does move, it is to just re-adjust his stance. After a while he moves a bit to grab a chair and pulls it over near the door.

Silas hasn't gone to the bathroom, not even once. A bladder of steel, Nick thinks, when several hours have passed and still nothing. When Nick tries to use the bathroom as a means of getting free of Silas, it doesn't quite work. Silas just comes into the bathroom with him. Silas doesn't even attempt to go to the bathroom; he just stands there staring at Nick while he goes. Nick doesn't know what is creepier, the fact that Silas has gone over 5 hours without going to the bathroom or the fact that he is watching him pee. Nick comes to the realization that getting out of the room is going to be more difficult than he initially thought.

Dr. Cyrus gives up on his escape ruse for a while and continues to work on his creation. He decides he is going to momentarily change his personality and become overly friendly and try to open up to Silas in hopes that he can convince him to grab him some dinner. It is not the most original idea, but after knowing Silas for close to five days now he realizes that Silas isn't exactly the sharpest crayon in the box and it has the potential to work.

"Silas, I'm getting pretty hungry here. You've got to be hungry as well. It's been nearly seven hours since we had lunch. We're going to go to bed soon and I don't want to go to bed on an empty stomach. I would really appreciate it if you went and grabbed us something. There is a delicious deli right up the street. I had it right before we headed for South Carolina and it really hit the spot," Nick says with his words full of hope.

Silas ponders Nick's request for a minute or so before responding, "I am getting pretty hungry. This big body of mine could use some fueling. I don't think I should leave you though. I can probably call up and ask for someone to grab us something."

Nick knew this was likely to be his likely response, but he is surprised that Silas is dumb enough to even have considered leaving him alone. He decides to try again with a little more pressure.

"I totally see why you would be concerned, Silas, but I promise you, I'm staying here in this lab until my eyes won't stay open any longer. To be honest, you're really the only person I trust here. I don't know how disposable Pierce thinks I am and I'd honestly rather not be poisoned. I can trust you, can't I?" Nick says cunningly.

Silas' eyes soften. It is almost like he has never felt friendship before.

Silas agrees, "Alright, I see what you're saying. To be honest, I don't know who I can trust 'round here neither. It is best if we stick together then, as a team, to get this job done so we can go on about our lives. You promise you'll stay put?"

Nick takes his finger and makes the 'cross your heart' sign across his chest and walks back to the lab table to get to work. Silas leaves the room and Nick calculates that even if Silas walks quickly and there isn't a line at the deli that he has at least 17 minutes before he would be back. Nick peeks in the hallway to make sure it is clear and then heads toward the stairwell. Before he makes it to the stairwell he walks past the quarantine room, the one where he met Adam Ardi, and pauses to look into the window. Instead of seeing Adam there, he only spots Ava. He knows he has to try to find Katie, but something in his gut tells him he needs to go into the quarantine room to find out what had happened to Adam.

He scans his card through the card reader and the light blinks green before the door opens. Ava immediately begins sobbing at the sight of Nick.

"What's wrong Ava? Where is Adam?" he inquires, looking around to see if anything about the room has changed since he last was there.

"They took him," she shouts through her sobs and sniffles.

"What do you mean they took him? Where did they take him? Why are you in the quarantine room?" The questions flow out of Nick's mouth.

Ava is now crying even harder than before. She tries to suck in a deep breath to slow her crying, but it doesn't work, and she begins choking over her own breath. After a second, she collects herself just enough to talk.

"The people took him. I'm not sure who, I know that Bruner man is behind it. He was the one standing outside of the door giving the orders," she points at the door while explaining.

Nick interrupted, "Why did they take him Ava?"

The tears are still streaming down her face at an alarming rate. "They didn't just take him. They took my husband, Derrick, and my other son, Ben also. They took them all. When you were here a few days ago Adam was the only one who had been developing the gills on his neck. They had my husband and other son held up in some hotel room or something while I was down here with Adam. The day after you left some men in hazmat suits rushed Ben and Derrick down here and threw them in the quarantine room with Adam. I tried to question them, but they wouldn't tell me what was going on. I peeked through the window for less than a second before a security guard came and locked me inside that waiting room. Ben was forming gills just like Adam had. I didn't see Derrick, but he must have been developing them too since all three of them were gone—taken somewhere else—when they put me in here," she explains.

Nick tries to process what Ava told him quickly. He doesn't have much time and now it is more important than ever that he doesn't get caught out of the lab room. He needs to be right there working when Silas returns so he can convince him to get him some face time with Bruner.

"Ava, I need you to be calm and smart about this. I am going to find them. There is no time for me to explain, but I need you to trust me. I'm going to do whatever it takes to make this right for you and get your boys back to you, but I need you to stay put and not make a fuss. It is best if you stay here for now," Nick says with fury in his voice.

He is so angry about the inhumane treatment the Ardi's are facing by Bruner and his people that he can barely contain it. Ava nods in between sobs and shivers. Nick retreats back to the door and slips out. He doesn't have time to try to find Katie now. He has to go back to the lab.

As the quarantine room door slides shut behind him he tries to think about what Ava must be feeling. Even with her hysterical crying she is taking being locked away from her family in a quarantine room much better than Nick ever would. He wants to go back and tell Ava that he is proud of how strong she is, but he knows that won't do any good. He has to think of a way to help her to reunite with her family.

Nick scurries down the hall and back through the door of the lab. He goes back over to his lab table and begins working on his creation. He is only working for 10 or so minutes when Silas comes back in with their sandwiches. It is now key for Nick to get Silas on his side. He walks over to an empty lab table and pulls two stools next to each other. He gestures to Silas to bring the food over. The two of them begin eating the pastrami sandwiches—at least that's what he thinks it's supposed to be—and critiquing the food as a means of conversation. Both of them agree that the sandwiches are good, but they miss food that is less processed. Silas even makes a joke about how even what they are eating is probably profiting Nathan Pierce and his companies. Nick knows it is true and even though it would normally be a funny joke, he isn't amused by it given the circumstances.

When Nick is halfway through his sandwich he swallows and asks, "Silas, do you think I could meet with Mr. Bruner now? I want to put in a request with him. I think that I may be able to have a better shot at creating this serum if he can give me access to another sample that he allowed me to look at when I first arrived here."

Silas finishes chewing what is in his mouth while he mulls over the plea.

"That sounds reasonable enough. I'll contact him right when we finish up our dinner."

Nick feels a sense of relief come over him. It won't seem out of the realm of possibility that he needs to see Adam and observe once again how the modification affected a human body in order to create a serum to stop it. Any reasonable person would be able to see the value in that. He just needs to convince Bruner to bring Adam and the rest of the Ardi family back. Having them back in quarantine might not be the best option with everything so undetermined, but it certainly feels like a better option than not knowing where they are at.

In order to make Silas think he is really trying to be friends with him; Nick needs to show a little interest in him as a person. Ya, know...to bond with him and all that relationship stuff that Nick was never good at. When making conversation about what Silas does in his free time, Nick is surprised to learn that Silas has a young daughter. He explains that she lives with her mother and he wishes he could see her more often.

Learning about Silas's family makes him seem more human to Nick and less like someone who is babysitting him for an evil corporation. He tells Dr. Cyrus about all of the things his daughter is interested in and he talks about how proud he is of her academic accomplishments. Nick wants to believe that because Silas works for MoonCycle that he is a bad man, but part of him knows that Silas can't be all bad. Silas wants to be there for his daughter and he wants to be a good father, that is more than Nick can say for his own father.

Silas turns the conversation to focus on Nick by asking if he has anyone special waiting for him at home. Nick wants to answer, but he really doesn't know what to say. He has no real family around, but somehow he doesn't feel like he is alone. He hopes that Katie will be the one he will eventually say is his special someone because he already feels like it is true. Nick can't tell Silas much about his interactions with Katie, as it would be obvious as to why he has moved them to D.C. Instead, he shares generic things about the girl he is fawning over—stretching the truth about the timeline and location.

Silas listens to the random details that Nick shares about his interactions with the girl he desires and offers suggestions like a close friend would. Despite how he has come to spend time with Silas, Nick finds it nice to be able to speak to someone about Katie so his thoughts of her can stop spinning inside of his head.

As soon as Silas cleans up the wrappers from their dinner and wipes the table down he messages Kenny asking if Dr. Cyrus can meet with Mr. Bruner. Kenny replies immediately that Bruner will meet with Dr. Cyrus first thing in the morning in his office. Kenny notes that Mr. Bruner can make himself available as early as 6:30 a.m.

Silas relays the message to Nick and they begin to wrap things up for the night. Mr. Preston walks Nick to the hotel accommodations half a block away. Nick hopes he will be lucky enough to have some alone time, but no such luck.

When they arrive at the hotel room Silas opens the door and announces, "This is where we will be staying. I'm a rather good house guest and I don't get in the way much."

Nick forces a smile. Great, he thinks, and sighs in his mind.

The morning can't come soon enough. Nick lays in the bed awake. He was able to sleep for a couple of hours, but as it turns out Silas snores incredibly loud and he wasn't able to sleep through what sounded like a train running over a cat.

He keeps checking the clock and waits patiently until 5:00 a.m. before he gets up to take a shower. Even if he is only pretending to be friends with Silas he still doesn't think it is fair to ruin his sleep and social norms make 5:00 a.m. seem like a reasonable time to move about the room.

When he exits the bathroom, dressed and ready about 25 minutes later, the designated babysitter is already up and ready to go. Silas asks Nick if he wants to grab something for breakfast on the way to the lab and Nick tells him that the hotel probably has a grab-and-go breakfast that they could take advantage of on the way out. He doesn't want to waste any more time eating so he thinks it is a good compromise. Silas nods and they are off to meet with Mr. Bruner.

When they enter the waiting area for Bruner's office, Kenny notifies them that Mr. Bruner is already in and that he will be with them momentarily. Nick checks his watch, surprised to see it is only 6:05 a.m. Bruner must have gotten an early start. Dr. Cyrus and Silas Preston go to sit in the chairs along the west wall of the waiting area, but before their bottoms hit the cushion, Bruner's door opens. He greets both men and they make their way into the office and take a seat. Kenny joins them for this meeting and closes the door behind him.

"Kenny told me that you wanted to speak with me, Dr. Cyrus," Bruner says looking for confirmation.

Nick pipes up, "Yes, that is correct. I think I will be able to be more successful in creating a serum that is suitable to MoonCycle's needs if I am able to see the boy you introduced me to before, the *Modified* one named

Adam Ardi."

David's eyes narrow as if he is finding the request suspicious.

"Why is it that you think that would help you with your endeavors, Dr. Cyrus?"

Nick takes a deep breath and huffs. He hates explaining that he knows how to do his job to people who have literally no idea what his job even entails. He is sure that David doesn't really even care much about what his answer is going to be but rather needs to see how confident he is in addressing this situation.

"Well, in order to create a serum that would essentially stop the *modification* process I would need to be able to do two things. One is to be able to look at the DNA of a live, *Modified* human being and the other is to test the developed serum on a live, *Modified* human being," he says in a condescending tone.

Brunner nods several times as if trying to convince himself that what Nick is saying actually makes sense.

"We're concerned that the boy is contagious. His little brother and father have both been showing signs of *Modification*. I've had them moved to our most secure quarantine zone for further studies."

Nick can't believe that they have to go over this again. He has already explained to him that *Modification* isn't airborne, but apparently, he is going to have to inform him again.

"I can assure you Mr. Bruner that it is not airborne. It is not contractible from human to human unless it is through gestation. His mother doesn't have it and she was the closest to him in proximity for many weeks. The other two probably began *Modifying* because of the same reason that Adam had. The best case scenario here for all of us allows me to work with the Ardi family to complete this task."

After some more convincing, he agrees to have the Ardi's all transported back to the quarantine room near the lab. Nick requests that Ava also be in the quarantine room so that he could have a specimen that isn't *Modified* to use as a control variable. He doesn't really need Ava in the room, but he wants her to be able to see her family again and know that she can trust him.

David nods at Kenny and the exuberant assistant bolts out of the room to get to work.

Chapter 16

April 29th, 2082 - AVA

Ava sits with her own thoughts in the quarantine room. She is destroyed inside not knowing where her children and husband are. The only bright spot in these endless hellish days was seeing Dr. Cyrus again. He's promised her help. She's hopeful that he will come through but knows better than to count on anyone but herself. Her whole life she has always been the one to fix everything. The one that people know they can count on. She admires that about herself. Even her husband Derrick counts on her to make everything better. She's tired of being everyone's rock, but it is all she's known and will continue to do what it takes to keep her family safe.

In this room there is nothing but time to reminisce. When she met Derrick years back he was a mess, just like her father was. She wonders sometimes if that is why she loves Derrick, because she wished she could have loved her father with all of his flaws. Ava's mother died during childbirth with her younger sister Molly and her dad could never cope with that loss. Ava, even though only seven years old, had to take on the role of mother, cook, caretaker, and, in many cases, even father. Her father would drink himself into oblivion each night. At first the drinking only led him being late to work, but eventually as Ava entered high school, it led to holes in the walls and broken glass on the floor. The drinking and erratic behavior only got worse as time progressed. Ava tried to reason with him and take care of him the best she could—hoping to salvage what family she had left—but he didn't make it easy. He couldn't hold down a job any longer so Ava had to get a part time job working as a receptionist at a nursing home. She was nervous at first about leaving Molly alone with her father, but she was nearing ten and old enough to take care of herself for a few hours at a time.

The nursing home eventually became like a second home to her. A place where she could laugh and joke again. A place where families visited their loved ones and shared stories of their daily lives. A place where some normalcy still lived. Last but not least, a place where she could do what she did best—help people. She would clock in day after day and see people living their last days in happiness surrounded by friends, joy, and entertainment. Each day she left there, she wished that she would eventually be able to give the same to herself and Molly.

The day after her 18th birthday she got a call at the reception desk and it was the hospital informing her that her father and sister were in a car accident. Her heart seemingly stopped. By the time she got to the hospital Molly was dead. Her father survived. He was charged with manslaughter and a DUI. As it turns out, Molly wasn't the only person he killed when he was driving. He turned the car into manual mode and hit someone crossing the street before he wrapped the car around a pole, killing Molly.

As far as Ava knows he is still in prison. She doesn't keep tabs on him anymore. Despite wanting to be forgiving, she hates him and what he did to not only Molly, but to her childhood as well. Ava in part understood the anger that led him to drink and to become that uncivilized, evil person she became used to. She was angry, too, at the cards she was dealt and the roles she had to take on, but she loved Molly and never blamed her for her mother's death. She didn't understand why she was being punished in life, but she didn't want anyone to be hurt the way she was, so when high school ended she decided to become a nurse to help others.

When Derrick became a patient she instantly liked him. They had a similar background growing up so they understood each other on a special level that most wouldn't understand. She also felt a small connection to him because he reminded her of all the good things about her father before her mother died. She thought that maybe she could have a second chance when it came to having a happy family. All she had to do was save Derrick and let go of the fact that she couldn't save her father.

She breaks away from her memories and looks around the cold quarantine room. She can't help but to realize that up until recently everything was going according to her plans. She worked hard her whole life to provide a stable, safe, happy environment for her children to live in. Her and Derrick were living their dream. Now she has to put all of her hope into a scientist that she doesn't even know to help rescue her and her family. If he comes through with his promise to help us, she thinks, 'I'm going to fight like hell to keep us safe and happy, like no one ever did for me.'

Chapter 17

April 30th, 2082 - NICK

Now that Nick is sure that the Ardi's will be moved back to this floor, he has to get back to figuring out how to find Katie. He doesn't know if Silas is quite dumb enough to fall for the same trick twice, but he decides he will give it a go.

He works for three hours and then he requests that Silas go grab him a tea from BeverageCabana next to the hotel. He thought for sure that Silas would just offer him a drink from a number of different places in the building, but he didn't even fight him on it. He just asks what he wants and leaves the room. Nick starts to feel a little bad about using Silas, not because he is dumb enough to fall for it, but because he thinks that Silas really is beginning to value their friendship and trust him.

The second Nick hears the door to the elevator open he looks through the window to watch it close with Silas inside it and sprints for the stairwell. He doesn't have time to console Ava again so he doesn't even look in through the quarantine room window as he passes by.

Nick decides that since his lab is on the lowest floor of the building that he will work his way up floor by floor until he runs out of time and then he will continue moving up whenever he gets another chance. He wishes Katie was more specific about where she was being held in her message, but he realizes she was probably in a panicked state and details weren't really on her mind. He can already eliminate floor 7, the floor that Bruner's office is on. Nick looked around the best he could when he and Silas walked down the hall to his office earlier and it didn't seem like there were any other areas where Katie could be on that floor.

The first door he reaches coming up the stairs opens to a parking garage. He continues to move up the stairs. Nick hopes that David Bruner and Kenny Nash really trust Silas and are not checking the security cameras. If they find out what is happening, Silas would be replaced very quickly by another person who may not be as easy to trick.

The next door opens to the main floor where the lobby is. There are no rooms off of the lobby so he continues up. The new door opens up to the second floor above ground. This floor looks almost identical to the floor that Bruner's office is on. Nick walks past two bathrooms, one on each side of him before reaching a conference room. He knocks and opens the door. It is empty. The rest of the rooms in the hall are a series of offices. Each of the offices have glass doors so it is unlikely any of them are where Katie is being held. He sprints back to the stairwell. He has only time for one more floor before Silas will be back. He opens the door to the third floor and the layout looks similar to the last floor, but these doors are solid and the offices aren't transparent. He immediately rushes to the first conference room he sees and tries the handle. It's locked. He doesn't want to make noise and draw attention to himself. He can tell from the buzzing of the voices in the background that there are people in the offices at the other end of the hall. He knocks lightly on the door hoping for a response. He waits for several seconds, but decides he needs to go before Silas returns.

Something in his gut tells him to knock once more before he leaves. He knocks again a little harder this time. A muffled voice says 'hello' on the other side. He knows immediately it is Katie. It is the voice he's longed to hear. He's replayed this moment a thousand times in his head over the last few days.

Nick presses his forehead up against the door and says in a volume a little above a whisper, "Katie, it's me, Nick. We don't have a lot of time." He can hear her laugh through tears on the other side of the door.

"Oh my god! Nick! I can't believe you came back for me. I can't open the door. It is locked from the outside. You'll have to get something to pick the lock."

Nick is feeling more adrenaline than ever before. He tells Katie to hold on and that he needs to buy more time. He picks up his phone in an attempt to stall Silas.

He sends Silas a text, "Hey Silas, getting a little peckish. Do you think that you could grab me a pastry from BeverageCabana as well?"

The 'read' checkmark darkens within seconds.

Silas replies quickly "Just started heading back, but I'll run back in and grab you something. I could use a little snack as well."

Thank God Silas is an empty tank that can eat forever, Nick thinks, as relief washes over him.

He walks over to one of the offices down the hall. He tries to act as normal as possible. He approaches a secretary sitting at her desk and asks her if she happens to have a letter opener or something of the like that he could borrow. He hopes that she even knows what something as antiquated as a letter opener is, given her younger age. She looks confused, questioning why a man in a lab coat is on her floor when there isn't a lab nearby.

Nick clues in on this and continues, "I have a sample in the lab that I wasn't able to open. It is sealed too tight. The person I share the lab with is utterly disorganized. I was told you may be able to help me."

The young girl smiles. She pulls open her drawer and hands him an old letter opener. Nick gushes many thanks at her and walks casually out of the office. Once the door latches closed, he runs quickly down the hall, back to the door that stands between him and Katie.

He begins poking and prodding inside of the lock. The letter opener slips around in his sweaty hands. Eventually he hears a click followed by a pop and he turns the handle, hopeful that it will open now. Nick slides the letter opener into his pocket for safe keeping. The door swings in and there she is.

Katie is standing there, her hair down in waves along the side of her face. He is surprised to see she isn't sporting her hair up in a bun, but he loves this look on her too. For the first time in his life, Nick doesn't hesitate. He grabs her arm and pulls her closer to him, pushing his lips up against hers. He realizes what he is doing and pulls back a little bit in fright that it isn't what Katie wants, but she pulls him back in holding the kiss longer. After a few seconds their lips part and their eyes meet. Katie smiles at Nick. He can't resist the feeling of joy and smiles back.

They don't have time for a conversation. Nick grabs her arm and closes the door to the room she is in as not to raise suspicion. He begins explaining, while they tear quickly down the stairs, that Silas is returning and he can't be caught out of the lab right now. Katie nods even though she doesn't have a clue what is going on. He tells her that he will hide her in the women's bathroom on the same floor as the lab. He knows there won't be anyone down there to use the bathroom since the only woman he has ever seen on that floor is Ava and she is stuck in a quarantine room now. He begs her to stay put and he will find a way to come for her as soon as he can. She agrees and runs out of sight.

Nick rushes back towards the lab room but is stopped by the elevator opening in front of him. It is Silas carrying a drink carrier with coffee in it and a bag of pastries. His eyes widen at the sight of Nick.

Nick greets him casually as if nothing happened even though his heart is about to pop out of his chest, "Had to use the bathroom. You got back quickly. Thank you for getting me something to eat. I didn't know if I could make it much longer without eating. I really hit a wall there."

Silas pauses for a moment but shrugs it off. The two of them enter back into the lab.

Nick works uninterrupted for three and a half more hours before announcing to Silas that he needs a break. It isn't quite a lie—he really does need a break, but he needs to see Katie more. He tells Silas that now is a good time for dinner because he wants to work for a couple hours afterwards before they turn in for the night. Silas agrees. Man, this guy is an empty pit that caves at any mention of food, Nick thinks, pleased by this characteristic of the bodyguard. They discuss food options for a few minutes and decide that they want to try the Italian place down the street. Silas is the one to really make the decision. He has a soft spot for Italian food, and he hasn't had a good Italian meal in forever. Apparently, the south isn't known for its Italian food. Nick loves this idea and agrees. It will give him a lot of time to get to Katie.

Nick moves quickly down the hall towards the bathroom when he knows the coast is clear. He peers into the quarantine room and sees that all of the Ardi's are now in there. They must have been transferred when Nick was working. He makes eye contact with Ava and she mouths 'thank you' to him. He doesn't know how she knows he was the one to get the boys transferred back, but that doesn't matter now. Adam turns toward the window when he sees his mother looking at Nick. Adam waves and smiles at him. As happy as it makes him to see them all together again, Nick just doesn't have time for this right now. He waves back quickly and moves on down the hallway. He doesn't stop until he is in the middle of the women's bathroom whispering for Katie to come out of hiding.

One of the stalls along the long wall opens and Katie appears. She rushes over to Nick and hugs him. He wants to look into her eyes and kiss her again, but he knows that there needs to be a lot of explaining done in a very short time frame. He pulls away from her gently so as to not hurt her feelings.

"Katie, I'm sorry that took so long. We have to get out of here and we have to do it now."

Katie is shaking and breathing heavily. He hadn't realized in his adrenaline rush that she is probably so shaken up from being held hostage for the last few days. He tries to comfort her by putting his hands on her arms and rubbing them up and down. His mother used to do that for him when he was little, and his anxiety got the best of him. It worked wonders to calm him down. Apparently it works for Katie too because within a minute she seems to be more comfortable and her breathing slows.

"Bruner, MoonCycle, Silas, Mayor Roy, Sheriff Santos, they're all working together. This is worse than we thought. I figured out it was MoonCycle who poisoned the water. It was easy to figure it out, they are one of the only companies that can get away with using those chemicals in their products. Plus, I found out that they have a plant relatively close to the Ardi's house. Now MoonCycle wants me to create a serum to block the *modification* process in humans. I can't do that. Well, I mean, I can, but I won't. It would backfire on me and on the country. I know it would. It is almost like they are trying to play both sides."

Katie looks in his eyes as he talks. Peering back at her he realizes how much he missed her. He thought of the moment when he would be able to meet her eyes again so many times over the last several hours and he can't believe the time has finally come.

"What do you mean by playing both sides?" she asks.

He tries to think of the words to describe the feeling that he's had all along.

"It's almost like they want a war, but at the same time they don't... like they want to benefit from whatever outcome happens. If a war starts they want to come out on top as the savior for creating the serum that can bring the country together and if a war doesn't happen, they want to be the ones that prevented it."

Katie takes in everything he is saying and agrees that it makes sense. Her expression changes.

"So, are you saying that there isn't anything we can do? If either way they come out smelling like roses, then what are we supposed to do?"

Nick smiles. Katie isn't expecting such a reaction out of him. She has seen him smile before, but it hasn't ever been one with all of his teeth showing. He seems so proud and excited.

"I'm glad you asked that, Katie!" he beams and continues, "I have a plan. We have to run by the lab and grab something and then get somewhere safe. I can explain more once we are safe to talk for a while. Do you trust me?"

Katie doesn't hesitate.

"More than anything," she says.

Nick grabs her hand and leads her to the lab. They move as quickly as possible, filling his case with what he's been working on. He leaves his cell phone on the lab table. He figures that they are probably tracing it so it will do him no good now. He throws his wallet in the case and closes it up. They walk out of the lab toward the stairwell once again. As he approaches the quarantine room he makes an impulsive decision. Better go big if I am going to take out MoonCycle, he thinks.

Chapter 18

April 30th, 2082 - NICK

The light flashes green on the quarantine room's card reader. The door opens and he waves the Ardi's over in a flustered motion. The family looks at him with confusion consuming them.

"We've got to go quickly. There is no time to explain," Nick shouts.

Katie is surprised at what is happening, but she trusts Nick and hopes he has thought this plan through before putting an entire family in danger. Tension is rising with each second that passes. Ava grabs Adam's hand pulling him behind her through the quarantine door followed by Derrick who has scooped up Ben into his arms.

The truth is that Katie couldn't be more wrong. Nick hasn't thought about bringing the Ardi's with at all, at least not until he figured out a well-developed plan, but when he saw them in the quarantine room he knew that there was no good ending for them here and they were better off fighting for a chance at a life again with him. The family of four follow Nick and Katie into the stairwell and out of the next door that opens into a parking garage. Nick doesn't have a car here, but he knows someone who does...Silas.

When Nick and Silas deboarded the plane a couple days ago there was a white, high end, fully loaded, steam powered SUV that was delivered for Silas to use to transport them around the city. Nick has seen many SUVs like this one in the cities he's lived and traveled in. Steam powered vehicles, despite the high price tag, have made a huge comeback due to the growing climate concerns. Technology and car companies worked together to update the old early 1900's steam powered vehicles to not only look modern, but to burn more efficient materials than fossil fuels and create cleaner exhaust mostly made up of water and carbon dioxide.

Nick remembers exactly where the SUV is in the garage. As far as he recalls, Silas hasn't used it since they've arrived and has been walking to pick up their meals at local restaurants.

The six crouch behind some vehicles and weave in between others until Nick stops leading them once they approach the white automobile. Ben, the smallest of the six, only three years old, begins to cry. Ava does her best to soothe him as quickly as possible. She grabs him from Derrick's arms and sways him back and forth while whispering soft sounds into his ear. He looks so sad and uncomfortable. Nick stops for a second and thinks about how scared Adam and Ben must have been this week. Nick has felt fear several times since this all began, and he is a grown man. He can't imagine how the small boys must feel.

The doctor takes in his surroundings and realizes that taking Silas' car would be too obvious. It will be the first car they look for once they realize that all six of them are missing. He has to come up with a better plan and stop flying by the seat of his pants. If he doesn't start being smart this whole thing could end badly, very quickly.

He looks around perusing the garage for a more suitable steal. In the corner of the garage, he notices an old silver Toyota. It is a small hatchback, but they can make it work. It is a less comfortable option for six people, but maybe that might make it less expected. The six huddle between the white SUV and a large, navy truck as Nick unveils his plan.

"We can't take Silas' car. The more I think about it, his car will be too easy to track. Everyone see that silver hatchback over there? That's where we are going to go. I want everyone to stay put here until I get it started. One person draws less attention than six. Once I get it started, I want you all to run and jump in. I figure we've got about five more minutes until they notice I'm missing, twenty until they figure out Katie is gone and maybe even less than that before they notice an entire family has disappeared," Nick whispers.

Ava and Derrick nod. Derrick seems to be nervous. He is sweating profusely even though it isn't really all that hot in the parking garage. Ava, on the other hand, looks determined and ready for whatever may come. What choice did they really have anyways? They are just pawns in a game that is already at play.

Katie speaks up, "How are you going to get into the car? It's likely locked. Everyone locks their car in D.C.. The city is notoriously known for car theft."

Nick gets another smart-alec smile on his face as he reaches into his pocket and pulls out the letter opener that he picked the door lock with earlier. The blade gleams in the fluorescent light. Katie looks at what Nick revealed, and her eyes smile with satisfaction.

Before Katie can even ask how he plans to start the car Nick hands her the case of his research materials that he's holding and begins walking to the car at a normal speed hoping not to draw attention. Every second they are able to avoid suspicion matters in their timeline.

Nick approaches the small hatchback and begins to try to jimmy the lock by sticking the letter opener down the window. He has never done anything like this before, but he's seen it in the movies, and he knows how locks work. Luckily this car is an extremely old model so he is pretty sure he can unlock it through the window. He can hear the letter opener hitting the lock and catching, but it isn't unlocking. He keeps jiggling the letter opener for what seems like hours but is probably only a minute before he hears the lock pop.

He opens the car door and slight relief rushes over him. He isn't in the clear yet but is feeling more confident in his plan now. He pops the board below the steering wheel free in one quick motion. He has to hotwire the car and he has to do it quickly. Similar to breaking into the car, he has never hotwired one either. This though, he feels confident in. Electricity is an easy concept for him. He knows he just needs to spark the live wires and they'll be good to go.

He pulls off the little plastic wire nuts that hold the twisted wire sets together and gets to work. Within seconds he has the vehicle started with a quick spark. Katie and the Ardi's run over once they hear the engine catch and the car begin to purr. Katie jumps in shotgun and the family piles into the back seat. It is tighter than they initially thought, but they make it work. Adam sits between his parents in the middle of the vehicle's small backseat and Ben climbs onto his mother's lap and snuggles into her, looking for safety.

The car drives slowly through the garage avoiding suspicion. Once they reach the exit they peel out as quickly as possible down the street. After they get a few blocks away from the lab building everyone calms down a bit and begins to feel more comfortable.

"What is our plan now? Where are we going?" Katie asks excitedly, filled with adrenaline.

This is the part that Nick isn't so sure about. He knows what he wants to do, but he doesn't know how to execute it. He will need some help putting his plan in motion, even if he isn't all that comfortable relying on other people.

"We need to find a way to get streaming on the internet. We need a safe spot to do this. The public needs to know what's happening. That's the only way we can make sure the right people get punished. It's also the only way to keep everyone safe. MoonCycle won't dare to come after the Ardi's once the truth is out, it would kill their public image," Nick explains.

Everyone begins thinking, filling the car with silence. After a few moments, Derrick speaks up. Nick realizes this is the first time he's heard Derrick's voice. The tall, slender man who has previously just been more of an extension of Ava, now finds his place in the newly formed group.

"I've got some family that lives in Virginia. We can go there if we have to," Derrick notes, with obvious apprehension.

Nick thinks about it for a minute; Virginia is probably 3.5 hours from where they are depending on traffic and depending on where in Virginia his family lives.

"Can you trust them?" Nick asks hopefully.

"It's my second cousin. We aren't the closest, but I think we could trust her. I haven't seen her in close to a decade though," Derrick responds, still not sounding all that confident about the option he presented.

That seems like a big risk, Nick worries. They can't handle a big risk right now.

"Do we have any other suggestions?" Nick inquires desperately.

Katie begins to respond, "I have a friend in Pittsburgh, where I'm from, I think he can help us. He is a police officer. When we were in college at Penn State, he ran the school's news and radio program. It was a really big deal. The program had a lot of followers. He was really into it and he probably still has a lot of the equipment. I trust him, Nick. I really do."

Nick's lips flatten into a line. A police officer? This is a really bad idea, he thinks, without showing uncertainty on his face. Nick trusts Katie and it seems like a better option than what Derrick offered. Off to Pittsburgh then, he decides.

Chapter 19

April 30th, 2082 - NICK, KATIE and the ARDIS

Pittsburgh is about four hours from D.C. This means that they will definitely have to stop to get gas since the car they chose is an old one and not steam powered but need to choose their spot carefully. The radio has been dead silent. They scan all the satellite channels the best they can to see if any news of them has spread, but it hasn't and it has been nearly two hours now. The entire car decides through discussion that no news is good news, but Nick knows it is too good to be true. Just because there isn't a public announcement about them doesn't mean there isn't communication traveling throughout the East Coast. Heck, there might be communication throughout the whole country by now with how widespread MoonCycle is and how many different facilities they have across the entire continental United States.

After a few hours of driving, they are now well into Pennsylvania and away from the coast so they know that if any of the Ardi males are spotted it may amount to trouble for them. The northern areas that don't have a lot of coastline are not the most tolerant of those who have become *Modified*, especially with gills. Having two 'aquatic type' *modifieds* in the car who are over the age of 4 would cause hysteria in any part of the country but having them spotted in the north could amount to an uprising of a whole new level.

The gas light popped on a few miles back and even though they have pulled off the road a few times in remote areas for the younger kids to go to the bathroom, the adults need a break now too. Nick had hoped that they would have been able to drive an hour or so more until it was dark, so they'd feel safer in public, but the car definitely won't make it another hour without fueling up. Nick is the only one who has a wallet with him. Everyone else's items were confiscated while they were being held captive, so it is up to him to fund this operation.

It isn't safe to use his credit cards, but he only has $82 in his wallet and the group will have to stretch it pretty far to make it another hour and a half in the car and provide some sustenance to the kids who've been whining for most of the car ride about being hungry. Nick understands the kids' frustration. He is hungry too. Since he didn't get to eat that Italian meal Silas picked up, it's been several hours since he's last eaten.

Gas is about six dollars a gallon and he decides he needs to get ten gallons to make it all the way to Pittsburgh, so that leaves him close to twenty dollars for everyone to get snacks. He doesn't want to spend all of his money, but with how expensive things have become over the last few years there is no way they'll be able to leave the store with more than just a few items for the kids.

They pull into a gas station off of route 76 in a small town called Mount Pleasant. The station seems like a good place to stop since there are only two other cars in the lot and only one of them is getting gas. The small-town atmosphere makes it more likely that they won't be judged for using cash. Cash nowadays is still legal tender but rarely used in the big cities. Most businesses in the cities have worked around having to accept it, but small towns still hold onto it for nostalgia of an easier time.

Katie heads in to pre-pay the gas pump. Ava also goes in to go to the bathroom and grab a few snacks with the money that Nick gave her. Nick gets busy filling up the car and Derrick is put in charge of entertaining the kids and keeping them quiet and out of sight.

Everything seems to be going as planned until Ben decides that he misses Ava and needs to see her right away. Being away from her the first time during the quarantine must have triggered some separation anxiety because he is absolutely losing it. He begins crying and screaming as loud as he can. Nick isn't around kids very often, but he imagines this is not just a 'normal temper tantrum' with how crazed the young boy is acting. Derrick does everything he can to stop him—he even covers his mouth with his hand, but the damage is done.

An older woman who is sitting in the car while her husband fills up their seemingly ancient town car looks over at what is happening in the small hatchback and becomes alarmed. Nick notices her and begins pulling the pump nozzle out of the car and placing it back on the stand even though the pump only reads 8 gallons at this point. Nick can't tell if she is alarmed because she thinks Derrick is abusing Ben or if it is because she sees the gills forming on their necks.

Nick tries to act as relaxed as he can hoping the woman will drop it, but she doesn't. She alerts her husband who has walked away from the pump and is now approaching the silver car that the boys are flailing around inside of. Nick looks back at the store to see if Katie and Ava are on their way out. Through the slightly tinted window he can see that they are at the counter still checking out. Katie, Ava and the gas station attendant are looking back at Nick through the window trying to see what the commotion is. Within seconds Katie throws the money on the counter and Ava grabs the snacks. The two start sprinting for the car. By the time they make it to the car the older man is already at Nick's window peering into the backseat to see what is going on. He has a horrified look on his face and begins shouting "MODs! They've got MODs in the car! One of them is a grown man!" The older woman exits the car and is trying to take a picture of them with her cell phone while she is screaming hysterically. As she gets closer to the car her emotions get the best of her and she faints with her husband catching her just in time—seconds before she hits the pavement.

Nick starts the engine and peels out of the gas station as quickly as he can back onto route 76. He hopes that the stereotypes are true about elders and technology and that the older woman wasn't able to take the picture of them in the car. Either way he knows their time is limited and everyone will soon know that the missing scientist, government official, and family of four have made it to Pennsylvania.

The six listen more intently to the radio now. Focusing on local stations first and then moving to a.m. frequencies. They hear nothing for close to

70 minutes, but then as they flip the channel to one of Pittsburgh's leading stations, a news broadcast interrupts the music playing.

"An important broadcast from WYEP - 91.3! Your station for alternative hits from all the decades. We've gotten reports that an elder woman and her husband were attacked by a group of *Modified* people at a small gas station in Mount Pleasant at approximately 7:10 p.m. The woman described the group as two men and two women traveling with two small children in a silver hatchback. She states that they headed north out of Mount Pleasant. The woman and man survived the attack and are not injured. For more information you can follow us on our Zoop social media app or turn to WTAE14 Action News sponsored by ABC9 on your smart device. The police are asking that if you see anything that could relate to this event or if you notice anything that looks suspicious you should contact your local police station."

The car fills with silence. No one needs to speak. Just looking each other in the eyes says enough. The government and MoonCycle know they are in Pennsylvania now and they probably know they are headed towards Pittsburgh. David Bruner knows that is where Katie is from and authorities have likely been alerted to keep an eye on the entire city.

Katie glances over at Nick once he clicks the radio off. She can tell he is nervous because he keeps tapping his fingers along the steering wheel with no real beat. She wants to try to alleviate some of his stress, but she doesn't want to break the silence and begin a conversation that might cause the kids in the back to worry. Instead of talking she just rests her hand on his right knee hoping that her touch can somehow heal him.

Ava sits smooshed in the small backseat and holds Ben closely trying her best to comfort him. Now that he has calmed down, he is trying to take a nap. Derrick tries to distract Adam from the news on the radio by playing 'I spy' with him. It seems to work for the most part, but Adam still seems a little uncomfortable. He is holding his dad's hand tightly. Derrick gives Ava a look that tells her he is concerned about the children. She returns the same sentiment without words.

After a few more minutes of listening to 'I spy' from the backseat, Nick pulls the car up to where Katie says Patrick Janes lives, a traditional style build in Shadyside on the east side of Pittsburgh. They pull as far into his driveway as they can, past the house and into the back where the garage is. Katie knows Patrick is home because they see the police car parked in the street right in front of the house. Katie requests that everyone sit tight in the car while she goes to the door first to talk to Patrick.

Nick doesn't like the idea of letting Katie out of his sight, especially when he doesn't know about the past the two have had with one another. She's already been tricked once by Bruner and he can't stand the thought of her being hurt again by another person in her life. In general, he doesn't trust police officers, but they have to give this a chance. Nick puts his hand on Katie's thigh and gives it a squeeze while he looks into her eyes, letting her know that she can do this and that he believes in her.

Chapter 20

April 30th, 2082 - KATIE and PJ

Katie walks up the cement stairs that lead to the backdoor of PJ's house. She knocks on the door and waits in anticipation for close to a minute before hearing footsteps nearby. The blinds that shield the light from coming into the top of the door separate only slightly enough for two small eyes to appear. The blinds slam back closed in a shutter and the locks on the door begin to make a clanging noise as they unlock.

Patrick opens the door with a confused expression. He hasn't seen Katie in years and he definitely wasn't expecting to see her now. Katie looks into his eyes with concern and sorrow and he can see she needs help. He doesn't speak but rather opens the door wider so she can slip into the kitchen.

They sit down at the kitchen table a few feet from the back door. Katie looks around—taking in the place. It looks pretty organized for a man that lives alone. It is an older, more retro-styled home, but still rather taken care of.

She thinks back to how gross PJ's apartment had been in college. She recalls one time that Patrick hosted a party at his house for a few of their closest friends and Katie asked to use his bathroom. When she got into the bathroom she couldn't find any toilet paper, only paper towels. She asked PJ if he had any toilet paper and he just told her to use the paper towels, but to be sure not to flush them. She used it only because there wasn't another option but was utterly disgusted by the experience. When she went to wash her hands after, she found there wasn't any soap in the bathroom either. At that moment she concluded that all men that live on their own must live like actual pigs in a pigpen. She just always assumed that he still lived like that without a wife to help keep him organized.

As Katie gets comfortable in her chair at the table, Patrick offers her some coffee or tea. She turns down his offer but is very thirsty and asks for a glass of water instead. Patrick nods and stands up and walks over to a cabinet to grab a glass.

As he is walking to the sink to fill the glass up, he asks, "What do I owe the pleasure of this visit, Katie? It's been a long while since we've seen each other. This isn't about that background check on that Preston fella' is it?"

Katie shakes her head indicating 'no' but then stops because she realizes that isn't entirely true. It does partly have to do with Preston. Patrick notices Katie's hesitation and decides he will let her take the lead in the conversation.

Patrick fills the glass and sets it down in front of Katie and returns to his seat across from her. Katie lifts the glass and downs the entire thing within seconds. She bats her eyes several times to clear them of the tears forming as she swallows her last huge gulp.

Patrick's eyebrows raise, "Thirsty, eh?" he laughs.

Katie puts the empty glass down in front of her and begins to clear her throat.

"I really need your help with something PJ. It is something serious and I don't think I can do it without you, but I need you to help me as my friend, not as a police officer," she pleads.

Patrick moves in his seat trying to re-adjust himself in a comfortable position now that he is starting to feel concerned.

"I don't know if I can promise you that, Kate," he says with seriousness in his voice.

Patrick always calls her Kate when he is trying to console her. She forgot what it is like to be near someone who really knows her—the real her—not just the professional version of herself. Things have been so lonely since she moved to D.C. and things going south with David hasn't helped her feel at home. Even though this discussion with PJ is going to be difficult, part of it still feels good, being able to talk to her old friend.

"Patrick, I wouldn't ask if I didn't trust you. You're one of my oldest friends. I really need help. It's not just for me, but for my friends as well. Things have really gotten out of control, and it could get worse if we don't act now," Katie explains with sincere distress in her voice.

Patrick, now more confused, responds, "What friends?"

Katie points towards the door and Patrick gets up and looks through the blinds again. He spots the car parked at the top of his driveway and sees that there are people moving around inside it. He can't quite see how many people are in the car, but concern grows as he sees a small child peering through the window looking up at the house.

"Who are they?" he asks, not sure what he is hoping the answer will be.

"Well, there's a whole family there. The Ardi family. It's the family that has been all over the news for having gone missing. I'm sure you've seen it on the news or at least heard about it at work," Patrick nods and Katie continues, "another co-worker is there too. A scientist. His name is Dr. Nicholas Cyrus."

Katie pauses to think about whether or not she is explaining who Nick is to her correctly. They are co-workers, but they are also more than that. With everything going on it isn't like they have had time to decide if they want to date, be in love, run off and get married or anything like that. After some thought she decides how she introduces him doesn't really matter as long as they get the help that they need from Patrick.

"Katie, I could lose my job for aiding and abetting you if you two kidnapped that family."

Katie laughs, "Oh get real, PJ! You think I kidnapped an entire family?"

Patrick shrugs, "I don't know! Maybe! You're acting all crazy right now!"

He throws up his hands in emphasis of how ridiculous the situation is. Katie laughs again. This time harder and more of a belly laugh at the thought that Patrick hasn't even heard the craziest part of the story yet.

"PJ, please let me go get my friends. It will make more sense if we can all explain what happened together," Katie begs.

Patrick agrees. It makes sense for him to hear whatever it is that needs to be said from the whole group. That way at least he can be sure that Katie didn't kidnap the missing family.

Katie walks out the kitchen door and to the car. Within a minute she returns with five people in tow. Standing in the center of the kitchen now, directly in the light from the ceiling light fixture, Patrick can see the Ardi men and their gills. He tries not to look too surprised. After all, they are people and he doesn't want to hurt their feelings, especially the little boys who already look shaken up.

"Welcome everyone, I'm sure Katie has told you already, but I'm Patrick. Patrick Janes. Can I get you all something to drink and maybe a snack? It was probably a long drive," he offers.

The boys shake their heads in appreciation. They haven't had much to eat and everyone who was in the car can tell they are not only hungry, but tired as well. This combination of emotions isn't good for anyone, especially children.

"Let me just make us all up some sandwiches then, I'm a bit hungry myself. Why don't you all get situated in the living room and I'll be right in," Patrick gestures toward the room and continues, "Katie, why don't you help me here in the kitchen. Four hands are better than two," he pleads, needing a second to take in what just happened.

Katie and Patrick don't speak, not even one word, while they work on the sandwiches. Katie decides it is best for Patrick to lead the discussion even though the silence is deafening. She doesn't want to scare him away from helping them. Once the sandwiches are ready, Patrick puts them on a large platter and walks into the living room with Katie following behind. He sets the sandwiches down on the antique coffee table and everyone digs in. None of them wanted to admit how hungry they are at risk of inconveniencing anyone else, but these sandwiches are a godsend. Everyone eats in silence for the next few minutes, just taking in how good it feels to fill their stomachs again.

"I have a spare bedroom in the back, down that hallway there," Patrick points towards the back of the house, "You can have the little ones go lay down and rest if you'd like. They're probably exhausted. It's nearing 9:45 p.m. now," he offers, really hoping that they will take him up on his offer so he can get some information from the adults without scaring the young children.

Ava and Derrick express their appreciation many times of how hospitable Patrick is being. Each of them picks up a child and carries them to the spare room down the hallway. A few seconds later, Ava returns, leaving Derrick to tend to the children in the guest room.

Patrick sits himself in a chair opposite of Nick, Katie, and Ava who are now sitting together comfortably on the couch. He stares into their eyes and requests an explanation. The three guests look back and forth at one another, trying to silently gesture 'you go first'. No one seems to want to be the first to speak.

Ava is the one to find the confidence to break the silence.

"Thank you so much for your hospitality, Mr. Janes. I can't tell you how much my family and I appreciate it. My name is Ava Ardi. I'm sure you've heard on the news about my family."

Patrick just sits emotionless, taking in her words.

He doesn't respond so she continues, "My son, the older one, Adam, started to show signs of *Modification*. He's seven, he wasn't born like that or anything. I tried to hide him, but once I took him into the doctor, word around the town spread like wildfire. Before I knew it, there were some men at my door carting him and I off to some lab. They took my husband and other son too, a few days later…to clean up their mess, I think. They weren't showing any signs of *Modifyin'* at that point. They, the scientists, put us in a quarantine zone in the lab and wouldn't let us go. They even separated us at one point," she explains, now with tears coming down her face.

Patrick's face goes from unaffected to upset from hearing the words coming from Mrs. Ardi's mouth. Inside he is feeling anger, but he doesn't know who to feel angry at yet. He decides to take in more verbal accounts before making a judgment.

Nick is the next to speak, "I was enlisted to work for the Human Biology Research Department in D.C. they asked me to look into what was happening with the Ardi boy. I didn't know anything about them being held in captivity until I got there. Honestly, they didn't tell me anything at all about the project until I walked into the room and saw the poor kid scared out of his wits sitting on a lab table. Things just got worse from there."

Patrick is beginning to understand that all of these people are on the run from something or someone and now he is being enlisted with the job of hiding them. As for Nick and Ava, he is starting to really feel for them, but he doesn't know if he can do what they need him to do.

Katie chimes in, "Nick and I were assigned to work together. In order to get more information as to what was happening, we decided to dig into things in South Carolina, where the Ardi's are from. Long story short, when we got there, we found out that the *Modification* was being "accelerated" or something like that, by chemicals being dumped into the water along the coast. I'm not the scientific one, but I think that is the jist of it. MoonCycle, that big cosmetics company, the one famous for the life elixir…what's it called…Half Moon. They're the ones doing this. They kidnapped me. Nick saved me and now we are here."

Patrick notices Katie turn and look lovingly at Dr. Cyrus when she mentions his name. He doesn't have romantic feelings for her at all—well at least not anymore, but he still doesn't like the way she is fawning over the doctor when he doesn't know anything about him. He has always been protective of Katie in the past and he knows he has to be protective over her now when it comes to the doctor and when it comes to saving her from the government and MoonCycle.

Patrick takes in everything they said, but he needs clarification, "What exactly do you need me to do? What is your plan moving forward? It isn't going to be easy to escape the entire government and one of the largest companies in the world."

Katie peers over at Nick waiting for him to reveal what is to come next. Even though they had been in the car for over four hours, they didn't really talk about the plan. She doesn't know if it was because he was still thinking about it or if he just didn't want to scare the Ardi's and their small children.

With all attention on Nick, he begins to unfold his plan, "We are going to expose MoonCycle for causing the super immune response that is sparking people who would not normally *Modify* to *Modify* at an extended age and accelerated rate. We are going to do this by some sort of video broadcast. If we can put the blame on them publicly then it will protect Ava and her family. It may not stop the societal issues across the nation—it may even fuel them, but it's the only way I can see to place the blame on the right people while protecting those boys sleeping in the room back there."

Patrick looks at Nick while he is speaking. Part of him can see why Katie likes him. He can tell his main concern is the safety of those around him and Patrick respects that, but at the same time Patrick may very well lose everything if he helps them. His job will be gone in the blink of an eye if he is found harboring the missing people. This is especially true if the government's involvement with MoonCycle is as deep as Nick and Katie are making it seem. Most people might not blink an eye at losing their job to do the right thing, but being a police officer is Patrick's identity.

PJ's father died when he was a young boy and right after he went off to college, he lost his grandmother, who was his legal guardian and caretaker for most of his life. He doesn't know much about his mother. All he knows is that she wasn't around and no one ever talked about her. When his grandmother died, he lost his last real connection to a bloodline relative. His college friends became his family. As soon as he graduated he immediately went into the police academy. Since then, that's all his life has been about. He gave up most of his hobbies right when he joined the academy because he worked odd hours and the only friends he keeps in touch now with are those he works with, aside from Katie, of course.

PJ carefully studies the three people sitting across the coffee table from him, wishing he could hear their thoughts. He looks at Ava first, a mother of two who never asked for this to happen but will do anything to protect her children. He can see the worry in her eyes and bags forming below them making her look as though she hasn't slept in days. For all Patrick knows, maybe she really hasn't slept in days. Ava can tell that Patrick is considering everything that was said. She doesn't want to disrupt his thought process, but she feels that she needs to advocate a little bit more for her family.

"Mr. Janes, I really do understand your hesitation. This is a very serious matter to involve yourself in. I do have to say, though, that all I've ever wanted in my life is to keep my family safe. My family is my entire identity. I live and breathe for them. I fear that if we don't stop what is going on that many other mothers like me will be put in similar, dangerous situations and may not have an opportunity like this to protect themselves and their loved ones from the hate that comes along with being *Modified,*" she stops and takes a deep breath, trying to hold back tears, before continuing.

Patrick stays still in his seat, staring directly at the mother who is speaking her truth.

"I know what a lot of people think of the *Modified*. They think that they're freaks and that they are ruining human civilization as we know it. It's not true. Since the night I first saw gills forming on Adams neck and ever since, my love never once felt any different towards my family. The only new emotion is fear and not because of the unknown, but because of the hate in people's hearts. I know my children's lives are going to be harder now that this has happened. I know that they are going to need me and my husband to protect them for most of their lives now and that will take a toll on all of us. It doesn't bother me that my life will now revolve around protecting them because honestly that has always been what my life has felt like. The thing that does bother me is that my children will, at times now, feel less than because of what MoonCycle has done to us. They need to be held responsible."

Ava stops speaking and turns her head ever so slightly to wipe the tears away that are forming in her eyes. Her blonde hair falls in front of her face helping shield her from the group's gaze.

Patrick slowly takes in everything Ava just said. While he isn't a parent himself, he can feel the love Ava has for her family and wishes he felt that passionate about someone. He knows he wants to help her, but he needs to be able to trust everyone in the room.

He turns his attention to Nick. He doesn't know much about him, but he knows that he is probably one of the smartest men he's ever interacted with. Why shouldn't he trust a scientist, he reasons. He knows that he likes the fire in Nick's eyes and intensity in his voice when he talks about keeping the group safe and thinks that maybe that should hold weight in his decision to help them.

Lastly, he looks at his longtime friend, Kate. Patrick knows that Katie would never ask for help unless she really needed it. Over the course of the decade or more that they've known each other, she has rarely asked for favors. She is more likely to be the one to fulfill a favor that others ask of her.

When Patrick's grandmother died their freshman year in college, Katie was the only one of his friends who showed up for the service. She didn't do it out of obligation either. She did it because she cares about Patrick and wants to genuinely be there for him. After the service she even came back to the house for the luncheon and stayed until everyone left so she could help clean up. At that time he couldn't believe that she had done that for a friend she had only had for a few months, but as time passed, he could tell that is just who she was. She has character and strong morals.

These enticing traits are probably why Patrick had a crush on Katie for several years after that. He never told her how he felt. He didn't want to ruin what they had. She became his family during that time away at school and he wasn't willing to lose her by expressing his feelings of interest. He was perfectly content just being her friend and being able to spend time with her. After they graduated college he thought about telling her how he felt, but he had just been accepted into the police academy and she was looking at internships all over the country. The timing never seemed right or at least that is what Patrick told himself to justify his fear of losing her.

Before Patrick is done reminiscing about his old friend, he already makes his mind up. Katie is the kind of friend worth saving and that's exactly what he is going to do. He has no choice but to help her even if it means he could lose everything in the process.

Chapter 21

May 2nd, 2082 - THE WHOLE CREW

Patrick climbs up the ladder to the attic that swings down in the middle of the hallway on the second floor of his home. He climbs into the attic and begins rummaging around. Nick stands at the bottom of the ladder ready to help in any way that Patrick will allow. Within minutes, Patrick appears at the opening in the ceiling carrying a large box. He hands the box down to Nick who is surprised at the weight of it. The way Patrick was carrying it with ease made Nick think it was light, but it has to weigh upwards of 75 pounds. This is the first time that Nick really notices Patrick's physique. Patrick is fit by most people's standards. He isn't the tallest guy around, but he's not short by any means. When Patrick climbs down the ladder, Nick looks at his arms and sees they are rather muscular and decides that he must weight train regularly or at least weekly.

Nick doesn't want to feel jealous of Patrick, but he still doesn't know where he and Katie stand and he's been left in the dark about how she knows Patrick. He hopes with everything in him that they are just old friends and not old exes. He knows better than to ask either of them about their connection because it isn't the time or the place. A day has passed since Patrick agreed to help them and his house has become nothing but chaos filled with six unexpected house guests. Adam and Ben's childish giggles have returned and while everyone is happy to hear their contagious laughs again, they are feeling a little sensory overloaded by everything going on around them.

Katie notices that Patrick is a little on edge. She doesn't know if it is because the situation is really overwhelming, because he isn't a fan of sharing his space with so many people, or maybe a combination of the two. She wants to check in with Patrick to see how he is handling everything, but when she finds him and Nick gathering equipment from the attic she decides to leave them to their work, hoping that the two of them might get to know each other a little bit. She watches from afar as the shaggy-haired doctor tries to do his best to help her old friend.

She tries to think back to the last time that she saw PJ. She can't quite put her finger on it, but she imagines it was when she came back to Pittsburgh to see her parents off before they moved to Arizona. Patrick looks really different in her memory. He looks older now with his hair darker and less red than she remembers it. The depiction of him in her mind from years ago displays a much scrawnier man than the one that is before her now. Katie wonders if anything else about her old friend has changed since they last saw one another.

The box that Patrick hands Nick has a couple old microphones, a video camera with a foldable tripod, and some cables. Patrick thinks it best to set up their recording location in the basement. He has a small office down there with a computer and some other technology equipment. He figures that it is quiet down there, away from the boys, so that they can talk logistically about how to ensure that this live presentation they are creating will be seen by as many people as possible.

Patrick hasn't messed around with any of his old news station equipment in years. It probably would have stayed up in that attic for at least another decade if Katie hadn't come asking for this favor.

Patrick shows Nick the path to the office downstairs so that they can set up while the rest of the group entertain the boys upstairs. The men make their way down the creaking wood stairs to the basement. Even now, a floor below everyone, they can hear the boys' deep laughs and feet pattering as they run across the living room above.

The basement is 'finished' in the most simple sense. There is an ugly, beige carpet on the floor in the main area, an old, 2060's style t.v. hanging on the wall in front of a tattered couch and barely any decorations or accents in the space. A sole picture hangs on the wall adjacent to the couch—a picture of Patrick graduating from the police academy with another uniformed man shaking his hand. There is a pool table in an open space at the bottom of the stairs, but it is dusty and looks like it hasn't seen action in years. Next to the office is a small half-bathroom that seems rather dated with blue mosaic tiles as the flooring and wallpaper that has a light blue background and bright yellow lemons scattered across it.

The decor looks like it is straight out of the late 2050's, a time when people decided that everything had to be bright and colorful otherwise it wasn't on trend. Nick thinks it is hideous, but he remembers that his mother had fallen into the trends of that time period later in the decade and changed their spare bedroom to be lime green with bright orange flowers all over it. That is one room he doesn't miss seeing after he sold his childhood home a few years back.

Trends seem to come back around after several decades, but he had hoped that wouldn't be the case with the 2050's. He remembers seeing pictures of the 1970's in museums, movies, history books and on the internet and he couldn't believe that the society of the 2050's thought it was a good idea to bring back the obnoxious color schemes and silly patterns. Luckily for him, the trend left as quickly as it had arrived.

Finally, they make it to the furthest corner of the basement and enter the office. Nick is expecting the office to be in shambles or poorly decorated based on what he's seen since they've entered the basement, but he is pleasantly surprised when the office looks updated. The desk looks like new, handcrafted oak with modern finishings. The walls have what looks like a fresh coat of gray paint, although it doesn't smell like a fresh paint job. There is a relatively new computer slate on the wall, hovering perfectly over the desk and everything atop the desk looks organized.

Patrick can tell Nick is surprised to see that the office doesn't appear as dated as the rest of the basement and says, "I've been doing a little bit of remodeling. I figured I'd work my way from the furthest point in the basement and then eventually make it up to the main level. I haven't had a lot of time lately so my efforts have sort of stalled after the office. Hoping to pick it up again when I find some time."

Nick is impressed that Patrick is making an effort on his home in order to create a space that is comfortable to live in. Nick has lived in and out of apartments for the last ten years and none of them really have felt like home. When he finished the Half Moon serum for MoonCycle he was hoping that he could find a long-term science position in a smaller town somewhere outside of Chicago so he could settle down and finally own a house and maybe even start a family. Those hopes diminished the second he began hearing the news about the *Modified.* He knew he would be headhunted right when his contract with MoonCycle ended and look where that got him.

Patrick begins to hook cables up to some sort of old converter that will allow it to work with the computer and the camera system. Nick pretty much stands there useless, just watching Patrick work. He obviously uses technology often in the lab and by his standards he is pretty good with computers, but the technology Patrick is working with seems foreign to him. The camera system that Patrick is using has to be considered extremely dated. It was probably considered dated even a decade ago when it was put into storage.

Newer technology is much easier to work with. In fact, the newest models of most devices pretty much tell you how to use it. Literally. Artificial intelligence has come such a long way that most tech devices now verbally tell you how to work them and can adjust to their user to make it easier for the user to learn to control it. Individual room bots are also programmed to work with the devices so that they can set up all technology and sync their user's preferences without the user even having to lift a finger.

Patrick is working with something that has to be adjusted manually and Nick watches in awe of his understanding of the old devices. Minutes pass before Patrick breaks the silence that fills the room, "So how many people exactly are you trying to reach? There are a lot of social media platforms online now that we can use. We can stream to multiple platforms if you'd like."

Nick likes the idea of millions of people getting this information through social media because he knows that once it is on social media it can be shared millions of times within minutes. If that happens there is no way that MoonCycle can stop people from seeing it even if the original posting gets taken down.

"If we stream it to a platform, it would be live as we are doing it, but then it would be saved and posted, right?" Nick asks for clarification.

Patrick nods, "Yeah that is pretty much how it works. We have to make sure we share it to the major news station's accounts because millions of people follow them, that should set everything in motion really quickly."

Nick is happy with the way things are set up by the time they are finished. They even hang a sheet from the ceiling as a background so that their location can't be identified. The sheet is Patrick's brilliant idea. Patrick has been really good about keeping things quiet and Nick appreciates that. When they finished their conversation after their sandwiches last night, he went out to the driveway and used an old car cover he found in the garage to cover up the car that they had stolen. Then when he awoke in the morning, he could be heard calling into work saying that he had come down with a pretty serious flu and can't get his fever to break so he will be taking a few days off. Now, he comes up with the idea to hang the sheet. Nick doesn't know if Patrick is trying to save his own skin or if he is trying to keep them safe, but to be honest, it doesn't really matter as long as both things stay true.

Evening arrives and Ava and Katie go through Patrick's kitchen to make dinner out of whatever they can find. They find some pasta, tomato sauce, and defrost some mystery meat they found in the freezer to make spaghetti and meatballs. They all sit around the kitchen table eating while Katie and Patrick tell stories about their old college days. It is nice for a few moments to forget the trouble they are facing and just focus on a few laughs with good company.

Patrick talks about how he and Katie met through mutual friends. Katie's roommate was dating one of the guys that Patrick shared his first apartment with. They met one time at a party that Patrick hosted early on during their freshman year and stayed friends long after their friends ended their relationship.

Katie talks about how Patrick became like a big brother to her. Always keeping an eye out at parties to make sure that the frat boys were acting appropriate in her presence. Nick enjoys hearing how they met, but he really enjoys hearing Katie confirm that their relationship is a platonic one.

Nick hasn't had a hot, home cooked meal, at a table, with company in who knows how long. He tries to soak in every minute of it. As he looks around the table at Patrick, Katie and the Ardi family he realizes that he's missed having people in his life that he cares about. He hopes that after all of this is settled that he can feel like this again with these people who now feel more like his family and tribe than strangers...even Patrick is growing on him.

The group finishes eating and Nick volunteers to clean up after everyone as a thank you for the wonderful meal. Katie and Patrick retire to the living room to catch up a little since they haven't had much time to talk with everything going on in the house. Derrick offers to get the kids cleaned up from the mess they created on their hands and faces from the spaghetti. He tells Ava to enjoy herself and rest for a while. Ava sits down at the table as Nick clears it, but finds she is incapable of resting while others do work. She hops up and begins to help Nick tidy up.

Ava begins to interrogate the doctor as they clear the plates.

"I see that you are sweet on that beautiful girl in there," she says, nodding towards the room Katie is in.

Nick blushes and squeaks out an embarrassing little laugh. He tries not to make eye contact with Ava in fear she might push the issue. His fear is rightfully placed because Ava's strong personality won't allow her to stop antagonizing him.

"Oh, c'mon now! You don't have to be embarrassed! I can see she has some strong feelings for you as well. She looks at you like you're the best thing she's ever seen!" she blurts in a playful manner.

Nick likes the words he is hearing coming from Ava's mouth, but he is still too embarrassed to talk about his feelings. He didn't have the opportunity to talk about his feelings a lot growing up without a father. His mother often tried to pry emotion from him, but he likes to keep his thoughts to himself. This was especially true when it came to girls and the conversation just seemed too awkward to have with his mother.

Ava stops what she is doing and sets the dirty plate that she is carrying down on the countertop. She turns her body towards him and just looks at him for a few seconds. Nick is thrown off by her actions and stops what he is doing as well and turns towards her. She takes her arms and wraps them around his neck, putting him into a tight hug.

She leans her mouth towards his ear and whispers, "I can't thank you enough for bringing my boys back to me and working to keep us safe. This world is a mess and it's people like you who are going to make it better. I don't want you to be shy around me. I want to be here for you as your friend, like you've been there for me."

She holds him for a little longer and Nick wraps his arms around her, returning the hug. It is nice to have a friend again, he thinks, remembering what it feels like to spend time with people that aren't in his work circle. He can't remember the last time he had a true friend that he could trust. She releases him from her grasp and turns back to the dishes, acting as though nothing happened.

She starts up again a few minutes later, "Now, tell me about how things are going with her."

Nick decides to give in and open up to Ava.

"I think things are going well. I'm being honest when I say that I don't know if I've ever had a connection this strong with someone before. She just seems to get me, almost in an unspoken way. It's like we are the same people when it comes to the important things, but different enough to keep it interesting. I don't know if that even makes sense," he explains, trying not to sound too gushy.

"That makes perfect sense. I know it doesn't seem like it, but Derrick and I have a similar connection. He and I appear opposite to the naked eye, but we're more alike than most people think. I am more outspoken than he is and I can be much more overbearing than him, but we both had rough childhoods and turned things around because having a family and a life together means more than anything to both of us. Deep down where it counts, him and I, we're exactly the same. He may not look it, but he is strong and he can be fierce when it really matters," she explains to the doctor, with pride carrying every word.

Prior to Ava's words pumping life and excitement into Derrick's existence, he just came off as a very bland person. For the first time since he had met the family, he is looking forward to getting to know the father of two. Nick continues to smile at Ava as she speaks. She is so down to earth and full of wisdom that he is in awe of her. Looking at her and even spending all this time with her, he would have never known that she came from a rough upbringing if she hadn't told him.

"When Derrick and I first started trying to have a baby we weren't successful. The doctors said it would be nearly impossible for me to conceive. They found out that I have unusual growths in my uterus likely due to nutritional deficits I had when I was younger. My mom died when I was little, and my dad wasn't really all that into taking care of me and my sister. Foods changed a lot in the United States when I was around that age with farms shutting down and factories picking up. At that time, it was hard to afford nutrient dense food, so whatever we could afford I tried to give most of it to my sister," she says without any regret in her voice.

Nick thinks hard about what Ava is saying, trying to compare his childhood to hers. He knows she is slightly older than him so she would remember the food processing changes better than he, but the truth is, his memory of his childhood with his mom is mostly positive and there weren't any real struggles at home when it came to money or access to resources. He feels grateful to his mom at this moment but also feels sorrow for Ava. It makes him sad to know that someone as loving and kind as her had to struggle so much as a child. Part of him wonders if the struggle is what has made her into such a positive person to be around.

She continues telling him about her past, "Even though it was super unlikely that I got pregnant, Derrick kept telling me that we should keep trying and that our dreams would come true. It finally happened after a little over three years of trying. Adam finally arrived and we finally had our happiest moment. I never thought I would be able to have one child, let alone two after hearing what the doctors had to say. After two years of trying, I wanted to give up but Derrick kept me going. He always says that I'm the one that is the strength in our family and sometimes he is right about that. I have spent my time rescuing him, but he's rescued me too. He's my person, my soulmate. Without him, I wouldn't really be me. Based on what I've seen around here lately, it looks like you've found your person too."

Nick isn't much of an emotional person, but Ava's words touch him to his core. He tries not to make it noticeable that his eyes are welling up a little bit. Despite his efforts, Ava notices and rests her head on his shoulder in a playful way and tells him not to be so mushy. The pair of friends laugh at the situation like they've known each other forever.

The two continue to chat about less serious topics as they clear the plates and wipe down the table. As it turns out, Adam and Ben made a much bigger mess than they initially thought. Spaghetti sauce is stuck on just about every surface near where the boys sat. Nick doesn't mind taking the extra time to clean, he feels grateful to have something to be thankful for at this moment.

When the kitchen is clean, they decide it is time to retire to the living room with the rest of the group, minus the boys who can be heard playing 'cars' in the back bedroom. When they approach the living room, they notice that the TV is going and it is a news broadcast. The news is displaying another violent act on *Modified* people. This time it is in the form of a riot outside of a hospital in Michigan. The newscaster explains that a woman reportedly gave birth to twins who are *Modified.* Their *modification* is of the northern kind—the thick skin. The woman reporting on the event is standing in front of a large group of people carrying signs with messages that are hurtful and threatening to the *Modified* and their families. The police are pictured standing outside of the entrances to keep the protesters out. The message that the newswoman is giving is proof that things are becoming more polarized than ever in all parts of the country now that more MODs are being born each day.

Patrick switches the television off, and the group sits and talks to one another about their surprise of how bad things have gotten. They've known that things are strained in many places throughout the country, but they didn't realize how many incidents have occurred that were newsworthy until they all began sharing their local stories.

Nick shares his story about the mother he saw on the moving sidewalk. Katie mentions the news story that she remembers from the grocery store in Texas and follows up with a horrific local story in the D.C. area about a father losing an eye when he jumped in front of men throwing rocks at his wife and baby when they were on a family walk.

Patrick talks about a story from the police station about a baby that was left on the doorstep of the station. He wasn't on shift that night, but his co-workers filled him in on what happened. He explained that a mother dropped off her baby, who couldn't be more than a week old, with a note at the station saying that she loved her son, but she doesn't know how to protect him because of his *Modification*. Patrick explains that at first when he heard that story the next day, it didn't seem to be so awful or out of the ordinary as people sometimes relinquish their children to the state because they can't take care of them for various reasons. The next morning Patrick was on shift and he heard about the night before. A few minutes later a call came in to check out a house due to a call from a neighbor who heard what they thought sounded like gunshots. Patrick and his partner went to check on the call and when they approached the house all of the lights were on, but no one was answering the door. They had to forcefully enter. It turned out to be one of the worst crime scenes that Patrick has ever experienced. The father hung himself and left a note saying that he couldn't handle knowing that he created a *Modified* child. It looked like his body had been there at least a day and that was confirmed by the coroner. A woman's body was also found. The crime scene and time of death indicated that she died by a self-inflicted gunshot wound to the head. The police records later indicated that these were the parents of the baby that was dropped off at the station the night before. The mother ended her life five hours after dropping her baby off with the police.

Patrick still thinks about this case to this day. He explains to the group that he isn't able to understand how parents could leave their helpless baby just because it didn't look the way they wanted it to. He understands that it is a scary situation, but that baby is their blood. The case got transferred to Child Protective Services and Patrick never found out what happened to the baby, but he still thinks about the boy and hopes that he is safe and loved.

Ava stays silent for many of the stories, trying not to store the new knowledge into the same mental folder as the rest of her fears. When her time to share comes she starts to tell a story she heard through the local parent group a year or so back. Derrick removes himself from the group to go check on the kids, but it seems the real reason is because the prospect of hearing one more story is not something he can handle.

Ava's recollection of the story is that one of the members of a parent group she was a part of has a cousin who lives in Massachusetts. The cousin is being shunned by the entire family, including extended relatives because they are in prison for attacking and almost killing a mother in the delivery room immediately after she gave birth to a *Modified* baby. The way Ava remembers the story is that the cousin was a nurse at a hospital in the labor and delivery unit. Immediately after the c-section birth of the baby, one of the nurses took the baby to clean them up and the doctor began to close up the mother's incision. While all of that was happening the 'cousin nurse' grabbed a scalpel off of the doctor's tray nearby and lunged at the patient stabbing her in the right breast. The husband tackled the nurse and held her down until security got there. Luckily the gynecologist in the room was well practiced enough in general surgery to tend to the woman until other doctors arrived. The most disturbing thing that Ava remembers from the story is that the 'cousin nurse', even after being tackled, continued to shout horrible things at the mother. She said things like "God is punishing you", "you and your baby need to die", and "this doesn't happen to good Christian people." Ava explains that hearing that story for the first time was the moment that she realized how difficult times ahead may be. She never believed she would have to worry about things like this for her own family though.

After sharing their insights into the polarization of society when it comes to the MODs, they collectively decide that now is the time to get to work on their public service announcement. They want to make sure that people's minds are on the MODs when they deliver the message and with the local news, now is the perfect time. Derrick comes back into the room carrying the boys as Nick begins to give directions. He tells Ava and Derrick that all four of them would have to be part of the announcement. Having them speak will help to alleviate any suspicion that people might have as to what happened to the missing family, and who is to blame. Nick and Katie decide they will take over the rest of the announcement once the Ardi's get done. They will explain what happened with MoonCycle and ask that people band behind them so justice can be served.

They all head down to the office in an orderly fashion. Ava and Derrick sit down with the boys in their laps in the middle two seats of the four folding chairs that Patrick placed in front of the white, hanging sheet. Nick and Katie sit down in the chairs left open on each side of the Ardis. Patrick begins tinkering on the computer and pressing some buttons on the camera. Ava takes this opportunity to remind the boys how important it is that they just need to sit very quietly while the grown-ups talk. Both boys nod in agreement. They can tell that their mom's tone is serious this time and they are prepared to follow through with her directions.

Patrick adjusts the lighting in the room using the dimmer on the switch to make it more illuminated and then stands back behind the camera. He takes one final look at the camera and then at the computer screen before he gives the group a thumbs up. It is time, it's a go.

Ava clears her throat and speaks clearly, "I am Ava Ardi and this is my family."

Derrick sits up proudly displaying his gills for all to see. He holds tightly onto his son as the woman that ties their family together speaks. Ava looks towards her sons and husband, grateful to be together again.

Ava continues speaking without missing a beat, "We are the family that everyone, especially folks in South Carolina, believe to be missing. I'm here to tell you that we aren't missing. We were taken."

Derrick takes over the speech as practiced, "My wife, children and I were taken by the Human Biology Research Department or at least those are the people who agreed to put us in containment. Rumors have been swirling for some time about our son Adam. He is seven years old and he was not born a MOD. As you can see though, he is currently a MOD and so am I and my other son. They took us with plans to study our DNA."

Ava's voice emerges again, as if her and Derrick are tag-team partners in a wrestling match, "The people sitting on each side of us are the people who have saved us. We're asking you to listen to their story."

Katie begins telling her story, "I am Katie Kleug and my job is or I guess, was, Junior Administrator at the Human Biology Research Department in Washington D.C. My boss, David Bruner and his associate, Kenny Nash, tried to coerce me into illegal actions to cover up an intentional chemical spill that had been recently determined to cause a super immune response in those who came in contact with it and forced the *Modification* process to accelerate and even begin in some individuals."

Nick takes it upon himself to conclude the Public Service Announcement as the camera pans toward him, "I am Dr. Nicholas Cyrus and I was the lead scientist that was enlisted by the HBRD, D.C. to not only look into the causes of *Modification* in the Ardi family, but also to come up with a way to stop it. I'm not here to create panic, but I am here to inform you as to what Ms. Kleug and I have found to be true in our research…'"

Nick pulls out a piece of paper that has his talking points on it. He briefly glances down at it to get his bearings. He gathers himself with a deep breath and makes eye contact with the camera again.

He continues, "…Number 1. Adam, Ben and Derrick Ardi have become *Modified* only because of their immune response to chemicals that have altered their DNA. Number 2. A MoonCycle factory has been dumping their chemical runoff into the water along the coast of South Carolina for who knows how long—until they found out about Adam, at which point they enlisted me. Number 3. I have zero doubt that the HBRD and MoonCycle knew exactly what caused the *Modification* process in the Ardi family and only enlisted me to either take the blame as a previous employee and/or to create a serum that could stall the *modification* process, which they directly asked me to do. Number 4. I have scientific proof that I have gathered during my time being held captive by HBRD and MoonCycle that without a doubt will prove I am telling the truth."

Nick reaches into his pocket and pulls out a vial. He holds it up to the camera for all to see. The blue contents illuminate in the light from the ceiling fixture and begin to sparkle. He puts his list in his pocket and steadies the vial in his left hand so that he can point to it with his right.

"This vial contains high doses of the chemical composition gathered from the areas of runoff along the coast of South Carolina. It has been treated for preservation. If injected into the human body it will create an immune response that will automatically trigger the *Modification* process. This process will take effect immediately due to the specific composition of the high levels of concentrated chemicals that I have created with the samples I have collected. A man by the name of Silas Preston, hired by MoonCycle, was there when I collected samples and worked on the serum in the lab. He can corroborate everything I am saying, that is, if he is not a coward. Number 5. I am not asking anything of you other than to join our side and seek justice for those involved. I believe that the government and MoonCycle are using the country's current division as a means to gain more control and power. Please do not let the government turn this into blame due to lack of action in the climate change crisis. That is not the only factor in play. While environmental factors may be how the *modifications* that we know of began, that is not how every person is *modifying*. As a scientist, I have always supported organizations for climate change action. We all need to be one with all life and find value in everyone. Please join us and help us see that justice is served. Thank you."

Patrick stops the recording on the camera and begins working on the computer immediately. The stream is live on the most popular social media app, Zoop, through an anonymous account that Patrick created using a virtual private network so the location's origin can't be traced back to him. Patrick then saves the video and shares it to feeds on other social media sites like Surge and FrameKick, also using anonymous accounts. He also shares the video to every major news outlet that he can think of. Now all they can do is wait to see what happens.

Within ten minutes the video has over 400 shares, 2,000 comments and 5,000 reactions. The video is taking off. Now all they have to do is wait. They will need a lot more traction than this to make a difference. They don't want to get their hopes up, so the group collectively decides it is best to take the night off from watching the feedback on the video and instead head up to bed early.

A few hours pass and Nick finds that he still can't sleep. He decides to head down to the main floor and grab a snack from the kitchen to distract himself from worrying about the video they posted. When he arrives in the kitchen, he finds Katie already sitting at the table eating a bowl of cereal and reading a book.

She looks up and smiles, "Couldn't sleep either?" she asks.

Nick shakes his head and sits down in the chair next to Katie.

"I'm worried that our video could make things worse in society. People are already growing so intolerant of one another. *Modification* has really polarized people politically and culturally," Nick explains.

Katie rests her hand on top of Nick's, her bright eyes gleam in the light as she stares into his dark, full pupils.

"We did what we thought was right. If there is going to be a war, it isn't going to be because of us. It would be because people can't stand the intolerance or inaction any longer. This problem is bigger than us. The government has ignored climate change too long and because of that biology took over. We can't control that. The government allowed MoonCycle to function without any real regulations for too long, now they've made a mistake and biology once again took over. None of these things are in our control. The only thing in our control are the choices we make next," she says, meaning every word.

He never realized how blue her eyes are until this moment. He thinks about what she said, and she is right. It isn't in their control, but they can control how they move forward. He decides that no matter what the outcome of the video share is, they will deal with it. The important thing is that they will do it together.

Nick smiles at her wisdom. He needs to try to get some sleep so he can have a clear mind as he heads into the aftermath of releasing the video. He leans forward and kisses Katie on the cheek. Her cheeks become red, and her heart begins to beat quickly. Nick pulls his lips away from her cheek, but she wants more. She needs more. She puts her hands on each side of his face, pulling him back in gently and kisses his lips ever so softly. Her heartbeat begins to slow as she slowly releases the kiss.

"Goodnight, Dr. Cyrus," she says playfully.

Chapter 22

May 3rd, 2082 - THE WHOLE CREW

Katie awakens to the smell of eggs and bacon coming from the kitchen. She rolls over and looks at the clock—8:05 a.m. She can't remember the last time she slept past 6:30 a.m. She can't believe her body let her get the extra rest. Maybe it is because she is still swooning over the kiss she and Nick shared in the middle of the night. She climbs out of bed and heads to the bathroom to relieve herself and clean up a bit. She eventually makes her way down to the kitchen to find that Nick is the one who is cooking. He is whistling a peppy tune as he removes the bacon from the pan and puts it on a plate.

"You're certainly in a good mood this morning," Katie remarks.

Nick chuckles. He knows he is acting giddy, but he can't help it.

"You've had that effect on me, Ms. Kleug. Plus, I have good news," he says.

Was he just flirting with me? She wonders, knowing he is, but trying to reassure herself that he is still interested. She didn't think he had it in him to flirt. It isn't his style, but she likes his effort.

"Care to share this good news with me?" she asks in a spirited tone.

Nick tells her how he woke up early, around 6:30, and couldn't wait any longer to see how the video did so he went downstairs to check the feed on the accounts that Patrick left open on the computer. He explains that there is so much action happening on the video that he can't keep up. The amount of shares is unknown, but he says there is already a huge impact. That isn't even the best part. Two amazing things happened that no one ever considered.

He explains that he was browsing through the accounts and he found inboxes full of messages asking us to start a resistance group. Nick knows that in his speech he was asking for people to help him seek justice and to hold the right people accountable, but he never imagined that so many people would want to be a part of a bigger cause. A lot of messages explain that some of the people are already creating their own subgroups to help support Dr. Cyrus's cause.

When searching earlier he also found that people are so inspired by the video that they are now sharing their own stories as videos to the accounts that Patrick created. Nick explains to Katie that apparently there are a lot of people who have become MODs along the coastal region. They have gone into hiding for fear that people would ostracize them. There are so many more people like Adam than the public is aware of.

Several videos express so much gratitude to the group for sharing a message that makes people feel protected and safe—a message that encourages people to tell others that they are MODs. There are countless loved ones of MODs who are expressing openly that they are delighted to hear people are fighting back against the intolerance fueled by the lack of governmental action.

#FightingfortheArdis is a trending tagline along with other related taglines like #DrCyrusforthewin, and #MODsarepeopletoo. The tagline with the most attention is #OnewithALLlife. It was taken from Nick's speech and apparently it speaks to the way a lot of people are feeling. It is exciting for Nick to see how much traction grew over the course of just one night.

Katie doesn't want to rain on Nick's parade, but she can't inflate his ego right now either. She is so worried that it all seems too good to be true. It isn't that Katie isn't excited for the success they've found in such a short time, but she knows there are going to be some drawbacks to having gone public. She decides to look through the accounts herself to see if there is anything that she seriously needs to be worried about.

She scans through hundreds of comments, threads, and videos that morning to find the downside of their fame. Searching for something unnerving is really easy because there are almost as many negative things being said as positive. Most of the comments are bigoted. The people who are fearful of the MODs in real life found their voice online and aren't afraid to use it. Dr. Cyrus is getting some of the backlash as well. A few of the comments about him can even be considered threats and that worries Katie. A few taglines against their movement are also picking up like #JusticeforMoonCycle and #DrCyrusisaquack. There is even some hate mail in the inbox on each of the accounts.

Katie tries to share her concerns with Nick about how some people who speak out online are, in fact, crazy enough to do something to hurt someone. He appreciates that she is worried about him, but he finds her fear unwarranted. He reassures her that throughout every event in history there have always been people on the wrong side of things and that time can sort it all out. He promises her that he will protect her at all costs. Katie's negativity has gotten inside his head a little bit, but he won't let her know that. He makes sure to express with confidence that he believes sharing the video is a win for them.

Chapter 23

May 6th, 2083 - THE WHOLE CREW

Things seem to be going well for two more days. The number of shares and views the video is getting continues to grow. Both positive and negative correspondence fill the inboxes each day. Even with some hate comments and a few threats, the group consensus is still that the video was overall a good idea and things are progressing on the right track. Even Katie has to admit that things are looking pretty positive as the group watches the videos of support together in the office.

Things change drastically when they turn on the news later that morning. Late last night there was a riot that broke out in Beaufort, South Carolina. The people of Beaufort are tired of being lied to about the Ardi family and feel that Mayor Roy and the police department are hiding things from them. Hundreds of people ended up storming the city hall building. The news story airs footage from a local station that shows people with torches and guns scattered across the courtyard entrance of the building. People have megaphones and are shouting 'No more lies'. It is noted on the broadcast that a few of the people broke into the building and ransacked some of the offices, spray painting hate words about the mayor all over the walls. The news story explains that there are not any injuries, but a lot of damage occurred to the premises. One of the protesters is on the screen being interviewed by the station and their interview consists of them calling for Mayor Roy to come out tonight to city hall and tell all of his constituents, who have trusted him, the truth at once and face his fate.

Before long the broadcast replays showing that the police department interrupted the riot by getting their swat gear on and breaking it up. The replay shows that it takes a while for them to break it up though, and at one point they even use tear gas. Several people got arrested for inciting the riot, but the reports show that they didn't go quietly. The television shows people screaming at the top of their lungs about the deceit.

One man shouts directly into the camera, "They knew about the Ardi's and they lied to us. The Ardi's are part of our community. They're like family. It's the government's job to protect us. Don't trust them! They are all liars!"

The T.V. pans over to what is currently happening in Beaufort. A press conference is being held by Sheriff Santos in front of City Hall. The aftermath of the riot can still be seen in the background of the camera shot. Pieces of garbage and makeshift weapons are lying all over the courtyard. Sheriff Santos looks defeated as he approaches the podium to speak.

"I'd like to speak to the events that occurred last night and that have been ongoing for several weeks now. I would like to start with what happened last night in the heart of our little town—at our city hall. There was a large group of insurgents who stormed our town's most important governmental building in hopes to send a message to our mayor. The message has been received and because of that our town is now suffering. I want to be very clear: those who pillaged one of our most valued community buildings last night will be held responsible. As the police force, it is our job to keep our community safe from rebels who are seeking to cause our community harm."

Sheriff Santos pauses for a long second and then looks deeply into the camera, as if the newscasters and citizens standing right in front of him no longer exist.

"As for Dr. Cyrus and Ms. Kleug, our town opened our doors to you when you came here to help solve the case of the missing Ardi family. You have taken a tragedy that has fallen on our town and have turned it into a conspiracy. You have brainwashed all of the people around you, including our dear friends, Ava and Derrick Ardi. Justice will certainly be served, and it will be you who suffers the consequences."

He takes a second to break from the staring contest that he is having with the camera. He refocuses on those citizens who have come to hear him speak.

"To the Ardi family, no matter what you've gotten yourself into, we are here to help you whether you've become a MOD or not. We can't control the environmental changes, and you shouldn't suffer because of that. All of the claims that Dr. Cyrus has made about our town are false and we'd like the chance to prove that to you. We support you and hope for you to return home safely."

As Sheriff Santos is finishing his speech, yells from the crowd come from all directions. Some in support of the Sheriff and some against.

One person shouts, "Is it true Mayor Roy has gone into hiding?"

Commotion fills the screen before the sheriff can address the question. A huge fight breaks out between the groups of people arguing over whether or not there should be support for the worn-down sheriff and the news broadcast ends abruptly.

The group is shocked by everything they've witnessed. Ava notes that she is so glad the boys are still sleeping and didn't have to see that. It would have been very confusing to them. She explains that they really liked Sheriff Santos because he had always been kind to all of the children in the town. The group spends some time really dissecting the speech Santos made and makes the observation that the sheriff looked spooked by what happened at the city hall and that he is losing control of his town.

Chapter 24

May 6th, 2082 - SANTOS & ROY

Sheriff Santos shouts for his police force to break up the fights that are occurring right in front of the podium that he just gave his speech on. He retreats from the stage and gets into his police car. He decides that the rest of the police force can deal with the mess going on. He needs to get some air and think. He is losing control over everything and now that Dr. Cyrus and Ms. Kleug have pulled the Ardi family onto their side, he doesn't think there is much he can do to rectify the situation.

He drives for some time mulling over his options. He can turn on Mayor Roy, like he had considered some time ago, but now that he has given that speech condemning the doctor and Ms. Kleug, it won't look good if he flip flops now. As he weighs his options, he realizes the only thing he can do now is to double down. He doesn't really feel an allegiance to Frank Roy any longer, but he knows that Nathan Pierce can really do damage to him and his family if he doesn't cooperate.

He pulls up to a beach cottage, just about as far south as you can go in Beaufort without leaving the city limits. He slowly approaches the door and knocks as loudly as he can. Mayor Roy peeks his head out of the door to see if Santos is alone before welcoming him in. He enters the small cottage and sits down. He takes in his surroundings for a moment. Even though the cottage is small, the interior has perfect, updated southern charm. Mayor Roy offers Rio some sweet tea, but the sheriff waves him off and gestures him to sit down on the couch adjacent to him.

Rio begins, "The press conference didn't go well. The public has already assigned you the role of the villain in this story."

Mayor Roy hangs his head. He doesn't just seem disappointed but annoyed as well. He has seen the broadcast on the television and knows that his options are limited as to what path to take next.

"I tuned in. I saw everything. I have been receiving calls from other mayors in surrounding towns and things aren't looking good. They've been putting out their own fires. Apparently, our riot hasn't been the only one and it is most certainly not going to be the last one. People are either mad about what happened to the Ardis or are taking this opportunity to show their true hatred of the MODs. Either way, violence is on the rise," he states with defeat in his voice.

The violence from the north has now made its way down to the south and pretty much every single state is facing some sort of backlash ever since the Ardis and Dr. Cyrus released that video. People have organized these events really quickly. There is only one play left and it is going to have to be a big one. The mayor doesn't want to make this call because of the suffering that will come from this, but it is the only way to protect his own skin.

Frank Roy looks long and hard at his old friend, Rio. It is a look of deep concern because he knows what is to come. Rio looks back at Frank and can see the uneasiness in his eyes. At that moment he knows that the 'last resort plan' has now become the only plan. Neither of them speak another word to one another.

Mayor Roy stands up from the lounge chair and walks over to the dining table that overlooks the ocean to grab his phone. He stops, but only for a moment, to take in the sight of the sun hitting the ocean as the waves crash into the sand. To an outsider it may look like he is second guessing his decision or trying to find another way, but that is the furthest from the truth. He made his mind up before Sheriff Santos even arrived, waiting for him was just a courtesy from one old friend to another. He picks up his phone, clicks a few buttons and waits until a voice on the other line picks up.

"It's time. We've run out of options," the now again confident Mayor said.

Chapter 25

May 7th, 2082 - THE WHOLE CREW

The popularity from the single video they posted keeps growing. People continue to reach out to the anonymous accounts that Patrick created to share the public service announcement on. There are too many messages to respond to. It would take hours if they tried.

Patrick tells Nick that they need to come up with a way to respond to all these messages, but all at once rather than individually. Nick agrees. Afterall, he started this movement, and he can't leave all the people who are now behind it in the dark forever.

Nick calls a 'family meeting' to talk to Patrick, Katie, Ava and Derrick. He doesn't want to proceed in any way without discussing it with them. After Ben and Adam are put to bed that night they all meet in the living room, around the coffee table—the same spot they met that first night when they arrived at Patrick's house.

Nick begins to explain what he thinks their next step should be, "Patrick and I talked, and we need to act now before we lose traction with social media. I think we need to rally all of our followers and start pushing for revolution. It's the only way to ensure that we see change and protect all the people who are counting on us to make the world a safer place for them. I obviously wanted to talk to you all first to see what you thought. I'm not in this alone and all of us will be put at risk."

PJ chimes in, "I agree with Nick on this. We're in deep now and we're going to have to make a bold move. Lots of people are counting on us."

Katie's eyes began to fill with tears. She isn't exactly scared of what's going to come next, but she is scared that everything is going to change. She likes how things have been the last few days in the house. She feels like everyone is becoming like a family. Since the second night in the house everyone has been sharing great conversation over meals each day. They watch shows together and play old board games and video games to pass the time when they aren't following the news or tracking their online success. Being held up in Patrick's house allows everyone to really get to know one another. Each adult spends time taking care of the kids and trying to make things seem as normal as possible to them, which in turn, makes things seem normal to everyone. It scares her that all of it could change in a matter of minutes.

Nick draws his attention over to Ava. From the very moment Nick met Ava in the waiting room that day near the lab he could tell she was one of the strongest people he had ever met. Nick feels closer to Ava each day that they spend together and he is sure that she will stand by him even with the risks involved. Nonetheless, she is the one that he wants verbal approval from. Afterall, she and Derrick have the most to lose.

Ava sees that Nick is watching her, so she inserts herself into the conversation, "The moment those men came and ripped my family from our home is the moment that our lives changed. I know we will be at risk, but you, Nick, aren't the one putting us at risk. The government and MoonCycle have made this world unlivable for my family and many others, and we are going to fight to make it a better place to live for my children and the rest of the children of the world, no matter the cost."

After talking about logistics for a while the group concludes their conversation. Nick and Patrick head downstairs to make another video and this time the video will feature Nick and only Nick. He takes a seat in front of the white sheet that is still hanging in Patrick's office. Patrick gets everything ready on the computer and camera the same way he did the other night. Once Patrick finishes adjusting the lights to make it look brighter in the room, he gives Nick the signal that they are good to begin.

"My new make-shift family and I have heard your cries and appeals. We aren't backing down. We are calling for every single one of you who wants to see this world become a safe place for all again, to join us. We can no longer sit by idly waiting for something to change. If we want change then we must will it into existence. I've seen all of the posts about OneWithAllLife or OWALs (pronounced ow-alls), as many of you call yourselves now on social media, and I'm asking the rest of you to become an OWAL as well. Fly into the night like an owl and make your presence known. I call for a revolution and I call for it now," Dr. Cyrus proclaims.

Chapter 26

May 8th-10th, 2082 - THE WHOLE CREW

The six spend the next couple days in and out of Patrick's living room watching the news. Patrick calls and asks for a leave from his job. He tells his supervisor that he needs to take a medical leave, but he is sure that the rumors swirling around the police station are that it is more of a mental health leave because Patrick cut off everyone around him out of nowhere. He hasn't responded to any communication from his friends down at the station other than the occasional text letting them know he is alive.

He is linked to the OWALs now whether or not that is something to be happy about. No one knows he is connected to them, but it is only a matter of time before the group ventures out in public and embraces the revolution that they have started. His place is here with them now and he is going to follow them into the trenches.

Each and every channel the group flips the living room's holo-screen television to shows riots, sit-ins, pillaging, marches and protests that are occurring across the nation. Mayors and governors are hosting press conferences in cities and towns across the country begging people to take to their homes and stop the violence. People refuse to stop. Men, women, and children band together in hopes of creating a more tolerable future for all. Young people, mostly those under forty years old, are what make up the majority of people who've become a part of the resistance groups but chanting and screaming by those young and old can be heard across the entire nation. People holding signs depicting an owl in many different likenesses fill the streets. The owl is now the symbol of the resistance group and everyone is embracing it.

Owl graffiti fills brick walls along main streets across the nation. Every social media source is inundated by the owl, but the most commonly used image becomes an owl with a set of eyes that has been artistically changed to look like an inverted MoonCycle logo. The eyes resemble two crescent moons facing one another with a small slit cut into each of them. A perfect artistic culmination of Dr. Cyrus's speech.

Despite the continuing action on television, there isn't much pushback from the government yet. Sure, the mayors and governors keep asking for things to stop, but that is about all that is happening. Some police forces work to control the crowds—if the crowds are small enough to contain, but oftentimes that isn't the case. Media announcers continue to report and with each report there is growing concern as to why there isn't anything being done to support the people of the communities who don't want to take part in what is happening. Many people are begging for protection.

Even though it isn't the intention to cause harm, most of the events turn violent. For every rally there is a group fighting back against the OWALs. Some people screaming how MODs deserved to be put in camps and segregated from everyone else. Other people calling the OWALs traitors of their own species. An unfathomable number of slurs and offensive words continue to be spewed across the rallies. No matter what is said, people become triggered and it almost always results in violence. The police let the violence occur unless it starts getting too out of hand. It is as if they want the people to destroy one another so they don't have to be the ones to do it. In the cases where things escalate to extreme heights, swat teams arrive and tear gas people. Some arrests are made, but not a lot. People often flee when the swat teams or police force arrive. Both groups know that getting arrested will do neither side any good. People from both sides of the division are getting out of control.

In some places people are causing terrible destruction. Buildings are being burned on main streets and people are being beaten if they get too mouthy. On most of the live news footage, broken glass can be seen lining the streets. It comes from windows being busted in or glass bottles being thrown into the crowd. As Nick watches the news, he realizes that he is, in part, responsible for the destruction of many towns and cities across the nation. But that is what they asked for in the videos—a revolution.

Nick, Katie, and Patrick know it is time to head to the front lines. They begin to call on some of the people that have reached out to them via social media about starting a Pittsburgh OWAL group. Many people are ready to get involved and respond to the call, or the WHOO, a clever little acronym that makes a nice word play of their new mascot. The term is being used by people across social media platforms to mean 'we help our organization'. The newly formed Pittsburgh group agrees to meet tomorrow to start their preparations.

Patrick agrees that since no one really knows he is involved yet that it would be fine if people meet at his house. After all, he already decided he no longer wants to remain just ankle deep in this. Ava and Derrick make the decision that even though it is the most important cause to them that they can't put their children at risk of physical violence out on the streets. Watching the news proves it is no place for children to be. They think it is best to take turns fighting for the cause so someone can stay back and protect the kids.

The WHOO has been sent out and the clock begins ticking. The newest part of the plan is in motion. It is time for the world to see Dr. Nick Cyrus in action as the face of the revolution.

Chapter 27

May 11th, 2082 - OWALS

The OWALs gather in Patrick's basement to begin discussing their plan of attack. Luckily, due to lack of decorating, he has plenty of room for the group to spread out and make preparations. One of the new members explains that she thinks they should venture out into downtown Pittsburgh this evening because her connections told her there are other branches of the resistance planning a march in protest of the intolerance that the city has for MODs.

The new member introduces herself to the group as Tamera Townsend but asks that she be called Blue. She doesn't explain why she wants to be referred to as Blue, but one can make the assumption that she had been given the nickname 'Blue' on account that she has the most beautiful, piercing blue eyes that most people have ever seen on a woman with such dark hair and skin. She is breathtaking and everyone makes sure to take notice when she enters a room. Tamera isn't a *modified,* and she doesn't really tell anyone if she knows any MODs personally, but she makes it clear through conversation that she knows from history what can happen if people are judged and punished by their looks or any other personal characteristics. She isn't willing to let that happen to America again.

Blue takes the lead on the plans for the evening. At 5 p.m. the group will gather near the Moorhead federal building and then march their way through the business district. Her half-brother, Terrence—who is also an OWAL, stands nearby discussing what each person should bring to the march. Each member is assigned to bring a sign or megaphone, a light source, and something to protect themselves with. The member meeting convenes and the individuals disperse so they can spread the word to like-minded people in the community with hopes that this protest will be the largest one yet.

As 5 p.m. approaches, the streets of Pittsburgh's business district are flooded with OWALs marching and chanting words of hope that echo off of the building faces. The protest starts off successfully. News trucks line the streets and the well-put-together reporters give a play-by-play of the events as they unfold. People from different OWAL groups all over the state are now working together to spread their message. Protest signs pump up and down in the thick evening air. By this time most of the news reporters have labeled the OWALs a liberal extremist group that is trying to cause havoc in a city that is otherwise generally safe. This is similar to all of the newscasts in other cities throughout the last few days. Despite the general consensus by the conservative media channels, there are a few stations that offer unbiased or even liberal views on the protests and how the requested changes can be positive for the nation.

From the very beginning of the OWAL meeting, Nick made it clear that as the face of the organization he wants everyone to understand what he is hoping for and that he wants to do his best to achieve it without violence, but he understands that sometimes for a revolution to be successful a few heads have to roll. He is hopeful that his message will be clear and that this protest will go off as a peaceful and impactful one.

Nick looks around and takes in the sight of what the group has accomplished in such a small amount of time. By his count he is surrounded by at least two thousand people who have come to support the cause that he spoke about only a few days ago on social media. The signs present in the crowd support his message: hope for safety and rights of those who have become *Modified.* A sense of pride swells in him. He is ready to finally show that he is a man of action and no longer a face on a screen spewing words of inspiration. Dozens of people are crowded around him—shielding him from view—but that doesn't save him from being inundated by people telling him what his vision means to them once they notice who he is. He enjoys the credit he is getting, but he isn't one for wanting attention placed on himself, so he begins to feel mixed emotions.

Katie stands in the crowd taking in the man next to her. Even though she is nervous for what is to come, she is proud of Nick and how he has stepped up over the past week to protect everyone in their tribe. She watches him as he looks into the crowd sizing up his success. He appears content with the turnout, but uncomfortable to be around so many people especially now that everyone's attention is on him. His discomfort is somehow appealing to her. She likes that he isn't overly confident and feels more drawn to him than ever.

Once the commotion fills the area around Nick, reporters pick up on what is happening and approach to try to get a story from the man in the viral videos. Nick tries his best to avoid the cameras, but the words "Dr. Cyrus, a word?" are being shouted in various locations around him until finally he speaks up for all to hear.

"We have arrived here this evening to show we are serious about creating change. It is our hope to secure safety and support for those who have become *Modified*. If we don't take action against the corporation at hand for trying to capitalize on the struggles of the people and put pressure on the government to turn their focus to supporting what our world is becoming since they refused to put an effort into slowing global warming and monitoring MoonCycle's company practices, then the world as we know it will be over. Join us and become OneWithAllLife," Dr. Cyrus says with unwavering strength in his voice.

The cameras pan in on his face as he concludes speaking. Nick, Katie, Ava, Patrick, Tamera and Terrence who have all stayed close to one another and their followers begin moving in the crowd to reach the front in order to lead the group. They are welcomed by the people around them once they settle into their places. Excitement rises and spreads throughout the streets as they begin marching.

At a cross street, after walking and chanting for a few blocks, the large group comes face to face with another group that seems to go on for miles in the opposite direction. At first glance it appears that the group may just be another batch of supporters of the OneWithAllLife cause, but that theory quickly diminishes as the incoming chants emit hate. The group is full of individuals who reject the cause and believe that segregation should be put in place to separate those who have been *Modified* from those who are considered 'normal' humans. They are here to stop the movement and instill fear in those who are fighting for equality.

The crowd looks like a wave of red. Almost every person in front of their eyes is wearing a red shirt or sporting the bright color in some fashion. Many, but not all, of the shirts display a logo on the front that has an image of an owl crossed out on it as if it were a no smoking sign. The blur of red goes on for what seems like miles. Nick tries to gauge which of the two groups have more people. He loses count as the faces before him blend together into one huge blob. The number of people on each side seems too close for comfort and he begins to worry. From the signs blocking his view of the crowd in front him, he gathers that this group calls themselves AmerEagles.

Clever name, he thinks. Since eagles eat owls, he determines that it must be a power play on words. The group has done a great job of keeping their existence under wraps since Cyrus hasn't heard of them before. They must be a direct retaliation of OWALs and fairly new.

The thing that Nick can't figure out is how the hate group found out about the OWAL protest. He begins to wonder if there is someone who has been brought into the organization that is working both sides. It's a possibility because it seems that the AmerEagles group knew exactly what time and what route the OWALs would be taking. He hopes it is a coincidence...stranger things have happened lately.

Katie takes in the sight of the crowd before her and immediately grabs Nick's hand. She can feel his hand clam up as she tightens her grip on him. The people before her are ready for violence. They carry automatic weapons, baseball bats and other pieces of improvised weaponry. Some of the men are even carrying Molotov cocktails ready to destroy the city. The OWALs have come prepared to protect themselves, but they have nothing close to the stock of weapons that this AmerEagles group came armed with.

She shudders at the thought of her friends being in harm's way.

Both groups come to a halt within 20 feet of each other. The stare off between the two seems to last forever before a glass bottle is thrown into the crowd of the OWAL resistance group by one of the AmerEagles members. That tiny action sparks violence. People from each side begin throwing themselves into each other. Some people in the crowds charge as quickly as they can—looking to make severe, violent, contact with anyone they can. Others chose their opponents strategically, fighting with their hands first before weapons.

Not before long things escalate. Someone near Nick has been stabbed and is bleeding out on the curb nearby. The man—he can't be more than twenty by Nick's account—holds his hands over the wound on his stomach as the blood gushes through where his fingers are weaved together. Friends of the man are surrounding him trying to stop the bleeding. A man rips his shirt off and balls it up to help apply pressure to the comrade's wound. Other people are pursuing their rivals with anything that they can use as a weapon. The first few rows in each group that have already clashed look beaten down. People are bruised, bleeding, limping, everywhere Nick looks.

Shots ring out abruptly and bullets begin raining down on the OWAL crowd. Some cower in fear and retreat, but others persist with full force. At the first sight of the bullet casings hitting the ground, Nick grabs a hold of Katie and pushes her to the ground. He throws his body on top of hers to shield her from the piercing metal falling from the sky. He tucks her under him and waits until there is a lul in the shower of bullets. Screams and cries are coming from every direction.

Nick shouts, "Retreat! Head to safety!" to anyone around him that will listen.

He rolls himself off of Katie and pulls her up at the same time as he rises from the ground. With their hands interlocking now, they try to head towards a side street that looks mostly clear of the crowds. They weave in and out of the groups of people the best they can without becoming a target themselves. Katie looks up and takes in her environment, trying to find a safe route. The street is full of bodies battling as hard as they can. Chaos ensues in every direction she looks. Trash riddles the streets as garbage cans are knocked over and used as a weapon or sometimes even a shield. She speculates that some people from the AmerEagles group must have used some of their Molotov cocktails because there are storefronts, buildings, and trash cans burning. Smoke begins to fill the already smoggy, polluted air.

As they approach the side street, Katie lets out a scream that shakes Nick to the core. She pulls away from Nick in an instant. He abruptly turns around to find Katie hovering over a body lying on the side of the street. Katie sobs and pulls her head back slightly to look at Nick. That's when he sees that the body Katie is covering belongs to Ava. She is laying on her side with her bright, blonde hair draped over most of her face. He can tell that it is her small body without even seeing her face.

Nick drops to his knees and tries to see if she has a pulse. He presses his index and middle finger gently onto her neck and waits—hopeful to feel a thump against his fingertips. He waits for a few seconds longer before moving his fingers around to other areas of her neck, wishing with everything in him that he will find a pulse. Nothing. He can't find one. She is gone. A rush of guilt spreads over him. It is his fault, he thinks—silently mourning. He shouldn't have allowed her to risk herself.

His mind is once again back to the moment that he first met Ava in the waiting room back at the lab in D.C. How strong willed and full of life she seemed and how she remained that way—fighting for her kids safety—until the very end. Her blue eyes were so fierce and loving when it came to her children. He had saved her once, but now she lay so lifeless before him and there is nothing he can do to save her now.

He checks her body up and down looking for a wound. He doesn't see anything on her front side, but he can see blood beginning to pool underneath her and he realizes the wound must be coming from her back. Katie helps Nick roll over Ava's petite body. Her sun kissed skin now looks as white as a sheet. A large blood-soaked spot in her upper back displays a bullet wound. He can't be sure, but to Nick it looks like it is right behind her heart. Although he won't ever know, he hopes that she went quickly and without pain.

His mind shifts to Adam and Ben sitting back at Patrick's house with Derrick. They lost their mother today and Derrick lost the love of his life, and they don't even know it yet. The thought of going back to the headquarters and telling Derrick what happened makes him feel ill. Nick can feel bile rising up, stinging the back of his throat. He manages to force it back down and focus on what he needs to do next. He can't leave Ava's body here to be trampled or defiled. He needs to return her to her family where she can be put to rest.

He looks over at Katie who is just staring blankly at Ava's body. Tears are streaming from her beautiful eyes and crossing her soft cheeks. Although she stopped screaming, there are still little whimpers exiting her body with each breath. He decides that he can't comfort her right now. There will be time for that later. His priority has to be to make sure that Ava's children can say goodbye to their mother—something he didn't realize until now that he himself was grateful for when he lost his mother. He reaches down and picks up Ava's limp body. He swiftly slumps her over his shoulder holding onto her small body with one hand and grabbing Katie's arm with his other.

Noise rises from overhead as a helicopter appears. It appears to be a news station helicopter recording the events of the evening. Sirens are heard in the distance, moving closer. People surrounding Nick and Katie begin to stop what they are doing and disperse in hopes that they can be in the clear and on their way to safety before emergency services arrive.

With Ava's body hanging lifelessly over his shoulder, Nick sprints down the side streets all the way back to Patrick's house with Katie's short legs working hard to keep up. Nick and Katie don't speak during their entire journey. There is nothing to say that can fix this anyways, he tells himself. He doesn't want Katie to console him and assure him it isn't his fault. That isn't what he needs right now. What he needs is to be sad and angry. He is glad Katie is letting him have this time to be alone in his head. He wonders if maybe she knows him even better than he knows himself.

Katie still hasn't stopped whimpering even as they approach Patrick's house. She can't seem to catch her breath no matter how hard she tries.

She wants to talk to Nick but doesn't know what to say. As much as she needs to be with her own thoughts, she knows he needs to be with his more. She doesn't blame him for what happened, but she knows he is placing the blame on himself, nonetheless.

She studies Ava's body hanging over Nick's shoulder. She still looks so pure and dainty. Katie now wishes she would have gotten to know Ava better. They talked while they cooked and played with the children over the last several days, but there were so many opportunities to learn about Ava that Katie didn't take. She knows she loved the beautiful mother of two as a member of her tribe and family, but she feels that if given more time they could have become the best of friends and even formed a more sister-like relationship. Katie would have loved that.

Now in front of Patrick's house, Nick pauses for a moment before lowering Ava onto the front lawn. He doesn't care anymore who knows they are there. They have made themselves targets and because of that, lost an important part of their family that day and that needs to be acknowledged. Katie waits with Ava while Nick tirelessly climbs the stairs to the front entrance. He slowly opens the door and enters, making almost no noise at all.

Nick finds Derrick and the boys in the living room. Derrick is sitting on the floor building lego towers with Ben and Adam. Ben giggles as Adam knocks over the tallest tower and it comes crashing down into pieces. Nick waits a second and takes in the sight of the three of them happily playing because he knows that once he speaks their lives will forever have a shadow of sadness running through them.

Derrick notices that Nick has entered the room. He stops playing and rises up slowly, showing his age. He moves quickly across the room so he can ask Nick how the protest went. As Derrick approaches Nick he can tell from the face he is wearing and how disheveled he looks that something is wrong. Before he can ask, Nick's eyes well up with tears. Derrick feels sick to his stomach. He looks down at Nick's blood-stained hands.

He frantically asks, "Where is Ava?"

Nick can't look him in the eyes as he begins to speak. "Things got really out of control when we were there. There was a huge group of anti-OWALs. They called themselves AmerEagles. The groups clashed and shots were fired. Ava was shot in the back. We found her, but it was too late. She was already gone. I brought her home so you and the boys could say a proper goodbye," Nick explains with deep sadness in his voice.

Derrick turns his saddened, brown eyes away from Nick. He covers his face and begins sobbing. The young boys take notice and run over. Derrick gets down on his knees, so his eyes meet theirs. He explains that something bad happened to their mom and that she fought for them until the very end. He tries his best to explain that they can say goodbye to mommy, but after they do, they won't be able to see her anymore.

The boys begin crying and begging for their mommy to come home. Derrick wraps his arms around the boys and they cry together until there are no more tears left inside. Nick stands by and watches the small family grieve for the woman who gave them everything. His heart breaks for the small boys who will now grow up without their loving mother because of the circumstances the world created.

Chapter 28

May 11th, 2082 - OWALS

Several minutes later, Nick, Derrick, and the boys walk slowly out to the front of the house so they can see Ava one last time. When they arrive on the front porch, they see Katie sitting on the ground with Ava's head in her lap. Surrounding the beautiful fallen soldier are Patrick and at least fifty of the OWALs that were notified by Blue to support the family and the cause.

Derrick sprints towards Ava the second he gets off the porch and falls to his knees before her. He picks up her head from Katie's lap and holds it in his hands, brushing her vivid, blonde hair from her face. He kisses her lips for the last time and pulls her body up into a hug and cries, deep, long sobs. Her limp body hangs in his arms as he tries to hold on just a little bit longer.

Nick takes the small boys' hands in his and guides them towards their parents. Adam squeezes Nick's hand as they approach. The boys stop and stand next to their father and place their hands on his shoulders. Derrick acknowledges their presence and places Ava's head down on the ground so the boys can see their mother's face. The boys lower themselves near Ava. Adam begins crying harder at the sight of her face. He runs his small fingers across her face, feeling the features one more time. Ben gets low to the ground and curls his body into hers, placing his head on her chest, cuddling her for the last time. He rises after a few minutes and tries to wake her, not understanding that she is gone for good. Katie tries her best to comfort Ben, but her emotions get the best of her and she needs to step away to collect herself before she starts to scare the children.

Derrick picks up Ben and hugs him tightly while whispering something into his ear. The youngest boy starts crying for his mother and for her to wake up, but Derrick just hugs him tighter, hoping to offer him some comfort. The hearts of every bystander shatter as the small, high-pitched voice recites the words "wake up, mama" over and over. After a short time, Ben nestles his face in Derrick's neck and sniffles. Adam moves towards his father and turns into him, resting against his side and hiding his face from the crowd.

Derrick calls Nick and Patrick over to talk to him. He requests that he be able to keep Ava here, near Patrick's house, so the boys can feel close to her—just until things calm down and he can move her to a proper burial place. Patrick agrees and is happy to help the widower through this difficult time. Derrick rises and publicly expresses his desire to bury Ava here where she lay in the yard, where she was last able to see her children. He explains he wants to allow the boys a chance to properly celebrate their mother, her love for them and her amazing accomplishments, with a small burial ceremony.

Blue once again takes on a leadership role and begins delegating tasks to the OWALs who showed up to show their support and give their condolences. Some people are sent to gather tools to dig a grave for the mother of two, others are sent to get candles and flowers for the memorial service that will be occurring soon. A few people who don't receive a role in preparing for the memorial service take it upon themselves to organize food and drinks for after the burial.

Derrick stays with Ava while everyone else gets to work. He wants a few more minutes with the woman who meant everything to him. Patrick and Blue stand nearby making sure that all of the helpers know where to go and what to do. Katie and Nick decide to take the boys in the backyard to pick some flowers for their mother. The boys feel safe with them and easily oblige their request.

Adam looks around the yard carefully at his options of flowers. He wants to be sure to pick the perfect ones. Katie watches the young boy mulling over his options and in that moment she thinks about how it is such a beautiful sight and if the circumstances weren't so grim, it could be a beautiful picture to add to her memory. Adam finally makes his selection and grabs a handful of daffodils. He runs back over to where Katie and Nick are standing to oversee the flower gathering.

Katie gets down to Adam's eye level and gently speaks to him, "Those are the most beautiful daffodils, Adam. Your mother would have loved these."

At the mention of his mother's approval, Adam smiles the largest smile while tears and confusion fill his eyes. For a moment he remains silent, and he looks like he is deep in thought or searching through his memory for something.

"I chose these because they remind me of my mom's beautiful, yellow hair," Adam explains as he pushes the bouquet into his face to hide his tears and to take in the soothing scent of the flowers.

Watching the interaction between Katie and Adam unfold is when the grief really hits Nick. He thought he had felt the deepest level of grief over losing Ava when he had to deliver the news of her passing to Derrick, but he finds this moment to be much worse. He can't look Adam in the eyes. The boy that once sat on the lab table in front of him, scared, longing for his mother, will now never see her again because Nick decided to free them from the lab and put them in danger. He thought what he was doing was the right thing, but at this moment, watching the young boy shield his eyes with daffodils that remind him of his mother, it doesn't feel like it was the right thing to do.

Science and the government should not have let things get this far, he thinks, mentally unloading his grief. He always counts on scientific reasoning as a way to explain why things are the way they are, and how to change them. Steps could have been taken early on to learn more about the *Modified*. Scientists could have been working on this for years. However, his trust in medical advancements once again let him down and has taken yet another important woman from his life too early. Nick thinks back to the loss of his own mother and immediately feels closer to Adam.

Dr. Cyrus recalls a time before he was a renowned scientist, when he was just a young man—still feeling like a boy, saying goodbye to his mother at her funeral service. He stood before the deep hole that they had lowered her into and held his own bouquet of flowers as if that was somehow supposed to help him get over the fact that she was gone forever. He dropped the pink lilies into the hole as a way of saying goodbye.

Nick begins picturing Adam carrying those freshly picked daffodils over to a freshly dug grave and tossing them in as his own way of letting go of his mother. Nick's mother's death helped guide him to become the person he is today and each step he has taken and will take in the future is because of her. Adam's loss will do the same to him now. The thought of the small boy taking on such a heavy burden pains Nick more than anything. Adam is only 8 years old and now he won't even get to spend some of his most personality-defining years of his life with his mother who fiercely loved him and even so, his entire life will still be shaped by her.

Adam clears his throat and holds his breath to avoid more tears. He hands the bouquet over to Katie and runs across the yard to help his little brother choose flowers of his own. The two boys return, hand-in-hand, with more flowers, this time a variety of colors fill the freshly picked bouquet. As Katie compliments the boys on their fine flower choices, Patrick appears around the side of the house making his way towards them.

When PJ is within reasonable talking distance he announces, "We're all ready for the memorial service." His voice creaks the words out and both Katie and Nick can tell he has been crying too.

As the group makes their way around the side of the house into the front yard their senses are inundated by the volume of food, people, and decorations. Blue and Patrick have done a great job delegating and helping set up. It looks like a proper celebration of life.

Folding tables with a hodgepodge of dishes line the side of the yard. The aromas of the different kinds of food fill the air, somehow making the environment more welcoming. Each small dish that resides on the nicely decorated tables represents someone who cares about the cause and about the Ardi family.

Along the sidewalk are potted plants that the OWAL members have gathered and lined up as decorations. The plants bring life back into the bare yard. The variation of flowers and colors welcome all of the guests who are attending the gathering, making it seem more like a normal funeral service.

Lit candles are placed all around the grave that was dug by some of the men. The ambiance of the lighting is calming. Ava is placed on a white sheet near the freshly dug hole. Her face is illuminated in the candlelight. It looks as though someone spent some time cleaning up Ava and brushing out her hair so she would look more like herself when it came time to say goodbye.

The yard and street is filled by the OWAL members sitting and waiting for the ceremony to begin while holding lanterns and candles to light up the area as the sun goes down. Each OWAL holds a single flower to honor Ava with. Looking out into the yard, it seems as though the number of people who initially arrived at the house after the riot has doubled, if not tripled, Nick observes. It is a good thing that the police in the area are too busy dealing with the aftermath of the downtown area to worry about such a large crowd gathered on the street in front of Patrick's house.

The young boys make their way to their spots near their father along the gravesite. They settle in, holding on to one another, supporting each other the way Ava and Derrick have raised them to. Blue stands up and gestures to the large crowd to quiet down so that the service can begin. A wave of silence flies through the air.

Derrick stands up tall, straightening his spine. He is a tall man by nature, but his presence grows larger in this moment. He clears his throat to begin speaking.

"Thank you all for coming out tonight and supporting my family in what is our most difficult and defining moment. As I look at my beautiful wife lying here, I can't help but feel a mix of emotions. I am so angry for what has happened to her and how my boys are going to be changed by this forever. I am, at the same time, extremely grateful for the time that I had with Ava. She was, is, and will forever be the love and light of my life. Not a lot of people know how we met and sometimes that is intentional."

Derrick stops to wipe his eyes and clear his throat once more before continuing.

"Ava was a nurse in a rehab facility before she became a stay-at-home mother to our two boys. We met because I was an addict. She met me while I was at the lowest point in my life. She is, without a doubt, the reason I am alive today. She saw the good in me even when I was unable to see it in myself. She had a way of always seeing the best in people and making sure that people lived up to the expectations that she set for them. Ava gave me a reason to live and showed me how beautiful life can be if we surround ourselves with the right people. While I am both angry and grateful, I am also filled with another emotion—hope. I am hopeful that I can use the strength that Ava has taught me and continue to be the best person I can for our boys. Ava would want us to continue fighting for what is right and to build a safe future for all and that is what we are going to do. I love you Ava and I always will. You'll always be my guardian angel."

Sobs are heard throughout the crowd as Derrick finishes his speech. He takes a deep breath to collect himself before he picks up a few flowers lying near his feet and places them on top of his wife's chest before placing her hands over them. The small boys begin to follow and do the same with the bouquets that they collected from the backyard. Adam holds his head high trying not to succumb to his tears again. Ben, being so small, doesn't know how to act and runs into his father's arms for safety, which he finds quickly.

Patrick and Nick move from where they are standing, behind Derrick, and each grab an end of the sheet that Ava's body is on. They move towards the recently dug hole and slowly lower her in. Her body slowly settles into its final resting place, and she looks at peace.

As Patrick stands back up he begins to speak to the crowd, "I think it is important that those of us who really got to know Ava over the last few days get the opportunity to say something about her in this moment and I would like to start."

Patrick pauses as he adjusts his stance and clears his throat.

"I wasn't expecting the Ardi family to show up on my doorstep. My long-time friend, Katie, brought them to me thinking that I could help save them from the government and corporations that are after them. I don't know why Katie chose me to be the one to help, but I am so glad she presented me with the honor of getting to know Ava and her family. I don't have a lot of family and frankly, I don't have a lot of friends anymore either. I've been married to my work since I got into the police academy. Meeting the Ardi's and watching the way Ava loved and protected her family makes me long for more than the life I was living. I hope to one day meet a woman like Ava and raise a family with her. Over the last few days, I am thankful to say that Ava, Derrick, and their boys have found a place in my heart. They have shown me what my life is missing, and I will no longer be married to my job, but rather committed to helping Derrick, Dr. Cyrus, and my friend Katie ensure that Adam and Ben are taken care of." Patrick finishes speaking and picks up some of the flowers along the side of the grave and throws them in as his final farewell to his friend.

Katie stands up from her seat in the front of the crowd and walks over to the backside of the grave so she can face the crowd in front of her and look down at her friend Ava for the last time. Katie feels in her heart that it is her turn to speak, but she doesn't know how to explain her feelings about Ava. She decides to just be honest about how the past few days have felt.

"As I look down at my friend, Ava, I feel regret. Over the course of the last few days she has shown me how unconditional love looks. She played with her kids even when she was tired and scared, just to show them normalcy and safety. She cooked meals and tended to everyone else's feelings because she was the strength in our group. While I helped her cook and watched her play with the boys, I didn't think to get to know more about Ava. I was so wrapped up in what was happening to all of us that I forgot to look at the bigger picture. I forgot to look at the 'why' behind it all. The answer to why we are fighting for the rights of the MODs. I look at Ava now, and I know why. It is because of people like Ava and her family that we need to fight. We must fight for the person who wants to protect their children. We must fight for the children who will lose countless family members to violence if this doesn't end. For Ava I will fight. For the woman who, if I spent more time looking at the bigger picture and lived in the moment, could have become like my sister," Katie says as her sadness fills the ears of all who listen.

Nick sees that Katie is hurting and walks closer to her and grips her hand tightly while she picks up flowers on the ground and drops them into the deep grave. It is his turn to speak now. All eyes in the crowd turn to him, awaiting his words.

Dr. Cyrus begins speaking slowly, "The first time I saw Ava Ardi was in a waiting room of the Human Biology Research Department's lab level. She was shaken up because they had taken Adam from her and put him in a quarantine room to study him. I was the one they had enlisted to study him, but from the moment I saw her in that waiting room I knew I had to do whatever I could to help them. I'll be honest when I say that I didn't plan to break them out of the lab and rush them into hiding here at this house before you. I also didn't know ahead of time that things would unfold as they have over the last few days with our online postings. One thing that I do know is that when I saw Ava in that waiting room, she reminded me a lot of my own mother and I chose my actions based on what I thought they both would want me to do. Ava's entire life revolved around her children and their happiness." Nick's voice begins to squeak and lose its volume as the tears once again fill his eyes. He stops for a moment to wipe them away with his hand.

He speaks up again, "The more I got to know her and watched her interact with everyone around her, the more I realized that this group of people is my family. Katie, Ava, Patrick, Derrick, Adam and Ben are more like family to me than anyone in my life has been in the longest time. A few nights ago, Ava and Katie cooked us a home cooked meal and we sat around the table enjoying it as if we had done it every night before. I don't think Ava knew how much that meal meant to me. It was not only the moment that I realized we had become a true family, but the moment that I knew I was in love with Ms. Katie Kleug."

Nick turns and looks at Katie. He holds his gaze on her as he wipes the tears from his eyes. Katie, who is still holding Dr. Cyrus's hand, squeezes it tightly while every other part of her body freezes. He looks back and smiles through his tears before continuing his speech.

"Ava was in part how I figured that out about myself because she and Derrick had shown me what a partnership looked like. My parents weren't together when I was younger and I always resented that part of my life, so much so that I never thought I would be able to find someone I cared enough about to ever stick it out. Seeing the Ardi's together showed me that even in the worst of times, working hard to find happiness together is always worth it. As I lowered Ava into her resting place, I knew I wasn't saying goodbye. Ava is here with us and her spirit will live on in everything we do next."

Similarly to everyone else, Nick takes a handful of flowers from the grass below him and tosses them on top of Ava. Blue rises from her seated position in front of the large audience and walks over to where Ava is put to rest. The large audience watches closely, looking for direction on what to do next.

Blue speaks as she drops a single purple flower into the grave, "For Ava, I will fight," she shouts.

Other OWALs began to rise and follow Blue in saluting their lost member. A line is formed and one by one each member in the crowd walks past the open grave and drops in their handpicked flower. When the procession ends people begin to spread out and it is time to celebrate the woman who was taken too soon.

Patrick begins to stream music from his phone to his outdoor stereo system that hangs from the porch. People join in by eating and dancing in celebration. Voices buzz in every direction, talking about the events of the day.

Somehow when the procession ended Katie and Nick got separated. Now that things are settling in she begins to look for Nick to address what he said in his speech about the way he feels about her. She weaves in and out of the groups until she finds him sitting on a short retaining wall along the side of the house that holds several well-kept rose bushes. He notices her arrival and smiles shyly, barely making eye contact.

Nick isn't really sure of where they stand now. He is relieved to finally tell her how he feels and to lay all of the cards out on the table, but they have never really spoken about their relationship before, and he isn't sure he made the right choice by choosing to start the conversation in front of hundreds of people. Katie sits down right beside him and grabs his hand, trying to force him to make eye contact with her.

He looks into her eyes as the pressure of her hand on his grows. Nick can't tell what she is thinking by looking into her eyes or at her facial expression. Instead of trying to guess how she feels, he decides it's best to hear it directly from her.

"I'm sorry that I put you on the spot during my speech. I was feeling very emotional. I shouldn't have done that to you," he says apologetically.

"Does that mean that you don't mean what you said?" Katie probes.

Her heart begins aching at the thought that he only said it in the heat of the moment, without really meaning it.

"No, I meant every word, but I shouldn't have come out and said it to such a large group of people without telling you first," he clarifies.

She starts to feel the ache inside disappear and in its place is something else.

"I love you, too!" Katie blurts enthusiastically.

She begins panting and tripping over her words, "I don't know how it happened. We haven't even known each other that long, but there is this unspoken connection between us that is unlike anything I've ever felt before. There's so much going on. It is all just such bad timing and such a bad idea."

Nick nods in agreement but turns his whole body towards her and grabs her other hand so that he is holding both of her hands in his on his lap now.

"I'll admit the timing isn't great," he says lightly, followed by a quick laugh.

"I know things are dangerous right now and I can't promise that it'll all turn out alright. You and I both know we are just playing each day by ear and doing what we think is right at the moment. I don't want to do this with anyone else, though. Derrick losing Ava has really clarified a lot for me. I want it to be you and me taking on whatever comes next," Nick explains with hope filling the air.

Katie leans in and kisses him lightly. She frees her hands from his and places them on his cheeks as she looks up into his eyes when she speaks, "Let's do this together then. This assignment brought us together for a reason. We can make a difference if we stick together."

CHAPTER 28

Before Nick can respond to Katie's last words, Blue comes around the corner of the house and interrupts them.

"I'm sorry to break up your conversation, but there is something that I think both of you need to know," she says, mustering up the courage to continue.

"I found out how the AmerEagles group knew about our march. It was Terrence..." she pauses, making a facial expression that could only be explained as anger and sadness mixed together.

Katie and Nick sit stunned hearing the words coming from Blue's mouth. Her stepbrother Terrence seemed so into the movement when they saw him earlier in the day.

"During the clash with AmerEagles downtown, I saw Terrence tear open his button up shirt and reveal the same red shirt that the others were wearing. He joined in the fight from the other side. During all the commotion I tried to confront him, but there was just too much going on that I couldn't talk to him. He knows I saw him. We made eye contact. He has been dodging my calls ever since," she says with betrayal in her voice.

"I can't believe he would do such a thing. He seemed so genuine when we met him earlier," Katie notes.

"I'm so sorry, you guys. I feel so guilty that I brought him into your lives. It's my fault that your group is going through this right now. It's my fault those kids are without a mother now."

A cry escapes Blue's mouth as she finishes speaking.

"It is not your fault, Blue. He is your family, and you thought you could trust him. Every single one of us went into today knowing it was a risk. None of this is on you. Ava's death isn't on you," Nick says convincingly.

Katie stands up and silently hugs Blue for what seems like forever. The two eventually part and wipe their tears. Blue, Katie, and Nick rejoin the party by making their way around the yard and meeting as many of the OWALs as possible. Blue tries to distract Derrick and the young boys by asking them to dance with her. Derrick doesn't have it in him to move on from his thoughts so quickly, but the young boys take her up on the offer and join her and her friends.

Eventually the music volume is lowered and people begin to call it a night. Blue makes her way around to all of the small groups that have formed to let them know to be watching and listening for OWAL updates as the days and weeks progress. Uncertainty hangs in the air, but at the same time everyone knows things aren't over. They have only just begun.

Chapter 29

May 13th, 2082 - OWALS

A worldwide broadcast stops the world cold. All radios, televisions, and streaming services go silent. The radio plays an automated message: 'The President of the United States of America to address the World within minutes'. All screens display the same message on a plain, neon blue screen.

Up until this point the executive branch has not been very vocal about the division that is growing wider between those who support the MODs and those who are fearful and hateful of them. The news outlets have been wondering for years when a formal announcement would address the changes that are occurring throughout the world.

The stance of the president and her counsel on the topic has been unclear because while she is generally considered conservative, she does have platforms on some topics that appeal to a more liberal crowd. She really is the people's president. Up until the *Modification* crisis started—at the end of her first term, she was known as one of the most loved presidents in modern history. She won her second term by a landslide. While most people don't blame her for the *Modification* crisis she has lost a little bit of support from her constituents because of her silence on the topic.

Everyone in the world is watching what is to come next, hoping the president will address these uncertain times and bring the country back to the solid foundation it had when she was first elected president. No one knows what stance the president will take or what support she will offer, but one thing is always true when it comes to politics: not everyone is going to be happy about the outcome.

Nick, Patrick, Katie, the Ardis, and countless other MODs and supporters that they have gained over the days, crowd around the small television in Patrick's living room to await the important announcement from the president. Patrick seems hopeful that things will turn out alright after this public announcement and that he can return to his job. It's been a difficult time since he made the decision that he would now be a part of the resistance and because of that he can't continue on as a police officer. He is glad to have met his new friends, but he misses the stability and comfort of his old life.

Derrick sits on the couch with his boys in his lap hoping the world can once again become a safe place to raise his children. He snuggles his boys tightly and feels lucky to be surrounded by other people who feel the same way that he does. Now that he's lost Ava to the cause, he is now, more than ever, invested in the revolution. He wants to make sure that her death wasn't in vain.

Katie doesn't feel much of anything at this point. Confusing emotions fill her body, causing her to be numb. She looks over at Nick and wonders what is in store for them next. She feels that no matter the outcome of this broadcast, they are now going to be in the limelight as a rebel group.

Nick returns the look to Katie. He can tell she is deep in thought. He grabs her hand and holds it tight. This is the moment when everything changes, he decides. Good or bad, something is about to give. The screen goes black for a moment before turning on to show the President of the United States up close. Her name fills the bottom of the screen in dark blocky letters, 'Madam President Karen Moros now speaking'.

"Good afternoon to all who are gathered around to hear this address. As president, I have had to make difficult decisions day in and day out during my entire presidency and today is no different," President Moros begins.

The camera pans out slowly to show the other people standing beside her on stage. Nick freezes. The room goes silent, as if all of the air had been sucked out. Standing to the right of President Moros with a smile plastered on his face is none other than Nathan Pierce, CEO of MoonCycle. On the other side of the president stands David Bruner.

David doesn't have a smile on his face the same way that Nathan does, but he still looks smug with the way he holds his head high while standing there as if he is better than everyone else. Nick can't believe what he is watching. A pain forms in the pit of his stomach and keeps growing. The pain feels as if it is consuming him. He can tell from the smile on Nathan's face and the way Bruner looks, as though he is untouchable, that what is about to come next isn't going to be good for anyone.

President Moros continues her speech, "With the consultation of some of my most important advisors on this topic..." She gestures to David Bruner first and then Nathan Pierce as their names flash across the screen, "It is our scientific belief that those who are *Modified* are a risk to the public. Not only are the characteristics of *Modification* dangerous to us as a species, but those who are now in support of the *Modified* and the process of *Modification* have become rebel forces that put us all in danger."

Gasps and cries of horror fill the room where Nick sits still holding Katie's hand tightly.

"The Human Biology Research Department and Mr. Nathan Pierce, CEO and representative of MoonCycle, have agreed to collaborate to find a scientific way to stop the *Modification* process. It is their belief that because they were able to alter DNA with their Half Moon product that they will be able to do it again for our purposes," she notes.

Nathan Pierce begins to wave at the crowd as if he just attended his coronation as king of the world. Nick's stomach turns as he watches the happiness fill the man who has already caused so much pain and suffering.

President Moros draws the attention back to her as she concludes, "At this time we are asking that all forces search out and bring in any person that they find *Modified* or in support of a *Modified* person and transport them to our holding facility in Washington D.C. or our containment facility located in Houston, Texas. Anyone who comes willingly will be provided assistance in receiving medical care as it becomes available. We are considering all rebel forces a threat and we are now declaring war on any individual who joins or shows support for Dr. Nicholas Cyrus and the rebel group he has started known as the One with All Life or the OWALs. You are all traitors of the state and we are coming for you."

Chapter 30

May 15th, 2082 - OWALS

It has been two days since the broadcast and the group, now including Blue, have stayed inside of PJ's house with the blinds drawn trying to figure out what comes next. No one was expecting the president to declare war on all MODs and now any plan they come up with just seems far too dangerous and nearly impossible to execute.

Derrick and Blue remove themselves from Patrick, Nick, and Katie to try to keep things as normal as possible for Adam and Ben. They are taking turns feeding them and entertaining them while the rest of the group sets up a planning headquarters in the living room. Patrick, Katie, and Nick have a holographic map of the city projected from Patrick's phone on the coffee table trying to figure out what the best escape plan is to leave the city.

Katie is trying to pay attention to Nick and Patrick but hears something loud outside. She moves herself to the window and peeks through the blinds to try to see what is causing commotion in the streets. Two police cruisers and a police van pull up to a house kitty-corner from Patrick's. Katie watches intently as the police, dressed in riot gear, use a battering ram to break down the front door and enter the premises. Katie interrupts Nick and Patrick's city geography conversation to get them to watch with her.

Minutes later, the police re-enter their view from the window as they exit the house with a woman carrying a northern MOD baby. Following behind them are two police officers dragging the body of a beaten, bleeding man. The family of three is forced into the van just seconds before it speeds off. The remaining police officers stand around schmoozing one another as if the situation that just occurred does not affect them at all.

Katie releases her fingers from holding the blinds open. She turns around and sees Patrick and Nick looking at her with stunned expressions. Katie takes a second to collect her thoughts before speaking, but she comes up with nothing except bringing up their escape plan again.

"Well, what plan did you both come up with to get out of the city?"

Nick is about to respond when Patrick's phone begins buzzing on the table behind them. He picks it up and looks at the screen. He pauses for a moment deciding if he should answer. He clicks the button and says 'hello'. There are no other words coming out of his mouth. He just listens for forty-five seconds before saying 'thank you' and hanging up. The call seems mysterious to both Katie and Nick.

"Who was that?" Katie quickly asks, interested in who was on the other end of the line.

"It was one of my friends from the police station. It was a warning call," Patrick says with his face still stunned.

"What do you mean, a warning call?" probes Katie.

"Exactly what you think it means...now that we just saw what happened down the street. My friend explained that he knows I am part of the resistance and that he doesn't necessarily disagree with me joining, but he needs to continue to do his job. He asked me to forgive him for what I'm going to see him and my other co-workers doing now. He told me that he can keep the police away for a little longer from the house—two days, three max—but he says after that the officers will come and try to take us all away for our role in the uprisings because it is only a matter of time they find out I am housing you all when they complete the block checks. " Patrick finishes his sentence and sits down on the couch feeling defeated.

The three sit silently thinking about what this means for their group. Their thoughts are interrupted when Blue enters the living room with more news.

"One of my OWAL sources just messaged me with some news. It is not good," she says.

"We also just received some news of our own," Patrick responds.

"What have you heard?" Blue retorts.

"My cop buddy let me know that the MODs are starting to be pulled from their homes and taken. He's keeping the heat off of our side of the block, but he can't hold the authorities back for more than a couple of days, so we have to come up with a plan and stat."

Blue nods and begins explaining what she's heard.

"I heard through my OWAL channels that people are already being taken, but that isn't why I came out here. One of my contacts told me that Nathan Pierce and President Moros just put out a smear campaign on national television and all over the internet about your credibility as a scientist, Nick. I think you should see it."

The group positions themselves on the couches so that they are in front of the television while Patrick begins streaming the campaign that he found on the internet so that they can all see it together. Nick is worried that this campaign will make people less confident in his leadership abilities and in the cause.

The screen starts off black with words across it that plainly state, 'This video is approved by President Moros and Nathan Pierce - CEO MoonCycle'. The screen changes to President Moros sitting at her desk in the oval office calmly speaking about how she has put her trust in Nathan Pierce because, he and all of his companies, especially MoonCycle, have done so much for the world. She recommends that the entire United States stand with her in support of Mr. Pierce. The screen changes over to Nathan Pierce in the Washington D.C. lab that Nick was working in just a few days prior. The video portrays Nathan Pierce as a scientist by showing him wearing a lab coat and surrounding him with other people in lab coats pretending to work in a lab. The others are likely MoonCycle employees that Nathan brought over to help him with the smear campaign, but when scanning the faces Nick can't confirm or deny their employment with MoonCycle.

Piece begins speaking, "As noted in our previous announcement, Dr. Cyrus is trying to steer you, the American people, away from safety and into danger and uncertainty. He lied about creating a chemical compounded serum in his last video using the water he collected in South Carolina. This is not true, and he is bluffing in order to gain more followers. Ever since I first met Dr. Cyrus when he started working for MoonCycle, he was always a fame chaser. Unfortunately, that is why my company had to cut ties with him. The prestige he gained from HalfMoon wasn't enough for him. In fact, he claimed that he created it mostly on his own, which just isn't true. There are many great scientists who put just as much work in on HalfMoon as he did. He's trying to bamboozle you all. Please don't listen to him. He does not know how dangerous *Modification* is. We need to work together to solve this world crisis and take back the human race as we know it."

The screen goes black after Nathan Pierce stops speaking and logos pop up all over the darkened screen. The Presidential Seal, MoonCycle's logo, numerous logos from Nathan Pierce's other companies and many city seals, including Beaufort, are displayed brightly for several seconds. Patrick closes the app on his phone and the stream shuts off. Each person in the living room turns their attention to Nick to see his reaction. Nick shakes his head, disapproving of what he just saw.

"It's a lie! I never cared about fame. I wanted out of that contract. I created that serum on my own and made him millions and now he tries to discredit me. I can't believe how he is spinning this to make me seem like a monster. It makes no sense. What kind of motive would I have for any of this?"

"We know it is a lie, Nick, but what do we do now? We can't lose traction now or OWAL members will get scared and go into hiding. Everything we've worked for will all be over before we know it," Blue explains.

"I'm going to send out another video. I know what needs to be done. Patrick, can you please get everything set up? I will be down in a minute. I need to explain to the people that I am innocent of the terrible things Pierce is putting on me. No one will want me as a leader if I don't respond to this with full confidence," Dr. Cyrus says assertively.

The group, minus Derrick—who is still protecting the children at all times since Ava's death, reconvenes several minutes later in the office. Patrick didn't have to do much to get ready because the setup they used in the last video was never taken down. Nick takes a seat in front of the camera and gives Patrick the signal to start.

The red light turns on and Nick begins to speak, "Hello OWALs and fearful citizens of the United States. I know this is a very uncertain time for us all and I, myself, am even scared of what might become of the great country we live in. I want to address the libel that Mr. Pierce is advertising about me all over the media. I can tell you for certain that the chemical compound serum that I created is real. It was created from the water I gathered in South Carolina, not too far from the MoonCycle plant there. I don't have all the money in the world, like Nathan Pierce, President Moros and all the other people that they have roped into this, so I know that all you are hearing right now are words that may not provide you with enough proof for you to trust me. Instead of continuing to ask you to trust that I am honest, I am going to show you."

Nick pulls out the shimmering, blue serum from his pocket, but this time it is in a syringe. He looks past the camera and makes eye contact with Katie. Her eyes grow large and fill with tears. She wants to scream, but knows it is too late. Nick takes the syringe, turns his neck to the left and jabs the sharp needle in quickly pushing down on the top of it until all the liquid flows out of the tube and into his body. He closes his eyes and takes a deep breath. Like magic, within seconds holes begin forming on the sides of his neck. Patrick zooms in on Nick's upper body to show the change. The holes on Nick's neck begin to grow larger and air begins to escape through them. Within a minute, he has full blown gills that are moving up and down with each breath he takes. Nick looks directly at the camera and smiles arrogantly. He doesn't say anything more and Patrick ends the live stream.

Once the feed cuts, Nick hops off the chair and quickly makes his way to Katie. But before he can reach her, she turns and abruptly runs out of the room, through the dark basement, and up the stairs, whimpering the entire way. Nick is surprised by Katie's reaction. He doesn't expect her to be happy about what just occurred, but he had hoped that she would understand why he went to such extreme measures without warning anyone. He had to make a statement, and this was how to do it, but if he talked to Katie or any of the group ahead of time he may not have had the courage to go through with it.

Nick races after Katie and eventually finds her when he reaches the kitchen. She is sitting silently crying at the table. He pulls out the chair next to her and slowly sits down, thinking about the best way to approach her. As she notices him settling into his chair, she slightly turns her face away from him so he can't make eye contact with her. She knows if she looks into his eyes and really takes in the changes on his neck that she won't be able to contain her emotions.

"Katie, please look at me," he begs.

His voice sounds so sad. She spends several seconds trying as hard as she can to resist him. It doesn't work and she turns her face back towards him with deep sorrow. As their eyes lock, Nick falls deep into Katie's gaze. He wants to tell her that he loves her, but he doesn't want her to see it as a ploy to get back into her good graces.

"I'm really sorry to catch you off guard. I just knew that if I talked to you about this that you would try to talk me out of it and tell me there was another way, when I knew nothing else would be as impactful as this," he says.

"I'm not upset with you about keeping it a secret from me, I get it. I really do. I'm upset with myself more than I am with you. The second that you injected yourself with that serum I felt something unexpected. I never really had a problem with anyone who was *Modified*, but in all honesty, I don't know anyone with young kids and the only people I've ever met before who are *Modified* are the Ardi boys, so I've had very little exposure," she says to clarify.

She pauses and takes a deep breath to try to calm herself so she can try to put her emotions into words, "I love the Ardi's. I swear I do. I'm not afraid of them or anything silly like that, but I have to be honest in that I really never pictured myself being with someone who is *Modified*."

Katie looks down at her hands as she twiddles her thumbs, still trying to calm her nerves. Nick notices and puts his hand on top of hers to stop the movement. He holds it there until she draws her eyes up to meet his.

"I know that you think I am judging you for what you said, but I'm not. I don't know how I'd feel if our places were reversed, but I know that our connection is strong, my feelings about you haven't changed. I really believe we can work through this. I know I look a little different now, but I'm still the same person," he explains.

"I know it's still *you* who is in front of me and I still feel the same way about you as I did before you evolved, but I just feel ashamed of my immediate reaction. I'm just scared. Things for people who are *Modified* are extremely dangerous now and this just adds another layer to things we need to be cautious about," she says.

Nick understands where Katie is coming from. He knew the risks before injecting himself but decided it would be worth it still to do so. He starts to lean in to kiss her and reassure her that it will all be alright, but before he gets close enough, Patrick joins them in the kitchen.

"Sorry to interrupt. I was just coming to get something to drink and check on you, Katie."

Katie abruptly pulls away from Nick and sits up straight in her chair. Both Nick and Patrick notice Katie's reaction but choose not to acknowledge it.

"No need to apologize PJ, I was just going to tell Katie that now that our traction should be renewed, we need to get out of the house and quickly", Nick says.

"I agree. Blue just told me she has some feelers out in the OWAL universe to see what our options are. She said she'll come upstairs once she gets off of some calls," PJ responds.

"Perfect, I know it's early, but I am going to rest for a while. I think all of the excitement of the day has tired me out. Please come get me if you hear any news," Nick says with exhaustion in his words.

Nick gets up and leaves the table and PJ replaces him in his seat so he can speak with Katie. She is also tired and doesn't want Patrick to make a big deal out of what happened in the basement, but she stays seated because the comfort she knows Patrick will offer her is very appealing.

He asks her how she is doing, but they both know that is a formality. He can see on her face that she isn't okay with what happened in the basement. She shrugs his question off to help contain her emotions. Patrick notices her attempt and leans over and pulls her into a long, tight hug. Her emotions get the best of her, and she releases the tears that she had been holding back as she snuggles her face into his shoulder.

“I really am okay,” she sobs.

She lifts her head from his shoulder and sniffles away the remaining sadness. As she regains her strength and pulls her head away from PJ, their cheeks graze and a second of sexual tension fills Katie causing her to flinch back into an upright position much quicker than both of them expected. She isn’t sure where the feeling is coming from because she hasn’t felt this way about Patrick before, well at least not since she was much younger—when a small part of her thought that their friendship could eventually turn into a happily ever after, but with who they were then it could have never ended well. She shakes the feelings thinking that it is just a product of her heightened emotional state. Patrick feels the tension too but decides the same thing: that it is caused by the situation.

“Katie, I know that things are off right now, but we can’t let emotion get the best of us. We need to be on top of our game to keep everyone safe. I need you to be strong right now.”

Katie nods knowing that PJ is right. At this moment she sees that PJ has grown up so much since she last visited him. Seeing him in a new light confuses her feelings for him a bit. The young boy she used to know was never someone she felt would take responsibility for himself or others, but this man in front of her now, is doing just that and is doing it knowing the consequences could be very dangerous.

After talking for a while, the two decide to take a mental break from all the stressful topics and make their way to watch something mindless in the living room. As soon as PJ’s bottom hits the couch cushion his phone begins buzzing in his pocket. He looks at it and sees it is his friend again, Joe, from the police station. He answers the phone and before he can even say ‘hello’, Joe begins talking frantically.

“Janes, don’t say anything for a minute. Just listen. I’ve been talking to a lot of guys down at the precinct just to keep tabs on everything and to make sure that they weren’t coming after your house next. They aren’t coming at this moment, so don’t worry about that, turns out you still have more friends here than you thought. The places that they are taking the MODs to are really bad. Worse than I thought it would be. I'm sure some news outlets will be outing the environment of the camps soon. I can't even stomach thinking that I am part of this...I saw the post of that doctor—scientist guy, online. It's going viral and things are going to get amped up in the morning. The problem is that I don't think I can protect you as long as I thought. While they aren't targeting your house at this moment, I think things are about to get much worse and if you're going to leave, I think you have to do it tonight. I can help you a little bit by taking over the patrol of part of your community area tonight so that you have a better chance."

"Thank you so much, Joe, for this information. I appreciate you trying to protect me and mine. We will take you up on that offer for tonight. I'll figure something out. Thanks again," PJ says and hangs up the phone.

Patrick gets up without saying anything to Katie and rushes to the basement to find Blue. Katie doesn't take offense to his behavior but rather follows him in search of answers. They find Blue sitting in the office on the computer and phone simultaneously trying to find answers. When she sees them both approach, she tells the person on the phone she has to go and hangs up, without a proper farewell.

"What is it now?" she asks, sounding annoyed and overwhelmed at the same time.

Patrick explains what Joe told him, being as detailed as he can with what he remembers. Blue explains that even though she doesn't have every single aspect of their escape planned out she has found some safe houses along the way to DC with people who are willing to help transport the group. She also found a safe place for Derrick and boys to stay for a while. Patrick and Katie are following Blue's detailed plans as she speaks and only Katie interrupts once to ask why they are going back to DC. Patrick already knows the answer, so he doesn't need Blue to respond, but he continues to listen as she explains the reasoning to Katie.

"It is important for us to go to the front lines and fight in this war and believe me, it is a war now. All of the OWALs that I have been communicating with all day are getting ready. They want to storm the streets of the capital and let President Moros, MoonCycle, and all their other minions know that we aren't afraid of them. It is important for us to be there and fight for this while we have the momentum," Blue responds.

Katie knows that Blue is right, but this isn't what she wants to hear. Things are moving too fast, and she doesn't like it. She announces that she is going to go break the news to Nick and Derrick about the plans and that she will leave Blue and PJ to themselves to work out all the details.

Katie first stops by Derrick's room and relays the information to him before telling Nick. After she explains the situation, the adults all convene in the living room to hash things out. Tonight, they will leave without looking back.

Chapter 31

May 15th, 2082 - SANTOS

Sheriff R. Santos sits in his kitchen eating dinner with his son while news feed of the MOD internment camps plays across every channel. His son, Javi, was so proud of how his father had been handling the town's outbursts in recent days, but now with news of the camps, things feel different. The camps show a new side to what being *Modified* means and it is a scary sight.

The feed on one channel shows a large area enclosed by a fence at least thirty feet high, topped with barbed wire, with guards on the ground and in the towers surrounding it. It looks like an old non-functioning prison that is being repurposed. The yard is filled with giant cages that are packed with people who must be considered overflow from the interior of the building. While the cages are very large in size, the quantity of people in each of them makes them appear much smaller.

It has only been two days since the president's announcement, but the authorities already have hundreds, if not thousands, of people in just this camp alone. The camera pans to and from cages showing the treatment of the people in them. There are no surfaces to sleep on, nor coverage on the cages to shield people from the weather. Small children curl up into their parents' arms for safety in some of the corners of the cages where there are thin sheets and small pillows for 'comfort'. Other older children are squeezing their hands and fingers through the chain links of the cages begging the guards for food. The lack of sanitation is inhumane and present for the world to see from the image on the screen.

The camera hones in on a boy, who can't be more than eleven or twelve, with his face up against the metal fencing. There is dirt on his face and sadness in his eyes. As the camera begins to pan away, the boy turns his face, and the sun highlights the side of his head. A gasp leaves Javi's lips. The boy's ear has a thick piercing in it with a numbered tag hanging from it. Javi has never seen anything like this before, but he knows it isn't right.

As the video feed scans throughout the camp, Javi grows silent. Anguish fills him. As the camera passes more people, he begins to notice all the numbered tags hanging from the top of their ears, even the small children have them. Without thinking, Javi reaches up with both hands and touches the piercings on his earlobes. As he runs his fingers across the small studs in his ears, he remembers how painful it had been to get them pierced. He almost stopped after the first one, but he didn't want his ears to look uneven. He scrunches up his nose just thinking about the pain that would come from having the tougher, upper part of the ear punctured.

The camera eventually turns to the fence at the back of the camp and zooms in on it to show what has become of those who fought back. Javi takes a second to count. He ends at seventeen. Seventeen beaten, bloodied, bodies hang from nooses attached to the top of the outer fence facing in towards the camp. The glimpse he catches of each body is quick, but they appear to be all adults. All men.

Javi changes the channel and finds more footage of the camps. He continues to move through each station quickly, trying to take in all of the information. His blood boiling hotter with each click. He can feel his father looking at him, but he refuses to acknowledge him.

Rodrigo wants to comfort his son, but he knows part of his anger, if not most of it, is now directed at him. Watching Javi's jaw clench tighter as he changes each channel makes it clear that it is going to be extremely difficult to calm him down. Rodrigo feels that the anger is partially misplaced, but when he sees Javi's eyes widen at the sight of the boy who is tagged and numbered, he realizes he feels ashamed of himself as a parent and as a police officer for allowing this to happen. Javi is too young to realize that this is how cattle used to be tagged, but Rio remembers it from his childhood and knows no one should be treated that way. He realizes that while the entire treatment of the MODs is not his fault, he did play some role in how things have escalated.

Rodrigo tries to break the silence in hopes to salvage his relationship with the only person who really matters to him.

"Javi, we should turn this off. I can see you're really upset right now."

"Why, dad? Are you ashamed to see how the police are treating people? Are you ashamed to see all of the MODs and their family members being punished for existing?" he retorts.

Before Rodrigo can even try to calm him down, Javi shuts the TV off and stands up abruptly. He turns and makes direct eye contact and holds it longer than necessary just to show how serious he is.

"Dad, I need you to know that I am going to protest. I am going to join the OWALs. I don't care what you think about it. I don't care if you try to arrest me. I don't care what happens to me anymore. What is happening isn't right and you know it. How would you feel if I was in one of those cages?" he says before he pauses for a second to catch his breath. His emotions are beginning to get the best of him, and his eyes are watering up.

He clears his throat and continues, "I've wanted to be just like you for my entire life. Even when you and mom split up, you admitted that you made mistakes and still tried to be a good dad—a good person. Growing up and becoming a police officer, like you, always seemed so great because you made helping people a priority. It was never about having the same job as you. It was always about becoming the kind of person I thought you were. In the beginning of this mess, I thought you were doing the right thing by trying to control the situation, but if you stand by what is going on right now, then I don't think I can stand by you as your son any longer."

Rodrigo inhales sharply, taking in what his son just said to him. The words cut him to the core. He knows Javi is right and that things have gone too far. He's scared of what Pierce, Frank and the rest of those goons will do to him, but he knows he won't be able to live with himself if he lets Javi down. He fears that Javi will find out that he knew about how involved the government has been each step of the way.

"I'll come with you, Javi. Please just don't do anything dangerous. You don't know what these people are capable of. Let's at least come up with a plan."

Hours later, emotions have leveled out. Rodrigo agrees to accompany Javi north, near the DC area, where most of the OWAL action has recently been occurring and will likely continue to occur because it is getting the most attention on the news. He calls Frank and tells him that he will be leaving town for a little while to survey how other areas of the country are handling the uprisings. Luckily, Mayor Roy applauds his initiative because the last thing he can handle right now is dealing with Roy being unhappy.

Chapter 32

May 15th- May 16th, 2082 - OWALS

The group patiently waits in the darkened living room until it's time to go. The plan is to leave around one in the morning after the police patrols drop down to just one car. It is nearly midnight, and the boys are nestled up in Blue and Derrick's laps on the living room couch. Everyone, including the young boys, is wearing dark clothing so as to not draw attention to themselves when they leave the house. The first stop on the way to D.C. is to stop by one of the designated 'safe houses' three blocks from here to drop off Derrick and the boys.

Finally, after discreetly peering through one of the front windows for what seems like forever, the patrol vehicles have shifted to just one vehicle every twenty or so minutes down the blocks in this general vicinity. The group makes their way through the house and quietly out the back door attached to Patrick's kitchen. Every member of the group is doing their part by carrying backpacks filled with things they need for survival. Luckily earlier in the day, one of Blue's close friends was able to bring a few changes of clothing for all of the adults and the boys so that they could put a few outfits into their backpacks along with snacks.

The group creeps along the retention wall in Patrick's driveway until they are able to see if the street is still clear. They walk slowly, but with purpose, past several houses until they reach an alley. Once in the alley they pick up their speed to an almost running pace. As they approach the block that the safe house is on, they adjust their speed back to a slow crawl and peer around a fence that is blocking their view of the street. The coast is clear, so they inch their way to a house four driveways down. The front porch lights are off and only a small back porch light is illuminated, to indicate it is safe to enter.

The group enters in through a stairwell in the back of the house that leads to a basement. To their surprise, there are four other families with *Modified* family members taking advantage of this safe space. Once the group settles Derrick and the boys into a comfortably cushion padded corner where they can sleep, they begin to say their goodbyes. Blue hands Derrick an untraceable pay-as-you-go phone that looks like it is from the stone age. She tells him that she entered her number, Patrick's number, and two new phone numbers seemingly belonging to Nick and Katie as she hands them burner phones at the same time. Patrick, Nick, and Katie give the small boys heartfelt goodbyes before making their way to Derrick to let him know how much they all mean to the group.

Blue kneels down to say goodbye to Adam and Ben. She tells them how proud she is of them and how well they did at following directions and being quiet on the way here. She grabs them into a huge bear hug and waits for the boys to be the first to let go. After a long thirty seconds the boys are still holding on to Blue. Ben begins weeping.

"I don't want to lose my new mommy," Ben manages to say through his tears.

This breaks Blue's heart. She didn't realize how attached the boys have become to her over the last few days, despite spending all of her time taking care of them and Derrick. She also feels a huge wave of guilt come over her as she doesn't want to take away from the loss of their real mother, Ava. She looks up at Derrick with a look begging him to forgive her.

"I'm so sorry, Derrick. I didn't realize they were getting so attached to me. I'm sure it is just because they are still processing the loss of Ava. I would never try to replace her. I was just trying to help."

"It is alright, Tamera. I know you have a good heart. You are one of the kindest people we have ever met. Ava would be so grateful to you for helping take care of her boys over the last few days. She was always someone who just wanted what's best for her family, it never mattered how that was accomplished or who accomplished it," Derrick thoughtfully explains.

Blue's eyes smile when she hears him call her Tamera. If anyone else called her by her real name she would immediately correct them and ask that they refer to her as her nickname, but somehow when Derrick says it, she feels warm inside.

"Thank you for understanding, Derrick. I am going to miss you and the boys so much. It was so nice getting to spend time with you," Blue says with genuine sadness that she is leaving.

Derrick whispers to Blue so the boys don't hear.

"I know this sounds crazy, but would you consider staying with us?"

Blue doesn't know how to answer. The question catches her completely off-guard. A huge part of her does want to stay with the boys. The last few days gave her a glimpse as to what it is like to have a family, and she is yearning for that feeling to stay with her. She glances over at Nick who has been quietly observing the entire interaction. She doesn't need to verbally ask him. He just nods at her, and she knows that he understands what she's asking.

Instead of responding directly back to Derrick in a whisper, she changes her voice volume back to normal and says for all to hear, "You know what? I think it is probably best if I stay here with you all, afterall. I want to be able to help protect the boys and you definitely have your hands full, Derrick.

Derrick smiles shyly. The boys, however, begin jumping up and down with excitement. Blue quickly begins to quiet them down so there is no unnecessary attention brought on to the house. She quickly says her goodbyes to Nick, Katie, and Patrick as they head out to complete their journey.

The three make their way back up the driveway of the now completely dark house. They have a car ready for them a few blocks away near a park, out of what they believe to be the patrol boundary, that Blue arranged with some of the other OWAL members. They sneak down the street trying to hide behind anything along the way so that the streetlight won't illuminate their shadows. After two blocks there is a loud slam. It is too hard to tell what the noise is coming from, but their best guess is a car door. They scramble to hide so they can get their bearings. Nick and Katie end up behind a group of large waste containers between two houses. They look around to see if Patrick is anywhere in sight. After several minutes of silence there is shouting between two men, neither of which sound like Patrick.

"There is someone over here!" one voice shouts.

Sounds of rustling take over the silence.

"You can't take me. I'm a police officer," shouts Patrick.

"You'll have plenty of time to prove that to us down at the station," another voice announces with dominance.

Katie and Nick listen to three doors slam one at a time before moving red and blue lights illuminate off of the surrounding houses. They wait in silence for several minutes before they deem it safe to even look at one another. Nick turns and puts his hands on each side of Katie's face and pulls her head toward him until their foreheads are touching. The perspiration on their skin mixes together as their breathing becomes one.

"What do we do now?" Katie asks, still slightly trembling.

"I think we have to keep moving. I think that is what Patrick would want. If I were captured, I would want you both to keep to the plan," Nick says confidently.

"Maybe Blue will be able to reach out to some of her connections to see if they can find out about when Patrick will be released. I mean…they can't hurt him, right? He is a cop. One of their own," she says not fully believing they will treat him fairly.

"Patrick is capable of taking care of himself. I'm worried about him too, Katie, but we need to be smart right now. We can send a message to Blue, but we have to keep going."

Katie nods and before she knows it, they are approaching the car that Blue arranged for them. She somehow can't even remember how they got here. Her mind is on auto drive as she replays Patrick being taken by the police over and over in her head. Nick reaches under the front wheel well and grabs the taped key fob from right where Blue explained it would be. They quickly get in the car and speed off before they find themselves in the same situation as PJ.

Chapter 33

May 18th, 2082 - SANTOS

Rio doesn't like that Javi is trying to be in control of the situation, but he knows not to push him right now. Since watching the news coverage back in Beaufort, Javi is becoming more and more distant with every passing minute. They finally make their way to Washington D.C. and are waiting inside of the hotel, adjacent to Capitol Hill, that Rio arranged for them to stay in while they are here. Javi is being very secretive about their plans for the evening. Rio asks what the plan is every few minutes, but Javi continues to ignore him and keeps going into the bathroom to take phone calls in private. Rio tries to listen in each time Javi sneaks away, but he can't hear anything but muffled noises coming through the door. After several hours of this back and forth, Javi is ready to let Rio in on the plan.

"It is time for us to go," Javi says without looking Rio in the eyes.

"Where are we going?"

"There is a protest that is about to begin right in front of the Capitol Building. It is going to be the biggest protest yet. You don't have to come if you don't think you can support this," he explains, still avoiding eye contact.

In the blink of an eye they are in the middle of a huge crowd that is gathering around the Capitol Building. Thousands of people sporting signs with the OWAL symbol chanting for change are in the front of the building. On the back side of the building an equally large group holding AmerEagles signs is forming and spewing hate. Even though the pair arrived only minutes ago, Rio can already tell that this is going to end badly.

He scans the crowd to see if they have the numbers to take on the

AmerEagles. As he is looking around, he locks eyes with someone unexpected. He quickly turns his gaze away, but it is too late.

"Sheriff Santos, this is extremely unexpected," Nick says in a condescending tone as he and Katie approach him slowly.

"Nice to see you, Dr. Cyrus and Ms. Kleug," he says flatly.

Nick smirks. By eyeing up the young man next to him, who is a spitting image of his father, he can tell that Santos is not here as a police officer, but rather as a parent.

"Is this your son? He definitely takes after you," Cyrus says.

Before Rio can respond, his son pipes in, "Dr. Cyrus, I'm so honored to meet you. I am so moved by everything you've set into motion."

Nick doesn't respond directly to Javi but rather nods while staring down Santos.

"Cyrus, listen…I have made some mistakes in my life. One of them being aligning myself with Frank Roy. I can't go back in time, but I can try to move forward with a new purpose. I'm here to support my son and if he believes this is the right thing to do then I will be standing here fighting alongside you," Santos says with an apologetic tone.

"That is very big of you, Sheriff. Forgive me if I don't quite trust your intentions yet," Nick says with slight disdain in his voice.

"I don't expect you or Ms. Kleug to trust me at this point, but after this rally I would like to meet up with you to show you that I can be trusted. Please meet me at the Old Independence hotel this evening. I want to help you both in any way that I can."

Nick opens his mouth to respond with something snarky, but before any words can leave his mouth, Katie quickly interjects.

"We will be there. Meet at 9 p.m. in the lobby of the hotel. Come with only yourself and your son."

Rodrigo nods and the two groups go their own ways disappearing into the large sea of people. The crowds grow even larger over the next several minutes. Helicopters fly above taking in the magnitude of the gathering. Swat teams surround the area ready to pounce if things get out of control. Camera crews are closing in around the edges of the crowd trying to get footage of anything and everything.

Javi makes his way towards the left side of the building approaching the outer layer of the crowd. He slowly inches his way closer to where the two opposing groups meet with his father following closely behind him. Within seconds of reaching the front of the crowd, a loud popping noise fills the air. It sounds like a car backfiring or an automatic weapon going off. Rodrigo finds the source quickly with his eyes. Fireworks set off in a metal garbage can. Not everyone notices this is the cause of the noise. Panic ensues and the groups collide with violence. Rio tries to gather awareness of his surroundings, but there is too much happening around him at once. Before he can turn towards Javi to protect him, a large man runs full force into Javi, taking him to the ground with brute strength.

Javi looks for his father while trying to catch his breath. As he stands, he sees that his dad is now on top of the man who tackled him, beating him violently with his bare fists. The man who is wearing a red AmerEagles shirt decorated with a faded flag is now covered in blood. Javi pulls his father off of the man but takes a second to take in the damage that his father did in order to protect him. The man's face is painted in so much blood that it is impossible to see where it is coming from.

As the father and son pair retreat from the front lines, they spot Dr. Cyrus and Ms. Kleug again. This time the situation is less flattering for Dr. Cyrus. A man much larger than Nick has him in a choke hold and Katie is hitting the man in the back over and over with an old wooden baseball bat that she must have acquired since their last interaction. Despite her efforts, the large man does not seem to be budging, and Nick's face is turning more purple by the second.

Rio pulls Javi with him towards the doctor. He and Javi both pry the anti-OWAL's hands off of Dr. Cyrus and manage to take him to the ground forcefully causing his head to hit the pavement with a bone chilling cracking sound. Nick stands and gives the sheriff a look of approval. The four silently decide that they've seen enough and try to make their way to the outskirts of the never-ending crowd. As they move between bodies, they notice that the SWAT team is now involved—trying to break up the fighting. They quickly push through the crowd, not worrying about what damage they are causing along the way. The four make it to an opening and slip through to find themselves finally removed from the chaos. On their way out of the vicinity of the Capitol Building they see six SWAT team members dragging three AmerEagles members towards their van. One of the men looks familiar to Nick, but he can't put his finger on why.

Katie sees that Nick's vision is fixated on the SWAT team and the people they are detaining. It takes her a minute to realize why and then she sees that Terrence, Blue's stepbrother, is one of the men flailing and trying to get away from the officer. She taps Nick and whispers what she's noticed. It takes a minute for it to register with Nick, but now he realizes that Terrence not only betrayed Blue back in Pittsburgh but is now continuing his destruction in the D.C. area as well.

The SWAT team is moving quickly and the gap between them and Nick, Katie, Javi, and Rio is closing rapidly. They don't want to get mixed up in anything, so they try their best to move at an accelerated pace. Their worry is alleviated when a black SUV pulls up in front of the SWAT team. Before they know it, Terrence is gone, but the rest of the detainees remain and are ushered off into the SWAT vans. The group isn't sure where he went, but they don't have time to worry. Their fast-paced walk turns into a run and they continue on like that for several blocks until they feel safe. The two pairs split up and go opposite ways.

Chapter 34

May 18th, 2082 - PJ

Patrick didn't think that the news stations were exaggerating when they talked about the containment camps, but now that he is in one, he realizes that seeing something and living something are not even close to the same thing. Being stuck in this cage means he has all the time in the world to think about what went wrong to lead him here.

He had high hopes that when the police picked him up a couple nights ago that he would be able to prove he is a police officer and be released immediately. Unfortunately, somehow, word about him aligning with the OWALs made its way through all the surrounding precincts. It took him less than five minutes of being detained in a cell at the station to know that things were going to end badly.

As he was escorted in, all the officers in the building on shift gave him a serious stink eye as he moved across the building. When he finally had a chance to speak to an officer about who he is, they laughed at him and said, "we all know exactly who you are" while pointing to a small "wanted" poster on the wall with his face on it next to Katie, Nick, and Blue's faces. His heart sank in that moment and hope floated away.

Patrick has only been in the containment camp for a couple of hours now, but the sounds and smells are becoming too much for him. Being newer to the holding facility means he is lucky enough to be put in a slightly less full 'cage'. Even so, there are far too many people near him for his comfort. The people in the cage across from him must have come here immediately after the president's national address because the smells of body odor, vomit, feces, and who knows what else, are emanating in the air and unfortunately reaching Patrick's nose. It is taking everything in him not to barf.

He considers that maybe the smell isn't what is getting to him. It could be seeing people treated so inhumanely, and knowing that police officers are responsible, that turns his stomach. There is nothing but buckets inside the cages for people to release their waste. Large jugs, resembling those used to feed rabbits or hamsters, are attached to the outside of the cages with a metal nozzle fitting through the links to provide water to those inside. He doesn't recall seeing these on the news of the Texas camp, so he wonders if this facility is considered the nicer of the two. He feels guilty even thinking that this place is 'nicer' than another. His surroundings remind him of what one would learn about in a history class or read about in an apocalyptic novel.

He manages to find a spot large enough to sit down along the metal chain links separating him from his freedom. He has plenty of time to be with his thoughts now. He finds himself feeling grateful that he was captured after Derrick, Blue, and the boys were brought to the safe house. He can't imagine how much worse this would be if the remaining members of the Ardi family had to go through something like this. He also hopes that Katie and Nick were able to get away and move forward with the plan. He didn't see any other police officers out that night in that area, but there is no way of knowing what really happened to everyone without any access to technology in this hell he is currently living in.

Patrick's alone time is interrupted by a petite, dark-haired woman who claims a small spot next to him. She introduces herself in what feels like too normal of an introduction given the circumstances.

"Hi! This place sucks, huh? My name is Emerson, but you can call me Em."

PJ glances at her and gives a small forced smile and a simple nod.

"Not much of a talker then. Alright. I'll do the talking. It will be worse in here if we isolate ourselves further," she says, narrating her thoughts to herself.

Patrick feels bad about not interacting, but at this moment he doesn't feel like anything he could say would make being here feel less than horrific. Emerson doesn't give up easily though and continues to talk to herself aloud for what seems like hours. Eventually, Patrick gives in and answers some of the questions that Emerson throws at him. He figures that he has to be here, so he might as well try to make it less miserable for someone else by entertaining their insanity.

The two discuss their pasts and what they want out of the future. Patrick learns that Em is a third-grade teacher who has only been here a day. She got picked up by the police when a colleague reported her for using *Modified* people as an example in a lesson about empathy. She explained that the school gave clear guidelines about talking about *Modified* people and she broke the rules. She doesn't care though. She stands by what she did. She believes that all people should be treated equally and that the school forbidding teachers to talk about *Modified* people doesn't mean they don't still exist. Patrick respects the decision she made as a professional. He feels like it puts them on the same level because they both lost their public service job for actually serving the public, which to him, seems pretty ironic.

Hours go by and PJ gets used to Emerson's voice. So used to it that he is starting to feel soothed by it. He nods off to her talking and hopes that when he wakes up, he will be somewhere else entirely.

Chapter 35

May 18th, 2082 - BRUNER and PIERCE

"Kenny, please come in here immediately," David shouts into his intercom. The loyal assistant rushes in before David's finger even releases from the button.

"What can I do for you, Mr. Bruner?"

"Nathan Pierce is on his way over right now. I'm guessing it has to do with that riot on Capitol Hill earlier. He wants to talk to us about what is next. Make sure you straighten up your desk quickly and bring refreshments in. We can't have him thinking we don't know how to host our guests," Bruner barks at him with what feels like unintentional anger.

Kenny just finishes setting out beverages and light snacks as Pierce arrives with bodyguards in tow. The guards take a seat in the lobby near Kenny's desk after turning down his offer of refreshments. Pierce doesn't acknowledge Kenny at all, even after the assistant verbally greets him with almost too much enthusiasm. He walks straight into David's office and closes the door behind him. Kenny, growing more and more frustrated with being treated like a minion, gets gutsy and quietly enters the office to join them. David nods at him upon his arrival and Pierce doesn't even appear to notice that he has entered the room.

"In hindsight, creating all of those hyper concentrated prenatal vitamins was probably not the way to go," Pierce says with a sigh.

"It's too late now. We have to accept where we are now and shift our focus. I promised President Moros that I would fund her campaign and help get the laws changed so she could run for president for additional terms if she supported me on this. I even told her that focusing on *Modifying* babies would be the easiest because we could blame it on global warming. It was the perfect plan, or so it seemed. I could make billions from the medical side, and she would benefit from having society so divided by hate that they wouldn't be paying attention when the legislation went through..."

Pierce stops talking without even finishing his thought. Kenny, hearing all of this for the first time, is trying to keep his face from displaying how truly astonished and impressed he is. David on the other hand is confused.

"So, what's the problem then, Nate? Everything is exactly as you predicted," David questions.

"You aren't wrong, but the issue now is that Moros and her team are getting spooked. She went into hiding with the cabinet members. She didn't anticipate anyone making as big of an impact as Dr. Cyrus did with this OWAL nonsense. The riot today was the worst one yet. It took five hours to get it under control. The SWAT teams couldn't do it alone. They had to call in help from surrounding areas, including militias from other states. The Capitol Building burned to the ground. I'm talking...ashes. Thousands are dead. It is going to take countless hours and millions of dollars to clean up this mess. Our only saving grace is that Moros paid off the news outlets to hold off on releasing anything about the death toll and imagery of the destruction."

"Obviously Moros going into hiding isn't ideal especially when society is looking for guidance, so what are you going to do?" asks Bruner.

"I have a plan, it will help both of us get where we want to be. You're going to have to do something outside of our initial agreement though," he says filling the air with mystery and dread.

Chapter 36

May 18-22nd, 2082 - SANTOS

The clock strikes exactly 9 p.m. when Nick and Katie enter the lobby of Rio's hotel. He is sitting on a stool at the bar enjoying a beverage when they approach him. He greets them gleefully.

"So glad you both were able to make it. Would you like something to drink? My treat," he booms.

Katie and Nick politely decline. Taking in their surroundings, they realize that there are many people in the lobby trying to check in. Too many for their comfort. While they are not in the near vicinity of the bar, they make the room feel like it is closing in on them. Cyrus and Kleug are technically on the run now, so being recognized outside of rallies and protests could leave them vulnerable to being harmed or taken by whoever Pierce has looking for them. Santos picks up on the awkwardness of their behavior and asks them up to his room so they can speak more privately.

Javi greets all three of them when they reach the room. The foursome sits in pairs on the beds looking towards each other.

"Again, thank you for coming to meet me. I am ashamed of the role that I played in Beaufort. I know you coming here is also a risk for you and I appreciate you taking a chance on me. I want to help you. I'm willing to join you in rallies, help bring awareness, whatever you need. Please let me try to make things right. My son deserves a better parent than what I've been lately," the officer pleads.

On the way over to the hotel Nick and Katie discussed whether or not they should trust Santos. Nick ultimately left the decision up to Katie. He figures that he has made most of the decisions for both of them lately and it is her turn to be in charge of their fate.

"Thank you for saying these things, Sheriff Santos. While I can't say that we entirely trust everything you are saying, I can tell that you want to be better for your son, so we are going to give you a chance. We do actually have a favor that we need from your connections in the police department," Katie explains, hopeful that Rio is serious about making amends.

"Anything. What do I need to do?"

"I need you to see if you can find my friend PJ. His real name is Patrick Janes. He is…or I guess, was, a police officer in Pittsburgh. He kept us safe when we were there and helped us escape after the OWAL revolution took off. He was traveling with us, but before we got out of the city he was spotted in the streets after curfew and was taken in. At first, we thought that since he is a police officer that he would be released right away and that taking him was obviously a mistake, but we haven't heard from him. Can you help us find him?"

Rio, eager to get back on their good side, but more so on Javi's good side, agrees immediately and picks up his cell phone to make a few calls. Javi, Katie, and Nick make small talk about the OWAL marches and riots they've heard about happening in other cities. A quick twenty minutes later and Rio is off the phone and has some answers for the group.

"My sources tell me that your friend Patrick is in the containment camp here in D.C. Luckily, one of my old lieutenants works in this area and has been assigned temporarily to be a guard at the camp. After several calls back and forth, he said that he arranged to sneak me in as a new guard so that I can help your friend escape," Rio says proudly.

"That's great, Santos, but can you trust this man?" The doctor wonders aloud.

"I trained him years ago. We came to be pretty close during that time, but since he moved north, we've grown apart. I want to believe that I can trust him, but I'm honestly not sure. Opinions on *Modification* changes people and causes them to choose sides. I don't know which side he really aligns with. I mean, a lot of people have personal beliefs, but have to go against those for their job or, frankly, for their own survival," he says, reminding himself that he, too, once had a moral compass before becoming Mayor Roy's whipping boy.

He continues, "Does it really matter if I can trust him? This is the only way we can get in. You do bring up a good point, though. We should be prepared for anything."

The four sit for the next several hours preparing for their upcoming encounter at the containment center. Nick starts to wonder if saving Patrick should be their priority right now. Not because he doesn't care for PJ as a friend, but because doing this puts them at risk.

He pulls Katie aside to talk to her about PJ. The conversation is really unnecessary because he already knows that Katie will say that they have to help Patrick, not only because he helped them, but because he is her friend. The entire conversation makes Nick feel like an asshole and for good reason. He claims to be brave to his followers, but shutters at the thought of being caught and put in one of the containment centers.

After a lot of discussion and planning, the four have what seems like a solid plan to break PJ out. Now they just have to gather supplies and wait for the right moment. Rio's old lieutenant friend works on the 22nd, a few days from now. They will just have to hold up in this hotel together until then.

……

The days stuck together in the hotel watching news coverage and eating vending machine food move at a snail's pace, but the 22nd finally arrives. The four are ready with a plan that doesn't seem good enough but will have to do. They grab a ride from a 'Sposta' car and request to be dropped off a block from the containment center so they can all get to their places.

Rio leaves the drop off spot first, heading to the side entrance of the containment center where he was told by his old lieutenant to meet at 10 a.m. Javi heads out second, moving towards the back of the containment center. Katie's role is to stay near the drop-off spot and keep the 'Sposta' car ready to go. Nick moves in the same direction as Javi but needs to go up the hill a block over to get a better view of the camp to report to Katie when it's time to start setting the car's directions to go. Katie would normally be annoyed that she has to stay back from the action, but after everything she's seen over the last few weeks she is glad to take a literal backseat on this one.

Santos reaches the guard's post along the left side of the camp and his stomach is already ready to turn inside out at the sight of the people in the cages and the pile of dead bodies slowly rotting along the inside of the fence. It is like a car crash. He doesn't want to look, but he doesn't know how to stop. The bodies already have swarms of flies around them so some of them have been here for at least a few days. Most of these deaths look like they are from guard related trauma, but he can't be sure if that's the cause. He can't believe that before his son shook some sense into him, that he was contributing, or at least helping to cover up, all of this hate.

His old lieutenant, Damien, walks toward the guard station and shouts to the guard on duty to let Rio in. He beams with a smile when he greets the sheriff with a bear hug. The sheriff returns the excitement and thanks him for his help. Damien shows Rio into the facility.

The inside of the facility seems a little better than the outside. The cells have more people in them than they should, but the conditions don't seem as grim because at least the people have access to indoor plumbing. Prisoners shout awful things at the guards and at Santos as they walk through the center of the building and to the left until they reach the back where they exit into the 'yard'. He tries to make small talk with Damien about how his wife and children are in hopes of distracting him from what Javi is planning.

From the moment he hung up the phone with Damien, he knew that he was being set up. He couldn't let Katie, Nick, or even Javi know that because they wouldn't agree to do this then, but he could tell the tone of Damien's voice wasn't normal. The amount of times Damien called him back with new updates solidified his thoughts. There was no way Damien wasn't considering him a traitor and planning to capture him or worse.

Santos positioned himself in such a way that he was facing the back of the camp. In order for Damien to look at him while speaking he would have to have his back facing the cages, as part of the plan. Santos pretended to brush something off of his pants which was the signal for Nick up on the hill to begin.

Nick uses the old-style binoculars that Santos borrowed to him to peer into the camp. He sees that Santos is outside and is giving the signal. He drops the binoculars and starts sprinting down the opposite side of the hill. He travels at least a quarter of a mile before he swings the backpack that he is carrying off of his back and pulls out several large fireworks. He sets them up so that they are facing towards the camp at such a low angle that they won't explode in the sky but rather hit the guard tower and fences. He lights a lighter in each hand and moves quickly to light each of the wicks. Once he confirms they are lit, he starts running back up the hill to safety and to view the outcome of the plan. The fireworks that were set off in the garbage can at the Capitol Hill protest gave him the idea. The idea is so simple, yet so effective in causing distraction and chaos.

Within seconds the fireworks go off one by one. Some slamming into the fences as expected, some slamming into the building and one hitting the guard tower. Commotion amongst the guards ensues. Some of the guards run to help the man in the guard tower. Others open the main gate and run towards where the fireworks are coming from in order to find the culprit. This works out better than they could have imagined. As the guards run away from the gate and it begins automatically closing slowly, Javi runs full speed and slips in, not even needing to use the bolt cutters that he brought.

Damien turns towards Santos and begins to angrily accuse him of having something to do with this. Santos puts his hands up and tries his best to explain that he has nothing to do with this. Damien doesn't buy it and pushes Rio as hard as he can until he bumps into the wall of the building. Rio knew things could come to this, so he pulls out a thin police baton hidden in his pant leg and clutches it like a deadly weapon. Damien reaches for his gun in his holster, but Santos slaps it away with the baton. They both dive for the gun that landed in the gravel and clash into one another with their heads colliding. They fall back in opposite directions and try to reorient themselves.

Meanwhile, Javi is inside running up and down the row of cages closest to the fence looking for someone that looks like the picture Katie showed him of PJ. He even begins shouting the name Patrick Janes. Three cages down from where he stops to look around, he hears someone say, "That's me. I'm Patrick Janes." He rushes over and starts clipping the chain link fence into a square big enough to free a full-size man. Patrick pushes hard against the area that Javi is cutting, helping to free it away from the rest of the cage. It doesn't take long before the pulled back fence is large enough to fit through. PJ slips through followed by Emerson and everyone else in the cage that is healthy enough to walk.

Javi and the newly freed people start running towards the gate that he entered the camp through. He sees that the guards are now aware of what is going on. The guards from the field are running quickly back to the camp, shouting "open the gate", so they can enter. The guards up in the watchtower are loading their rifles in anticipation. Emerson shouts at Javi to toss her the bolt cutters. He does so without a second thought. She begins cutting the fence in the cage closest to her to free more people while she has the chance. The gate opens to allow the guards in and as they enter, they clash with the people trying to flee. PJ looks behind him as he is reaching the gate and notices that Emerson is still cutting the fence. He turns around and grabs her. She didn't cut the hole big enough for anyone to get out, but she shoves the bolt cutters through the small opening and runs—hoping to allow someone the opportunity to save themself.

The guards on the ground are pushing and punching the people near the gate to try to keep them inside as the gate tries to automatically close again. Patrick and Emerson somehow slip through past the clash occurring in front of them and make it out the gate. Javi juts around a guard as if he is a football player and manages to escape when the guard loses balance. As they turn and run parallel to the gate, they freeze with the sound of a single gunshot ringing in the dead air. It feels like everything is paused in time. The quarrel near the gate stops dead with everyone looking for where the shot was fired.

Javi sees a guard standing facing his father with a gun pointed straight at him. He makes eye contact with his dad as life drains from his eyes before he hits the ground. Javi shouts, but no one can hear it because the quarrel by the fence recommenced. The guards from the tower begin shooting into the quarrel and many of the prisoners back off to save their lives. Two men get shot. One guard and one prisoner. The gate slams shut once again, with only Javi, PJ, and Emerson making it out. The tower guards turn their guns towards those on the outside now. PJ grabs Javi's arm and runs alongside Emerson, pulling Javi against his will while dodging bullets.

Javi snaps out of it after a few minutes of running, realizing where he is, and begins to usher PJ and Emerson towards the drop off location. Katie and Nick are already waiting for them with the car ready when they arrive. Nick asks where Santos is. There is no response, but PJ shakes his head 'no' and the car takes off.

Chapter 37

May 22nd, 2082 - DAVID

David wakes up today knowing that what he is about to do for Pierce is going to have horrible consequences. He reasons that if he doesn't do this that dealing with Nathan's punishment for disobeying would be even worse. David is the only one who has a reason, besides Pierce, to get near Moros while she is in hiding. He is going to talk to her about what she wants to do next from a medical and scientific standpoint because obviously things have gotten so out of control that she feels the need to be in a safe room.

He finishes getting his pressed suit on, straightens his tie, and kisses his beautiful girlfriend goodbye while she's still in bed. For a moment he wishes it were Katie that he is kissing. Things with her were so simple and he could have at least talked with her about what is going on. She always listened to him and gave him good advice. His new lady, while beautiful, is nothing more than a showpiece for him to tote around to gatherings. He shakes Katie from his mind as he leaves his apartment. He needs to make one stop on the way to see Moros.

He arrives at his office where Kenny is eagerly awaiting his arrival.

"Do you have it?" he asks the overzealous assistant.

"Yes, sir. It's here…in this bottle."

"Are you sure this is enough? This doesn't seem like much," he asks, taking in how small the container is.

"Positive. A little goes a long way. Anything else you need from me, Mr. Bruner?"

"No, but please be ready at a moment's notice, just in case."

The assistant nods and smirks at the notion of being needed.

David quickly leaves his office and makes his way towards where Moros is hiding. Pierce explained to him that there is a safe room in the basement of the White House and that the news only depicted Moros and the cabinet leaving and getting into SUVs with bodyguards so that the public would think they are all somewhere else in safe houses.

He finds himself approaching the outer gate and using his badge and a face scanner to enter followed by a second checkpoint where his badge is checked again by secret service. Once inside he is greeted by another secret service agent who is expecting him. They walk together through all the visitor areas before making their way to the restricted areas of the building. They arrive at a door that opens into a hallway with an elevator in it. They enter the aged, gold-plated elevator. David takes in the craftsmanship of the elegant elevator as it moves slowly down to the basement level. They exit the elevator, and the secret service agent leads David to a room at the end of the hallway before stopping and asking if he needs anything before he leaves him. David has been waiting for this moment. He requests beverages and asks that he can have a whole tray to bring in since he knows they will all be here discussing things for a while. The agent nods but doesn't speak. He is gone before David knows it, leaving him to sweat all his anxiety out alone.

A few minutes later the agent appears again, carrying a tray of tea and lemonade along with some freshly baked pastries. He hands the tray to David and abruptly makes his way to the end of the hallway where he stays pacing the area near the elevator. David reckons that must be where they told him to take post during the meeting. David Bruner turns his back towards the agent and opens the small bottle as quickly as possible, pouring in only a few drops of the mixture into all of the beverages except one lemonade in the left corner of the tray. He enters the room quickly to avoid him looking suspicious to the guard down the hall.

As he enters the room, all eyes turn towards him, and he joyfully greets the group. President Moros verbally announces David and his title to the cabinet members surrounding her.

"Thank you for having me. The agent outside handed me some refreshments to bring in. I've heard you've all been here for some time now," David says loudly so his voice reaches across the long table.

He takes his lemonade off of the tray, passes the tray down one side of the table as he takes a seat. Before he knows it, the tray makes its way around the long table ending at him once again but empty this time. Moros begins to debrief David about their upcoming plans in front of the entire group. Within minutes of her long speech, the members at the table begin looking flush. Some of the men loosen their ties and unbutton their top button on their dress shirt. A commotion picks up around the table questioning if the room is getting hotter or if it's just them. David knows he will be the first one suspected of something nefarious, so he starts acting affected as well, unbuttoning his shirt and fanning his face. He starts to feel churning in his stomach, but not because of the lemonade. Turning these people into MODs is what he agreed to do for Pierce, but he is feeling guilty at this moment. He waits a few more minutes to see if they develop gills or if their skin thickens. He's not sure which concoction Kenny grabbed from the lab, but it's taking longer than he thought.

One of the women at the table begins vomiting and panic ensues. He doesn't remember this happening when Cyrus turned MOD on the stream. He's surprised to see no one is attacking each other with blame, but as he looks around, he realizes that everyone is in so much agonizing pain they probably can't focus on anything else. One by one their bodies lose control. Some of them fall to the floor, others end up face down on the table. Moros, the only one that was standing, bends and groans before falling into the wall and eventually molding down into a ball on the floor. He stands up and walks around to each of the people to check if they are alive. To his confusion, all of them are dead, including Moros. He doesn't understand. The potion was supposed to turn them to MODs in order to help restore some structure and remove the toxicity that society is seeing with the imbalance of power between the two entities. At least that's what Nathan told him.

He realizes that the guard in the hallway likely doesn't know what happened. The room is mostly soundproof so there would be no way he could hear them groaning and pleading in their last moments, especially being all the way down the hall. He grabs his lemonade and wipes his fingerprints off with a napkin and does the same along the rim of the glass. He exits the room as normally as possible and closes the door quickly behind him. He walks at an average pace towards the guard and greets him.

"They'd like some more time to discuss. Can you please take me towards the exit? I have another meeting I must get to," David says, as calmly as he can while every inch of him is sweating beneath his suit.

The guard agrees and they move at the same pace on the way out that they did on the way in. David feels a small sense of relief as he exits the outer gate and gets into the car that is awaiting his arrival. He touches the side of his head above his ear acknowledging his virtual assistant before he asks it to call his real-life assistant. He pauses and wonders if Kenny set him up or if all of this is just a huge mistake. He decides against calling Kenny or even Nathan and sits with his thoughts on the way back to the office.

By the time the car pulls up to his office David decides that Kenny and Nathan must be pushing him out of the plan for some reason. While he doesn't know why, he knows that this is bad for him. They set him up to take the fall for the deaths of the entire executive branch. Instead of getting out of the car he requests that the driver bring him back to his apartment.

He arrives at his building and asks the driver to wait out front. He tells him that he just needs to run and grab a few things before heading to the airport. As he approaches his apartment door, he realizes that it isn't fully closed. He quietly pushes the door open enough to slip in. It's eerily quiet in the apartment, but he tries to remain calm believing that his girlfriend left and was just being ditzy by accidentally leaving the door open. His mind changes when he sees her lying face down in a pool of blood on the living room floor, still in her lingerie from last night. He becomes instantly more aware of his surroundings, looking for abnormalities around the apartment. The bathroom door is open and so is the sliding door to the balcony. He quietly goes to the kitchen that is connected to the living room and grabs a large, serrated knife and holds it close. He inches himself back to the living room and past his now deceased girlfriend. He begins to head towards the bathroom but pauses and realizes that someone would have heard her scream if the balcony door was open during her attack. He pivots and turns towards the balcony moving in slowly. He slides himself along the wall to try to see around the glass door that is shielded with hanging curtains. As he gets closer to the glass door, someone leaps inside the opening lunging at him with a long blade. David jumps back quickly, and the dark skinned, tall man drops to the floor. They do a shuffle for several seconds before coming at one another again. The man's long blade falls to the floor in the collision, but he grabs David around the throat tightly with his large hands.

Bruner is turning a dark shade of pink and trying to gasp for breath. He attempts to turn his knife blade towards the man, but before he can do it, he is brought to the ground, and the man is on top of him draining his life from him. He manages to readjust the knife in his hand and tries to stab the man in the side, but the mocha skinned man is quick and releases one hand from David's neck and forces his knife holding hand to the ground. David takes the man's hand moving as an opening and kicks up, hitting the man between his legs. The man groans in pain and shifts his hand back to Bruner's neck so that both hands are once again working hard to end his life. David has almost no strength left in his body but manages to adjust his hand once more with the knife and makes a swift jab with it into the man's rib cage. He curls up in agony and David is able to roll him off of his body. Once David is able to get on his feet again and regains his breath, he realizes he's seen this man before. It's Kenny's boyfriend, Terrence.

David searches his memory for snippets of Terrence. He first heard his name a few months back when Kenny was on the phone at his desk and the door to David's office was open. He didn't think much of it at the time, but then a couple weeks later Kenny requested to leave early because his boyfriend, whom he met online, was coming in for the weekend from Pittsburgh and he wanted to spend as much time with him as possible. David didn't know prior to that conversation that Kenny is gay. They never talked about it, but it made sense. Kenny never talked about women or dating. Every time there was a company event he always showed up alone and talked only to the other assistants, as where most of the men used the company events as a way to show off their women or to pick up women.

After that weekend that Terrence visited Kenny, there were pictures of him posted all over Kenny's social media. Terrence even came in that following Monday, before heading back to Pittsburgh, to take Kenny to lunch. That is when David met him. Kenny introduced Terrence to David beaming with so much pride that he snagged someone so tall and handsome. Terrence, too, seemed excited to be associated with Kenny. The pair looked really good together. Kenny, smaller in stature and darker skinned, but handsome. Terrence, tall and lean with a little lighter skin than Kenny and an interesting shaped white birthmark on his neck.

The birthmark is how David knows the man curled up on the floor trying to regain his strength to attack him again is Terrence. The white diamond shaped birthmark on the side of his neck is now facing up towards David.

Now that Bruner has regained his ability to breathe, he sees that Terrence is rearing to come at him again. Instead of letting him up, David takes the knife and plunges it into chest, ending the fight all together. He leaves the knife where it landed, next to Terrence's heart, and backs away. He runs to his bedroom and grabs a small travel bag. He quickly shoves a few changes of clothing inside of it, not worrying that everything will surely be wrinkled. He grabs his passport and his handgun from the floor safe, now that he doesn't have to worry about being attacked from behind. He shoves both items into the bag, zips it up, and leaves quickly without looking back at the destruction left behind.

Once on the ground level, he walks quickly outside to get into the car that dropped him off. As he approaches where he was dropped off, he sees that the car is nowhere to be found. Kenny must have gotten to the driver as well. It's probably better that he moves on his own now anyways, to remove himself from the danger that his assistant has become. He clicks a few buttons on his phone and a self-driving car from the most lucrative taxi company around, 'Sposta', pulls up within seconds. He hops in and sets the address to the airport in Virginia. He's planning to fly as far west as he can and look for a place to lay low. This would be so much easier if he could leave the country, but the travel restrictions are still put in place for Americans.

He is about fifteen minutes from the airport when he realizes that he will never be able to outrun Pierce or Kenny for that matter. He plays with the car's navigation screen in the back and resets the location. The car turns around and heads back towards D.C.

Chapter 38

May 23rd, 2082 - OWALS

The sun rises across D.C., but Javi isn't sure how. It feels like everything is over for him. He never got to tell his father how proud he is of him for admitting his mistakes and trying to correct them. Not having the opportunity to say these things feels like it will haunt Javi forever. He pulls the curtains to the hotel room window closed again. Katie and Nick are still sleeping in the bed they previously occupied. Emerson and PJ took the bed that Javi and Santos were using, but they are awake now watching the news silently with closed captions on so they don't disturb anyone. It doesn't matter that Javi's bed has guests in it. He didn't sleep anyways, well…at least not much. He spent most of the night sitting up against the wall near the window peering through the small opening in the curtains at the moon, feeling sorry for his own loss.

Seemingly out of nowhere, the volume is turned up on the television and the noise wakes up Katie and Nick.

"You have to see this," Patrick says with astonishment.

Everyone's attention is drawn to the screen that now displays Pierce standing at the presidential podium. A banner scrolls continuously across the bottom of the screen saying: 'President Moros and cabinet members are dead'.

"I, first, would like to thank the American people for taking the time to listen to me speak. I am saddened to be the one to deliver the news that President Moros and the cabinet members of the executive branch were found dead yesterday evening. It is our understanding that their deaths were orchestrated by the OWAL group. There is an ongoing investigation into how the OWALS infiltrated the safe room where the executive branch was convening. It is our suspicion that one of my own trusted advisors turned on us. David Bruner, who all of you saw stand on this stage with me mere days ago, was having an inappropriate relationship with OWAL co-leader, Kathryn Kleug. It is believed at this time that he became compromised and took matters into his own hands by poisoning our beloved president to help move the OWAL agenda along. I have taken the opportunity to reach out to Congress to assist them in these terrifying times. We have come to the agreement that it is best to keep all politicians out of the limelight for a while. I have humbly accepted their nomination of me as interim president until the next election."

The banner along the bottom of the screen immediately changes to say 'Nathan Pierce named Interim President of the United States'. Pierce ends his speech with a salute to the nation and walks off stage. The screen goes blank but the banner across the bottom stays, continuously scrolling across the screen.

Katie is the first one to react out loud.

"I wonder what happened to David. I doubt he really killed those people. He's an absolute jerk, but he isn't a killer."

"I'm sure he didn't kill them, Katie, but I doubt he's even alive at this point. If they are pinning the president's death on him, he's as good as dead," Nick states matter of factly.

Patrick chimes in for really the first time since they rescued him. He hasn't had more than a few words to say since leaving the camp and everyone else is too scared to ask him or Emerson what it was like there.

"How does this change things for us now?"

"It doesn't. We move forward," Javi says in an emotionless tone.

"He's right. We move forward. The president being gone doesn't really matter to our cause. Pierce was always the one pulling the strings anyways. I think we need to step it up though. It's time to end this once and for all. I don't think us going from riot to riot is going to make much of a difference at this point," Nick explains.

The group discusses their options and decides they need to reach out to Blue to gather the OWAL leaders on a virtual call. Blue gets back to them quickly with a time to meet virtually later in the evening. In the meantime, there is not really anywhere safe for them to go so they stay in the hotel having nothing to do but talk.

Emerson, being the social butterfly that she is, offers up information about herself easily. She talks about how she and PJ became fast friends while they were 'doing time' in prison. She playfully says it, but the rest of the group thinks it's a coping mechanism to distract from how horrible it really was in there. She talks about some of the people she met while she was there and how she hopes they were able to escape or at least remain alive.

PJ watches her while she is talking and notices that she is much prettier than he remembers. It's probably in part because she is showered and wearing clean clothes now. Luckily, she and Katie are close in size. He even finds her to be less annoying than she was when they were in the camp. He reasons that is likely due to the fact that he is free and fed now.

Katie can't help but notice that PJ is watching Emerson intently while she speaks. She feels a small rush of jealousy come over her. She doesn't know why. She loves Nick. She guesses that a small part of her always thought that PJ had feelings for her. She tries to will the feeling of jealousy from her body because she doesn't want to be selfish. She cares for PJ and wants him to find someone. Maybe that someone could be Emerson. They don't exactly have a 'meet cute' story, but they do have a shared experience that most people wouldn't understand.

After a while the conversation dies down, and everyone begins to find their own things to do around the small space. Nick begins creating a plan and noting it down on Javi's tablet. Emerson decides she is going to take a nap. Javi leaves the room to gather some food and supplies for the group. That leaves only Katie and PJ to find something to do. They decide to head out to the room's balcony to catch up one-on-one for a while.

"How are you doing, PJ?" Katie starts off.

"As best as I can, given what happened. I'm really sorry about your friend—Javi's dad," he says in a sympathetic voice.

"He wasn't really my friend but thank you. He was making amends with us. He was the sheriff that I told you about before. The one from Beaufort," she explains.

"Oh, that makes sense. That poor kid. He just lost his dad. It sucks, even if he wasn't always such a good guy," he notes.

"I know, it is awful. Javi is a really cool kid. We need to try to make him feel like he has a place with us. He really needs us right now," she says, trying not to get choked up.

"You're such a good person, Kate. You always think about the people around you. When I was in the camp I thought about you a lot. I really missed you. I thought that I was going to die there. I ran through all my regrets in my head during those seemingly endless days," his voice trails off.

"What regrets? You've led a great life up until I came and disrupted it. I'm really sorry about that by the way—getting you involved in all of this. I never knew things would get this out of control," she says apologetically.

"Katie, what I'm trying to say is that my life isn't really what I thought it would be. Well, that isn't entirely true either. I guess what I mean is that I wasn't happy before you came busting back into my world. Sure, I had a good job, but that's all I had. I didn't have anyone to share it with. I barely had any real friends. I worked all the time and ate meals alone," he says staring off into the distance of the view from the balcony.

"Why didn't you call me? Why didn't you tell me things weren't going well? You know I would have come to visit more. We could have talked more. I could have helped you to meet more people, even more women," she explains, feeling guilty for not knowing how sad her old friend was for so long.

"I don't know, I guess I didn't want to talk to anyone about it, especially you. Ever since the first night that I saw you all those years ago, I've loved you. I thought about telling you once, but I was scared to ruin our friendship. Years later when we were graduating, I was going to tell you, but you told me you were going to take a job outside of Pittsburgh and I couldn't ask you to stay. Long distance would have been a nightmare. Plus, I didn't even know if you had feelings for me at that time or ever really," he says, still looking off into the distance.

"PJ, I don't know what to say," she says, trying to process his love confession.

"I don't really need you to say anything. I regret not telling you all those years ago. When I was in that cage, listening to Em go on and on about all of the things she wants to do when she is free again, I decided that when I got out the thing I wanted to do most is to not have any more regrets. I don't expect you to fall at my feet and tell me that you love me. I know you and Nick are in love. I see the way you look at each other. You've never looked at me the way you look at him. I'm happy for you. I really like Nick. He's a good guy. I guess I had to say it out loud in order to let go and move on. I'll probably always love you, but I need to find someone who loves me back now."

Katie doesn't say anything back to PJ. Instead, she gets up from the chair she is sitting in and moves herself in front of Patrick so he can't avoid looking her in the eyes any longer. She leans down and gives him the tightest hug and a small kiss on the cheek.

Before removing her body from his, she whispers in his ear, "You don't know it yet, but you've found the one you're supposed to be with. You're hurting right now, but once you get over that you'll see what I mean. She's already here."

She slowly releases her grasp on him, straightens herself up and walks inside closing the sliding door behind her. Patrick is left alone with his thoughts once again. He knows that Katie is talking about Emerson. He can't see how she thinks she is the one he is supposed to be with though. He spends a few minutes thinking about his interactions with Em in the cage. Without even realizing it, throughout their conversations, he's learned more about her than he has about anyone. She also likely knows more about him than anyone else does because of how many questions she asked him. At the time he thought that maybe it was because she was bored, but he wasn't the only man in the cage. She could have chosen to pester anyone, but she chose him.

Patrick joins the rest of the group back in the room once he hears Javi arrive back with supplies. The group eats a few of the snacks that he brings back and gets ready to join the virtual call that Blue organized. They stream the tablet to the television screen so that the whole room can hear and see the call. Blue joins first and Nick asks her to wait to let others in so they can chat for a second.

"Hey, I forgot to mention on the phone earlier that we saw your stepbrother, Terrence, the other day. He was at Capitol Hill the day that rioters burned down the Capitol building. He was taken away by the SWAT team," Dr. Cyrus explains.

"I figured he was there. I have been carefully keeping in touch with my mother. She doesn't know where I am, but I wanted her to know I am safe. Anyways, I talked to her last night, and she said that my stepdad got a call saying that they found Terrence's body in some apartment in D.C. They said he was stabbed to death. Apparently, there was another body in the apartment too, which is how they found him. I guess someone was looking for the other person and couldn't get a hold of them and sent the police. I don't know much else. I would have mentioned it earlier, but ever since he betrayed me, I don't really talk about him much," Blue says without showing any emotion about losing her stepbrother.

"Oh, wow! I'm sorry to say it, but at least he is one less AmerEagles supporter we need to worry about," he says only half joking.

Blue gives a half-assed laugh to Nick's mildly insensitive joke. She changes the subject by noting that she is so happy that PJ is safe again. After a few minutes of catching up with PJ she notifies the group that she is going to start the meeting. Within minutes there are over five hundred OWAL group leaders from various locations across the U.S. on the call. Nick is overwhelmed with the amount of support Blue was able to gather in such a short time. He is, once again, in awe of her connections.

Blue, as the organizer, begins the conversation.

"Thank you all for joining us. It is time for us to once again join together to fight for our *Modified* brothers and sisters. Dr. Cyrus has worked out a plan and is ready to share it with you. All of this information needs to be kept confidential. Any leak and everything could be ruined. Please don't share any information other than what is necessary to carry out the plans. We are counting on you all to help end this once and for all. Please take it away Dr. Cyrus…"

Chapter 39

May 23rd 2082 - PIERCE

"Kenny come in here," Pierce shouts.

The newly promoted assistant rushes into the oval office sporting a sharp new suit.

"How can I be of service, sir?" he asks submissively.

The newly appointed president swivels around in his chair to face Kenny before he begins to speak.

"Any word on the whereabouts of Bruner?"

"None yet, Mr. President. I'm thinking he skipped town. He likely heard your speech and figured that if he stuck around, it wouldn't take long for the police to pick him up, given that he is the only suspect in the murders."

"He better stay gone. The last thing we need is more trouble. Now that Moros and her minions are gone, we have the opportunity to get things back in order. She was so weak in the country's time of need. We had everything going for us until she decided to back out and go into hiding," President Pierce explains.

"What is the next order of business?" inquires Kenny.

The president plays with his hands while he is running through his thoughts.

"My original goal in all of this was to sell more of my products and make more money, which I now realize is silly since I have plenty of money. Now I have all the power and control too. I mean, not only do I have the presidency, but I am basically a God. I can take humans and turn them into whatever I want. Look at all those little MOD babies that my products have created," he pauses.

Kenny tries to be aware of his facial expressions because he is utterly disgusted at the God complex that this man has. No wonder David used to complain about his cockiness, he thinks, realizing that he didn't fully realize the kind of person he is dealing with until now.

"The way I see it, things can go one of two ways. I can blame everything on the MODs, divide the country further and begin on a path to building a kingdom with many loyal subjects. Saying it out loud makes it sound even more appealing. Or I provide the people with support to come together while my company begins working on another serum to try to reverse the effects of the current *modifications*. I still look good if I go with this option, that is, assuming I can find someone to create a serum that doesn't have any side effects. Which shall it be?"

Kenny shrugs. He knows that Pierce isn't really asking him what he thinks. He is here to stroke his ego and be a wall to bounce ideas off of. Pierce opens an old wooden box on the desk in front of him and picks up a quarter. He studies it, noting that the date on it says 1993. He finds it hard to believe that this is how some people still pay for things. He spins it around in his hands feeling the weight of the nickel-copper mix.

After a few seconds he rests the quarter on his thumb and says "heads, I become a king, tails, I become a savior."

The coin flips off of his finger and rotates in the air before landing back in his hand. He cups his hand over it before revealing the result and saying, "King, it is."

Chapter 40

May 25th - June 15th, 2082 - PIERCE

Nathan wakes up feeling more powerful than ever. He always thought the desire to be rich is what drove him to greatness, but in reality, it is power. Of course, money provided him with power in the past, but nothing like what he is feeling sitting in the oval office looking out the window of the White House. He feels untouchable. He realizes that if he wants to be different than any other leader, he needs to act differently than any other leader has in the past. He presses the intercom button and calls in Kenny, for what feels like the millionth time, to the agitated assistant.

He comes in the room smiling despite wanting to punt Mr. President out of the window.

"Yes, Mr. President?" he says sweetly.

"We are going to paint the White House," President Pierce declares.

"I believe it is on a rotation to be painted every few years, sir." he says, growing more irritated.

"Red. We are going to paint it red," the president says with excitement in his voice.

"Sir, it is the White House. The president has always lived in the White House. A house that is...literally white," he says stating the obvious.

"That is precisely why we are going to paint it. Presidents have always lived in the White House. Kings, however, can live in whatever color castle they like and I...like...red. Call in all the maintenance people to start at once. I want it done within two days. Tell them we will pay overtime if necessary."

Kenny Nash immediately turns around and walks out of the room to fulfill the request. Within an hour painters begin to arrive and start to transform the White House into the Red Palace. He will never tell Nathan how stupid he thinks painting the building red is because he needs him, but he truly can't think of anything more idiotic. Every inch of him wants to think of Pierce as an unintelligent person, but that just wouldn't be true. You don't get to be where Nathan is without extreme wit and confidence.

Once the painting is finished, Kenny forces himself to go back into the oval office to update Nathan.

"Sir, sorry to interrupt your busy schedule, but the Red Palace project is complete," Kenny Nash says with condescension in his voice knowing that Pierce has been doing nothing but watching people paint the building for two days.

"It looks majestic, doesn't it? We must now move onto phase two. It is time to get me back in front of the cameras. That is where I shine. I want to make an announcement about the fate of those that have *Modified.* I will need you to get me the head of the Department of Defense and bring him in for a meeting in the next few hours. Tell him to meet me in the War Room. Also, keep checking in on Bruner. It is suspicious that no one has seen him since the murders in his apartment," the president orders.

Kenny's face grows warm at the mention of Terrence's death. He knew it was a risk sending him in to take care of David, but he really thought that he'd come out alive. His heart sank when he heard the news of his death. He wouldn't go as far as to say that he loved Terrence, but he did have strong feelings for him and enjoyed spending time with him. A big part of Kenny believes that Terrence loved him. Why else would he agree to do something so dangerous for him? It doesn't matter now he reckons. What's done is done. The same could be said with betraying Bruner. He didn't dislike Bruner, in fact, he thought he was a decent man. However, he needed to become collateral damage just like Terrence. Kenny doesn't mind, he got what he wanted in the end…to align himself with true power and money.

…….

Nathan Pierce appears in front of the camera once more to share news with the country. He looks sharp in his blood red suit and matching tie. His gold cufflinks bring elegance to his suit, making him look even more stately. Kenny thinks Nathan is taking this 'red' thing a little far, but he must admit that he looks really good.

"I've come before you once again to address our country's issues and work towards a solution. I have spent days working closely with members of our strong and able government to come up with a plan to help put the shattered pieces of our society back together. Our first step is to deal with those that are *Modified.* President Moros addressed this nation with a plan weeks ago, but due to her inability to lead was unable to follow through with her promises. I, however, will follow through with the promises that she made and show the American people what a strong leader looks like. Beginning this evening, similar to immediately after Moros' speech, anyone aiding and abetting someone who is *Modified* will be taken into a holding facility. We have opened up two in every state over the last few days. Police officers and militia members will enforce a strict curfew in all states that begins at 8 p.m. Anyone who leaves their home after that time without permission or in case of an emergency will be assumed to be aiding a *Modified* individual and will be placed in a holding facility. This is, of course, unless you are a public service employee or healthcare worker. Those who are presently in a holding facility will have two options. The first option is to be moved to a work camp to help bring prosperity back to our country. The other option is to try your fate by staying in the holding facilities. Infants and young children who are *Modified* will be taken and transported to a secure facility where they will be cared for by healthcare professionals to see if there is a chance to reverse the *modification*. America, we are about to enter our Crimson Era, and I promise you, it will be better than the Golden Age the Greeks spoke of," Pierce says exhibiting nothing but confidence.

The camera cuts out and Pierce leaves the podium. Once he is back in the oval office he immediately gets on the phone and makes sure that his plan begins immediately. Within the hour police cars are once again patrolling streets looking for MODs. By 8 p.m. the streets across America are empty. Dark houses with shaded windows line the streets of every city in the country. People who aren't *Modified* are scared too. One wrong move and anyone can be placed in a containment center.

Two mornings later and almost every holding facility across the continental United States is at capacity. All guards are to report to the holding facilities bright and early to transfer all the people who agree to go to the work camps in order to free up space in the holding facilities. The president had construction workers working overtime to get as many camps up overnight that they could. The television networks and streaming applications pause all activity to show coverage of the makeshift camps.

Hundreds of vans and buses are lined up along the outside of the holding facilities. Thousands of people, some *Modified,* some not, are ushered inside of the vehicles. The stations shift their coverage to the 'work camps' that are set up in remote areas of the states. These work camps consist of large open areas that new fences now surround. The electric fences are like those in the containment or holding facilities, tall and lined with barbed wire. In the center of the work camps there are shabby tents for housing. A huge screen is along the back fence on posts holding high above the camp. The screen displays 'code names' consisting of letters, numbers and symbols that the camp prisoners are assigned upon arrival. The 'code names' are assigned roles each day and it is to be updated on the screen. The screen today doesn't have anything other than directions on how the screen will work. It displays examples, 'AB12-1: Road Construction, report to Gate 2' and 'QR54-11: City Hall Refurbishment, report to Guard Station 14'.

The campers that are entering the facility are tagged, or retagged depending on their previous location, on the ear with their 'code name'. They are then lined up and marched to their sleeping quarters. Small children who were transferred with adults are removed from their care without explanation and taken from the camp. The news stations zoom in to ensure that those who are at home watching can see what their fate will be if they don't comply with President Pierce's requests.

One station shows a camp in Arizona. A woman began attacking a guard because her child was removed from her care and the guard shot her on site and dragged her body along the perimeter fence. The feed follows the guard pulling the woman and shows him putting her next to other bodies of women who likely ended up there the same way.

Guards are being trained as the new campers arrive. The coverage shows the new guards being issued their uniforms at the same time the campers get theirs. The guards have been assigned new uniforms that are crimson red with gold accents. Instead of wearing orange like people in prison wear, the campers that arrive are given a royal blue sweatsuit. The material depends on the location due to climate differences, but the stations show that the color remains the same at all of the camps.

As the days go by the campers are forced to work long days with very little food provided to them. One meal a day is served in the work camps. The food is brought in by trucks that gather leftovers from restaurants nearby. Much of the food is highly processed and has very little to no nutritional value. Despite some of the people only being in the camp for a week or so their quality of life is visibly declining.

Media coverage continues to run 24/7 on most networks to continuously spread fear. At times the coverage shows fights that break out in the work camps. One would think that the quarrels are between guards and campers, but more often than not it is campers versus other captives. Some of the camps have become divided by those who are *Modified* and those who ended up in the camp because they were wrongfully accused of aiding a *Modified*. The tents provided are small, so discomfort is the source of many battles.

Pierce and Kenny are sitting in a meeting room in the Red Palace and have all of the holographic media footage of every major station lining the walls of the room. Pierce looks around at all of the footage and is proud of what he has accomplished in such a short time.

Chapter 41

June 20th - June 21st, 2082 - OWALS

So much planning has gone into what is to come. Nick and Katie have been held up in the same hotel room with PJ, Emerson, and Javi for what seems like forever, but in reality, it has only been 28 excruciating days.

"Nick, I can't believe we've been living together for almost a month now," Katie says in a joking manner, trying to lighten the mood because tensions are high.

"Katie, I love you and I have loved being able to sleep next to you, but we have not been alone in all this time, and I feel like I am losing my mind. Literally. I feel like I'm becoming insane or schizophrenic or something," Cyrus states as they lay in bed whispering to each other trying not to wake any of the others.

"What do you think our lives will be like after all of this is over?" she asks.

"You know I'm a realist and it is hard for me to sugarcoat things. We don't know what the outcome of the next two days will be," Nick says, not able to play along with her little game.

"Nick, please. I need some normalcy in my life. Please just tell me what you would *like* our life to be like when all of this is over. I need something to hold onto to get me through this," she begs.

"After all of this is over and we are safe I want us to buy a house. A cute little beach house like the Ardi's, where our future kids can play along the sand. We can even get a dog if that would make you happy," he says with sincerity.

"You've thought about us having kids?" she replies.

"Of course. Two, maybe three. That is, if you'll marry me after all of this is over."

Her heart skips a beat at the thought of becoming Mrs. Cyrus. Of course, she has thought about it many times while she has been trapped in this drab hotel room, but to hear him say it brings it closer to reality.

"I'd love to become your wife after all of this."

"Well, please pretend to be surprised when I ask you for real then," he says while winking at her.

She makes a small little giggle whisper and pulls him in for a kiss. They stay that way for a while. Things start to heat up so she pulls away. This has been the norm each morning and night in bed. They can't take things too far with the crowd in the room. She starts to talk again to bring her mind away from his lips.

"I don't want to sound insensitive, but because you are *Modified* now does that mean our kids would be *Modified* too?"

"Would it bother you if they were?" he quickly replies.

"No, I'm just wondering how it works...you know...genetically. Like... because you are now genetically *Modified*, right? So, that means that our kids could inherit those traits?" she asks, a little embarrassed that she doesn't scientifically understand how it all works.

"Yes, our kids will most likely be *Modified*. It is genetically dominant," he clarifies.

"That's what I thought. Could you maybe *Modify* me one day? So that I could be the same as you?"

"Yes, I could. If that is something that you want. I won't do that until you are without a doubt positive that it is something you want. At this point there isn't a way to reverse the DNA from *Modification*, at least as far as I know," he explains.

She smiles at the thought of their future children walking around with his eyes. She starts to pull him closer again to kiss him, but his phone starts buzzing. He grabs it off of the table next to the bed and answers it.

"Hey Cyrus, it's Blue. I'm sorry it's so early. I have some news and I couldn't wait another minute to tell you."

"Hey Blue! No worries. I've been up for a while anyways. Are you, Derrick and the kids alright?" he questions.

"Yes, thanks for asking. We are great. This is unrelated to us. I got a message from David Bruner. At first, I didn't know how I knew that name, but then I remembered that he was the Human Biology Department guy that you told me about back at PJ's place. He says that he needs to speak with you immediately. I told him that wasn't going to happen, but he is very persistent," she says not knowing how Nick will respond.

"What?" he says, extremely confused and not really looking for an answer.

"Right? So weird. He says that it is incredibly important that he speaks to you and that he has disconnected himself from 'the real problem'. Whatever that means," Blue says.

Everyone in the room is awake now waiting for the conversation to end so that Nick can fill them in.

"How does he even know who you are? I didn't even know you when he and I were in communication. I mean, I guess he has resources, but still, it seems odd."

"I asked him that very question through the Zoop app that he messaged me on. He said that he had a brief interaction with Terrence due to his old assistant and that's how he found my account. I guess he has enough resources to know that I am connected to you through our OWAL organization and the location. He said that he couldn't find an account linked to you or Katie anywhere, so I was his next best choice. He wouldn't tell me what he wants to talk to you about, but he left me a phone number."

"I don't know what I'm going to do, but I'll take the number just in case," he decides.

Nick jots down the number on his hand using a pen he found in the drawer next to him since the burner phone he has now is basically prehistoric. He thanks Blue and hangs up. He immediately fills in the group. An hour-long conversation commences on whether or not contacting David is a trap or just a bad idea. Everyone unanimously decides that they want to know what he wants and that he can't trace a burner phone anyways so it's probably pretty safe.

He calls the number on his hand and within two rings David picks up. He doesn't speak; he waits patiently for Nick to start the conversation.

"'Hello? David?"

"Dr. Cyrus. Nice to hear from you. I appreciate you going out on a limb and calling me. I know you're probably really pissed about how things turned out with Pierce and myself. Obviously, they turned on me as well."

"What do you need, David?" Nick asks, keeping their interactions short.

"Still a man of few words I see. I know you think that I am reaching out just because I'm on the outs with Pierce and most definitely have a target on my back. That is partly true, but more than anything I want to take him down and I know you are still working on that yourself. He ruined my life. I didn't kill those people, Cyrus. I really didn't do it. I know I am at fault for a lot of the situation I am in, but I didn't kill anyone. He and Kenny tried to have me killed in my apartment," David explains.

"David, let me call you back in a few minutes. I need to think about all of this," Cyrus says, being logical as always.

"Take your time, Dr. Cyrus," David says immediately before disconnecting the call.

Nick sets his phone down and all eyes are on him. No one speaks. They all just wait for Nick to share the pertinent information. He explains the phone call in detail to the group.

"Well...what do you guys think?" Cyrus questions after laying out all the details.

"I have an idea. It will fit in with the structure of our plan, but everything would have to play out perfectly for it to work. Call David back and tell him we can meet," says Patrick.

Chapter 42

June 28th, 2082 - OWALS

The alarm goes off and it reads 2 a.m. Katie is the first one to hear it. She hits snooze and she rises out of bed immediately and begins to coax Nick awake. Javi wakes from the makeshift bed on the floor and heads for the bathroom to relieve himself. The alarm goes off once more. This time Katie shuts the alarm off because she sees Emerson waking up. Em rolls over and pokes Patrick who is still deep in his REM cycle. He flinches and opens his eyes.

"It's time," she says with a mixture of anxiety and excitement.

Chapter 43

June 28th, 2082 - OWALS

The guards at the Richmond, Virginia work camp begin to change shifts at 4:30 a.m. One by one the men in red leave their posts as their counterparts walk towards them. A long row of headlights shows up in the distance, gradually moving closer. One newly trained guard points out the lights to his colleague who brushes it off and chalks it up to a new delivery of campers. Several large 18-wheel trucks pull up and stop at the gate in a straight line. The first truck pulls the strap in the cab and the horn blares. The doors to the back of the trucks swing open simultaneously and hundreds of armed OWALs, wearing all black with small logos representing the group on their back, jump out and immediately begin charging the camp.

The men guarding the entrance to the camp are quickly taken out and the gate begins to open. The guards try to prepare themselves with their automatic weapons but are disadvantaged by the element of surprise. Most of the guards are eliminated quickly with only a few OWALs sustaining injuries and an unfortunate single casualty.

The rebellious OWALs help the camp prisoners into the trucks, removing them from the inhabitable conditions they've been living in. The same exact thing happens at every single containment center and work camp in the United States all at the exact same time. The trucks all depart from their locations and have one more stop before true freedom is obtained.

Chapter 44

June 28th, 2082 - PIERCE

The sky over Washington D.C. glows of pink and orange as the sun rises in the east. Pierce steps outside onto the Red Palace lawn to enjoy his morning coffee. The hot coffee lines his throat as he warms his face in the rising sun. It feels eerily calm out today, he mentally notes. There aren't any birds chirping or cars honking. He doesn't hear the trains running in the distance. He tries to take the silence as a positive sign that things are finally calming down. There haven't been as many riots across the country over the last few days and security informed him that most of the OWAL sites have been taken down.

He finishes the last sip of his coffee and begins to walk back into the large red structure to begin his day. A huge explosion goes off in the distance and he sees a large cloud of smoke fill the air a few miles away. He drops his mug, and it smashes into pieces on the brick pavers. Two secret service agents run towards him and start pulling him inside while shielding his body with theirs. He sprints to the control room where walls of what seems like infinite cameras surround him. The cameras cover most of the metropolitan area. He scans them to find where the explosion occurred. It appears to be near the Federal Reserve. The on-shift Department of Defense employee confirms this.

Seconds later another explosion occurs on the screen this time in the middle of the National Mall. The screen shows the streets filling up with people who seem to appear out of thin air. The people are chanting, carrying signs, and shouting that they want Pierce to resign from his position and that they want equality for the *Modified.* Large military grade tanks spray painted navy with the OWAL symbol on them roll in behind the swarms of people coming from each cardinal direction. The crowds slowly make their way towards the Red Palace. The large semi-trucks carrying those who were released from the containment centers and work camps roll up behind the crowd that already exists. News stations that caught on to the early morning happenings closely follow the trucks in but keep their distance as to not interfere or put themselves at risk. Thousands more people join the efforts as the doors to the trucks open. Blue and black smears of color disperse making the group gathered more diverse.

The crowd entirely surrounds the crimson building. Nick, Katie and the rest of the crew make their way to the front of the crowd and position themselves along the tall, barred gate standing between them and victory. Within minutes of the crowd forming a circle around the building, local AmerEagles groups have joined the party. A red outer ring develops and slowly moves inward to fight against those trying to enter the Red Palace. Nick hops up on the ledge holding up the iron gate and looks out trying to size up the strength of the AmerEagles group. There appears to be a lot of members of the anti-OWAL group, but somehow not as many as Cyrus expected. He begins to wonder if the harshness of President Pierce's executive orders has scared some of his followers away. An OWAL leader from another city standing below where Nick is on the ledge hands Nick a microphone that is connected to speakers that were wheeled in on carts.

"Thank you, OWALs. I can't express how elated I am feeling at this moment to know that there are so many good people fighting for equality and for the safety of ALL human beings. Nathan Pierce, who now calls himself 'President Pierce' is inside those walls that used to mean something before he stained them with the blood of the *Modified.* I am asking you right now to risk everything to not only take him down, but to challenge the AmerEagles groups. ONE WITH ALL LIFE!"

People begin to storm the gates. Hundreds of OWALs start to climb the gates to enter the premises, but many are shot down by snipers on top of the Red Palace. Other OWALs run around the tall fence looking for an opening near the guard posts and force their way through. Noise fills the air as the tanks roll in closer and lock into place for an attack. The wind picks up as a couple of helicopters begin to fly low. OWALs dressed in blue sporting faux owl wings jump from the base of the helicopters and soar in, landing on the well-manicured lawn.

Within minutes the lawn is filled with alive and dead OWALs alike. Those who are able to dodge the shots fired at them work their way to the building to overpower the guards who are on the ground. Nick is handed the microphone once more.

"Pierce! Come out and show us what you're made of. You can't hide in there forever. Hiding didn't work for Moros and it's not going to work for you. Come out you coward!"

Nathan hears the racket occurring on the outside of the building from all the way in the basement safe room, the same room Moros met her end in. There are three agents stationed outside of the room and countless others on the floor above to protect him from the mob trying to make their way in. Pierce thinks that he can wait this entire thing out if he is patient enough. He sits down and pressed a few buttons on the computerized table to display the holographic cameras covering the outside of the Red Palace. He remains calm and cocky while sipping on some whiskey from the rolling bar cart in the back of the room. He hears a thud hit the outside of the heavy metal door followed by two additional thuds seconds later. He waits patiently for several seconds and hears nothing else. He goes to the door and cracks it enough to peek into the hallway. He sees nothing until he looks down and all three guards have tranquilizer darts sticking out of their necks. He flings the door open wider to see who is there. Standing down the hallway he sees his old friend, David Bruner, pointing a tranquilizer dart gun straight at him.

David shouts down the hallway, "No need to worry. I won't need a dart to take you out."

He walks slowly and confidently towards President Pierce. Nathan finds himself impressed with the level of swag David is presenting at this moment. When he comes within a few feet of Pierce he asks, "aren't you going to ask me in?"

Intrigued, Nathan moves out of the way and holds his hand out in the way one does when they welcome someone through a door. Nathan closes the heavy door behind them once they are both inside.

"I didn't think I'd be seeing you again David. What a lovely surprise."

"I couldn't leave town without thanking you for setting me up for the murders of the entire executive branch," Bruner says playfully.

"You could have mailed a card. No need for such formalities, David," the president says, growing irritated with the game they are playing.

"You make a good point, but if I didn't come in person then I wouldn't get to see you take your last breath."

"Enough with the games, Bruner. It's growing old. I need to focus on what is happening in my yard right now."

David begins to laugh maniacally. Pierce grows even more agitated and shouts, "What could possibly be so funny?"

"Oh, nothing. I just find it amusing that you are worried about what's happening outside when you should be worried about what's happening in here…or rather what happened in here. Oh, by the way, did you enjoy the whiskey that I left for you," Bruner says with a jokeresque smile.

Pierce is so caught off guard by David's claim that he can't even see straight. He leans forward to put his hands on the glass, computerized table in order to keep his balance. His eyes shoot across the table to the short glass with only a few small drops of whiskey left in it. He starts to sweat.

"I never really wanted to get involved with you in the first place, but you promised me so much money that I could finally leave my job and start my own company. How could I resist? I'm going to assume your bribes are how you got Kenny to turn on me," David says, trying to get everything off his chest while he has the chance.

"Getting Kenny to turn on you was one of the easiest things I've ever done. He doesn't give a damn about anyone but himself. If he wasn't so incredibly unlikable, I would actually say that I see a bit of myself in him," Pierce claims, trying to act unaffected even though he is screaming inside trying to figure out if Nathan really poisoned him.

"It shouldn't be long now," David says looking at his watch and then back at Pierce.

Nathan feels a little pain in his stomach, but he convinces himself that David is bluffing and that the discomfort is all in his head. He sits down and stares at Bruner.

"Where have you been all this time? No one has seen you since Moros died. It's very rare that I can't find someone that I am looking for," David questions.

"I'm glad that you asked. It's actually a rather funny story about how I ended up here. I'll skip the part where you trick me into poisoning seventeen people because I think you already are familiar with how that all went. After I figured out that I wasn't *modifying* the people in the room, I headed to my apartment and was greeted by someone trying to kill me. I'm sure you know about that part too. So, I fled, but as I was heading to the airport, I realized that no matter what I did you would be able to find me. I would have to spend the rest of my life on the run or hiding and, frankly, that didn't interest me. I also knew that there is nowhere in the city that would be safe for me, so I did what felt like the least obvious thing to do. I came right back here, to the White House or I guess the…Red House," David explains.

Nathan interrupts him. The pain in his stomach getting worse by the second.

"That is impossible. There is no way that you've been here the entire time."

"Actually, it isn't as impossible as you think. I've been coming and going for days. You don't have as many friends as you think you do here. I've been paying a few guards at the main gate to let me in and out. One of the guards even helped me with my disguise so that I could look just like him at times. One day I worked an entire shift as him and no one batted an eye. I've been sleeping here too. There are so many rooms in this building that are off limits and not a single person checks, especially if you look like you work here," David proudly smiles as he explains his feat.

Pierce is getting dizzy now and barely able to hold himself up. He is trying to focus on what David is saying because he needs to know how he bested him.

"You obviously saved some of the poison from the vial Kenny gave you, but how did you get tranquilizer darts? You haven't been to the lab. I know that for a fact. That building has been under lock and key since you became a murder suspect."

"You're right, I haven't been there at all since then. It turns out I didn't need to get into the lab. I have a scientist that was willing to help me. Turns out he really hates you too. I think you probably remember him—Dr. Nicholas Cyrus," David says slowly, watching Pierce twist and turn in pain.

Nathan can't take it anymore. He collapses to the ground taking a few shallow breaths before his eyes glaze over and his heart stops beating. David drags Nathan's lifeless body past the three guards in the hallway who are still out cold and into the elevator. Once inside he admires the craftsmanship and elegance one last time as he makes his way to the main level.

As he leaves the elevators, he sees that OWALs and members of AmerEagles have entered the building and are fighting to the death. He dodges around several small warring groups, pulling Pierce behind him. He doesn't have the energy to get involved in any quarrels, so he tries to move quickly, but Nathan's limp body is heavier than it looks. Slowly, but surely, he makes it out to the front entrance and scans the crowd ready to end his participation in this event. It takes several lengthy seconds, but David and Nick's eyes meet.

Nick is somewhat surprised, but not disappointed that David followed through on his promise. He nods at him with approval and David Bruner returns a nod before he disappears into the crowd leaving Pierce lying right on the doorstep of the Red Palace. The fighting ensues for hours before the state militias arrive and are able to put a definitive end to things.

By then the yard and corridors of the once white house is littered with bodies of those who fought for what they believed to be right. The building itself is still standing, but barely. The once beautiful structure is now full of broken windows and smashed doors. Carefully curated portraits and furniture no longer look pristine.

The director of the Department of Defense makes an appearance on the Red Palace lawn to partner up with the FBI director in order to work through the mess that plagues the capitol. A thorough search is conducted on the premises to find President Pierce's body once the militia is able to clear everyone out. He is nowhere to be found. They try to find his assistant, Kenny Nash, but it is as if he vanished into thin air leaving no trace that he ever existed in the first place. They begin sweeping the city, but before they can even leave the perimeter of the palace calls come in notifying government officials that news stations are showing footage of the president's corpse on national media outlets.

The sun is slowly setting across Washington D.C. as television screens across America pan in to show Pierce lying lifeless on the steps of the Lincoln Memorial in his trademark red suit. A cardboard sign hangs from a rope around his neck that reads, 'You are not our president, and certainly not our king'. Arching over his body the steps display a gigantic, spray-painted message. The camera zooms out to show the blood-colored art that says, 'Equality for ALL'.

Chapter 45

June 30th, 2082 - DR. NICHOLAS CYRUS

Nick wakes up in Katie's apartment and creeps to the bathroom to hop in the shower without waking up Katie who has been sleeping for the past 18 hours. Nick can't stop smiling. It feels so good being able to finally relax in their own space. He gets in the shower and turns the water hotter than he normally would to really feel like he is washing away the last few days.

After a long forty-five-minute shower, he steps back into the bedroom and finds that Katie is awake but still cuddled up in bed. He walks over to her with his shaggy hair dripping wet and nothing but a towel on. He leans down and kisses her deeply, like he's wanted to do since they met. They spend the next couple hours in bed getting to know one another on a new level before they decide that they must get up and make some decisions about what their lives will look like now that Pierce is gone.

They sit down at a diner down the street from the apartment to eat lunch and discuss what they envision the next few years to look like, but before a fork can reach either one of their mouths a secret service agent enters the diner and makes a beeline for the couple. He greets Katie first and then immediately asks if he can speak to Cyrus in private. Nick gets up from his chair and walks a few feet away from the table while the man begins talking.

"Thank you for agreeing to speak with me. Obviously, things over the last few days have been a mess to say the least. Vice President Prossima would like to speak with you if you'll agree to meet him. He is right outside in the car," he says as he points through the glass window at the large car with tinted windows.

Nick doesn't answer and instead walks out of the diner and to the car awaiting his arrival. He opens the back seat door and enters the empty seat waiting for him.

"Dr. Cyrus! I am so pleased you agreed to talk with me," Vice President Prossima says with a thick Italian accent.

Cyrus shakes Prossima's dry, rough hand. He isn't impressed by him at all. All the respect he had for leadership was lost with Moros and Pierce.

"I know it seems weird, me hunting you down here and all, but I would like to enlist your assistance," Prossima explains.

"I have to be honest with you when I say that I have little confidence in you or Congress after you abandoned the country, went into hiding, and allowed Pierce to take over the entire executive branch," Nick says with resentment.

Prossima swallows the lump in his throat. He isn't used to being talked to in such a disrespectful way, but he knows Nick isn't wrong.

"Dr. Cyrus, the lack of action on my part and on the part of the Congress was a huge mistake. There isn't much I can do about the past, but we are ready to move forward and in order to stabilize the country we need to make some changes."

"How could I possibly be any help to you?" Nick inquires.

"I want you to run the Department of Science and Innovation and become one of my cabinet members. I will be sworn into the presidency in the coming days. Within that role I will ask you to not only represent the *Modified* people as a government figurehead, but I want you to offer opportunities to people in order to level the playing field of genetics," the soon to be president vaguely explains.

"What exactly does that mean…'level the playing field of genetics'? You obviously have something in mind already," Dr. Cyrus says, growing tired of Prossima's cryptic delivery.

"It is our, the government's, belief that being *Modified* may be advantageous to us as a country. There are a few things that you don't know quite yet. The first thing being that the reason we have been isolated from the rest of the world, as you may have suspected, is because there are no other countries with MODs. The *Modification* of everyone in the United States is the doing of MoonCycle," Prossima explains explicitly.

"What do you mean it is the doing of MoonCycle? There are babies born with the *Modification* without the parent's holding those genetic abnormalities. This is only possible if the parent's exposure to something..." Nick stops and the wheels in his brain work overtime to double check his logic before he speaks.

Prossima doesn't say a word. He lets the doctor work through his thoughts.

Nick continues after organizing his thoughts into formulated sentences, "MoonCycle has been giving something to pregnant women in order to force the inheritance of the *Modified* genes. Why would they want to do that? Just to make money?"

"Money, yes, but Pierce and Moros had other plans that obviously didn't work out for them. What we'd like you to do is be the face of *Modification* products. We believe that it will benefit us down the line by making us genetically superior—Darwinism and all. Despite this not occurring naturally, global warming is going to affect us and this puts us in a really strong position to survive. Physical superiority isn't the only thing we believe would come out of offering this to people. We believe that the polarization of society would be eliminated or at least severely diminished if people became *Modified* at a quicker rate than just through gestation. You've created a super serum that works immediately, and we'd like you to mass produce it for both types of *Modifications.* Please seriously consider this. Take some time if you need to," Vice President Prossima thoroughly explains.

"I'm in," Nick says with confidence that things can't possibly be any worse than they were under Pierce's reign.

Chapter 46

January 1st, 2083 - MAYOR ROY

Frank Roy adjusts his tie and makes his way to the podium outside of city hall. It's a particularly warm day for Beaufort in January, but he's not surprised by the erratic weather any longer. It's been almost eight months since he was notified about Rodrigo's death. He still thinks of Rio often. Sometimes the guilt of involving him in everything becomes too much and he doesn't even get out of bed. He knew eight months ago when he received the call from an old lieutenant named Damien, who he had by the pocket for many years before, that he was going to have to choose between himself and his old friend.

The guilt consumed him for days after telling Damien to take out Rio, the traitor, anyway he saw fit. His wife noticed the depression sink in and requested that he go to therapy with her to work through his issues, but being old fashioned he refused. Two months later Mrs. Roy had enough and moved out. She still doesn't intend to return anytime soon, or at least that's what Frank believes. He threw himself into his work, trying to get some of his constituents to trust him again. When that didn't work he hired a new assistant—an old acquaintance by the name of Silas Preston. He didn't hire Silas because he could help him win over the town, but because he needed someone to lean on who could understand his guilt.

Silas now stands a few feet back and to the left of the podium that Frank Roy is about to give his speech on, ready to pounce on anyone who tries to interrupt the event.

"Thank you all for coming out to city hall today. I've called this press conference to tell you all that I am stepping down as mayor effective immediately. I lost your trust and justifiably have not been able to gain it back. I want the people of Beaufort to know that I regret my actions and plan to live my life looking for redemption with not only the people of this fine city, but my family as well. Before I leave the office for the last time today, I wanted to introduce you to the candidate that I am endorsing for mayor of this lovely town—Javier Santos. Don't let his young age deter you from electing this strong-willed man. He may only be twenty, but he has seen and learned more than many do in their lifetimes. His father, the late Sheriff Santos, lives on in this bright young man. I'm going to hand the remaining time in the conference over to Mr. Santos. Thank you again, Beaufort. I'm going to miss serving you."

The old mayor steps down from the stage and makes his way to see his office one last time. He picks up the one remaining box that June packed up for him and takes in the sight of the room one final time. He walks past June's desk and their eyes meet. Her disappointment in him over the past six months, after the news broke about his involvement with Nathan Pierce, has affected their relationship to the point where words are rarely exchanged. Her eyes appear damp as if she had cried earlier. They hold the gaze between them for a few seconds before intentionally turning away. The mayor walks out of the office for the last time leaving nothing but regret behind.

Chapter 47

April 15th, 2083 - PJ and EM

"Hey, PJ! Don't forget to tip the movers before they pull away!" shouts Emerson.

PJ sprints down the driveway towards the moving truck and asks one of the men getting inside of the truck for their CashCube so he can leave them a tip. The man hands him a silver cube no larger than a fist. PJ quickly types in his username on the flat face as words illuminate on the mirror-like screen. He confirms the amount he's sending from his account, logs out, and hands the man the cube back, thanking him for all of his work today.

He turns away from the truck and slowly walks back up the driveway towards the house that he and Emerson just moved into. The salty air reaches his nose, and he turns to look out at the ocean. He reminisces about the last six months and how quickly things have moved with his and Emerson's relationship once they both admitted their feelings for one another. Katie was right. His person was right there in front of him the whole time. His attention shifts from the ocean to the large porch that wraps around the house. He stops moving and watches as Em confidently moves around shifting furniture and placing trinkets, trying to make their new house a home.

She stops what she is doing when she notices him in the driveway. The smile she forms is so full and pure that he can't help but smile back.

She calls to him, "Blue just called. They'll be over in a second. They're bringing us dinner. Benefit of having best friends as your neighbors, I guess."

PJ laughs and moves towards the porch. Around the corner he spots two little blonde-haired heads bouncing past the row of bushes separating the property. He hears Adam and Ben giggling as they run towards him, and he knows that he found his home.

Chapter 48

July 19th, 2083 - NICK and KATIE

Patrick, Em, and Javi sit across from the Ardi family and Blue in the hospital waiting room. Patience is wearing thin throughout the group. Adam and Ben are becoming irritable, so Blue and Derrick try to appease them with snacks. The long drive back to D.C. took a toll on the boys. Patrick, growing antsy himself, stands up and walks across the room to the secret service guards near the door and asks them if there is any news yet. Both of the grumpy, large men shake their heads indicating 'no'. PJ returns back to his seat feeling more restless than before.

A few moments later the doors swing open and Nick sprints over to the group quickly. The gills on his neck flap quickly as he tries to catch his breath.

"It's a girl!" he shouts.

The 'chosen' family jumps up and celebrates with hugs and tears. Dr. Cyrus leads the rest of the family into the delivery room to meet his daughter. Katie is in the bed with her blonde hair loosely pulled into a bun at the top of her head—her signature look, according to her husband, Nick. Her face is glowing with joy and maybe a little bit of sweat. Snuggled in her arms is their daughter, wrapped up tightly in a white muslin blanket with a tiny pink hat on. The tiny little gill holes on her neck mimic those of her father and mother. The group moves in closer while complimenting the baby and congratulating the couple.

"Everyone, we'd like you to meet Ava Lynn," says Katie.

Derrick's eyes get glossy and tears start to form, but he wipes them away before they leave his eyes.

Chapter 49

August 23rd, 2083 - The Ardis

Adam and Ben run across the beach towards the water at their beach house. Derrick and Blue sit in matching navy-blue Adirondack chairs in the yard above them, watching the boys play.

"Tamera, I can't thank you enough for coming to live with us this last year and helping us adjust to life again. The boys love you. Now that things are beginning to feel normal again, I've been meaning to ask you...would you like to officially go on a date with me?"

Blue giggles and nods.

"Of course. I'd love to."

Adam pauses playing in the sand and looks up at his dad and Blue feeling a sense of relief that he is home. He finally feels safe again and gets to be with his family. He turns around and walks closer to Ben who is sitting where the water meets the sand. His legs are in the water splashing while he is playing with something. He crouches down next to Ben to examine his new toy. Ben smiles and lifts it in his hands to show it off to Adam.

Adam's eyes grow large, and he screams. As the shrieks leave his body more of them leave the water. Adam is chased up the beach by several spiked, sharp-toothed, walking fish.

He shouts as he runs towards his father, "Daaaaaaaaaaaaaaaaaaaaaaad... you need to call Dr. Cyrus!"

www.ingramcontent.com/pod-product-compliance
Lightning Source LLC
Chambersburg PA
CBHW071743300326
42091CB00051B/333

* 9 7 9 8 2 1 8 7 2 8 7 1 7 *